DEATH AMONG THE STARS

The Y-wing let a proton torpedo go at point-blank range, but it shot past the eyeball and would have hit the X-wing had Corran not rolled fast. "Break outside, Champions!"

The Y-wing pilots complied with Corran's order, but did so slowly. The TIE spun in on Champion Five, pouring verdant laser bolts into its shields. The Y-wing pilot continued his roll and dive, and the TIE corrected to follow him, allowing himself to fly a level arc as he pursued his quarry.

You're mine, now. Corran eased back on his stick, millimeter by millimeter centering the Imperial fighter on his targeting crosshairs.

Whistler shrilled a warning.

Behind me? Who? He glanced at his sensors and saw the other TIE closing in on him and he wanted to break away. *Can't, Five is history if I do.*

Corran hit his trigger and prepared for nothingness.

The Sensational *Star Wars* Series published by
Bantam Books and available from all good bookshops

The *Empire* Trilogy by Timothy Zahn
**The Heir to the Empire • Dark Force Rising
The Last Command**

The *Jedi Academy* Trilogy by Kevin J. Anderson
**Jedi Search • Dark Apprentice
Champions of the Force**

The Truce at Bakura
by Kathy Tyers

The Courtship of Princess Leia
by Dave Wolverton

The *Corellian* Trilogy by Roger MacBride Allen
**Ambush at Corellia • Assault at Selonia
Showdown at Centerpoint**

The *Cantina* Trilogy edited by Kevin J. Anderson
**Tales from the Mos Eisley Cantina
Tales from Jabba's Palace • Tales of the Bounty Hunters***

Crystal Star
by Vonda McIntyre

The *X-Wing* Series by Michael Stackpole
**Rogue Squadron • Wedge's Gamble
The Krytos Trap* • Rogues Unbound***

The *Black Fleet Crisis* Trilogy by Michael P. Kube-McDowell
**Before the Storm • Shield of Lies*
Tyrant's Test***

Children of the Jedi
by Barbara Hambly

and in hardcover

The Illustrated Star Wars Universe
by Kevin J. Anderson & Ralph McQuarrie

Darksaber
by Kevin J. Anderson

Shadows of the Empire
by Steve Perry

*Forthcoming

X - W I N G

BOOK TWO

Wedge's Gamble

Michael A. Stackpole

BANTAM BOOKS
TORONTO · NEW YORK · LONDON · SYDNEY · AUCKLAND

WEDGE'S GAMBLE
A BANTAM BOOK : 0 553 40923 9

First publication in Great Britain

PRINTING HISTORY
Bantam edition published 1996

Bantam Books are published by Transworld Publishers Ltd,
61–63 Uxbridge Road, London W5 5SA,
in Australia by Transworld Publishers (Australia) Pty Ltd,
15–25 Helles Avenue, Moorebank, NSW 2170,
and in New Zealand by Transworld Publishers (NZ) Ltd,
3 William Pickering Drive, Albany, Auckland.

Printed and bound in Great Britain by
Cox & Wyman Ltd, Reading, Berks.

ACKNOWLEDGMENTS

The author would like to thank the following people for their various contributions to this book:

Janna Silverstein, Tom Dupree, and Ricia Mainhardt for getting me into this mess;

Sue Rostoni and Lucy Autrey Wilson for letting me get away with all they have in this universe;

Kevin J. Anderson, Timothy Zahn, Kathy Tyers, Bill Smith, Bill Slavicsek, Peter Schweighofer, Michael Kogge, and Dave Wolverton for the material they created and the advice they offered;

Lawrence Holland & Edward Kilham for the **X-Wing** and **TIE Fighter** computer games;

Chris Taylor for pointing out to me which ship Tycho was flying in *Star Wars VI: Return of the Jedi* and Gail Mihara for pointing out controversies I might want to avoid;

My parents, my sister Kerin, my brother Patrick and his wife Joy for their encouragement (and endless efforts to face my other books out on bookstore shelves);

Dennis L. McKiernan, Jennifer Roberson, and especially Elizabeth T. Danforth for listening to bits of this story as it was being written and enduring such abuse with smiles and a supportive manner.

DRAMATIS PERSONAE
ROGUE SQUADRON

COMMANDER WEDGE ANTILLES *(human male from Corellia)*
CAPTAIN TYCHO CELCHU *(human male from Alderaan)*
CAPTAIN ARIL NUNB *(Sullustan female from Sullust)*
LIEUTENANT CORRAN HORN *(human male from Corellia)*
LIEUTENANT PASH CRACKEN *(human male from Contruum)*

OORYL QRYGG *(Gand male from Gand)*
NAWARA VEN *(Twi'lek male from Ryloth)*
RHYSATI YNR *(human female from Bespin)*
ERISI DLARIT *(human female from Thyferra)*
GAVIN DARKLIGHTER *(human male from Tatooine)*
RIV SHIEL *(Shistavanen male from Uvena III)*

ZRAII *(Verpine male from Roche G42)*
M-3PO *(Emtrey; protocol and regulations droid)*
WHISTLER *(Corran's R2 astromech)*
MYNOCK *(Wedge's R5 astromech)*

ALLIANCE MILITARY

ADMIRAL ACKBAR *(Mon Calamari male from Mon Calamari)*

ALLIANCE INTELLIGENCE

GENERAL AIREN CRACKEN *(human male from Contruum)*
IELLA WESSIRI *(human female from Corellia)*
WINTER *(human female from Alderaan)*

CITIZENS ON CORUSCANT

ASYR SEI'LAR *(Bothan female from Bothawui)*
INYRI FORGE *(human female from Kessel)*
FLIRY VORRU *(human male from Corellia)*
ZEKKA THYNE *(human/alien male from Corellia)*

CREW OF THE *PULSAR SKATE*

MIRAX TERRIK *(human female from Corellia)*
LIAT TSAYV *(Sullustan male from Sullust)*

IMPERIAL FORCES

YSANNE ISARD, DIRECTOR OF IMPERIAL INTELLIGENCE *(human female from Coruscant)*
KIRTAN LOOR, INTELLIGENCE AGENT *(human male from Churba)*
GENERAL EVIR DERRICOTE *(human male from Kalla)*

1

Even before his X-wing's sensors had time to scan and identify the new ship, Corran Horn knew it was trouble. That knowledge was not based on the ship's unscheduled, unannounced reversion to realspace in the Pyria system. In the month since the Rebel Alliance took the planet Borleias from the Empire, more ships than Corran cared to remember had popped in for a quick survey of the place. Some were on diplomatic missions from worlds that had already joined the New Republic coming to inspect the latest conquest of their forces. Other ships had been sent by the rulers of planets who wanted to separate fact from propaganda before they decided if they wanted to shift allegiances in the galactic civil war.

Still others had been Imperial vessels on reconnaissance missions, and a goodly proportion of the rest were Alliance ships with legitimate business in the system. All of them had to be checked out, and the hostiles discouraged, but the patrols had produced no serious incidents or fatalities. This spawned a complacency among the pilots that was not conducive to long life, but even Corran had found it hard to keep his edge when no serious threats presented themselves.

The new ship's arrival slashed away his peace of mind like a vibroblade. The sensors reported a modified freight cruiser that had started life as a Rendili Star Drive ship—not in the *Neutron Star*-class of bulk cruiser, but something roughly a quarter that size. That in no way made it remarkable or unusual—dozens of ships built on the same design had been through the system since its conquest. The name, *Vengeance Derra IV*, followed the naming convention common among New Republic ships of recalling some event in the course of the civil war. It had even entered the system on the course and at the speed the Rebels had dictated for freighter traffic.

Still, something is not right here. During his brief career with the Corellian Security Force, hunting down smugglers and other criminals, he'd learned to trust his gut feelings about things. His father, Hal, and even his grandfather—both CorSec officers themselves—had encouraged him to follow his instincts in dangerous situations. The sensation frustrated him with its elusiveness, as if it were no more tangible than the faint scent of a flower teasing his nose and defying identification.

It's enough that I know something is odd. Exactly what isn't important at this point. Corran keyed his comm unit. "Rogue Nine to Champion Five, you handle the challenge. Wait here with Six. I'm going to go out and do a flyby."

"I copy, Nine, but we are supposed to expedite all shipping in this area. They aren't in the challenge zone yet."

"Humor me, Five."

"As ordered, Nine."

The system patrols had been broken up to cover four zones around the planet of Borleias. The plane of the ecliptic split the system up and down, with sun side and out splitting it core and rim. Corran and two Y-wing pilots from General Salm's Defender Wing had up-and-out, which was by far the busiest sector because the planet's moon had moved out of it and sunward two days previously.

"Whistler, see what you can do about boosting our sensors to pick up any anomalous readings from that freighter."

The green and white R2 astromech blatted harshly at him.

"Yes, fine, there's likely to be lots of things wrong with that freighter." Corran frowned as he nudged his throttle forward and the X-wing started off toward the freighter. "I was thinking about inappropriate weapons or other odd things."

As Corran's fighter came in closer he began to get a visual feed on the ship. All of 150 meters long, it had the gentle curves of smaller ships, or the larger Mon Calamari warships. The bridge was a bulge on the top of the bow that tapered back and down into a slender mid-ship. Two thirds of the way back toward the stern the ship's body flared out again to accommodate the star drives. A communications array sat right behind the bridge, and quad laser turrets bristled off the bow and in a ring around the middle of the ship.

Whistler splashed a report on the ship onto Corran's primary monitor. It was a Rendili Star Drive's design, from the *Dwarf Star*-class of freighter. It shipped roughly fifteen hundred metric tons of equipment, ran with a crew of four hundred, and had nine quad lasers as well as one tractor beam that could be used to pull salvage into the belly storage area. The guns and carrying capacity made it a favorite for short-haul traders who were willing to work in areas of the galaxy where authority had broken down, or Imperial entanglements could be a problem.

"Champion Five here, Rogue Nine."

"Go ahead, Five."

"I challenged the *Vengeance* and it answered with a code that is good."

That surprised Corran because he couldn't shake the feeling that something was wrong with the ship. "Did they get it on the first try?"

Five's comm unit didn't filter the surprise out of his voice. "No, second pass. Why?"

"I'll tell you later. Stay where you are, but get some-one to lift from Borleias in an assault shuttle. You and Six be ready for trouble."

"As ordered, Nine."

Whistler chirped an inquiry at Corran.

"Yes, I think it's exactly like the doubletaker case." Back on Corellia he and his partner, Iella Wessiri, had investigated a series of burglaries where things had been stolen from houses, but there were no signs of forced entry. All of the security systems were manufactured by different companies, and installed and monitored by different agencies. The key to cracking the case was that the ROMs used in the security systems all came from the *same* manufacturer. An employee had sliced the code that got burned into the chips so when a particular password was used on the locks, the system would spit out the correct password. On the second try the thief would enter the correct code, get in, and rob the place.

The Y-wing fighters the Alliance used were old, but still vital, and most of them were a patchwork of new and old systems. Spare parts were not easy to come by, and whatever were available were used quickly to keep the fighters in service. It was conceivable that a sensor/comm unit integrator had been fitted with odd chips that gave away codes when checking them. Arranging for such things would not be beyond the Empire's Director of Intelligence, Ysanne Isard, especially if it would help prevent the Rebel Alliance from taking Coruscant away from her.

Corran punched his comm unit over to the frequency the freighter was using. "*Vengeance Derra IV*, this is Lieutenant Corran Horn of Rogue Squadron. Stop now. Stand by for boarding."

The freighter did not even slow, much less stop. "Is there a problem, Lieutenant?"

Corran shifted the targeting crosshairs of his heads-up display over to lead the freighter, then sent a quad burst of red laser fire across the ship's bow. "*Vengeance*, stand by for boarding. There will only be a problem if you make one."

"Standing by."

The freighter began to roll to port, exposing its top toward Corran's ship. *Not good.* "Five and Six, prepare proton torpedoes. Link fire and lock on the freighter."

"Nine, they've done nothing."

"Yet, Five, yet."

Swinging up and around from the belly of *Vengeance*, four TIE starfighters raced in toward Corran's X-wing. Without waiting for them to start shooting, he slapped the stick to the right and brought the fighter up onto its starboard S-foil. The TIEs started their own turns to port and began to dive, anticipating his escape maneuver. Corran punched his left foot on the etheric rudder pedal, skidding the stern of his ship to starboard, then shot off straight in the opposite direction from his pursuit.

"Nine, we have two TIE bombers deployed."

"Five, fire on the *Vengeance*, then take the dupes. I've got the eyeballs. Let Borleias base know we have trouble." He knew the Y-wings would have little trouble out-flying the dupes—pilot slang for the double-hulled bombers. If he could keep the TIEs occupied, they wouldn't be in any position to harass the Y-wings. If the missiles the Y-wings launched at *Vengeance* were enough to take down the forward shields, the freighter's captain would have to think about running, which would distract the TIE pilots, since without him, they were stuck in the Pyria system.

Lots of ifs there. Time to make some of them certainties. He used a snap-roll to bring the fighter up on the starboard stabilizer again, then dove into a long loop that took him down to where *Vengeance*'s bulk hid him from the TIEs. Rolling his ship and applying some rudder, he arrowed straight in at the freighter. This put him in position to watch as the quartet of proton torpedoes launched by the Y-wings nailed the ship's bow. Each missile exploded against the shields like a star going nova.

The astromech droid whistled up a requiem for *Vengeance*'s bow shield.

Corran tightened on the trigger and sent a quad burst of fire toward the ship's bridge. Without waiting to see if it hit or did damage, he barrel-rolled to port, moving toward the middle of the freighter, and pulled back on the stick to bring the fighter's nose up. His targeting crosshairs hung just above the horizon of the freighter's hull.

A TIE starfighter, shying from the series of explosions against the forward shield, streaked over the freighter's edge and right into his sights. Corran triggered a quad shot that caught the eyeball on the port side quadanium steel armored solar panel, slicing the hexagon into a dozen or more pieces. A secondary explosion suggested a failure in one of the ion engines that the fighter's subsequent careening off through space confirmed.

Corran rolled up on the left stabilizer foil and drifted to port for a heartbeat before snapping over onto the starboard S-foil and hauling back on the stick. The maneuver allowed him to evade the fire coming in from *Vengeance*'s lasers. It also put him on the vector the TIE had used coming in over the freighter's hull. Adding a bit more to the starboard roll and pulling back on stick again took him out past the ship's damaged bow and let him swoop in on the tail of another TIE.

The eyeball broke back left, but Corran rolled his ship through a corkscrew that kept him on target. He fired twice. The first quad shot missed, but the second tagged the ball cockpit full on. The lasers blew through the engine, then an explosion ripped the fighter apart. Corran dove into and flew through the expanding ball of incandescent gas, then rolled and dove again.

"Five, report."

"One dupe dead, one sleeping."

Corran laughed aloud. "Nice shooting, Five. Good thinking." The Y-wing pilots had shown the presence of mind to engage one of the bombers while using their ion cannons. The weapons were inferior in power to lasers, but they had the advantage of knocking out a ship's electronics by overloading the electrical system. The ion cannons could render a ship inoperable, allowing the pilot to be picked up later.

Chances are, though, this Imp pilot will kill himself to avoid capture. Still, the ship might teach us something.

"Nine, the freighter is turning to run. Do you want help with the eyeballs?"

"Negative, Five."

Whistler scolded him with a harsh blatty sound.

"It's not that I think I'm that good, Whistler, it's that I know they aren't." Refusing assistance to deal with enemies that outnumber you was usually ascribed to unending egotism or terminal stupidity, but Corran had a third reason in mind. The Y-wing pilots, while enthusiastic and decently trained, were insufficiently experienced in dogfighting to be much help to him. If they entered the fight, he'd have to worry about hitting them. Without their intervention, his only possible targets were Imperial ships, and that fact gave him some freedom.

"Nine, we'll take *Vengeance*."

"Negative, Five, definitely negative." *If they go in on the freighter it will pick them apart.* "Hang off there and try for torp locks on the TIEs."

Glancing at his sensor displays, he marked the positions of the Y-wings, then rolled his ship and dove. Angry green laser bolts slashed through the blackness in front of him, but neither of the TIEs' shots hit. The sensors reported the last two eyeballs had just pulled through a crisscross maneuver and were looping up and around to make another pass on him. That told him the last two pilots were good enough to have survived more than one fight in their ships.

They rolled through their double-helix maneuver and Corran shot through the center of their spiral. Rolling out to the right he cut in front of one, inviting a hastily snapped shot. The TIE pilot took it, splashing lasers against the X-wing's aft shield. Ignoring Whistler's shrill shriek, Corran reinforced the rear shield, then rolled and began a dive.

The eyeball rolled and started after him. Corran chopped his throttle back, then rolled and dove sharply. He remained in the dive for a couple of seconds, then rolled again and climbed. Rolling back out onto his original course, he popped in behind the TIE that had previously been on his tail and took a shot of his own.

The eyeball juked at the last second, so the four laser bolts only clipped the top of one of the solar panels. The TIE starfighter began to whirl away, but it never exploded. Damaged as the ship was, it would be an easy target to follow and finish, but the last TIE sprayed laser fire against the X-wing's shields, giving Corran a more immediate threat to deal with.

Because it was coming in from the left, Corran rolled right, then cruised down through a diving turn that aimed him back along its inbound course. The TIE looped up, then rolled and came down through an inverse loop to cut across Corran's tail. Corran let the X-wing sideslip right, but not before the eyeball had taken a shot at him. Whistler screamed, then a bank of lights started flashing on the fighter's command console.

Sithspawn! My shields are down. Corran stomped on the right rudder pedal, swinging the X-wing's nose in that direction, then rolled up on the port stabilizer and pulled back on the stick. As the ship started to climb, another snap-roll to the left broke it off at right angles to the climb and away from pursuit. "Whistler, get the shields back up, fast."

A counter appeared on his main screen and began counting down from one and a half minutes.

"Not good, not good at all."

The major advantage an X-wing had over a TIE starfighter was shields. The two fighters matched each other in speed and the TIE actually had the edge in maneuverability. Shields allowed the X-wings to survive more hits during a fight, and in dogfighting, the goal was surviving to the end and beyond. Corran felt he could outfly the TIE pilot, but engaging in combat while naked was not something that made him feel at all confident.

He punched the throttle to full and pushed the fighter through a series of twists and loops that carried it away from the TIE, but no closer to the Y-wings. Time seemed to be passing very slowly to Corran, with each second on the counter seeming to take a minute to click off. The TIE pilot seemed content to circle around, trying to close with Corran, then he broke off and streaked in toward the Y-wings, coming up from beneath them.

"Heads up, Five. Invert, you have incoming."

The Y-wings executed the flip in good order as Corran allocated power that would have normally gone to shields over to propulsion. That provided him a bit more speed, which let him close the gap with the eyeball.

"Nine, I have missile lock."

"Shoot, Six, shoot."

The Y-wing let a proton torpedo go at point-blank range, but it shot past the eyeball and would have hit the X-wing had Corran not rolled fast. "Break outside, Champions!"

The Y-wing pilots complied with Corran's order, but did so slowly. The TIE spun in on Champion Five, pouring verdant laser bolts into its shields. The Y-wing pilot continued his roll and dive, and the TIE corrected to follow him, allowing himself to fly a level arc as he pursued his quarry.

You're mine, now. Corran eased back on his stick, millimeter by millimeter centering the Imperial fighter on his targeting crosshairs.

Whistler shrilled a warning.

Behind me? Who? He glanced at his sensors and saw the other TIE closing in on him and he wanted to break away. *Can't, Five is history if I do.*

Corran hit his trigger, tracking ruby energy darts along the TIE's flight path. Even as he saw the lasers hit the eyeball's wings and cockpit, he braced for the other TIE's lasers burning through his ship. He saw his target explode and knew, as green laser bolts scythed down toward his ship, he was a dead man.

He prepared himself for nothingness.

He was not wholly disappointed.

Nothing happened.

Corran rolled left and climbed. "Find him, Whistler."

The droid gave back a negative report.

"What about *Vengeance?*"

Whistler reported it had gone to lightspeed.

At least we're clear there. Corran felt a shiver run down his spine. His left hand rose up and, through the fabric of his flight suit, touched a gold medallion he wore. *It appears all my luck has not run out.*

"Five, Six, what happened to the other eyeball?"

"I got him, Nine."

"With what, Six?"

"The missile I launched."

It took Corran a second to make sense of the reply, then he remembered the missile that had almost hit him as he had come in on the TIE starfighter. "Six, you were aiming at the *second* TIE?"

"Yes, sir, Lieutenant. Did I do something wrong?"

Corran wanted to yell at him about choosing targets that have a higher threat factor—by virtue of being closer and, therefore, more likely to hit their target—but he stopped before he gave in to temptation. "Not wrong, Six, but it could have been more right."

"Yes, sir," came a sheepish reply that remained full of nervous energy. "Next time, sir."

"Yeah, at least we can all be thankful there will be a next time."

Whistler tootled triumphantly as the X-wing's shields came back up.

Corran smiled. "Yes, I do appreciate your shaving seven seconds off the estimate, Whistler." He keyed his comm unit. "Five, Six, mark the coordinates of your sleeping dupe, then we head in. We'll have reports to fill out but the fact that we *can* fill them out means this has been a very good day."

2

Wedge Antilles shook hands with both of the pilots standing in his office. "Sorry to keep you waiting but we apparently have had another probe of the system by Imperial forces. The Imps didn't make much of a fight of it, but we almost scrambled the rest of the squadron." He walked around to his side of the transparisteel-topped desk, then waved the two of them to chairs. "Welcome to Rogue Squadron."

Both pilots smiled and thanked him.

Wedge looked first at the Sullustan female. "Captain Nunb, I hope you do not think the fact that you were not selected to join Rogue Squadron six months ago reflects in any way a lack of respect for your skills as a pilot."

Aril Nunb shook her head, the slender plait of brown hair lashing one shoulder and another. "I harbored no such thought, Commander."

"But you were aware that I chose Captain Tycho Celchu to be my Executive Officer, not you?"

A red-purple light flashed in her big garnet eyes. "Rumors to that effect were easily heard, but more easily ignored, sir."

Wedge smiled. *Frank* and *practical, this I like.* "Those rumors were true, Captain. My reasons were . . ."

"Excuse me, sir, but you have no need to explain yourself to me."

"I think you will find, both of you, that Rogue Squadron is full of very good pilots. Our discipline is a bit more lax than in other units, and I tend to explain orders when I can because we rely on each other very heavily. No one shirks duty here, no matter how dangerous. I think it is important that every member of the squadron knows where he or she stands."

The mouse-eared Sullustan nodded her head. "Yes, sir."

"I'd heard stories about you and your brother, especially concerning your exploits on behalf of the Alliance in stealing supplies from SoroSuub Corporation and turning them over to us. I saw firsthand how well your brother flies when he piloted the *Millennium Falcon* into the second Death Star and enabled Lando and me to blow the reactor and control structures. I saw then, and later in reviewing your performance tests, that the both of you have a native ability in a fighter that wasn't learned and can't be taught. Since the rebuilding of Rogue Squadron involved training pilots to higher and higher levels of efficiency, I didn't think you were well suited to a role with us in such a training period."

"I understand, sir."

What she left unsaid told Wedge that she understood a lot more about the situation in the galaxy than she cared to mention. Rogue Squadron had lost four pilots, a full third of its strength, in the last six months. Under normal circumstances new pilots would be brought in and trained up to the squadron's level of efficiency, but such training required time. Events in the galaxy did not give the New Republic's forces much in the way of time, so the replacement pilots were being drawn from the best available candidates who expressed an interest in joining the unit.

Wedge turned to the redheaded man seated next to

the Sullustan. "I was surprised, Captain Cracken, to see your name appear on a list of candidates willing to replace pilots in Rogue Squadron. You've got your own flight group out on the Rim and you're used to flying an A-wing, not an X-wing. Won't you find us a bit slow for your tastes?"

"I hope not, sir." Pash Cracken frowned slightly.

Wedge thought for a moment that the question had irritated the young pilot, but the reply had come in a voice that maintained its emotional neutrality. Cracken was the son of General Airen Cracken, one of the Alliance's legendary leaders and the New Republic's answer to Ysanne Isard. Airen Cracken had fabricated an identity for his son that allowed Pash to enter the Imperial Naval Academy. On his first assignment after graduation, Pash led his entire TIE wing in defecting to the Alliance. They became known as "Cracken's Flight Group" and their killing of a *Victory*-class Star Destroyer had made them and their leader legendary as well.

"If you don't mind my asking, why do you want to leave your people behind and join us?"

Cracken's frown deepened and he shifted uneasily in his chair. "It's a kind of hard to explain, sir."

"But your reasons must be strong because you'll have to take a reduction in rank to Lieutenant to join us."

"I know that, sir."

Wedge opened his hands. "You may share as little as you want with the others in the squadron, Mr. Cracken, but I really do need to know why you want to be a Rogue."

Aril Nunb leaned forward in her chair. "Perhaps if I were to leave, sir?"

Pash shook his head. "No, that's not necessary." Breath hissed in through clenched teeth. "This is going to sound odd."

"Perhaps, but we won't know until you get it out."

"Yes, sir." Pash sighed. "Pretty early on, because of time I spent fooling around with old Z-95 Headhunter simulators, my father realized I had a bit of a talent for flying. He encouraged my interest in flying and made all sorts of opportunities available for me to use simulators and then real starfighters. I soloed before I hit puberty and simulator battles had me beating some fairly good pilots. I knew I was good, but I didn't know *how* good because I thought people praised my skill to get in good with my father.

"When I went to the Academy I got a handle on how good I was. I was better than most of my instructors when I started, and by the time I graduated none of them could touch me. We were flying TIE starfighters and my squadrons weren't losing a single pilot. I graduated right up at near the top of the class, and the guys who finished ahead of me were the guys in my squadron that I'd forced to leave the simulators and work on their academic studies."

Cracken's hands curled into fists as strain entered his voice. "When we defected, when we killed the *Exsanguinator*, all my people followed my lead and most of us survived. Attrition has worn the unit down, that's why we're now part of Commander Varth's wing, but the people that have been with me all the way along think I lead some sort of a charmed life. They think I won't fail them, that I can't be beaten. Those who have died along the way are accused of having done the wrong thing at the wrong time, and in some cases they're right, but I *have* sent people to their deaths.

"The new kids coming into the squadron are inculcated into this myth of my invincibility. My pilots are getting careless, and that's going to get people killed. I know that happens, but because of the legend they've built me up into, I can't get my people to listen to me or do the things I need them to do. If I stay there and some Imp outguesses me, everyone will follow me down in flames."

Wedge sat back and nodded slowly. Rogue Squadron's unit roster had a lot of names on it, and save for a Jedi Knight, a couple of pilots assigned to training squadrons, and a few pilots who had left for other pursuits, anyone who wasn't active duty was dead. Biggs Darklighter, Jek Porkins, Dak Ralter, and Bror Jace were all among the most talented and famous pilots the Empire had killed, but Wedge could attach faces to all the names on the roster, and knew the details of how each of them had died. That they had perished under his command did overwhelm him at times, so he found it very easy to understand Pash Cracken's dilemma.

"I would say, Lieutenant, that a change is due for you. Your unit will have to reassess how it operates in your absence, and that will certainly be a good turn of events." Wedge tried to read Cracken's expression, but he could not. "It strikes me, however, that there are plenty of other fighter units in the Alliance that would welcome a pilot of your skill—and most of them are A-wing units."

"Yes, sir, true, but they're not Rogue Squadron."

"Why is it that important that you join Rogue Squadron?"

Cracken's shoulders slackened slightly—not so much that Wedge would have said he slumped in his chair, but Cracken had clearly decided he would withhold nothing from his answer. "Any other unit would put me in command and that would solve nothing. You see, because of my previous situation, I no longer have a perspective on how well I fly. I'm beginning to question myself and my performance, and that means I'm a hairsbreadth from doubting myself. If I've lost something, I need to know I'm not flying as well as I can, but if I lose my confidence, I lose everything.

"Here, in Rogue Squadron, I'll be measuring myself against the best our side has to offer."

Wedge pressed his hands together, fingertip to fingertip. "What does your father think of this change?"

Cracken's face slackened for a moment, then fire flared in his green eyes. "My father had nothing to do with this decision."

"But you have spoken to him about it?"

"Yes."

"And he approved?"

Cracken's head came up. "He has nothing but the utmost of respect for you, Commander Antilles."

"That's good to know." Wedge frowned, drawing brown brows together to hood brown eyes. The conquest of the Pyria system had required two operations because Alliance Intelligence had failed to uncover some information about the Imperial installations on Borleias. The idea of Imperial operatives or traitors having set the Rebels up for their first defeat could not be ignored and any investigation of such allegations would fall to General Cracken and his people.

While Wedge had absolutely no reservations about any of his people, his trust was not shared by others in the Alliance. General Salm, the leader of Defender Wing, had long been suspicious of Captain Tycho Celchu. While Salm had admitted to Wedge that he knew Tycho had not leaked information concerning the first Pyria assault to the Empire, he believed Tycho was an Imperial agent who would betray the Alliance at the worst possible moment.

The conquest of the Pyria system had opened the way for the Rebel Alliance to strike at Coruscant, the Imperial homeworld. Taking Coruscant would confer upon the New Republic a legitimacy it had not yet earned in the eyes of much of the Empire's citizenry. Those who were aware of the state of the Empire could find little to differentiate the Rebels from the Imperial warlords who were carving their own little realm out of the Empire. Though they might not believe assurances from Coruscant that the threat presented by the Alliance or people like Warlord Zsinj was minor, they did not yet see the Empire as a cadaver waiting for scavengers to carve it up.

Coruscant was the key to establishing the New Republic as the new ruling force in the galaxy. Taking it was a bold step—a serious gamble that required thousands of factors to fall into place to win. Since Admiral Ackbar had ordered Wedge to attend the Provisional Council's deliberations on the project, he knew Rogue Squadron would be heavily involved in the campaign. Airen Cracken had to be aware of that eventuality, too.

In his place I'd consider planting an agent in Rogue Squadron to watch for any suspicious activity. But would I use my own son? Wedge looked at the younger Cracken for a moment and read disappointment on his face, not outrage or wounded pride. *I'd be angry and indignant, fighting the implication of being a spy with an appeal to honor. Pash is not. Is he innocent, or just very much his father's son?*

The Corellian leader of Rogue Squadron sat forward and rested his forearms on the desktop. "Trust is the key to this unit, but that doesn't mean you have to tell your fellow pilots your deepest, darkest secrets. The people here are the best and I'm sure you'll both fit in. Again, welcome to the unit."

"Thank you, sir."

Wedge handed each of them a small strip of plastic. "The facilities here are a bit more comfortable than we've been used to—Evir Derricote ran this operation until we took it away from the Empire. He was devoted to a certain level of creature comfort. Captain Nunb, you'll have your own quarters. Lieutenant Cracken, you will share a room with Nawara Ven, a Twi'lek pilot. I think you'll like him."

Pash took the strips and handed one to Aril.

Wedge glanced at his datapad, then frowned sharply. "I've only got an hour until I have to fly out to rendezvous with *Home One*. I will be taking our *Lambda*-class shuttle since I'll be bringing General Salm with me. Lieutenant Cracken, you may use my X-wing for the time being—we should have one of the others up and repaired inside a week for you. Captain Nunb, I'll introduce you to Captain Celchu. Because of his status, you'll actually be in command of the unit in my absence. Tycho will help you with anything you need."

He stood up. "Is there anything else we need to discuss?"

The Sullustan shook her head. "No, sir."

Wedge looked at Pash. "Anything?"

"No, sir."

"And if I see your father at the meetings?"

Pash smiled. "Just tell him he was right about the grilling he said you'd give me, and let him know I passed."

"It will be my pleasure, Lieutenant." Wedge kept a smile on his face as he led them to the door. "I think you both will find the trials of being a Rogue a bit more difficult than any interrogation I'll give you, but I have no doubt, being as how you *are* Rogues, you'll survive and then some."

3

Corran welcomed his visitors to the small suite of rooms that he and his wingmate, the Gand named Ooryl Qrygg, had been given on Borleias. Since the Rebel assault had severely damaged most of the surface buildings in the Imperial installation, the New Republic occupation force housed itself in the underground warrens that formed the foundation for the base. Aside from the occasional blaster scars and a couple of blown-out walls, the facility was in fairly good repair.

Corran's suite had two bedrooms that had been built on to either narrow end of a rectangular room. The walls had been painted an Imperial grey. That color, combined with the deep blue of the carpet, made the room fairly dark. Corran had countered the color scheme by bringing in as many lights as he could find and rigging a small holoprojector to flash up images of other worlds and cover a huge chunk of the longest wall.

He'd begged, borrowed, and bartered for the furnishings installed in the room. Most of the functional surfaces were the tops of spare parts crates. He'd managed to keep one of the couches that had originally been in the room and swapped the one with the blaster-burn hole for two

Y-wing ejector seats. A small refrigeration unit doubled as the holoprojector stand and, though filling the room with an occasional rattle or wheeze, managed to keep beverages cold and food from spoiling.

A slender, brown-haired man entered the suite first and smiled as an image of Alderaan appeared on the wall. "It has been a long while since I saw Wuitho Trifalls." He pointed at the promontory from which a river fell in three spectacular waterfalls. "I visited there with my family the week before I went off to the Imperial Academy. NovaCom maintained a repulsorlift cabin in the area, so that's where we stayed. It was as beautiful as that picture, but without the roar of the water, it seems . . ."

Dead. Corran didn't need to see the sorrow and pain on Tycho Celchu's face to know what word had gone unspoken. Save for the coldest-hearted Imperialist among the survivors of Alderaan, the Alderaanians had suffered a deep, emotional wound when their homeworld had been destroyed. It crushed some but others, like Tycho and Princess Leia Organa, seemed to be driven by that loss to forever put to rest the Empire and its evil.

"I apologize for that, sir. The projector chooses images at random."

Tycho's face brightened. "Don't apologize. I may miss my home, but that does not mean I like seeing holograms of it any less. The planet may be dead, but its beauty lives on in images like that."

The second visitor shuffled through the doorway, then took a hop forward as it shut behind him. The black droid had the body of a 3PO unit, but the crested clamshell head of a spaceport control droid. "Good evening, Lieutenant Horn. May I say I was pleased to receive your invitation to visit this evening because I am finding Captain Nunb a bit brusque for my tastes . . ."

Corran flicked a green-eyed glance at Tycho. "Do you want to do it or should I?"

"Do what? May I help?"

Tycho smiled. "We couldn't do it without you, Emtrey. Shut up."

"Sir, I must protest . . ."

"Shut up."

"But I . . ."

"Shut up."

With Tycho's third repetition of the command, the droid's arms snapped to its sides and its head canted forward sharply until its chin almost touched its chestplate. At the base of its skull, back at the top of its neck post, a glowing red button became visible. Emtrey shook once as if hit by a blaster bolt, then stood still and, most remarkably, silent.

"Every time I see that little routine I'm amazed." Corran shook his head and waved Tycho to the couch. "I think I've gotten to the bottom of what's going on with him, though."

"Great." Tycho sat down and turned to face away from the picture wall. "Tell me what you've got—or at least as much as you can."

"Sure." A shiver worked its way down Corran's spine. A month previously Tycho had reported that Emtrey, Rogue Squadron's M-3PO unit, had exhibited odd behavior when told to shut up repeatedly. The droid had been acting strangely for a time before that, but no one had complained because he was talking less and had managed to cobble together some excellent exchanges on the black market and within the Alliance's quartermaster corps to get the Squadron needed supplies. That behavior Corran had been able to trace to his suggestion that the droid "scrounge" some parts to fix his X-wing.

"I managed to track records back to right before the evacuation of Hoth. Emtrey was there working for a Lieutenant in the Quartermaster Corps. Her name was Losca or something like that. Anyway, she was having to work hard to try to build up stores after the losses at Derra IV and she wasn't having much luck. At that point in time the defeat made things look bad for the Rebellion, so resources began to dry up."

Tycho nodded. "I remember. We had a difficult time

getting our equipment to function in the cold because we didn't have the proper conversion kits."

"It appears this Lieutenant Losca was getting killed on negotiations and wasn't getting the job done to her or Alliance Command's satisfaction. She wanted to create a database that would allow her to function like a commodities trader, but computer resources were limited and tied up coordinating things like defenses. Apparently the Alliance leadership wasn't too high on the idea of becoming a commodities exchange, so they forbade her from doing anything that ambitious and urged her to keep doing what she was doing."

"The Hoth base was supposed to be top secret." Tycho frowned. "Setting it up as some sort of marketplace would have led to its discovery even earlier than Vader's tactic of using probe droids surveying worlds."

"That may be true, but this Lieutenant Losca appeared to think that without some sort of trade, the Rebellion would run out of supplies. The base would remain hidden, but be out of everything that made it possible to rebel. In desperation she had some techs cobble Emtrey together out of spare parts. She sliced some commodities-brokering code together and burned it into some chips which were implanted into Emtrey. The brokering chips give him a second personality that operates without the normal 3PO personality being aware it exists. The scrounger can be brought to the fore by asking it to scrounge something, or telling it to shut up, as you discovered. When you use that latter technique, the droid becomes a simple terminal that gives you access to all its data."

The man from Alderaan leaned forward and rested his elbows on his knees. "What were the security precautions Losca took with the droid?"

"I don't know, and I can't ask because she died on Hoth during the assault. Emtrey got off the planet and has been kicking around from unit to unit until we got him. No one else learned about his secret until we ran across it. I had Whistler do a basic diagnostic scan of

Emtrey and the scrounging circuitry is the only unusual stuff in there. I don't think he's a security risk."

"That's good." Tycho smiled. "And it was good work getting the data from Hoth. Most of those files are still classified, aren't they?"

"All of them are, but Whistler's got slicing code that can get him through low-level security stuff." Corran shrugged. "Those files are easy to break—unlike the routines used to seal portions of your record."

Tycho barely missed a beat. "Good. I doubt there is much damage that could be done by people learning details about Hoth. My adventures, on the other hand, could cause problems."

Corran made no effort to hide the surprise at Tycho's words. "Aren't you angry with me for trying to crack your file?"

Tycho smoothed his light brown hair at the back of his neck. "Anger isn't going to do me any good, is it? I might be a little disappointed, but not angry."

"Why disappointed?"

"If there was something you wanted to know, you could have asked."

"Would I get a straight answer?"

Tycho blinked. "Why would you think I'd lie to you?"

Corran jerked a thumb toward the closed door. "There are two Alliance Security officers at my door, correct? They're waiting to escort you back to your quarters, right?"

"Yes. So . . . ?"

"So General Salm thinks you're some sort of threat to the Alliance. Shouldn't that make me wonder about you?"

"It could." Tycho shrugged his shoulders. "Then again, you could think about what you know about me and decide for yourself if I can be trusted or not."

Corran sat back and folded his arms across his chest. In his career with the Corellian Security Force, Corran had questioned all manner of people—humans, aliens, and even the occasional droid. He'd always had a sense about who was telling the truth and who was lying to him. He'd gotten used to following that feeling, playing his hunches to find the chinks in the stories suspects used to build.

From Tycho he was getting no sign of deception, but what he *didn't* know about the man seemed to outweigh what he *did* know. There was no question that Tycho Celchu had been a valued and valiant member of Rogue Squadron from before Hoth until after Endor, Bakura, and dozens of other little battles. He flew an A-wing in the assault on the second Death Star and managed to draw pursuit away from Wedge and the *Millennium Falcon*. Well after that he had volunteered for a classified mission and all trace of his records up to six months before he rejoined Rogue Squadron had been encrypted. The gap only amounted to three quarters of a year, but it marked the end of trust in him by a host of Alliance figures. *It seems Wedge Antilles was the only person who still had faith in him.*

Corran had only known Tycho for six months, but in that time Tycho had repeatedly flown an unarmed shuttle into dangerous situations to recover pilots who had been shot out of their ships. On one of those occasions he had saved Corran's life by providing him a datafeed that let him target incoming TIE Interceptors. It had been a brave thing to do, and one that could have gotten Tycho killed, but he took the chance to keep Corran alive.

Despite owing Tycho his life not once but twice, Corran still had reservations about him. Tycho had been secretive about the gap in his record. Corran could have easily ignored that, but the ease with which Tycho had overpowered his security detail and slipped away from supervision on the second occasion when he saved Corran's life made Corran wary. He knew his suspicion was the residue of having been a CorSec officer whose father and grandfather had also served CorSec, and he'd hoped learning the truth about Tycho would ease his mind.

The problem was that the only place he could learn the story would be from Tycho who, for better or worse, had to be considered somewhat unreliable as a narrator. *Still, it's better than unfocused suspicion.*

"Sir, I have trusted you in the past, and I'll go on trusting you in the future because I've not seen you do anything wrong. And I apologize for trying to slice out your file. I guess having worked with CorSec has just honed my sense of paranoia. Not knowing why Salm has you under guard has that sense working overtime."

"But you'd still like to know what happened to me two years ago?"

"Yes, sir."

"Fine." Tycho shrugged with resignation, but his voice carried with it some relief. "It'll be good to share this with someone else, but it goes no further, right?"

Corran held his hand up. "On my honor."

Tycho fixed him with a crystal-blue stare for a second, then nodded. "I volunteered to fly a TIE starfighter into Coruscant. The Alliance impounded it at Bakura and modified it heavily to fill it with sensor packages. In coming in I made several orbits of the planet and picked up all sorts of interesting data on the Golan space fortresses, the defense shields, the orbital solar collection mirrors, the skyhooks, the dry docks and ship factories, and everything else orbiting the planet. I then took the ship in, landed on Coruscant, and the data was downloaded. It was shipped out by various routes and within two weeks I was asked to fly the eyeball back out, taking readings as I went, then hook up with a freighter and return to the Alliance. I knew getting out would be tough, but we had all the proper codes to get out, so I chanced it."

"And the Imps got you."

"They did. Two ion-cannon blasts shorted every system I had in the ship, including the self-destruct. A Star Destroyer pulled me on board and I was captured. They hit me with a Stokhli stun spray and I was out. When I finally awakened again I was on a transport coming out of hyperspace. We grounded and I found out I'd been taken to Lusankya."

"Lusankya?!"

"You know it?"

"Only by the most vague and nasty of rumors. It's supposed to be Iceheart's own private prison. Weird things happen to people there."

Tycho nodded. "The guards, when they deign to speak to a prisoner, take great delight in noting that no one leaves unless Ysanne Isard is through with them."

Corran shook his head. It was easier for him to believe that the *Katana*-fleet existed than it was to accept the existence of Lusankya. Corran had first heard the word mentioned after a rival of Corellia's Diktat had been murdered by a trusted aide. The aide had been taken away by Imperial authorities about a year before the murder, but had been returned three months later. After he killed his boss he was reported to have repeated the word "Lusankya" over and over again. After that incident Corran had heard of a dozen other, similar situations where a seemingly normal person had turned on friends and family, betraying them or performing some hideous act of terrorism against them. Each of these incidents had a link to Lusankya in some way or other, but that link only became apparent after the crime had been committed.

Corran frowned at Tycho. "People who come out of there are human remote bombs. They do horrible things when the Empire activates them."

Tycho's hands convulsed into fists. "I know, I know. What's worse, no one has ever mentioned Lusankya *before* they have acted. The clues are always found later. But with me, after three months of interrogation and detention, I guess they decided I was useless. I was in bad shape—catatonic for most of my time at Lusankya so I remember almost nothing, then I was let go. They shipped me to Akrit'tar. After three months I managed to escape from the penal colony there and made my way back to the Alliance. I was debriefed for two months but they couldn't find anything wrong with me."

"And they hadn't found anything wrong with the other people who had been to Lusankya either, right?"

"No. The only difference between me and them was that I remembered having been there. It is the opinion of General Salm and some others that I was allowed to retain my memory, and that my escape was engineered, just so I could return to the Alliance and betray it."

Without any evidence to prove he was a sleeper agent, the Alliance couldn't imprison Tycho without seeming as much of a heartless entity as the Empire itself. Even so, Corran reminded himself, lack of evidence was not evidence of lack. Salm's suspicions about Tycho could be one hundred percent correct, and the utter lack of evidence pointed to the skill of Ysanne Isard and her people.

Corran's eyes narrowed. "So, you don't even know, really, if you are an Imperial agent waiting to happen or not?"

"I *know* I'm not." The Alderaanian's shoulders slumped. "Being able to prove it is something else again."

"But being constantly under suspicion, that's got to wear on you. Why put up with it? How *can* you put up with it?"

Tycho's expression drained of emotion. "I put up with it because I must. Enduring it is the only way I can be allowed to fight back against the Empire. If I were to walk away from the Rebellion, if I were to sit the war out, I would have surrendered to the fear of what Ysanne Isard might, *might*, have done to me. Without firing a shot she would have made me as dead as Alderaan, and I won't allow that. There's nothing in what I have to live with on a daily basis that isn't a thousand times easier than what I survived at the hands of the Empire. Until the Empire is dead, I can never truly be free because I'll always be under suspicion. Living with minor restrictions now means someday no one has to fear me."

Tycho slowly opened his hands and scrubbed them

over his face. "I don't know if any of that sets your mind at ease, but that's all there is."

Corran shook his head. "It helps, a great deal. Whether you are or are not an Imperial agent in a Rebel uniform, the fact is that you've saved my life twice. That definitely counts for something—a great big something, in fact."

"Good." Tycho pointed at the droid. "What do we do about him?"

"I don't think he's much of a security risk, provided he doesn't trade in futures for commodities that are present on whatever targets we're heading out to hit. Whistler's already modified his purchase parameter programming to cover that situation." Corran smiled. "I don't think General Salm will think Emtrey any less of a threat than he considers you, *if* we report on his scrounging personality. As long as we don't activate it, except in very specific cases, we should be safe."

"So you think we can reactivate him?"

"Yeah, I suppose so." Corran stood and walked over to the droid. "Brace yourself."

He hit the button on the back of the droid's neck.

Emtrey's head snapped back and locked in its proper position. The droid looked around for a moment or two during which his elbows crept out away from his body. "I don't know what got into me. Please, forgive my rudeness." The droid's head tilted to the right and his eyes brightened. "Did I miss anything?"

Corran slapped him on the shoulder. "Nothing you'd find useful, Emtrey. We were just swapping gossip and repeating rumors that had no substance to them at all."

4

At first the giddiness bubbling up inside him surprised Wedge, then gratified him as he slipped into his chair behind Admiral Ackbar. *They're actually here, the Provisional Council. I never thought I'd see the day.* He felt the same excitement inside him that he'd known as a child when some alien or famous Corellian had come to his parents' refueling station. Had he been asked he would have assumed that being in the same room with the leaders of the New Republic would not seem that special, but it *was* and made him think that the war hadn't burned all of his innocence out of him yet.

Mon Mothma, still looking strong and serene despite the traces of grey creeping into her hair, stood at her place at the circular table. "I call this meeting of the Provisional Council to order. Councilor B'thog of Elom sends regrets at being unable to attend, but we have a quorum, so we will be able to proceed. Councilor Organa, if you would be so kind as to update us on your attempts to open a dialog with Warlord Zsinj."

The woman at Mon Mothma's right hand stood. Though she wore a pale green gown gathered loosely at the waist with a silver belt, Wedge couldn't help but see

Princess Leia ready for battle, the way he had seen her so many times before. It struck him as odd that a martial image could so easily replace the elegant vision before him, but he was reading the fight in her eyes and the fire in her spirit. Those qualities had made her one of the Rebellion's most respected leaders, and clearly sustained her in her governmental activities.

"I have attempted through numerous channels to make contact with Warlord Zsinj, but have been rebuffed every time. It appears he believes his possession of the Super Star Destroyer *Iron Fist* has made him into a force to be reckoned with in the galaxy. What little of his Imperial career we know about indicates he is a man who embraces the idea that the ends *do* justify the means. He is a survivor, and shows cunning at playing his enemies off against each other. The leadership vacuum in the Imperial Navy post-Endor allowed him to rise further than was previously reasonable, then declare himself a Warlord and begin his drive to take control of the Empire."

Borsk Fey'lya's cream-colored fur rippled as he stood. "Councilor Organa, it would seem that this Zsinj, if he is as cunning as you suggest, would be open to negotiations. How have you approached him?"

A trace of weariness tightened the flesh at Leia's eyes. "We have tried contacts at various levels within his organization. Messages sent via the Imperial HoloNet have gone unanswered, though *your* people have assured me they have been collected by Zsinj. More light escapes from a black hole than information that comes back out from him and his fleet. I suspect he wants to see how truly strong we are before he begins any negotiations with us."

The Bothan's violet eyes narrowed. "If there is no information coming out of his organization, how do you know he is seeking data on us?"

Admiral Ackbar nodded to Leia. "If I might answer that, Councilor."

The hint of a smile on her lips banished the fatigue from her face. "Please, Admiral."

Ackbar remained seated and waited until the Bothan sat back down before he spoke. Borsk's fur rippled again, this time quickly, which Wedge took as a mark of irritation. "A little less than a standard week ago a freighter appeared in the Pyria system. It was challenged and responded with the proper passage codes, but a member of Rogue Squadron chose to do a closer check. The freighter launched six TIEs, four starfighters, and two bombers. The freighter fled and all but one of the smaller ships was destroyed. The one that survived was a bomber that had been disabled by two Y-wings. Examination of it and interrogation of the pilot indicates the ship was sent by Warlord Zsinj to confirm our conquest of Pyria and, if the opportunity presented itself, to strike at the base."

Borsk's face hardened. "And your people let the freighter escape?"

Ackbar's lids drifted down for a moment. "Councilor Fey'lya, the freighter was fully armed and deployed six fighter craft. On post we had two Y-wings and one X-wing. Despite being outnumbered, our forces eliminated the six fighters and damaged the freighter, driving it off. The freighter fled before the fighter screen was eliminated, but even if it had not, engaging it would have been suicidal."

"I thought such missions were Rogue Squadron's specialty."

Wedge felt color rising to his face. *The last time that was suggested, it was another Bothan who did the suggesting.*

Admiral Ackbar opened his hands. "I would point out that to so easily dismiss Rogue Squadron's sacrifices is to denigrate the sacrifices made by all peoples who have died in service to the Rebellion."

The Bothan councilor sat back and Wedge's admiration for Ackbar grew. The Admiral's veiled reference to *sacrifices* echoed the oft-heard Bothan lament about the number of Bothan agents who had died to secure the information about the second Death Star. Because the Bothans did not possess a strong military—as opposed to the Mon Calamari fleet forming the backbone of the New Republic's Armed Forces—they used the sacrifices of their people as their justification for sharing power in the New Republic. If Fey'lya devalued Rogue Squadron's contribution to the Rebellion, he likewise eroded his own basis of power.

Doman Beruss, a flaxen-haired woman who represented the Corellian exiles on the Council, stood. "I believe we are heading toward the focus for this meeting, but I would prefer to cut directly to it instead of watching my colleagues scratch and claw their way there. Zsinj knows, as do we, that whichever force is able to wrest Coruscant from the grip of the Imperial government will be seen as the legitimate, or at least strongest, claimant to governance. The Pyria system was taken to be a stepping stone to Coruscant, and Zsinj now knows we do have it."

The Wookiee and Sullustan representatives nodded in agreement with Doman. Mon Mothma looked up. "Admiral Ackbar, if you are prepared to give your presentation."

"I am." Ackbar stood and General Salm, a small, balding, thickly built man, slipped into the chair the Mon Calamari had vacated. Salm linked his datapad into a jack on the edge of the table. Above the mirrored plate centered on the table the holographic image of a world appeared.

"This is Coruscant. It was the administrative center of the Old Republic and retained that function when the Emperor seized power. Palpatine made an attempt to rename it Imperial Center, but it is known as such only in Imperial decrees. Coruscant is still seen as the heart of the galaxy and many look to it as the center of order and authority, no matter who controls it.

"After the Emperor's death, a government was formed under the leadership of Sate Pestage. His suzerainty lasted six months until a coup by a coterie of other Imperial advisers forced him into exile. It appears that his ouster was organized by Ysanne Isard—she was definitely behind Pestage's hounding and death. She deftly undercut the bureaucrats she had used to vanquish Pestage and took control of the Empire for herself. While she maintains her title of Director of Intelligence, and has suggested she is holding the planet in stewardship, there is no doubt that she is in full control."

As Ackbar spoke, the planet dissolved into an image of Isard. A tall, slender human woman, she still seemed possessed of the vitality that the Rebellion had begun to sap from Mon Mothma. Isard wore her hair long. Except for white sidelocks, her hair was as black as night and served to accentuate her severe beauty.

Her most striking features became apparent as the image shifted to a close-up of her face. Her eyes were mismatched. The right one was an icy blue that had contributed as much as her demeanor to her nickname of "Iceheart." By contrast the left eye was a molten red. Wedge felt a shiver run down his spine just looking at her hologram—and he had no desire to make a closer acquaintance with her.

Ackbar continued. "Despite her not being from a military background, she has, in no way, allowed the defenses of the Imperial homeworld to slacken. Outermost we have Golan Space Defense stations. They are comparable in power to a Star Destroyer. They are not mobile, so eliminating them from a section of the sky over Coruscant will give us an area in which to operate, but eventually all of them will have to be neutralized.

"In addition to these defense stations, there are approximately seven *Victory*-class Star Destroyers on station at Coruscant. There are ground-based fighter groups as well as the fighter wings stationed in and around the ships, shipyards, and orbital factories. The orbital mirror stations and low-orbit skyhooks may also have been armed."

Ackbar clasped his hands behind his back. "As formidable as all that is, the primary problem in taking Coruscant is the overlapping defense shields."

The image of the world had long since returned. As the Mon Calamari had described aspects of the defense, representations of them appeared in orbit around the planet. With his mention of the defense shields, two spheres constructed of hexagons appeared to encase the world. One moved in the direction of its orbit, the other moved in the opposite direction. The neon-blue lattice-work shrouded Coruscant and occluded any good view of it.

"To take Coruscant we must eliminate the shields. There are a number of ways to do this, but none of them is simple. A direct assault would cost us more dearly than both Death Star battles combined. I think the only reasonable approach to taking Coruscant is to blockade the world. It is hardly self-sufficient—even the defense stations only carry three standard months' worth of provisions. Faced with dwindling supplies, a negotiated surrender would be possible."

Mon Mothma frowned. "The problem with a blockade is twofold. The first is that it would keep our fleet at one place for an extended period of time. This would allow Isard to recall the Imperial fleet to drive us off."

Ackbar nodded. "Or it could encourage naval officers in far-flung regions to sever their ties with the Empire, breaking it up further."

"Giving us many warlords like Zsinj to worry about." Borsk's words came so softly they seemed almost purred. "Pinning our fleet in one place would also allow Zsinj to prey upon New Republic worlds."

Ackbar opened his hands. "Yes, what you suggest might happen."

Mon Mothma raised a hand and cut him off. "The second problem with a blockade is that the people of Coruscant will suffer. My friend, you visited Coruscant when you were with Grand Moff Tarkin. You know there are vast populations of outcasts who dwell deep in the shadowed canyons of that metroworld. They barely survive as it is. If supplies are cut off to Coruscant, they will suffer the most and we cannot afford to be responsible for their suffering."

"This I know very well, Chief Councilor Mothma,

but you face me with an impossible task." Ackbar pointed a hand at the floating hologram of Coruscant. "You want the world taken, but the means that will deliver it to us with the minimum of bloodshed is one that is unacceptable. It is possible to batter our way in there. I cannot say there will not be a significant amount of collateral damage—damage that may harm people as much as any blockade. Yet, even if that sort of damage is more acceptable from a diplomatic and political point of view, it leaves us with a reality that is militarily unacceptable: the world we take will be a world we cannot hold."

Wedge nodded. To bring the shields down on a planet, standard doctrine dictated that the shields were to be probed for weaknesses, such as places where an atmospheric anomaly was causing a disruption. That weakened sector would be targeted and a hole would be punched through it. The gap would then be used as a hole through which shield projectors would be destroyed by bombardment or laser fire. While that would bring the shields down and allow for a planetary assault, it would leave the planet defenseless until the shield generators could be repaired or, most likely, replaced.

"What you ask of me and my troops is not possible." Ackbar shook his head. "Coruscant, if taken in haste, will fall to another just as quickly, and all we have fought for in this Rebellion will be for naught."

5

Wedge opened his arms wide and stretched. Standing on the patio of the Noquivzor facility's only aboveground building, he looked out over rolling hills carpeted with golden grasses. The breezes that stirred eddies and currents into them warmed him and began to take the chill out of his clothes. He pulled off his jacket and slung it over his shoulder. *I need an hour or two of sun and warmth before I head back in there.*

After the morning Council session had adjourned, Wedge and Salm had returned to Admiral Ackbar's quarters and discussed the problems with conquering Coruscant. Because of Noquivzo's arid climate, Ackbar's quarters had been fitted with a humidification system that made the environment more comfortable for the Mon Calamari. For Wedge and General Salm, the humidity thickened the air to the point where it seemed to drag on them and tire them out.

Wedge smiled as he watched a herd of wilder-nerfs spread out and over a far hill like an inky black stain on the golden carpet. He recalled a promise he had previously made to himself to return to Noquivzor and take some time to relax. He had wanted to remember what he was fighting for, and this world had seemed the sort of place where he could find some peace. *Now I'm back, but there's no peace to be had.*

"Would that some of this tranquillity would sneak into our deliberations."

Wedge spun around. "Highness."

Leia smiled at him. "Wedge, please, not so formal. We've known each other for too long to stand on ceremony."

He nodded sheepishly. "I know that, but things have changed. Look at you. I can still see the Leia Organa who waited anxiously for Luke's return from the Death Star at Yavin, but the others, they all see you as Alderaan's representative to the Provisional Council. I have no intention of seeming familiar or disrespectful."

"Things may have changed, Wedge, but not us."

"I don't think I can agree with that idea entirely." Wedge hung his jacket over the back of a metal chair and leaned heavily upon it. "Yavin was over seven years ago. I've gone from being a pilot who thought he was very good to someone who leads a squadron of hotshots and aids an Admiral in planning assaults on the Imperial capital."

Leia nodded and drew a chair up beside the one upon which Wedge leaned. "Back at Yavin we didn't have any Admirals."

"We barely had any ships at Yavin. We had General Dodonna, but he's gone." Wedge seated himself beside her. "You've gone from being the youngest person ever to be elected to the Imperial Senate to the fusion reactor for the whole Rebellion. Mon Mothma may lead us, and Admiral Ackbar may fight for us, but you're the one who keeps all the disparate parts of the New Republic working together. How you do that, I can't even begin to guess."

She laughed lightly and Wedge smiled in response to the sound. "Keeping Han and Luke out of trouble has often been far more easy, to be certain. There are times it feels as if this Rebellion could be measured in decades, not years."

"I was thinking centuries, but your point is well taken." Wedge shook his head. "Are all the Council meetings this difficult?"

"Some are. This one in particular is prickly. Borsk Fey'lya has some issues he wants dealt with and he has taken steps to see to it that he gets his way."

"I think Admiral Ackbar is holding his own."

"That's because Fey'lya is playing for a longer game. He has things well thought out, and he is a stickler for details."

"What do you mean?"

Leia looked at him with a mixture of surprise and pity in her eyes. "Oh, Wedge, you wouldn't believe how well Fey'lya has orchestrated things to work against Admiral Ackbar."

"Try me."

"You're on." Leia swept a hand out to take in the nearly treeless landscape. "Fey'lya arranged for this meeting to be held here, on Noquivzor. He is right at home here—these savannahs closely resemble his home range on Bothawui. Mon Mothma, you, me, and the other humans find the climate and setting pleasant enough that we are at ease. Kerrithrarr, the Wookiee Councilor, does not like a world with wide blue skies and a lack of trees. Asking him to live underground is to come within millimeters of violating his personal honor, and you know how touchy Wookiees are about that."

"Yeah, now that you mention it, Noquivzor and Kashyyyk have very little in common. Admiral Ackbar and the other Mon Calamari don't like the dry air here."

"Sian Tevv and his Sullustans find it a bit hot here." Leia shrugged. "As a result, most of those who oppose Borsk Fey'lya are ill at ease here. It will be easy for tempers to flare and people to decide someone . . ."

"Admiral Ackbar . . ."

"Right, someone is being stubborn. This could influence votes and could go against Ackbar and his plans."

The Princess sat back and smoothed her gown against her thighs. "Of course, Ackbar knows all this, which is why he advanced the blockade plan. He knew it would not work, so now if he retreats from that position, he shows himself to be reasonable and willing to compromise. This means the other side must compromise, too."

Wedge frowned because until after the meeting, when Admiral Ackbar had explained these things to him, he'd completely missed the significance of what Leia had just indicated was blatantly obvious. "I think finding enemy ships and shooting them up is easier than this politics stuff."

"Possibly, but it's a matter of scale. You lead your people against several dozen Imperials at a time. Each of us represents millions and billions of individuals and our goal is the overthrow of billions. We cannot afford to be so direct or free."

"Once upon a time we could."

"True, but then we were all self-elected members of an outlaw movement. Now we speak and act for whole worlds." Leia reached over, took Wedge's hand, and gave it a squeeze. "Back in those days I scarcely dared dream we'd have these problems to deal with in the future."

Wedge patted the top of her hand. "Yeah, in those days it seemed as if our children and grandchildren would still be fighting the Empire."

"Indeed." She laughed again. "So, Wedge Antilles, any prospects on the horizon for you contributing to the Rebellion's next generation?"

"Me? I have all the children I need in my squadron." He saw sadness wash across her face. "It's not that bad. I have friends, I just don't have the time to go courting. You found someone, and you weren't even looking. It seems to happen that way, so I'm not terribly worried. Now what about you and Han?"

"We're happy, when we get to see each other. It's kind of rough on a woman to finally admit you love someone and then have him frozen in carbonite for the better part of a year. Then again, during that time he didn't find little ways to irritate me."

"That's his nature, though—he's chaos incarnate." Wedge smiled. "Han Solo, you have to love him . . ."

". . . or freeze him in carbonite, I know." Leia stared wistfully off into the distance. "He's a good man. Even with his quirks and rough edges, I don't think I can find better in this galaxy. And I'm not really interested in looking, either, but there are times when I wonder 'Why him?' "

"If you ever have doubts, serious doubts, come see me. I can give you a dozen reasons to answer that question." *Not the least of which is that it takes a guy as fast and sharp as Han Solo to keep up with you, Leia.* Wedge let go of her hand and stretched again. "What about Luke? How is he doing?"

"He's doing well. He's continuing his Jedi training. He's also been traveling around the galaxy trying to recover any artifacts or documents that will fill in the background of the Jedi Knights. The Emperor's attempt to exterminate the order was very effective. Only the histories written at his order remain and they're long on fabrication. Luke says they have nothing serious to offer by way of instruction for a Jedi, though a couple of the texts suggest exercises that are designed to lure a potential Jedi over to the dark side."

"That's nasty, and rather typical of the Emperor."

"He was evil and, just as bad, quite thorough in his methodology." Leia sighed. "Luke has designed a regimen of exercises and has convinced me to start training. I do them when I can, but a Jedi is supposed to be tranquil and at peace when she acts, and the frustration inherent in my position often keeps me away from the proper frame of mind."

"I can imagine. The next time you see him, or speak with him, tell him he's welcome to fly with Rogue Squadron whenever he wants. I've got a good bunch of people—a solid core group to which I'll be adding new people as they become available." Wedge sat forward.

"We've rebuilt the squadron by filling it with good pilots who also have other skills. Ackbar wanted and we've now got an elite group that can handle everything from pitched battles to covert entry and scouting operations. Adding a Jedi Knight into the mix wouldn't hurt a bit."

"I suspect Luke would like flying with you again, but the responsibility of being the last or, rather, the first *new* Jedi Knight weighs very heavily on him right now. He's busy discovering as much as he can about the tradition to which he has become heir. I will give him your message, though."

"Thanks."

A comlink bleeped and Leia produced it from within the sleeve of her gown. "Councilor Organa here."

"Leia, it's Mon Mothma. If you have a moment, I have some things to discuss with you."

"On my way." Leia snapped the comlink off, then leaned over and gave Wedge a kiss on the cheek. "You may be right—we have changed, but I'm thankful that it's not so much that I can't sit with an old friend and relax for a minute or two. I'll see you later, Wedge."

"Good-bye, Leia." Wedge stood as she departed. *Change we have, Leia, but change for the better, I think. Seven years is a long time, but I think we can handle seven more.* He smiled. *And maybe another seven after that.*

A man came out onto the patio and turned in Wedge's direction. Though white hair dominated the red on his head, his green eyes and sharp cheekbones made the resemblance to his son unmistakable. Wedge snapped to attention and saluted.

The man stopped and returned the salute, then offered Wedge his hand. "Pleased to make your acquaintance, Commander Antilles."

"Likewise, General Cracken. Is there something I can do for you?"

The General pointed Wedge back to his chair. "If you have a moment."

Wedge resumed his place. "Go ahead."

"I wanted to thank you for taking my son in as a member of your Rogue Squadron."

"Thank me?" Wedge chuckled. "There are very few parents that would consider their children joining Rogue Squadron a good thing."

"I think you will find I am rather unlike most parents, Commander." The elder Cracken had the same general build as his son, though he had thickened a bit in the middle and jowls were just beginning to form on him. "Many other commanders would have rejected him just because of his connection to me. They would assume I was using him as an agent to audit their activity."

"Are you?"

"Should I be?"

Wedge shrugged. "I don't think so, but General Salm has concerns over the security of my unit."

"I'm aware of the Celchu situation but I am not overly concerned by it. I trust you will report any problem in that regard."

"Of course."

"I expected nothing less." Cracken rubbed his hands together. "Pash is a very talented man—I say this as his father and as a New Republic officer. His early success put him in a position where it was difficult for him to do anything else of apparent consequence, which meant he would have to push himself above and beyond his abilities to succeed. While I have no doubt he has not yet found the upper range of his talents, clearly his people could not keep up with him. His desire to do more was tempered by his knowledge that he could easily get them killed. It was a situation that would end up with him hating himself—either for having done nothing, or having gotten his people killed.

"By joining you he will be challenged. You're a good man, Antilles. You don't take chances when you don't need to, but you don't shrink from doing the jobs that need to be done. You've found the balance my son needs to find for himself. I don't expect you'll get him killed, but if he does die as a Rogue, I know he'll have been doing the best he could to do the best for the Rebellion. I'd hate to lose him, but if he has to go, doing so in that way isn't bad."

"I hope Rogue Squadron will live up to your expectations."

"I'm sure it will."

The confidence in Airen Cracken's voice made Wedge's stomach tighten. "Should it concern me, sir, that the head of Alliance Intelligence has just told me that his son will find his time in my unit *challenging*?"

" 'Concern' you, Commander?"

"Yes, sir."

"Oh, I should think so, Commander Antilles." Cracken nodded solemnly. "Very much so, indeed."

6

Whistler's warble made Corran look up at the timer on his green and white X-wing's main display. "Five minutes until we come out of hyperspace, thanks." The countdown marked the end of a two-leg run from Borleias to Mrisst that took a total of five hours to complete. Taking the precaution of hitting a transit system before arriving at Mrisst struck Corran as unnecessary, if the intelligence they were reacting to was correct. *Our target already knows where we live.*

Mirax Terrik had arrived at Borleias aboard her ship, the *Pulsar Skate*, after a trade run that had included a visit to Mrisst. Being a smuggler of no small amount of skill, she had pulled a copy of the local system traffic reports from Mrisst control to see who was operating in her area and might prove to be competition. One of the ships on the list was a freighter by the name of *Vengeance Derra IV*. When she arrived on Borleias she asked Emtrey for any information he had on the ship, and that resulted in their recon flight.

Corran fought to clear his mind and focus on the mission. That was not an easy task because of two bits of information the squadron had received a couple of hours prior to the mission being planned and launched. The first was confirmation by Thyferran officials of Bror Jace's death. He had been the hottest Rogue pilot in the squadron's first five missions, amassing twenty-two kills to eclipse Corran's mark by one. Upon his return from his last mission, he was called back to Thyferra because of a relative's impending death, but he had never arrived at his destination. Everyone had feared the worst, but until Thyferran officials backtracking his intended route had found debris from a destroyed X-wing, everyone had hoped for the best.

Though Corran and Bror had been rivals, they had also understood each other. Without that understanding, Corran probably would have accepted news of his death as easily as the others did. The Thyferrans reported that an Imperial Interdictor cruiser had been working in that general area, so the scenario appeared to be that Jace had been pulled out of hyperspace a bit prematurely and jumped by TIEs and destroyed. It seemed plausible to Corran except that no one reported finding any TIE fighter debris.

If I got jumped, I would have taken some of them with me. Corran did admit to himself that Bror could have been surprised and killed with a lucky shot or two, but that struck him as unlikely. If his ship had malfunctioned or something else had gone wrong, then Bror would have been helpless. The problem with that theory was that the unit's chief tech, a Verpine named Zraii, kept the X-wings in prime condition. Unless someone had tampered with the ship, the chances of a malfunction were slim and none.

The Interdictor cruiser had been reported to be the *Black Asp*. It might have been coincidence, but the Rogues had fought against that ship in their first engagement. Corran had come as close to dying in that fight—one where they had been dragged out of hyperspace by accident—as he ever wanted to get again. If not for Tycho Celchu's intervention he would have been dead or, worse yet, a guest at some Imperial penal colony.

He would have been inclined to let the *Black Asp*'s appearance pass for coincidence except for the second bit of information that came through to him. Emtrey had been trying to locate information on Gil Bastra, the man who had been Corran's superior at CorSec. Gil had been the one to fabricate the identities under which Corran, his human partner, and her husband had fled from Corellia. Corran had asked the droid to look for information because of a spurious report indicating that Gil had been caught and killed by Imperial authorities.

Emtrey had found a report that confirmed the original death notice, but this one elaborated on the cause of death. Gil had been killed during a botched interrogation by Intelligence Agent Kirtan Loor. Loor had been the Imperial Liaison to Corran's CorSec division and no love had been lost between them. *I never liked him even before he let my father's murderer walk free.*

A lump rose in Corran's throat. He rubbed at it with his right hand, the heel of which pressed his medallion against his breastbone. His father had kept the medal as a lucky charm. It was the only memento of his father he had left since he fled from Corellia and Mirax had identified it as a commemorative medal struck to mark a Corellian Jedi Knight's elevation to the rank of Master. The feel of the gold medallion helped him remember the good times with his father, and that eased the tension in his throat.

Corran knew it was a fallacy to think that two facts linked by time had a causal relationship, but he could not shake the gut feeling that Kirtan Loor had been involved somehow with Bror Jace's ambush and death. The report about Gil's death had indicated Loor had been summoned to Coruscant and assigned "new duties." Corran had no doubt that no matter what Loor was supposed to be doing, he would continue to look for a way to get back at Corran for eluding capture at Corellia. *If Loor found out that I was with Rogue Squadron, he'd do anything he could to strike at me, even if he could only kill my friends.*

Corran bounced his helmet back against the ejection seat's headrest. "Think about Loor later, now you have a mission to run." He glanced at the cockpit chronometer. "Ten seconds to reversion to realspace. Hang on, Whistler, we're going in hot."

The wall of light outside the cockpit exploded into a million pinpoints of light as Rogue Squadron burst into the GaTir system. Their jump had been plotted with spectacular precision—exceeding even that for which Sullustans were renowned—so they appeared below the planetary plane, heading in toward Mrisst via the south pole. Pash Cracken had suggested that approach since the austral-polar continent was known to be too geologically unstable for the Mrisst Trade and Science Academy to have set up any astronomical observation posts.

Rogue Squadron had not expected to arrive unnoticed, but they wanted as little data about them collected for as long as possible. If *Vengeance* was monitoring the same sort of traffic control reports that Mirax had pulled, the arrival of eight X-wings would attract attention. The arrival of eight mongrel snubfighters—for that was what Rogue Squadron's navigational beacons proclaimed them to be—would barely be noticed.

Data collection from stations on the planet would eventually be collated with the traffic data and point out that the "Uglies"—to use the Corellian nickname for such rebuilt craft—were performing like X-wings in good repair. With sufficient luck this anomaly wouldn't be noticed until after the mission was over. Corran was willing to settle for it being overlooked until they'd found *Vengeance*.

The X-wings swept up and around the fringes of Mrisst's atmosphere and caught their first glimpse of *Vengeance* glinting in sunlight. "Whistler, what's the ship next to *Vengeance*?"

The droid chittered for a moment, then displayed the answer on Corran's secondary monitor. The ship was a medium-sized transport calling itself *Contruum's Pride*. Whistler appended to his identification a criminal behavior code that Corran recognized as meaning the ships were moving in tandem, remaining steady to facilitate the transfer of cargo. *This is just like spotting smugglers back with CorSec.*

Before Corran could key his comm unit and let the others know *Pride* was in league with *Vengeance*, Pash Cracken's voice filled the comm channel. "Twelve, *Pride* is bad."

"How do you know that, Four?" Captain Nunb asked.

"Contruum's my homeworld. Naming conventions for ships restrict virtues to capital ships. Transports are named for beasts of burden and rivers."

Corran keyed his comm unit. "Four is correct, Twelve. *Pride* is transferring cargo to or taking it from *Vengeance*."

"We have two for the taking, then. S-foils in attack position."

Corran reached up and hit the appropriate switch. The fighter's stabilizers split and locked into the position that gave the X-wing its name. Off to the starboard side of his ship he saw the four fighters in Two Flight move out under Cracken's command. Corran served as Captain Nunb's wingman, with Rhysati Ynr and Erisi Dlarit in Rogues Seven and Eight completing One Flight.

Captain Nunb's voice filled the comm channel. "Starships *Vengeance Derra IV* and *Contruum's Pride*, this is Captain Aril Nunb of Rogue Squadron. You have violated New Republic space. Stand down. Drop your shields. Prepare to surrender your vessels."

Corran's green eyes narrowed as the ships began to move apart. "Be alert, Rogues. They're moving and the one thing we know *Vengeance* needs more of is TIEs."

As if summoned by his words, a dozen TIE starfighters and interceptors boiled out of the gap between the two ships.

"They needed pilots, too, Nine."

"Which they apparently got, Four."

"Cut the chatter. Two Flight, take *Vengeance*. One Flight, we have cover."

"As ordered, Twelve." Corran flexed his right hand, then took firm hold on the flightstick. He thumbed his lasers over to dual-offset mode that fired them in pairs. Doing that meant each shot packed less power, but he got a faster rate of fire. In the sort of wheeling, twisting dogfight the eyeballs and squints promised, rapid fire was devoutly to be desired. "I have your wing, Twelve."

No sooner had he said that than Nunb's ship sideslipped to port, then dove toward the planet. Corran had no idea why she'd done that, but he followed her as best he could, remaining off her starboard stabilizer and back a bit. As he started to follow her as she pulled up and out of the dive, he saw her lasers flash and the lead eyeball exploded.

"Nice shooting, Twelve."

Her only reply came in a snap-roll up onto her port stabilizer that she quickly reversed. The stern of her ship slid to starboard as she applied rudder, swinging the nose of her craft to port. It tracked along the course of the TIE that had taken her snap-roll feint. Nunb's quad shot clipped the port wing on the eyeball and sent it spinning off into space.

"You have lead, Nine."

"As ordered, Twelve." Corran glanced at his scanner and found a pair of Interceptors angling in from above. He pulled back on his stick, rolled, and acquired his first target. He set up for a head-to-head pass, then cut his throttle back. Bringing the port stabilizer up, he let the fighter sideslip to the right, then he applied port rudder and repeated Nunb's tracking shot on the lead squint.

It took him four shots to do what she had done in one, but the effect was no less spectacular. The scarlet laser bolts burned a line of holes in the Interceptor's canted port wing. It began to tear away from the front and smashed into the ball cockpit. When the top half of the stabilizer finally ripped free, the port wing twisted. The Interceptor began to gyrate and spin, then shook itself apart. Finally the twin ion engines exploded, one after the other, sowing ship shards on the Mrisst atmosphere.

The second squint kept coming and Corran's maneuver had left him presenting his profile to it. Whistler whooped a warning, but Corran felt no panic at all. He rolled the ship over onto its top, then hit more left rudder. This reversed the effects of his previous move and left him going nose-to-nose with the squint. Corran centered the Imp in his targeting cross and when it went green, he tightened up on the trigger.

The laser bolts perforated the cockpit and filled it with fire. A secondary explosion shredded the squint. The wings sailed away from the fiery red and blue ball, then the ion engines blew, engulfing the remains of the ship in a silvery cloud. It imploded and tiny bits of debris struck sparks from Corran's shields, but did no damage.

On ahead Corran spotted *Vengeance* because of the sheer volume of laser fire coming from its bow and waist lasers. The green darts formed striated cones of fire that spiraled around as the gunners attempted to hit their targets. While the freighter's guns had not been intended as antifighter weapons, the tight spirals meant the gunners were having a very difficult time tracking their targets.

Apparently Lieutenant Cracken can fly very well.

Corran saw four pairs of proton torpedoes head in at the waspy freighter from widely disparate angles. Even if the gunners had been good enough to actually shoot the torpedoes out of the void, covering all the shots would have been difficult. Some shots were going to get through, the only question remaining was how many.

All the torpedoes hit, bringing down *Vengeance*'s forward and aft shields amid a storm of brilliant explosions. *Vengeance* began to rotate in space, exposing a gaping hole in the port side. Escape pods shot out in all directions. The freighter continued to move away from Mrisst, but it was clearly drifting and would eventually succumb to the planet's gravitational pull.

"Nine, break starboard."

Corran rolled his ship to the right hard, but still

caught a couple of green laser bolts on his aft shield. He shunted power from his lasers to the shields, then evened their strength out. Back where he had been, a TIE starfighter swooped through a dive, and one of the squadron's X-wing's flashed past, hot on its tail.

"I can't shake this squint on me."

"Twelve is on the way, Eight."

Erisi has one on her and Captain Nunb is on her way to help. Corran saw two TIE starfighters streak down and past him, coming in on an oddly angled vector. He wondered what they were doing until Whistler put a track up on his screen that showed them to be on an intercept for Rogue Seven, the ship that had called for him to break. *Her target is pulling through a tight loop and she's following, while the two* garrals *try to cut across the circle and nail Rhysati. Not if I can help it.*

"Seven, watch your aft. I'm coming, but be prepared to break up and right if I call."

"I copy, Nine. Almost have him."

Corran rolled the ship to port, then hit enough rudder to stand the X-wing on its nose. He punched the throttle full forward and angled in at the two fighters following Rhysati's ship. He switched his targeting system over to proton torpedoes, but didn't target the TIEs immediately. *Some models have a target lock warning system. If I give them a chance to dodge, they will.* He took a quick breath, blew it out, then let his range on the lead TIE drop to one kilometer. Nudging his stick forward, he impaled the eyeball on his targeting crosshairs. The HUD went red, Whistler sounded a solid tone, and Corran hit his trigger.

The proton torpedo lanced out and hit the lead eyeball dead on. It pierced the starfighter's port wing, then exploded right in front of the cockpit. The central ball crumpled as the wing disintegrated. The bulk of the craft went tumbling off down Mrisst's gravity well.

Corran switched back to lasers and sideslipped right. He snapped a quick shot off that dinged the other TIE's starboard wing, but failed to get enough of it to do significant damage. The TIE broke hard to port, so Corran rolled the X-wing to the port, applied some rudder, and cut his speed back to remain on the TIE's tail.

The eyeball rolled right, then climbed sharply. Corran started to climb, then the TIE came over to complete a loop. Corran snapped the X-wing over on its right S-foil, presented his port side to the TIE. The starfighter's first shots passed wide on either side of the snubfighter, but the eyeball started to roll to correct his aim.

Corran hit hard left rudder, then rolled ninety degrees to starboard to face the eyeball head on and give him the worst targeting profile possible. With a flick of his thumb he brought the torpedo targeting program up and immediately got a tone from Whistler. Ignoring the hail of green laser bolts hammering his forward shield, Corran squeezed the trigger.

The proton torpedo tore the TIE's starboard wing off, sending the starfighter into a flat spin. Whistler reported the ship's thrust had cut in half. Corran would have put that down to damage done to the starboard engine, but the spin began to slow. The pilot had clearly shut down the port engine so he could counter the spin. Restarting the port engine would give the pilot maneuvering power, but an explosion on the port side of the fighter showed the restart had not worked as intended. Blue lightning played over the fighter, then it burst into a fireball that streaked in toward the system's sun.

"Whistler, targets."

The droid displayed an image of *Contruum's Pride* on the scope, but it wasn't going anywhere. Corran hit a few buttons on his console, shifting around to see if there were any more fighters available, but he found none. Whistler's negative bleat chastened him for doubting the droid.

"Just checking."

Whistle rebleated his comment.

"Yes, perhaps I *should* know better." Corran keyed his comm unit. "Nine is clear, Twelve."

"I copy, Nine. Come to a heading of 173 and orbit

Vengeance at three klicks. Four has convinced *Pride* that it wants to help stabilize *Vengeance* so it doesn't do an atmosphere dive. Mrisst Disaster Control is scrambling for recovery operations."

"As ordered, Twelve." Corran smiled. "And, Captain?"

"Yes, Nine?"

"Impressive flying out there. Welcome to Rogue Squadron. You're definitely one of us."

"Thanks, Nine. It's nice to be home."

7

At the sound of her voice a jolt ran through Kirtan Loor. He whirled away from his workstation and dropped to one knee before the towering holographic projection of Ysanne Isard. "Madam Director, I am at your service."

"That was my impression."

The chilly tone in her voice warned him that her mood was not one in which she would tolerate mistakes. He couldn't think of any he had made, but he killed the stirrings of anger that being unjustly accused started in him. *You have been accused of nothing. Her mood may not have anything to do with you or your service.* "What would you have of me, Madam Director?"

Some of the venom in her varicolored stare survived transmission from her office kilometers up and away from his work space in the bowels of the Imperial Palace. "I would have of you the best effort you can produce."

"Always, my lady."

"Your report on the incompetence of the *Black Asp*'s flight coordinator in the Bror Jace matter was quite thorough. I wanted Jace alive so I could utilize him at Lusankya. Your report makes it quite clear that Major Wortin knew this, but took no steps to guard against a kill. And you were correct in pointing out that his insistence that the ship blew up by accident was nothing more than a sham."

"Thank you."

"I did not need your editorializing in the conclusion you drew. It is true that in the past Major Wortin would have been executed, but we cannot afford to squander our personnel with such abandon anymore. I have approved your suggestion that he be transferred to the *Inexorable*. Under Thrawn he will learn lessons he should already know, or he will die."

"Yes, Madam Director."

"I have received another request from General Derricote for subjects. This time he wants Quarren?"

Loor brushed a hand back over his black widow's peak, then looked up at her. He had often been told he looked like a young Grand Moff Tarkin, but he was fairly certain Tarkin would never have let Isard intimidate him. *Tarkin had real power, almost as much as Iceheart wields here on Imperial Center. I have only the little bits I have assembled. I must wait and accumulate more.*

"Yes, Madam Director, that is his request. General Derricote's cadre of scientists have made the initial breakthrough in their research on Gamorreans. The virus has an incubation period of a month and is fatal in seventy-five percent of the cases."

"The incubation period is too long. It must be faster."

"Yes, they know that."

"How long are the subjects contagious?"

Loor reached back and pulled his datapad from the desk. "Four days, during the final throes of the disease. Transmission occurs through bodily fluid and can survive in contaminated water supplies for almost a day. It can be frozen and survive indefinitely."

Isard's expression hardened. "It cannot be made airborne?"

"The current theory is that the same genetics that would make it transmissible by air would greatly facilitate a spontaneous mutation allowing it to affect humans."

"Unacceptable."

"As I have told them, Madam Director." Loor glanced at his datapad again. "Derricote believes part of the incubation period problem is tied to the sluggishness of the Gamorrean metabolism. Quarren are not as good a platform to guarantee cross-species susceptibility, but their metabolic rate is higher than that of Gamorreans."

"Very well, give him what he wants. Organize sweeps in the undercity for Quarren. There should be enough of them in the warrens to suit his needs." Isard rubbed at her eyes with slender fingers. "Collect extras—Derricote's estimates of what he will need are always conservative."

"Yes, Madam Director."

"And tell Derricote I want the incubation period cut to a week, and I expect that breakthrough in a month, no more."

"I saw the reports of Zsinj's forces showing up near the core. Do you think he is coming here?"

Ysanne Isard laughed aloud and Loor decided he'd heard more pleasant sounds during difficult interrogations. "Zsinj? Never while I am here. He knows I would pluck out his heart and fling it into the streets from the highest tower in the Palace. The only way he will come here is after someone has taken the world away from me, and he can slink in like the coward he is and take it away from them. No, his probes are to evaluate my defenses and the Rebellion's strength. He will compare them, then put himself into a position to become the victor after the Rebels and I exhaust ourselves in the fight for Imperial Center."

Despite having only read it once, Kirtan Loor recalled very clearly the details contained in Zsinj's Imperial datafile. Everything there correlated well with the conclusion that the man was an opportunist, though Loor hesitated at deciding such a label defined the man completely. *I would have done that before my association with Iceheart, but I have been made painfully aware that relying on conclusions I had drawn was the source of the difficulties in my life.*

"If it would please you, Madam Director, I can arrange for efforts to discourage Warlord Zsinj's scouting
missions."

"No, absolutely not. The man may not be terribly
brave, but he compensates for this by being venial and
vengeful. Strike at him and he will feel compelled to strike
back." Isard's expression grew distant as her voice trailed
off. "No, we must concentrate on the Rebellion. All must
be ready for them when they decide to strike at Imperial
Center."

"As you wish, Madam Director."

"You had better hope so, Agent Loor. If Derricote
does not have his distraction for them available then, I
shall have to take drastic steps to assure that anyone connected with his project does not fall into Rebel hands."
She smiled coldly. "And if I were you, the implications
thereof would frighten me to death."

8

Wedge dried the palms of his hands on his thighs as he watched Admiral Ackbar rise in response to Mon Mothma's invitation. "Thank you, Chief Councilor. My staff and I have spent a considerable amount of time since yesterday's session reviewing and analyzing all pertinent files concerning Coruscant. While we are still of the opinion that a blockade of the world is the preferable course of action from the military point of view, we are willing to concede that other factors may make this option unavailable to us."

Mon Mothma smiled with genuine pleasure. "I appreciate your efforts in this regard, my friend. Have you discovered another way to approach this problem?"

"We have identified a number of them, Chief Councilor."

Borsk Fey'lya tapped a button on the datapad in front of him. "A more logical course would have been to identify the greatest problem preventing our conquest, would it not?"

The Mon Calamari nodded solemnly in the Bothan's direction. "We have done this as well. Clearly the overlapping planetary shields are the primary impediment to achieving our goal."

The large black Wookiee seated to Princess Leia's right growled a question that Leia's gold 3PO unit translated. "Oh, my, Councilor Kerrithrarr wishes to know if you have found a way to bring the shields down?"

The Wookiee snarled and the gold droid's arms flapped for a second. "I conveyed the meaning of your message, Councilor, without using the colorful analogy you suggested. For clarity, sir."

"I understand the question." Ackbar held a hand up to forestall further elaboration from the Wookiee. "In reply, perhaps an analogy *is* appropriate in that Coruscant can be likened to the first Death Star."

Borsk Fey'lya barked a quick laugh. "You suggest we let Skywalker and Rogue Squadron fly in and destroy the planet with a well-placed proton torpedo?"

"I am terribly sorry to disappoint my esteemed colleague from Bothawui, but I was thinking to the prior visit to the Death Star, when Obi-wan Kenobi succeeded in sabotaging the facility to allow the *Millennium Falcon* to escape." Ackbar pressed both of his hands against the tabletop. "The overriding problem we have in deciding how to approach Coruscant is determining exactly what is where. Huge construction droids are constantly grinding up old buildings and creating new ones. While we do have agents on the ground who are trying to supply us with as much data as possible, most of it comes from assets placed within the Imperial administration. While this has allowed us to react to things the Empire is doing off-planet, these resources are poorly positioned and trained to provide us with the sort of military data needed to enable us to effectively plan for conquest."

Doman Beruss looked over at Ackbar. "You want to send a team of military specialists to Coruscant as a prelude to moving on the world?"

"It is a stormy sea, but this venture is the first stroke in calming it."

Doman looked over toward Mon Mothma and beyond to one of the Chief Councilor's advisers. "General Cracken, this sort of intelligence operation falls into your area of expertise. Are you prepared to handle it?"

"Councilor Beruss, I have reviewed the general guidelines for the operation and I approve of them. I am prepared to use the assets I have developed on Coruscant to aid Admiral Ackbar's effort. However, the general division of labor within the Alliance—a division caused by our limited resources—means most of my people lack a prime requisite for being able to carry out this operation."

The Bothan craned his neck around to look at Cracken. "That requisite being?"

"None of my available people are fighter pilots." Cracken gestured in Wedge's direction. "Admiral Ackbar has suggested, and I agree, that Rogue Squadron is a natural choice for the operation."

"Rogue Squadron?" Borsk Fey'lya made no attempt to cover his surprise, and Wedge thought he might have been exaggerating it a bit for dramatic effect. "Here your analogy to the Death Star comes back to haunt you, Ackbar. Rogue Squadron may have worked miracles before, but they could not possibly succeed in rendering Coruscant defenseless."

"Rendering the planet defenseless is not the purpose of the mission, Councilor Fey'lya." Ackbar turned and pointed at Wedge. "In rebuilding the squadron care was taken to choose the best individuals possible—both in the area of their flying skills and for a host of other skills. Rogue Squadron is uniquely qualified for this mission."

"Do you think this as well, General Cracken?"

"I do, Councilor Fey'lya."

"You would risk your son's life in this?"

"That is a question that has been answered many times over."

The Bothan's creamy fur rippled along his shoulders. He fixed Wedge with a violet stare. "You accept this mission, Commander Antilles?"

Wedge waited to answer until after he got a nod from

Admiral Ackbar. "In principle, yes. The details are still being worked out."

"Do you think you could be effective on the ground there?"

Wedge thought for a moment before answering. "Given the parameters of the operation, yes."

Leia casually raised a hand. "Perhaps you could explain what you mean by that, Commander Antilles?"

"Of course, Councilor Organa." Wedge gave her a smile in thanks for breaking up Fey'lya's interrogation. "Because of the virtually total urbanization of the planet, Coruscant presents some unique problems for an incoming force. As we saw at Hoth, the Imperials correctly took our shield generators down first, then worked on other targets of military importance. On Coruscant we need to be able to pinpoint power plants, communications centers, and other sites that we can hit to disrupt Imperial command and control functions. We need to pull the shields down, then make them deaf and blind. If we give them no power to operate their defensive weapons, we further guarantee our success."

Leia nodded thoughtfully. "You said you needed to pinpoint targets. In what way does your piloting skill enhance your ability to do this?"

Easy questions with important answers—hitting Coruscant should be this simple. "Councilor, it is one thing to identify the locations we need to hit, but hitting them is another thing entirely. As a pilot I can identify and evaluate the possible approaches to a target. I can also help determine how much in the way of firepower will be necessary to eliminate it.

"I should also point out that we really do need to be running a precision operation because we have to take into account the possibility of Warlord Zsinj or some other Imperial leader trying to take Coruscant from us while we are trying to bring its defenses back up. For example, hitting a power conduit is preferable to hitting the reactor creating the power it carries because the conduit is much easier to replace."

The Bothan smoothed the fur on his chin with his left hand. "Bribing a custodian to shut the power down would be much easier, wouldn't it?"

"Yes, sir, but handling that sort of thing is outside my area of expertise."

"I see." Borsk Fey'lya sat forward and clasped his hands together. "Despite my reservations about this mission, I do agree with my Mon Calamari compatriot that the gathering of information is necessary if the conquest of Coruscant is to happen. I would also vouchsafe that any interim disruption of normal Imperial functions on Coruscant by Rogue Squadron, or General Cracken's people, would not be seen as a negative."

Ackbar blinked once, slowly, then clasped his hands behind his back. "Disruption is not necessary, but it could be effective and even helpful."

"I would think it could be very helpful, especially if it served as a distraction for Imperial authorities who might be working against Rogue Squadron." Fey'lya opened his hand. "That seems reasonable, does it not?"

Ackbar nodded. "Perhaps."

Wedge sensed in the slow delivery of Ackbar's reply an extreme reluctance to grant the Bothan his point. *Leia suggested Admiral Ackbar would have to compromise, and he has retreated from the blockade. It would seem Borsk Fey'lya wants him to concede more.*

"Good, for I have a little operation that I think will function very well as an adjunct to what you want to do."

"And that is?"

Fey'lya hit a button on his datapad and the holoplate in the middle of the table displayed a small, dirty red ovoid planet whose atmosphere escaped into space like smoke drifting from dying embers. A single large moon orbited it, plunging in and out of the wispy tendrils of atmosphere trailing from the planet. Wedge didn't recognize the world until the Bothan sigils running down the edge of the image area resolved themselves into Basic letters and strung themselves together at the planet's southern pole.

Kessel! Wedge shook his head. He knew that the Empire had maintained a penal colony there and used the prisoners as slave labor to harvest spice. One of Rogue Squadron's recruits—the first of the new members to be slain—had come from Kessel and still had family there who worked as educators. After the Emperor's death, the inmates had overthrown their masters and had taken control of the planet. They administered the mines and the vast atmosphere factories that freed enough oxygen and other gases from the rocks to let people exist on the surface using nothing more elaborate than a rebreather. It was a brutal existence with very little in resources being available to the residents—that the world was considered viable was more a testament to the tenacity of the residents than any measure of scientific analysis.

Borsk Fey'lya stood. "Kessel was one of the detention centers the Empire used to house dissidents as well as hardened felons. When the inmates took control of the center they chose a Rybet by the name of Moruth Doole to administrate. He was a minor official at the prison and appears to have been connected to the spice trade, hence his easy alliance with the prisoners. The Imperials and the political prisoners were sent to work in the spice mines. A few of each have been released, but only after off-world friends and family have paid a substantial ransom."

Threepio again translated for the Wookiee Councilor. "Kerrihrarr wishes to know what criminals and Kessel have to do with Coruscant?"

"Coming to that point directly." The Bothan smiled, but Wedge read a hint of threat in the toothy grin. "On Coruscant there are substantial remnants of the Black Sun organization. As did many of you, I thought Prince Xizor's grab for power was doomed from the start, but it was the Black Sun organization that allowed him to contemplate opposing the Dark Lord of the Sith. I propose selecting and freeing certain Black Sun officers from Kessel and bringing them into Coruscant. There they would bring the disparate parts of Black Sun together and work to sabotage the Empire."

Ackbar sat down slowly and gave Fey'lya a wall-eyed stare. "You want to revive the scourge of the Black Sun?"

"Not revive, just focus. The enemy of our enemy is our friend. Isn't that the principle behind Councilor Organa's approaches to the Hapans? That certainly was the principle that guided our alliance with Imperial forces at Bakura to fight the Ssi-ruuk." Fey'lya stared incredulously at Ackbar. "By granting selected felons their leave of Kessel—in effect taking Doole's obvious rivals for power off his hands—we can also ransom some of our people who are trapped there. And to guarantee Black Sun's compliance with our wishes, we can trade them more of their people when they perform as we want them to."

"I don't like this." Ackbar shook his head adamantly. "You are talking about unleashing thieves and murderers on Coruscant."

"To let them steal Imperial goods and kill Imperial officials, or do you want to reserve the killing for *your* people, and the *dying*, too? Shall that be a privilege reserved for the military, or will you take help where you can find it?" Fey'lya crossed his arms. "You have already admitted that added distractions could be a help to Rogue Squadron's mission. Certainly having an army of irregular troops at your disposal to disrupt Imperial operations when the invasion begins would reduce bloodshed."

Doman nodded. "It seems Councilor Fey'lya is merely suggesting you fight fire with fire."

The Mon Calamari half closed his eyes. "I do not like fire analogies. As we say on Mon Calamari, 'Frolic in the surf and get drowned by the undertow.' "

Leia stood. "I would agree, as one Corellian has put it, if you anger a Wookiee, you shouldn't be surprised at having an arm torn off, and it may well be that in the future we regret any sort of alliance with the remnants of Black Sun. On the other hand, I think none of us can truly comprehend the difficulty of neutralizing the Imperial forces on Coruscant. Indeed, as you have said, Admiral Ackbar, until you have Rogue Squadron on the ground to assess the situation, we cannot be a hundred percent certain what taking Coruscant will entail. The fact is, however, that winning the goodwill of at least part of Coruscant's underworld cannot hurt us."

Mon Mothma nodded. "I would also point out that some of our greatest leaders were thought to be nothing but ruffians, confidence men, and spice smugglers. In being given the opportunity to join us, they have managed to redeem themselves."

"But if they are the exceptions that prove the rule?" Ackbar slapped his hands impatiently against the table's surface. "I do not like this operation at all, but I believe many of you see merit in it where I do not. If this Kessel run is to be authorized, I want to go over every detail to make certain what we want to happen is what actually happens. No one, not even an idiot like Zsinj, has been foolish enough to free the dregs of the galaxy from Kessel. I do not want a situation to arise where my people are taken hostage and our equipment is converted to the use of the criminals. This will be a strictly military operation and I will not have it turn into the sort of disaster we faced on Borleias."

Councilor Fey'lya's fur rose on his neck and formed a crest between his ears before he smoothed it back down. The first assault on Borleias had been planned and led by General Laryn Kre'fey, a Bothan who, according to scuttlebutt, was distantly related to Borsk Fey'lya. The mission had gone from bad to worse, costing General Kre'fey his life and putting almost half of Rogue Squadron out of commission. Had General Salm not violated a direct order, all of Rogue Squadron would have been destroyed and the Rebel Alliance would be in no position to even consider a mission to Coruscant.

Fey'lya's voice began soft and low, causing Wedge to strain to hear him. "Far be it from me to wish a repetition of Borleias on anyone. You are the military leader here, Ackbar—I have no wish to supplant you. You should handle the military details, but I have prepared a list of people I think should be our targets. I have appended full files to my list so you may determine what efforts and precautions need to be taken."

"Your understanding in this matter is most appreciated, Councilor Fey'lya."

"Good. We really are on the same side here, Admiral. I want the conquest of Coruscant to proceed as swiftly and efficiently as you do." Fey'lya smiled, but Wedge found no warmth in the expression. "I *would* hope you will use your best people to see that this mission comes off perfectly. Perhaps if you were to employ Rogue Squadron as part of the operation, their efforts will establish a rapport with those they free and that will work in their favor."

"I will take that suggestion under advisement, Councilor."

Wedge leaned forward in his chair and dropped his voice to a whisper. "Sir, freeing criminals from Kessel is not a mission Rogue Squadron wants to perform."

The Mon Calamari turned his head enough to watch Wedge with one eye. "And Ysanne Isard does not want to surrender Coruscant to us. We all have to do things we don't want to do, Commander. Let us hope we can just make the best of them."

9

Wedge hit a button on the datapad, causing the holo-projector in the center of the pilot's briefing room to re-create the long-distance view of Kessel he'd first seen at the Provisional Council meeting. "All right, people, let's get this briefing under way."

The various members of Rogue Squadron took their places. Wedge noticed that Corran Horn and Nawara Ven, a Twi'lek who had been a lawyer before he joined the Rebellion, were sitting together in the back. When going over the initial planning stages of the operation with Captains Nunb and Celchu, he'd anticipated the greatest resistance to the operation coming from those two. *One sent people to Kessel; the other tried to keep them from being sent there. They've both got connections to the population there, and that could mean some complications for me.*

Wedge shifted his shoulders around to loosen them, then began. "This operation is going to be accomplished in three distinct parts. Each one has to go according to plan or we abort the whole thing. Admiral Ackbar is leaving the decision to proceed or stop to me. I may not like what we're being asked to do—and I don't—but the Provisional Council wants this done, so we're doing it. But we're doing it *our* way."

He pointed to the moon orbiting Kessel. "The Imps used to keep a base on that moon. It is supposed to be abandoned, but we don't know what the Imps may have left behind in the way of automated defenses or booby traps. Our first step is to run a flyby on the base, neutralize automated defenses, and knock down anything launched at us from there. Lieutenant Page and his commandos will then come in and secure the base. Alliance Security will follow up and relieve his troops. That's phase one. Everyone got it?"

The pilots before him all nodded with degrees of enthusiasm going from great to none.

"Phase two is a repeat of phase one, but it takes place on Kessel. We do a flyover and clear a landing zone for Page's people. The commandos will secure the LZ. When they do, Horn, Ven, and I will land. Captain Nunb will be in charge of the rest of you and you'll fly cover for the LZ and for Tycho. He'll be using the shuttle *Forbidden* to ferry our people from Kessel to the moon. On the moon the people will be processed, then shipped out on a number of different ships for insertion into Coruscant, or for repatriation to their own worlds or exile communities.

"The processing and out-shipping is phase three. It will run concurrently with phase two. Trouble with outbound people will cause the termination of the operation." Wedge crossed his arms. "Two key points here. The first is that this is an extremely sensitive and dangerous mission. The people we are dealing with will be very dangerous. Our rules of engagement will be simple: We offer a general warning when we come in, then we use whatever force we need to preempt problems.

"The second point is this: We're getting some of the good along with the bad. We have our want list of scum, but they won't know who it is that we want. Our job is to ransom as many people from political lists as we can for those on the criminal list we'll be taking away. Doole is the key to this strategy working. We'll be taking his enemies away and lowering the general population. This will ease his resource strain and increase his control over the spice operation. He'll see this plan as better for him than it is for us."

In the back Corran raised a hand. "Commander, what will we do in the very real situation of some of these people threatening to kill innocents if we don't take them? Lujayne Forge had . . . has family on Kessel. The people sentenced to Kessel are likely to do anything to get off that rock. For all we know, Doole wants to leave, too."

"That's all possible, but there are contingency plans to prevent that from happening. You'll note in the supplemental material in your briefing bytes I have a list of strategic sites on Kessel. They include the atmosphere plants and, most importantly, a list of spice storage facilities. Moruth Doole has supplies hidden away so he can meet demand well into the future. I will make it very apparent to him that if he cannot exert control over his people, I will be forced to destroy his storehouses. Since greed seems to drive the local economy there, I think he'll see his way clear to working with us."

Corran nodded. "When persuasion fails, coercion works."

"I hope so, Lieutenant Horn."

Nawara Ven sat forward, letting his brain tails dangle over his shoulders. "Commander, I've reviewed the list of ransom candidates. Am I mistaken, or do I notice a significant portion of them are Bothans?"

"Is there a problem with that, Lieutenant Ven?"

"On the surface of it, no, sir. On the other hand I noticed that a number of people—many of whom were my clients, in fact—people who truly *are* political prisoners, have been left off the list. I don't mean that there was any campaign to keep my clients from being pulled off the planet, just that the list of 'good' people has some people on it who could easily be on the other list, and some very deserving, innocent people have been left off the list."

Wedge smiled, a response that seemed to surprise his

pilots. "I'm glad you pointed that out. In presenting this plan to the Provisional Council Admiral Ackbar made very clear that we'd have to be dealing from a position of strength. Councilor Fey'lya provided some deal packages indicating who should be asked for in exchange for this or that person on the 'bad' list. With your help and experience in negotiations, Lieutenant Ven, I intend to win more people for each of our prisoners than the Council suggested we might. I do have clearance to supplement my lists to account for marriages and children. I intend us to exploit that latitude as much as possible."

He looked around. "Any other questions before I deal with Lieutenant Horn's next objection to the plan?" No one said anything, so Wedge nodded to Corran. "Be my guest, Lieutenant Horn."

"Not really an objection, sir, but a question—can we exclude any of the people on our 'bad' list?" Corran winced. "There are a few on here who really shouldn't be allowed off Kessel, unless we're going to dump them in the Maw on our way out of there."

The image of spacing any number of the criminals into the black hole near Kessel brought a smile to Wedge's face, but he killed it quickly enough. "These are the people that have been determined to be useful to us. Who did you have in mind?"

"Zekka Thyne—he's also known as 'Patches,' but not to his face. He's on Kessel because my father and I got him on a smuggling pinch, but he's been tied to the murders of nearly a dozen people—all of them rivals of Black Sun. Patches was being groomed as Prince Xizor's man on Corellia. Xizor tried to slice some files to get Thyne shifted back off Kessel but he couldn't because Corsec's Imperial Liaison, Kirtan Loor, had accidentally altered the structure of the files with Thyne's information. But for that bit of incompetence, Thyne would have been long gone from Kessel—it was the only good thing Loor ever did."

"If we're lucky, Lieutenant Horn, Thyne will be dead."

Corran smiled. "We could see to it that he is."

"Murder, Lieutenant Horn?" Wedge frowned. "Even if he is as bad as you say . . ."

"Wait, wait, wait." Corran held his hands up as everyone turned to stare at him. "I'd be the first person who would be glad to dance on his grave, and if he steps out of line at all, I'd be happy to vape him, but I'm not suggesting murder. It does strike me, though, that we could slice some files and report some deaths that prevent us from taking certain people."

Corran's suggestion sorely tempted Wedge. The list of criminals Borsk Fey'lya had supplied did scan like a directory of organized crime. Wedge had no love for the Empire, but it had been fairly ruthless at dismantling the upper levels of Black 'Sun. Black Sun was a cancer. The Empire hadn't been able to cut it all out, but they *had* forced it into a pretty serious remission. Reviving it to distract the Empire had some merit, and Corran's suggestion offered a possible way to excise some of the more malignant elements from the group.

The spark of hope burning in Wedge's mind died very quickly as reality set in. "The purpose of our mission is to take from Kessel and insert into Coruscant the people who will complicate the lives of Ysanne Isard and her people. The guys who are the most vile are also the ones who can cause the most trouble. We're going to be making the most out of the confusion they create."

Pash glanced back at Corran. "If we make Black Sun too weak, the Empire squashes it."

"Sure, but if we make it too strong, we lose the trust of the folks Black Sun hurts *and* we might find ourselves having to compete with them for the ownership of Coruscant." Corran shook his head. "Xizor would have deposed the Emperor if he could have, and Zekka Thyne will make a run at Isard if he has the chance."

Wedge shrugged. "Sounds like he is just the man Councilor Fey'lya wants to have on Coruscant."

"And the last person most of us should want there."

Corran's eyes narrowed. "Can we put him on the list of strategic targets to take out?"

"I'll trust your judgment in that matter, Lieutenant Horn. That's why you'll be with me down on the planet. If Zekka Thyne is a problem there, we'll deal with him there." Wedge looked around. "Anything else? No overall objections? Lieutenant Horn?"

Corran shrugged, but not fluidly enough to convince Wedge he was without objections. "It's a mission, sir."

"But I would have thought freeing criminals would have caused you to have reservations."

Corran smiled. "I'm not saying I *like* it, sir, but in CorSec we made deals with criminals on a daily basis. The goal then, just as it is now, is to trade a lesser evil for a greater one. I'd just as soon use Zekka Thyne and some of this other scum as rancor bait, but if they'll help bring Iceheart down, I guess my reservations don't really mean that much. I'm good to go with this, Wedge. I think I'll be fine."

Wedge nodded slowly. *He has a point, though I don't think he likes this any more than I do. But it's a mission and we're Rogue Squadron, so we'll get it done.* "Last-minute questions, anyone?"

No one had anything to ask, so Wedge killed the projection of Kessel. "We're mission go in twelve standard hours. You'll want to get some sleep, but before you do, give Emtrey a list of your belongings. While we're on the Kessel run, our headquarters will be relocating back to Noquivzor. We'll be operating from there for the immediate future."

Pash looked surprised. "Afraid of reprisals by Warlord Zsinj?"

Wedge just smiled. "Those are the orders, straight from the Provisional Council, the wisdom of which, I am certain, will make itself clear once we finish the mission to Kessel."

10

Kessel's weak atmosphere slowly smothered the fires burning amid the ruins of the two concussion missile launchers on the ridge overlooking the landing zone. A little smoke and even more dust rolled in a lazy mist down the escarpment, pouring like a vapor stream across the unpaved roadway carved from its face. The mist dissolved before it hit the flat of the plain, leaving a clear field of fire for Page and his people as they set up a perimeter around the hillock at the center of the plain.

Whistler hooted in a low tone.

"Looks pretty clear to me, too." Corran began a long turn to starboard that took him out over the main mine complex. The only surface features visible were the administration buildings and some storage sheds for surface vehicles. One track led off to the north on a nearly direct line for the nearest atmosphere plant. The other major track led south to the hills and the plain where he would be landing.

"Nine is clear, Rogue Leader."

"I copy, Nine. Come in and land. Don't forget your breathing mask."

"Thanks, Lead." Corran brought the X-wing about

and flew back to the plain. He eased his throttle back and cut in the repulsorlift generators. The X-wing glided down gently and hovered five meters above the ground. Using the rudder pedals, Corran swung the nose around and positioned his fighter so it formed the third point of a triangle with Wedge's and Nawara's fighters. His covered the southern defensive arc of the Rogues' position and left enough space for Tycho to easily bring the *Lambda*-class shuttle down in their midst.

Corran extended the landing gear and brought the ship to rest, then killed the repulsorlift generators and engine. "Whistler, remember, shoot first if you have to, *then* go for an engine start to give you more laser energy. If you have to, hover out of reach until the rest of the squadron comes and covers you."

The droid keened mournfully.

"No, nothing will happen, I promise, but I want you to be careful." He missed a chunk of Whistler's reply, but took it that the annoying tone carried the meaning of the missing content. He doffed his helmet, drew the blaster from his shoulder holster, checked it, took it off safe, and reholstered it. Finally he pulled on a breathing mask and a pair of goggles, then popped the release on his cockpit canopy. It slid up and he crawled out.

Corran jumped down and found Kessel to be just a bit lighter in gravity than Borleias or Noquivzor. He ran over to where Wedge and Nawara stood beside an orange, mushroomlike tent that the commandos had assembled. "How did your conversation with Moruth Doole go?"

Wedge frowned slightly. "I think I got my points across, but he's right on the edge of paranoia, and it doesn't take much to push him over."

"Doole's probably a glit-biter."

The Twi'lek twitched a head tail in Corran's direction. "I don't believe I've heard that term before."

"CorSec slang, sorry. Glitterstim is the most potent form of spice—the stuff most people get is cut and diluted so heavily that the most they get from using is a little euphoria. Glit-biters are taking the real thing and it seems, in some folks, to punch up their latent mental abilities. They can read minds, or so they think, and they assume any mind they can't read is closed because the person is plotting against them. Doole probably forgot he was seeing a hologram of you, Commander. You were hostile, he couldn't read you, hence he figured you really had it in for him."

Lieutenant Page, a dark-haired man of medium height and build, came over and pointed toward the horizon. "Landspeeder coming down the road."

Wedge hit his comlink. "Lead to Twelve. How does it look?"

"One vehicle, Lead."

"Thanks, Twelve." Wedge turned to Page. "It's coming alone. If you clear it, let it come in."

"As ordered, sir." Page went running off in the direction of the big, boxy landspeeder and a squad of folks fell in behind him. The landspeeder slowed, then stopped, and a door opened. Page spoke through the open door with someone while his people checked in and around the vehicle. Apparently satisfied with the inspection, Page closed the door and jumped back off the vehicle's running boards. He waved it forward and it headed in.

Other commandos stopped the landspeeder about a hundred meters beyond the perimeter at a point where it remained under the guns of Wedge's X-wing. Two people got out and a trooper escorted them forward toward Wedge. The man stood very tall and seemed to Corran to be painfully thin. What little hair he had left on his head was white and wispy enough that Kessel's weak atmosphere could make it float. The woman came up to the man's shoulder and had deep brown hair. Corran guessed from the way she moved she was younger than the man, but her face was deeply enough scored with wrinkles that he would have matched them in age were he looking at still holograms.

The commando moved the two visitors into and through the tent's simple airlock, then Corran and

Nawara followed Wedge through. Once inside they were able to remove their breathing masks, though the acrid stink of hot plastic almost made Corran put his back on. Resolving to breathe as little as possible, Corran joined Nawara in front of some folding camp chairs.

Squeezing past the table with the holoprojector on it, Wedge extended his hand to the man. "I'm Commander Wedge Antilles, New Republic Armed Forces. I lead Rogue Squadron. I knew your daughter."

The man shook Wedge's hand firmly and kept a brave expression on his face, but the slight tremor in his lower lip betrayed his true emotions. "I am Kassar Forge. This is my wife, Myda. I want to thank you for the hologram you sent after Lujayne . . ." He fell silent for a moment and his wife rubbed his back with her hand. "She always said she wanted to be a hero and show something good could come from Kessel."

"She succeeded." Wedge turned back toward his own people. "This is Nawara Ven and Lieutenant Corran Horn."

Kassar shook their hands as well.

Corran didn't release the man's hand, forcing himself to smile as he looked up into Kassar's dark eyes. "Your daughter really *was* a hero. She kept the unit together. She told me about what you do here, about teaching people so they don't have to return to crime. She spent a lot of time teaching all of us, too."

"Thank you."

"No, thank you." Corran patted the back of the man's hand. "I owed her a big favor I never got a chance to repay. If there's anything I can do for you, please, don't hesitate to ask."

Kassar nodded, then freed his hand from Corran's grip and turned back to Wedge. "I guess I have to ask what it is I can do for you, Commander? I'm sure all this wasn't just so you could say hello. Your strike on the moon base caused a lot of excitement, and Doole is not happy about losing his missile launchers."

"If Doole wants to be happy, today will not be his

day." Wedge ran a hand along his jaw. "We're here to take some people away from Kessel—some very bad people. We are also going to take as many of the good people from here as we can. On the top of my list is you and your family, *if* you want to go. And go or stay, I want you here to point out people who should be on the list but aren't."

The tall man clasped his hands together against his stomach and stared at the orange fabric floor for a moment. "I came here by choice a long time ago—well before any of you were born. Back before the Clone Wars even. I don't know if I have done much good here, but I think I've done very little evil. I'll stay. Myda?"

Her hand grasped the back of his neck and shook him gently. "I didn't come here willingly, but I did stay because I wanted to be with you. *We* will stay, and our family will, too." Myda's voice took on an edge at the last of her statement and Corran saw her exchange a sharp glance with her husband.

Kassar nodded slowly. "I am willing to help you, Commander, but I don't want to make decisions about who goes and who stays. I'll offer what I know."

"If you are afraid of reprisals . . ."

"No, no, I've long since been judged harmless by everyone here. You're taking them, the decision is yours to make."

"I understand. Lieutenant Ven has my list of the good folks that we want to get out. I'd like you to review it with him." Wedge twisted around and touched the holoprojector. "I've left Moruth Doole with the impression that this is very much a rogue operation. He thinks I'm setting myself up as the middleman in this hostage operation. I've told him I am willing to transport prisoners off Kessel—prisoners he'll be well rid of—in return for getting my people off. That's an accurate description of what will happen, but not my focus in this project. Still, Doole has to think I'm willing and able to kill his prisoners, blow up his stores of spice, and toss him into the Maw."

Myda looked over at Wedge and Corran with a piercing stare. "Are you capable of doing that?"

"Capable, yes," Wedge nodded, "and not particularly reluctant to do so."

She smiled. "Good. Fear is as much a part of life on Kessel as spice or air. Control it and you'll do fine."

Wedge hit the power switch for the holoprojector. An image of Moruth Doole the size of a pilot's helmet glowed to life. The batrachian Rybet hopped impatiently from one foot to the other, then stopped and clapped his webbed hands together. He twisted his whole body around to peer closely with his good mechanical eye at the holocam in his dark office. The green of his flesh melded with the similar hue of his jacket, while the tan tracery on his flesh looked as if he'd been drizzled with paint. Because of the way he leaned forward to get near to the holocam, his head swelled out of proportion with his body and nearly made Corran laugh.

"Is that you, Antilllles?" The Rybets voice jumped sharply between octaves and added more l's into the center of Wedge's name than necessary.

"It's me, Doole. I've got my first exchange to offer you." Wedge looked over at Nawara Ven and the Twi'lek nodded. Wedge smiled tightly at the holoprojector. "I have a group of ten Sullustans. For them I'll take Arb Skynxnex."

"No!"

"No?"

"I am selling them to you, I decide what I am paid. Skynxnex is mine—he does not leave." Doole hopped up and down angrily, then searched around until the metal and glass mechanical eye again spotted the holocam. "For these Sullustans I will give you Zekka Thyne."

The name didn't surprise Corran, but Kassar's reaction to it did. The old man shuddered and Myda clung to his arm. *They look as afraid of Thyne as Doole sounds.* Corran raised a hand and Wedge hit a mute button on the holoprojector. "Commander, he's too anxious. He wants to be rid of Thyne. We can get more for him."

Wedge nodded, then unmuted the communications device. "Thyne isn't of interest to me. I'd have to be mad to let someone like that leave this rock."

"You *will* take him, or you get nothing else."

Wedge pulled a comlink from a pocket in his flight suit and held it up where Doole could see it. "Rogue Leader to Twelve, you're free to fire on warehouse number one."

Doole's image capered away from the holocam, then hunched itself over, as if the Rybet was looking at a monitor built into an unseen desk. Doole reeled back, then ran to the holocam. "You wouldn't dare."

"No?"

"Twelve here, Lead. I have acquired the target. Commencing run now."

"Antilles!"

"You have something you want to say to me, Doole?"

"The Sullustans and more . . ."

"Twelve, abort the run, but don't clear your targeting data."

"As ordered, Lead."

Doole's thick purple tongue played out over the thin line of his mouth. "The Sullustans you can have. What else?"

Wedge turned away from the projector as if giving the problem due thought. Nawara held up fingers to indicate which of the target groups he thought should be added to Thyne's ransom. Wedge nodded, then turned back. "We're sending you the data on a group of five Bothans, including Esrca Plo'kre."

"Plo'kre." Doole's mouth snapped shut, then he bowed his head. "Done. And Thyne brings with him another."

"Who?"

"His cutter."

Wedge looked back at the Forges, but they gave no sign of even having heard Doole, much less understanding him. "Corran?"

I know I've heard the term before. He thought back, then nodded. "It's a spicer term, used a lot of years ago when Thyne was still on Corellia. A cutter is someone who prepares spice for use or sale. It came to mean someone close enough to a person that they could be trusted with cutting their spice. He probably means aide."

Kassar's head came up. "He means lover."

Corran shrugged. "That, too."

Wedge nodded. "Do you know who it is?"

Kassar hung his head and Myda answered. "We do. Her name is Inyri."

Corran checked his datapad. "I've got nothing on anyone by that name."

"You wouldn't. She's done nothing wrong."

Something is not right here. Corran frowned. "You don't get sent to Kessel for nothing. How well do you know this Inyri?"

"I thought I knew her very well." Myda swiped at a tear rolling down her cheek. "She's our daughter."

11

"Is it a deal, Antilles?"

"Send them out." Wedge hit another button that froze the transmission. On the other end Doole would only see a holographic representation of Rogue Squadron's crest. He turned toward the Forges. "Say the word and we'll make sure they are separated. We'll find her a place to stay, away from Thyne."

"Do it!" Myda reached out and clutched one of Wedge's hands in her own. "Please, don't leave her with him."

Kassar's hands settled on his wife's shoulders and drew her back. "Myda, we can't do that. She has made her decision."

"But it is a bad one."

Inyri's father slowly shook his head. "And so this means we can deny her freedom? Making bad decisions is not a crime, not even under the Empire."

"But I've seen plenty of people end up headed for Kessel because of making bad decisions." Corran saw the pain in Myda's eyes, and saw no small amount of it reflected in her husband's expression. "I know Thyne—he is as bad as they come. Your daughter's choice will land her in trouble."

Kassar straightened up. "Only if she acts on it."

"But she's leaving with him."

Kassar shrugged helplessly. "She has found something to value in him. Perhaps she can save him from himself."

Corran winced. "Thyne's pretty much a black hole as far as saving is concerned."

"My whole life has been spent here training people how to live away from Kessel. That is all I can do, though. I cannot make their choices for them. I cannot live their lives for them." Kassar looked down and wiped tears from Myda's face. "We gave our daughter—all of our children—all the love and support we could. We trust them. Just as we trusted Lujayne to go off and join the Rebellion, we must trust Inyri."

Corran shook his head. "I'm not liking this at all, Commander."

"It doesn't thrill me, either, Corran, but it's not our fight and not one we can win, not right now anyway." Wedge looked down at his fists, then opened them slowly. "Perhaps she will serve as a brake on him."

"And when the brake burns out?"

"I expect you to have something arranged to cover that contingency."

"As ordered, sir." Corran started going through the list of criminals on his datapad. The original list had been drawn from Imperial files and annotated with rankings that determined the value of each individual to the Rebellion. Out of thousands of convicts, only seventeen had been identified as useful by New Republic officials. Those seventeen—now reduced to sixteen since Doole had eliminated Arb Skynxnex from consideration—clearly had been rising stars in the Black Sun organization. While none of them had achieved upper-level status, they had shown the sort of initiative and drive that made it clear, had their careers not been interrupted by arrest and conviction, the best of them would have been on a rough par with Jabba the Hutt in terms of power and influence.

Corran remembered his father having complained about the changing nature of organized crime. Once upon a time Black Sun had been an honorable organization—with its own morality, of course, but with a code that its members lived by. Black Sun had always been ruthless—dump a load of spice and blaster-packers would worry about collecting the cost, or its equivalent, from the smuggler in question. Members who informed on others would be killed in a most grisly manner, and law enforcement officers were legitimate targets for reprisals, but these things were all done on an individual basis.

The new breed was willing to use a bomb in a crowded cantina just to get one individual. The idea of killing an informer *and* his family became standard. The spice that started to be sold was stronger than ever before and the assassination of political figures who opposed the crime cartel became the rule, not the exception. Hal Horn had assumed the Rebellion's success in defying the Empire had contributed to a general easing of moral standards that carried into Black Sun and allowed savages like Zekka Thyne to thrive.

Three silhouettes appeared on the other side of the airlock's translucent inner seal. The soldier inside the tent opened the airlock and tugged Thyne through first. The hobbles on the man's feet made him stumble, but Thyne managed to recover his balance despite having his arms bound behind him. He shook off his breathing mask, then held his head up defiantly. "I am Zekka Thyne."

Five years on Kessel hadn't done anything to Thyne but make him a bit leaner and, as the hateful glow in his eyes suggested, a whole lot more malevolent. *It's as if the years here have distilled him down to his core essence.* Only a couple of centimeters taller than Corran, Thyne had a wiry build that made him seem somehow even taller. Clean-shaven and bald—he appeared to be congenitally hairless—his head and exposed flesh gleamed like polished leather.

More remarkable than in its glow, Thyne's flesh came in two shades of color. Most noticeable was the light blue because it seemed to have been layered on over the whitish-pink color, as if he had been splashed with midnight-blue dye that never quite washed out. The biggest splotch cut right down along the bridge of his nose, then back under his cheekbone to his left ear and on up to the midline of his skull again. It gave the impression that he had one massive black eye that was slowly fading.

Aside from the color, his sharply pointed ears, and black, equally sharp serrated teeth, his eyes separated him from the realm of the wholly human. The orbs were red throughout, the color of arterial blood, except for where a slender diamond pupil bisected them. Flecks of gold outlined the black diamond and, in the dark, would reflect a little light. Those diamonds had betrayed him on Corellia, letting Corran and his father send him on his Kessel vacation.

Wedge raised an eyebrow. "It is truly him?"

Corran nodded. "It's Patches all right."

"Horn, here?" Thyne hissed. "Perhaps you never got the message I sent you?"

"What message was that?"

"Your father's dead, isn't he?"

The venom in the man's voice combined with the surprise of the question to make it feel as if Corran's heart had been slammed back against his spine. He wanted to shout something back at Thyne, but first his breath, then words failed him. Thyne had always been full of threats and intimidation, but Corran and his father had refused to acknowledge them. Thyne had not been the first criminal to threaten him, nor the last.

And not the first to be blamed for my father's death. With a moment of thought Corran realized that Thyne had probably heard of his father's death and decided to claim responsibility just to get at him. Corran thought Thyne more than capable of ordering a murder, and Black Sun more than capable of carrying that order out, but Hal Horn had been killed over a year and a half after Thyne had arrived on Kessel. *Black Sun preferred things a bit more immediate than that, as I recall.*

Corran's eyes became green slits. "I suppose you *could* have been the one who had my father killed—after all, you threatened us both and left the whole job undone, which means it's in keeping with your usual sloppiness."

The riposte had no visible effect on Thyne. He looked away from Corran, then watched Wedge for a moment. "Are you the Jedi?"

"No, I'm just the man who decides if you leave here or not." Wedge jerked a thumb toward Corran. "That wasn't a good start."

"Oh, forgive me, I've forgotten the Rebels are all sweetness and light. That's what they tell us, you know, all the pols who were sent here." Thyne smiled carefully. "Then again, you're here taking someone like me away from this place. Expediency wins over purity, it would appear."

The commando at the airlock brought Inyri Forge through and Corran saw the resemblance between her and Lujayne the second she removed her breathing mask. They both had the same brown eyes and trim bodies. Inyri wore her brown hair longer than her sister had and had dyed a forelock the same shade of blue as Thyne's patches. She appeared shocked to see her parents, but her face closed up quickly as she turned away from them and rested her hands on Thyne's left shoulder.

Wedge studied the woman for a moment, then looked up at Thyne. "The New Republic has authorized me to give you transport from Kessel to a destination you will learn later. You will be given tasks to perform. If you succeed in performing them to our satisfaction, the New Republic will grant you a conditional pardon for your crimes. Do you understand?"

"What if I decide to accept your offer, then I just go away."

Wedge smiled openly. "We'll hunt you down and bring you back here."

"The galaxy is a big place."

"You might think that, but it's getting much smaller

all the time." Wedge shrugged nonchalantly. "The Emperor couldn't hide from us, don't assume you could."

Corran nodded. "You weren't that hard to find before, Patches, you won't be again."

"You don't scare me, Horn."

"I'm not interested in scaring, just catching, Thyne." Corran bent down, retrieved Thyne's breathing mask, and shoved it onto the man's face. "No matter where you go, I'll find those double diamonds of yours, just like last time. Count on it."

Wedge nodded to the guards. "Take him outside and prep him for shuttle transport." Inyri started to follow, but a guard stopped her in response to Wedge's hand signal. "Ms. Forge, I'd like to speak to you alone."

Inyri turned slowly and stiffly. "We're hardly alone."

"You're not required to go with Thyne."

She glared at her parents, then looked at Wedge. "I've made my choice to be with him. Leave it alone. It is no one's business but my own."

"Look," Corran began, holding a hand out toward her, "we can protect you from him."

"Oh, like you protected my sister?"

Corran's hand dropped back to his side. The same horrible sensation he'd felt when Lujayne had died rippled through him. He knew the pain in Inyri's voice had triggered the memory, but he felt he was also sensing the part of her that had died when she found out about Lujayne's death. Asked to choose between the memory or Inyri's pain, he couldn't have decided which hurt him more, but the inability to redress either frustrated him like nothing else.

"I did, we did, everything we could to protect Lujayne." Corran tapped a hand against his chest. "We didn't know her as long as you did, nor as well, but you know what your sister was like. You know how good she was at making people feel welcomed and at ease and valuable. She did that with us, too."

He pointed at the airlock. "It may not be my business what you do with Zekka Thyne, but I'm certain your sister wouldn't have wanted you to go with him. Lujayne's gone, but that's no reason for the people who loved her and respected her to let you get into trouble. Thyne is everything your sister was not."

"You don't know him."

"And maybe you don't either." Corran held his hand out to her again. "You don't have to do this."

"I do." She folded her arms resolutely. "I am."

Wedge shook his head. "You will have time to reconsider—up to and including your final drop-off."

"Is that all?"

Wedge frowned. "You might want to say good-bye to your parents?"

"Why? That didn't keep Lujayne safe."

"It didn't get her killed, either."

Wedge's reply seemed to soften Inyri for a moment. Her gaze flicked toward her parents, and for a heartbeat, Corran thought she was going to come to her senses. Then her eyes hardened and she fitted the breathing mask back over her face. Without a word she turned on her heel and stepped into the airlock.

Wedge turned and looked wordlessly at her parents.

Kassar hugged his wife. "You tried, Commander. That is all we could ask."

The rest of the exchanges went fairly smoothly. Wedge resorted to threats a couple of times when Doole balked at giving him the people he wanted, but by the end of things they had managed to pull 150 political prisoners from Kessel in exchange for picking up sixteen of the most hardened and despicable criminals the galaxy had ever known.

And by the end of the process Corran had found someone they could use to keep Thyne in check. Wedge suggested a deal to Doole but the pretentious Rybet dismissed it as one where he got nothing. Wedge had suggested he consider it goodwill and after a flyover by the airborne portion of Rogue Squadron, Moruth Doole decided it was in his best interest to play along.

"And this is the last time I deal with your Rebellion. Kessel stands alone from now on!"

Wedge smiled at Doole's image. "Then we won't come back, unless we're returning some of your friends to you." He disconnected the transmission before Doole's howl rose to painful levels.

Ten minutes later two commandos escorted the last prisoner into the tent. The human was old, though not frail. The holograms Corran had seen of him had not had flesh quite so loose or sallow, but the dark eyes still sparked with life. While smaller even than Corran, the man exuded a certain power. A full shock of white hair crowned him and granted him some of the dignity his dirty jumpsuit stole.

Even Wedge seemed impressed. "Moff Fliry Vorru, I am Commander Wedge Antilles."

Vorru smiled graciously. "Charmed. Do I detect a trace of Corellia in your Basic?"

"You do."

"A loyal son come to free me from this prison?"

"Perhaps."

Corran had never met Moff Vorru before, but his grandfather had told stories of the man. As the administrator in charge of the Corellian Sector under the Old Republic, Vorru had turned a blind eye to smuggling activities, which made Corellia a center for smuggling and gave it a reputation that had not changed over the years. When Senator Palpatine declared himself the Emperor, he found Vorru to be a rival of sorts. Prince Xizor betrayed Vorru to the Emperor, but the Emperor did not slay him. It was thought that Vorru had ransomed his life by causing his datafiles about others in the Imperial Senate and throughout the Empire to be doled out to the Emperor bit by bit.

Though it had been decades since Corellia operated as an open sector under Vorru, many criminals thought of Vorru's Corellia as a shining utopia of unparalleled prosperity. Vorru had become a legend in the Imperial under-world and at CorSec there always were new rumors about an attempt by someone to raid Kessel and free Vorru.

The ex-Imperial Moff shrugged as much as his bonds would allow. "What do you want me to do for you?"

"Do you know Zekka Thyne?"

Vorru sighed. "I do. Aggressive and intelligent, though aggression is his default setting. Surprise him and he strikes out. Unpredictable beyond that."

"We're going to use him against the Empire, but we do not want him to become excessive and hurt others."

The old man smiled slowly. "Using strategic weapons to gain a tactical advantage is a sign of desperation."

"These are desperate times." Wedge nodded toward Corran. "Lieutenant Horn thinks you can control Thyne."

"Control him, no." Vorru closed his eyes for a moment. "Control those he needs to be able to go too far, yes, I can do that for you."

"Will you?"

"Gladly." Vorru's confident smile carried on up into his reopened eyes. "It will be dangerous, but seeing Imperial Center again will be worth the risk."

Corran blinked and looked at a stunned Wedge. *How did he know he was going to Coruscant?*

The old man read the surprise on their faces, then laughed. "Don't be astonished I was able to figure out where I would be used, *rejoice* in that fact. Were that simple a deduction beyond me, I would have no chance of fulfilling the mission you have given me."

12

Walking through one of the long dark corridors built beneath the Imperial Palace would normally have depressed Kirtan Loor, especially as he was on his way to a meeting with General Evir Derricote. When Derricote had summoned him the General had seemed quite manic—a state Loor had seen crumble into a tantrum filled with demands on previous occasions, yet even that prospect could not dampen his mood.

Corran Horn was on Kessel freeing prisoners. Loor allowed himself a laugh that echoed sinisterly through the passage. Over the past two weeks the freed criminals had been filtered back into Imperial Center. The Rebels had been careful in their insertion efforts—security was maintained at normal levels, which meant a substantial bribe could make almost any datafile look like it had never been sliced. Had he not been tipped to their arrival, Loor would have missed their reentry into Coruscant's underworld.

Loor even allowed himself to admire the Alliance for its plan. Criminals had a penchant for making themselves highly visible targets. The Empire did need to maintain order on the capital world, but their resources would only extend so far. By bringing to Imperial Center the people they did, the Alliance managed to breathe life back into the corpse that was Black Sun, causing some fairly alarmist reports to start filtering up from the constabulary.

Somehow, though, even their dire predictions amounted to nothing against Loor's mind's-eye image of Corran Horn helping to escort criminals from Kessel. Three of those on the list had actually been arrested on Corellia during Horn's time with CorSec. *It must have killed him to let someone like Zekka Thyne escape justice. What I wouldn't have given to be there and see it.*

Kirtan Loor forced himself to laugh again and willed himself to remain feeling triumphant, but could not. His basic fear of Corran Horn undercut his sense of superiority. Corran Horn, Gil Bastra, and Iella Wessiri had managed to deceive him long enough on Corellia that they were able to escape before he could have them arrested and jailed. He had found Gil Bastra after over a year and a half of searching, but Bastra maintained that's because he had given clues to draw Loor after him. Prior to that he had thought he was close to Corran once, but that had been a mistake, and Loor had no idea where Wessiri or her husband was.

The fact that they had been able to fool him once meant he had to assume it was possible for them to fool him again. In the old days, before Ysanne Isard had summoned him to Imperial Center and pointed out his penchant for making unwarranted assumptions, he would have *assumed* he could not be fooled again. That would have guaranteed his being deceived. *And that would have doomed me.*

Because he worked to no longer allow himself to assume too much, he had reassessed Corran Horn. From this reassessment his fear had grown. Loor had always known Horn was capable of being a killer, and he had labored under the assumption that Horn had actually murdered a bunch of smugglers in cold blood. When it became apparent that those murders were a sham—Loor's face still burned as he realized he had based his assumptions about those murders only on reports created by Gil Bastra—he saw Corran Horn as someone capable of using violence, but also as someone who could control his temper. Horn emerged as more cunning and that trait became more dangerous when coupled with his relentlessness.

To "motivate" Loor in his supervision of General Derricote's project, Ysanne Isard had released the fact that Loor had killed Bastra into channels that would carry that data to the Rebel Alliance. She also let it be known that Loor was on Imperial Center. She had said at the time that she hoped such information would serve to distract Horn from looking into other matters very closely, but Loor knew it would just draw Corran to Imperial Center like vice draws Hutts.

I will have to be very careful when he gets here. If he gets to me it will be because I want him to, but on my terms and to my benefit.

As Loor neared his destination, the door to Derricote's lab opened to an inrush of air and the General himself stood there beaming. Though cadaverously slender, there was no way Loor could squeeze past the General's rotund form and enter the lab with the man just standing there. "I thought you wanted me to see something in the lab, General."

Derricote brushed a hand back over his thinning black hair, then clapped his hands. "I do. The Quarren were very helpful, very helpful."

"Put it in a report, General."

"No, you must come see for yourself."

Loor hesitated. The holograms appended to the first of Derricote's reports had been enough to make him queasy. The idea of looking at experimental subjects in person did not appeal to him in the least. *Well, perhaps just a bit, but only out of morbid curiosity.*

"Lead the way."

Derricote stepped out of the doorway and Loor entered the lab. Unlike the majority of suites in the Imperial Palace, the laboratory had stark, functional appointments. Bright lights reflected from white and silver surfaces and the only things even approximating decoration were red and yellow signs warning of biohazards, live wires, and operating lasers. Glass walls allowed them to peer into a labyrinth of rooms where white-smocked individuals appeared to be taking creatures apart or putting them back together with the help of surgical droids of various configurations.

The door closed behind them, with the air whistling in as the opening narrowed. Derricote glanced back. "It sounds like that because we are under negative air pressure in here. That way if something breaks out it will not be carried by a draft out of the lab."

"I thought humans would be immune to this plague."

"No, that's not exactly correct." The General smiled and Loor knew the man just loved exposing any weakness in Kirtan's knowledge of the project. "We are starting from a number of viruses for which aliens show a high susceptibility. It is possible that spontaneous mutations could change it enough that humans could be affected by it. The chances of that are very limited, primarily because the genetic sequences we're using would have to be massively altered for humans to fall sick. It is possible, of course, that this might happen, but at the average mutation rate, it would take a thousand years before that would happen."

"But you could make a vaccine, couldn't you?"

"Building up immunity to a virus is not all that simple. It could take years to perfect a vaccine for this disease." Derricote smiled casually, as if talking about an inconsequential amount of time. "It could be done, but it would take a concentration of resources that would exceed these by ten or twenty times."

At least, then, the Rebels won't have a chance at doing it since they don't even have this facility. Loor lowered his voice. "You can cure it, yes?"

Derricote nodded. "Bacta."

"Is that all?" Bacta was the treatment for everything from a simple cut to severe combat trauma, from a sniffle to the virulent Bandonian Ague. "If Bacta will cure your disease, the disease is useless."

"Hardly. The more severe the case of the disease, the greater the amount of bacta needed to cure it." Derricote's dark eyes glittered in a way Loor found rather unnerving. "In the very late stages of the disease bacta can hold the disease at bay, but some organs and extremities may be so damaged that they will require cybernetic replacement. Come and see."

Derricote led him deeper into the laboratory complex and through a doorway into a stainless-steel corridor. Transparisteel windows lined the walls and gave them views of detention cells with one or two individuals in them. On the left were piggish Gamorreans—naked, as were the squid-headed Quarren on the right side— looking miserable in their clinically spare environs. Those nearest the doorway through which they entered appeared relatively normal—though they were such a sight that Loor couldn't bring himself to study them in any great detail.

"You will notice the transparisteel windows are triple-paned. That central sheet is reflective on their side, so they cannot see us. The walls between the cells are soundproofed. We found that necessary to maintain order."

"I see," Loor said, but he really saw no need for security precautions. The first few Gamorreans were placid, though they did seem to know people might be observing them through the windows, so they sat in such a way that they preserved their modesty. Farther along they appeared to be in some sort of a stupor. Their black eyes had become quite glassy and fixed on one point. They just lay there, barely moving, in whatever position they seemed to find themselves, no matter how uncomfortable.

Loor did notice a splotchiness on the Gamorreans' flesh. Angry black boils seemed to radiate out a spider's web of lines that connected them one to another. One creature had a boil on his tongue and several others showed them on the bottoms of their feet. Loor assumed the boils were painful since what little movement he did see seemed to be an attempt to relieve pressure on them.

He also noticed these Gamorreans seemed very dry. Mucus and saliva did not decorate their faces the way it normally did. Clearly the creatures were sick, but Loor somehow took that to be the most telling sign of their disease.

Then he saw the final-stage patients.

The boils had broken open and the Gamorrean's flesh had cracked along the spiderweb lines. Black blood oozed from the wounds and the Gamorrean left bloody footprints everywhere it wandered. And wander it did, darting left and right, backward and forward, dancing as if the floor were made of molten lava. The creature slammed into walls, leaving runny silhouettes of itself on the transparisteel, then it would rebound and fall to the ground. There it thrashed around, vomiting up liters of thick black fluid, then somehow clambered back to its feet and hurled itself around the room again.

Loor reeled away as the Gamorrean he was watching splattered himself against the window. The Intelligence agent fell to his hands and knees, fighting valiantly to keep from vomiting. He forced himself to breathe in and out through his nose and the nausea passed. "That's horrible."

"I know." Derricote slapped him on the back. "The Quarren go black all over, then their autoimmune system goes insane and liquefies their bones. They become a sack of fluid just teeming with Krytos."

"Krytos?"

"My name for the virus—it is a combination of the world names for the viruses I've combined here." He sighed and Loor could tell he was savoring the vision of the dying Gamorrean. "A milliliter of an end patient's blood is sufficient to infect an adult. The incubation period is falling slowly, but the period from first symptoms to final stage is remaining fairly constant. I doubt we will improve on that."

"Why not?"

"What you saw, the boils and the bleeding out, part of the whole process. The virus is replicating itself in the host body. Once it has filled a cell with virus, that cell explodes and those next to it are infected. The circulatory system carries the virus throughout the body. Cell by cell the creature dies, and the process escalates until you get the end stage. By then the pain is incredible—did I mention the virus doesn't seem interested in destroying pain receptors? Most remarkable, really."

Loor reared back onto his haunches, then stood. He focused his gaze on Derricote and consciously ignored the movement he caught out of the corner of his eyes. "How long from onset to final stage?"

"There are seven stages. One for each day of the disease." Derricote pointed to the right side of the corridor but Loor refused to look in that direction. "The Quarren die more gracefully, if liquefaction can be seen as graceful."

"How much tinkering did you do to make the disease jump species?"

"Not much. With the Quarren version we should be able to attack the Mon Calamari population. I will need other subjects, of course, to test other crosses. I was thinking a raid of Kashyyyk might . . ."

"Kashyyyk?" Loor looked at Derricote to see if the man had finally lost the last of his sanity. "I will check with Madam Director Isard, but I think eliminating a species that proved useful as slave labor before would be unwise. I suggest you and your scientists should compare the known susceptibility of alien species and try to group them so you can tailor a virus that will do the most harm to the largest number."

"We *could* do it that way, though it would be more elegant to engineer a specific . . ."

"There is nothing about your Krytos that is elegant."

Derricote took a step back and blinked. "What? Not elegant?"

"Don't take that the way it sounded, General, take it the way I meant it." Loor forced himself to smile. "Your work is most impressive, utterly unforgettable." The image of billions of aliens falling down and dissolving into fetid puddles in the canyons of Imperial Center almost made Loor sick. "The Rebels are coming here to take the center of the Empire. What they will get is a world of death and they will be powerless to save it."

13

Corran Horn waited behind the transparisteel blast shield until the *Pulsar Skate*'s repulsorlift drives had shut down and the gangway started to descend. The modified *Baudo*-class yacht looked a lot like its namesake, primarily because of the long, gentle curving lines of the wings. He realized he thought of the ship as quite beautiful, and that surprised him because both he and his father had worked hard to put the *Pulsar Skate* and its skipper out of commission.

Its old *skipper*, he reminded himself. Booster Terrik and his father had been each other's bane. Booster had a facility for hauling all sorts of contraband, not just spice, and enough of his cargo was made up of things that powerful people wanted that he made a number of influential friends. Booster easily could have become a broker of goods, but he loved flying too much. Eventually Hal Horn caught him and Booster did five years on Kessel.

Booster's daughter, Mirax, was unbraiding her long black hair as she came down the gangway. She stopped when she saw Corran and smiled. The fierce rivalry their fathers had known gave them a link—a link strengthened by the fact that they also were both raised on Corellia—

and that link had allowed them to avoid inheriting their father's enmity.

Corran returned her smile. "How was your run?"

"No Imperial complications." She rolled her brown eyes. "On the other hand, having two dozen utterly jubilant Sullustans aboard the *Skate* for a week is sufficient to remind me why I prefer moving inert cargo."

"Eat their weight in rations?"

"Yes, but that wasn't the problem. They're rather *perky* when they're happy, and perky can wear on you pretty fast." She jerked a thumb back toward the bridge of her ship. "Liat wasn't any help. He fell instantly and madly in love with one of the refugees. She seemed thrilled, as did the others. I think there may even have been a wedding in the hold, but I'm not sure."

Corran shrugged. "I don't know anything about Sullustan customs. We could ask Captain Nunb."

"That's a possibility." Mirax's smile slackened just a bit as she reached out and laid a hand on his shoulder. "Any bad effects from the trip to Kessel?"

"What do you mean?"

She shrugged. "A lot of good people made it off Kessel, but I know some real rancor bait had to have been let free to win their release. After all, I don't think the guy running Kessel is going to take New Republic promissory chits in exchange for prisoners. Doole doesn't do anything for nothing."

"Unlike some smugglers?"

Her smile brightened again for a moment. "I'm counting on you and Wedge to finish this Empire off so I can begin collecting what I'm owed."

"And if we don't?"

"Then just like that Jedcred you wear, the chits will become collectible and I'll make the money back later." Her hand shifted from his shoulder, allowing her to give him a light punch in the arm. "Nice change of subject, though."

"Sorry." Corran hadn't answered her question because he hadn't allowed himself to think about it very much. It was all well and good to tell Wedge before the trip that he didn't have any problem letting criminals loose. It was true that CorSec, like any other security force, made deals with a lesser evil to get rid of some greater evil. That clearly was what the whole Kessel operation was about—they'd be pitting a resurgent Black Sun against the Empire. With Fliry Vorru included in the mix of people freed, the chances were Black Sun wouldn't run hopelessly wild.

On the other hand, Corran would have felt a lot better if the list of criminals they freed had been a list of folks lost on a ship that flew into the Maw and never came out again. The criminals were capable of doing the job the New Republic wanted them to do, but it was precisely because they were as ruthless and cruel as any Grand Moff that had ever served the Emperor. And while it was true that their activities would help break the Empire down, Corran knew plenty of innocent people could get hurt by any violent spillovers—and the people they had released could easily be described as sloppy when it came to violence.

"I guess I'm having some second thoughts. I know the Empire wouldn't hesitate to use any weapon against us, so they're definitely the target to shoot at." He frowned heavily. "Once we take Coruscant, I'd be happy to help hunt down and ship back to Kessel any of the slime we released."

"If you need someone to do the hauling, I'm in, free of charge."

Corran smiled. "But we won't tell your father you're working with a Horn on such a thing."

"No, I like him alive too much to shock him with that news." Mirax laughed a bit. "Has the food here on Noquivzor gotten any better than the last time I was here?"

"It actually has. Lots of good things were shipped in for a meeting here last month and Admiral Ackbar left the surplus here. I think Emtrey has traded some of it away, but there are still some surprises. Want to get something to eat?"

"Please."

They headed off toward the central corridor that eventually sent a branch running down to the mess hall. As they walked along Mirax related some of the odder antics of her Sullustan pilot and his bride to be. The stories were funny, and Corran laughed in all the appropriate places, but he was laughing because of more than the humor in the stories. He realized that with Mirax he felt very much at ease, providing one more reason why he found her attractive.

He knew he wasn't in love with her, but he knew himself well enough that he'd be poised at the top of that very slippery slope if he just let himself go. Falling in love, for him, had never been one of those one-look-and-passion-ignites things. When that happened to him he knew it was lust, pure and simple. While Mirax was pretty enough to inspire lust, Corran knew things that burned hot burned out fast, and he'd been raised to think relationships should be stable, not supernova events that collapse into an emotional black hole.

The fact was that his father's murder had cut him adrift emotionally. While he was still with CorSec he had Gil and Iella keeping him pointed in the right direction, but he had only made one new friend during that time, and she left after six months. Then, on the run, he couldn't get close to people for fear of being unmasked and turned over to Imperial authorities. Even when he joined the Rebellion and applied for admittance to Rogue Squadron, the fierce competition with other pilots to get accepted created a wall. Lujayne Forge had made the first big breech in it, then others exploited that breech and helped him get used to being with people and trusting them again.

"Corran."

Both he and Mirax stopped at the high-pitched squeal of his name. They turned back as a tall, blocky Gand came down the corridor from behind them. The Gand's exoskeleton appeared uniform in color except where shadows edged the plates and on his right forearm and hand. There the exoskeleton was much more pale and even chalky. The latter half of the limb matched the left one in length, but was not quite as big around.

Corran pointed at his right arm. "They removed the bacta capsule."

"Yes. Ooryl is most pleased." The Gand forced inflections into his Basic, mostly at the right places, and added volume to emphasize his pleasure. Two months before, at the first battle for Borleias, Ooryl Qrygg had been shot out of his X-wing and had lost his right forearm in the process. By circulating bacta through a capsule, Rebel medics had been able to speed up the Gand's rather remarkable regenerative abilities—abilities no one in the Alliance had known Gands possessed.

Ooryl flexed his three-fingered hand. "Once the carapace hardens, Ooryl will be fit enough to be your wing-Gand again."

"I can't wait. Trying to keep up with Captain Nunb is tough. She's good enough she could fly through a nova and her ship would stay dark."

Mirax smiled. "We're going to get food. Do you want to join us?"

"Ooryl would be pleased, but Ooryl was sent by Commander Antilles." Armored lids flicked down over the Gand's multifaceted ebon eyes and back up again. "He wants to see you, Corran."

"Why would he want to see me?" Corran couldn't remember having done anything unusual. *I hope Emtrey doesn't have Whistler slicing some files for him.*

Mirax tugged on Corran's hand. "Let's go and get this over with. I can say hi to Wedge, then we can get some food."

Ooryl laid his left hand gently on Mirax's forearm. "Qrygg regrets to tell you that Commander Antilles said this is official business. The Commander knew you would be together—Ooryl was sent first to your ship—and he wants Corran to go alone. Commander Antilles said he would see you later and explain everything."

"If it's official, it's official." She shrugged and let Corran's hand go. "I'm still going to get some food. I'll eat slowly, so if you get done fast, find me."

"I will."

Mirax looked at Ooryl. "You are still more than welcome to join me."

"Ooryl is honored."

"Good, I like having company, and since you share a room with Corran, you can tell me all sorts of embarrassing things about him." She slipped her right arm through the crook of his left and winked at Corran. "Take your time with Wedge. I'll be well taken care of."

Corran laughed, more at Ooryl's discomfiture than her remark. "Have fun—the fun I can bet I won't be having."

Corran walked past Emtrey and into the office space Wedge had been given on the unit's return to Noquivzor. The room, which was not really that big, seemed far too large to suit Wedge. Other officers would have had the walls lined with holograms and the shelves packed with trophies from their various adventures. Aside from a few holograms of his dead parents and of him posing with squadron mates, Wedge didn't have much reflective of his time with the Rebellion.

Wedge pointed Corran to one of the two chairs in front of his desk. "Be seated. This won't take long, but it means some changes that are going to require some action on your part—both of your parts."

By way of his statement Wedge included the woman seated in the other chair. Erisi Dlarit had been another of the recruits that had joined Rogue Squadron at the time Corran did. She wore her black hair cut short and tight against the back of her neck. She had blue eyes that sparkled like sapphires and an elegant beauty that definitely made her prettier than Mirax. Erisi, having been raised among the privileged humans on Thyferra, had benefited greatly from the riches her kith and kin made from the bacta cartel. Mirax had referred to Erisi more than once as "the bacta queen" and Corran thought the remark was uttered with an equal mix of envy and disgust in Mirax's voice.

Though Mirax would deny any of the envy. Corran slipped into the seat and smiled at Erisi. "This should be interesting."

"Indeed. We finally get to fly together."

Wedge cleared his throat. "Emtrey will be giving you access codes for some datafiles. They include a self-extracting virus that will destroy the data once it has been viewed. Read carefully and memorize the points about initial contact."

Corran's mind flashed back to the sort of briefings Gil Bastra used to give him and Iella before they started on an undercover assignment. "You're not preparing us for some escort run, are you?"

"No." Wedge looked down at his desk, then back up again. "For a variety of reasons the Provisional Council has decided the New Republic needs to take Coruscant. To be able to do that we need reliable data on the defenses and the locations of tactical targets. Someone has to get that information and you're it."

"Us?"

Erisi looked as surprised as Corran. "Commander, there is no way the two of us can do that job alone, even *if* we have help from forces already there." Her blue eyes shrank to slits. "We're *all* going in, aren't we?"

"That's an assumption that I'm not at liberty to confirm or deny, Lieutenant Dlarit." The Commander shook his head. "You both know how a cell system works—no one is allowed to know about more than their portion of the network. What you don't know will keep others safe."

"Who do we report to?"

"All that will be in your briefing file—even I do not know what your cover will be or what your travel arrangements will be and I doubt sincerely I'll have a way to contact you."

"You'll be going, though, won't you?" Erisi frowned. "It only makes sense they would send all of us, not just two."

Wedge shook his head. "What makes sense to General Cracken is its own subset of reality. He says the precautions are necessary. It's all to keep you safe."

Corran scowled. "Since when was 'isolated' made a synonym for 'safe'?"

Erisi patted his left hand. "Don't worry, you'll be with me."

"That's something." Corran flashed her a smile. "How long before we head out, Commander?"

"You're off as soon as you leave this office. The *Forbidden* is waiting for you."

"Is Tycho flying us to wherever?"

"No. General Cracken has one of his people in command."

Corran nodded slowly. *The operation is sensitive enough that they don't want to trust him with a part of it.* "If you can, say good-bye to him for me. And good-bye to Mirax, too."

"Will do." Wedge folded his arms. "One last thing— and this is awkward—we need your permission to have Emtrey transfer money out of your personal accounts, slice it through some cutouts, and funnel it into the accounts you'll be using on Coruscant."

Corran laughed. "Get receipt bytes and we'll be reimbursed?"

Wedge chuckled right along with the two of them. "It's not enough they want our bodies, but they want us to finance the war. I understand there is a budget for this operation, but I know it's not going to be enough. If things go wrong, having the extra credits available . . ."

"I've had practical experience in this area, and I'd not care to relive it. I've got ten you can have."

Erisi looked at Corran, then up at Wedge. "Is ten enough?"

Corran smiled at her. "Ten thousand is what I meant."

"Oh, I meant ten million." She batted her eyes. "Is that enough?"

Wedge coughed into his fist. "I think it will do."

"Yeah, being able to buy a whole wing of snub-fighters could be handy in a pinch." Corran shook his head. "Do we have to come back after this operation?"

"Have to? I don't know, but I certainly hope you are able to." Wedge came around from behind the desk and offered Corran his hand. "May the Force be with you."

"And with you, sir." Corran shook Wedge's hand. "As much as we need, and then some."

14

I guess now is the time we will see if this disguise really works or not. Wedge sat back in the starliner's plush seat, barely glancing at the screen built into the rear of the seat in front of him. On it played little holographic reports about the nature of the Rebellion and the war being fought against it by the Empire. The gist of the reports was to suggest that the battle with Palpatine's murderers was going well and justice was being restored to the galaxy as victory after victory over the treasonous Rebels was gained.

Wedge, disguised as he was, presented an argument that belied the Empire's propaganda efforts. A metal mask covered his forehead, right eye, and cheek on down to the edge of his jaw. Part of the mask continued on past his right ear, flattening it utterly, and on back to the rear of his skull. Another piece curled down along his jaw and wrapped around his throat. A round lens set in place over his right eye enlarged it and made it very easy to see how blue the contact lens he had on was.

Surface pressure kept the mask in place, making it decidedly uncomfortable to wear. It also made the rounded edge on his face dig sufficiently into his skin to appear as if the metal had replaced flesh on that side of his face. The mask also unbalanced his head enough that his neck hurt too much to hold his head straight all the time. As a result he let his head loll to the right for the most part, and that added to his disguise.

The Customs official who had come aboard right after the Dairkan Starliner *Jewel of Churba* entered the Coruscant system stopped in the aisle opposite him. "I need to see your identification."

Wedge slid an identification card from inside the breast of his black Imperial uniform. He used his right hand that had been encased in black leather. The glove did little to hide the blocky, angular nature of the hand, though even if it had been smooth, the fact that it consisted of two thick fingers and a thumb would have given the Customs man the idea something was wrong. Gentle whirring sounds emanated from the glove as Wedge's fingers tightened on the card and his wrist rotated to hand the card over to the official.

"Here you are, sir." Wedge's words came in a buzzing croak, half because of the pressure on his larynx and half because of the voice modulator built into the mask.

The Customs official gave the ID card only a cursory glance before he swiped it through a slot on his datapad. "Colonel Antar Roat . . ."

"Ro-at."

"What?"

"My name is pronounced Ro-at." The buzz made the words all but unintelligible, though the emphasis he placed on them appeared to get through to the Customs official.

"Pardon, sir. Colonel Ro-at. You are bound for Imperial Center for reconstr . . . yes, of course." The man's voice trailed off. "Everything seems in order here, Colonel."

Wedge raised his hand to take the card back, but did not let his claw close on it yet. "Are you certain? My baggage is in my sleeping berth."

"Yes, I am certain." The man impatiently tapped the card against Wedge's thumb.

"I understand the need for security, sir."

"I'm certain, sir."

"If you have trouble, I will help." Wedge let his voice fall to a whisper, as if suddenly overcome with fatigue. His head dipped slightly at the same time, then he brought it back up. "I will help."

The Customs man nodded. "I will remember that, Colonel."

Wedge took the card and fumbled a couple of times before he slid it home again. "I live to serve."

The Customs man moved on, mumbling under his breath. "You're dead and still serving. The Emdee-fours should have let you die."

Wedge would have missed the remark, but the hearing enhancement built into the mask and fed into his right ear allowed him to catch it. He killed the smile the comment threatened to produce because he knew Colonel Antar Roat would find little in life that was funny. *And getting caught by Customs as I try to land on Coruscant would not be funny at all.*

It had not occurred to Wedge to wonder how he would be inserted into Coruscant until he was on his way for his briefing about his cover. He'd known, of course, that he couldn't fly an X-wing in there, and he sincerely doubted much in the way of contraband or illegal immigrants made it onto Coruscant without someone knowing and approving of it. He'd assumed he would be disguised somehow, but it never crossed his mind that he would head into Coruscant in an Imperial Naval Officer's uniform.

The briefing about his new identity had been fascinating. General Cracken's people had fashioned several identities for him. One, Colonel Roat, was designed for insertion and possible reuse later to get back out again. He had another one for the time he would be scouting around on Coruscant and a third as his exit identity. He had been informed about the latter two identities, but all datacards and other things for them would be supplied on Coruscant after he had been met and had a chance to settle in.

The Intelligence division had chosen Colonel Antar Roat as his insertion cover for a couple of reasons. The first was that the prosthetics hid Wedge's identity almost completely. Moreover, they were a forbidden attractant—they made him unusual enough that people would pay attention to him, but they would see the parts, not the man wearing them. And people caught staring at him would look away in shame. They would remember a man with war injuries, but any details would concern his mechanical parts. Since the parts could be removed and discarded, authorities would be looking for a man who no longer existed once Wedge had shed that disguise.

The second reason Roat had been created for Wedge was because Wedge was a pilot. He could accurately and intelligently converse about starfighter combat if pressed. His cover story indicated he had been shot down in the defense of Vladet, in the Rachuk system, and Wedge could talk about that battle since he'd been there.

I was on the Rebel side, but I was there.

A slight tremor rippled through the ship. Wedge hit a button beside the screen in front of him and the view shifted to an external one being flashed from a holocam mounted in the aft of the *Jewel of Churba*. A shuttle lifted off from a spinal docking port on the top of the ship. The ultra-class passengers had traveled in what was supposed to be unparalleled luxury on the starliner's upper decks and those who could afford it clearly took their own shuttles down to the planet to avoid waiting to disembark with the other travelers.

It amazed Wedge that people would or could exist in such luxury in such a time of turmoil. He found their desire for pleasure and ease less disturbing than their apparent lack of foresight. From the Rebellion's point of view the end was nigh for the Empire—though whether the Rebellion or someone like Warlord Zsinj was going to emerge as the new force in the galaxy was open to conjecture. The fact was, though, that no matter who won, avoiding unnecessary expenditures of money in such dire times seemed just to be common sense to him.

He did realize that some people would spend money to spin around themselves a cocoon within which the Rebellion did not exist. Maintaining the illusion that the Empire was hale and hearty was not difficult if price was no object. Wedge had no doubt that in some far-flung enclaves of the Empire not only were there people who did not believe the Emperor had died, but there were people who would keep on believing he was alive and well for years if not decades and possibly even centuries.

Ignorance I can understand, but not willful ignorance.

He killed another smile before it could blossom, though this one was more difficult to kill than the first. The very same people he considered willfully ignorant would find him deluded and misguided. Half of them would deny there were any problems inherent in the Imperial system—as if slavery, anti-alien sentiments, and weapons that destroyed planets could be so easily forgotten. The other half might admit there were problems, but they would shy from accepting open insurgency against the legitimate government as a solution to them. For those people, working within the system was the way to achieve change, but they failed to realize that when a system had become as corrupt as the Empire, significant change was impossible without a shattering of the power structure.

The trick of it all—and what tempted him to smile—was that all sides could make reasonable and logical arguments for their points of view. Therein was the problem with politics. Since it was the art of compromise, round upon round of discussion could end in no solution being reached. The only time serious change was made was when an individual was willing to die for what he believed. Absent that basic commitment—a commitment most Imperial citizens were not prepared to make—the

Empire would continue to exist in one form or another, institutionalizing evil.

A man appeared at the end of his row of seats. "Colonel Roat?"

Wedge looked over slowly, then nodded. "Prefect Dodt. It has been, well, years."

As Parin Dodt—an Imperial Prefect with greying brown hair and brown eyes—Pash Cracken nodded. "It was last at the ceremony ending the year of mourning, as I recall, just before you were transferred away. I would not have known it was you, but the Customs man told me who you were. The galaxy gets smaller as time goes by."

Wedge stiffly patted the seat beside his. "Join me, if you do not mind. My body has been broken, but my brain was unaffected. You are coming to Imperial Center on business?"

"You know better than to ask such questions, Colonel, just as I know not to ask where you were injured." Pash settled himself into the seat and loosely fastened the restraining belts on. "This has been a very smooth flight."

"It has indeed." Wedge nodded. Pash's comment had confirmed what Wedge had decided about the journey to Coruscant: security was not so tight as to uncover them, nor as lax as might have been expected were the Empire's core institutions breaking down. It also told him that Pash had encountered no trouble fitting in with the other passengers. While the two of them had known they were traveling on the same flight, they had not made contact previously. Had there been any difficulties they would not have made contact prior to landing, and only did so now to facilitate pickup in the spaceport.

A smiling flight facilitator's face appeared on the flat screen. "We are beginning landing operations. Please bring your seats into a full and . . ."

Wedge killed the sound on the display. "I hope our landing is as smooth as the flight."

"As do I." Pash sighed convincingly. "I hate spaceport tie-ups. If things are going to go wrong, it's generally there."

The spaceport at which *Jewel of Churba* set down was a multistory facility built atop a triad of towers approximately fifty kilometers from the Imperial Palace. The docking bay had multiple levels that allowed passengers from the various classes to disembark without having to mix with the others. The rich who had not left in their own shuttles were received in an opulent, spacious area that Wedge saw through the porthole as *Jewel* settled in for a landing. The keelrunners—aliens and low-class humans—were off-loaded in a secure cargo area.

The first- through third-class passengers exited the starliner through multiple ports and into a clean but crowded waiting area. Customs officials ran spot checks on some of the passengers, but Wedge saw no one hustled away. Beyond the Immigration area was luggage retrieval, but before he or Pash could worm their way into the crowd to get their things, a brown-haired woman in a prim grey medtech uniform approached them.

"Colonel Roat?"

Wedge nodded. "I am Roat. This is my friend, Prefect Parin Dodt. You are?"

"Irin Fossyr. I am from the Rohair Biomechanical Clinic. I was sent to meet you."

"You were."

"I had been told you were notified. I left word with your aide, Captain Seeno."

"That explains it. Seeno was killed just before I began my journey."

"You have my sympathies, sir."

"Accepted." Wedge nodded solemnly. The woman had used the correct phrases to introduce herself, proving she was one of Cracken's agents. Wedge waited while she and Pash picked up the luggage, then she led them out to a waiting lift-car. It had labels on the side proclaiming it to be from the Rohari Biomechanical Clinic but otherwise looked utterly ordinary. Their luggage was loaded into the external rack, then the three of them climbed in and the driver in the forward compartment headed them away from the spaceport.

The woman sat back on the bench seat that faced the rear of the craft. "It will take us fifteen minutes or so to get where we're going. We could get there faster, but . . ."

Wedge smiled as much as the mask would allow him to. "Precautions, we understand. I was wondering, though, if I can't take this mask off."

"By all means."

Wedge subvocalized the command that let the air out of the built-in bladders, loosening the mask. He worked it off, then coughed and finally shucked his hand out of the claw glove. "Luke doesn't seem to mind his replacement hand—it must be that Jedi training."

Pash chuckled politely, but the woman just sat there and stared for a moment. Then she blushed and looked away. "Forgive me. I had been told you were important, but I didn't realize. I remember your face from some early Imperial warrants. You're Wedge Antilles, right?"

Wedge nodded. "You saw Imperial warrants with my picture on them?"

"They had limited circulation—the Diktat might have been with the Empire, but not so all Corellians." She extended her hand to Wedge. "I'm Iella Wessiri. It's a pleasure to meet you."

Iella Wessiri? Why is that name familiar? Wedge shook her hand and let her introduce herself to Pash Cracken—eliciting another blush—while he thought about her name. Then it came to him. *That's what Corran's human partner was called.*

"You saw the Imperial warrants when you were with CorSec."

Iella blinked, then nodded slowly. "They must have given you a thorough briefing."

"Not really, but I have heard of you." He shrugged. "I can't say from where, of course."

She shook her head. "No, of course not."

"What I can say is this"—Wedge smiled—"what I have heard makes me think this mission's smooth start should extend yet further and give us a chance to accomplish everything we set out to do."

15

Corran Horn felt miserable. The cover story prepared for his entry into Coruscant called for him to be swathed in multiple layers of cloth—most of it oppressively heavy and hot—forming the purple and red robes he wore. The collar on the shirt he wore closest to his skin had been starched and pressed until its edge felt like a razor, especially where it pressed up against his larynx. A big, old, rounded cylinder hat crowned him while the skirts of the outermost robe dragged on the deck of the *Jewel of Churba*'s exclusive ultra-deck.

He kept his hands hidden in the sleeves of the robe, as he had been instructed a good Kuati *telbun* would do. The goal of the clothing was to render him all but genderless, and were he traveling on Kuat with Erisi, he would be considered all but invisible by the upper crust of society. On *Jewel* he had been a curiosity and the combined object of envy and pity.

Erisi's appearance had been the source of envy for every male in ultra-class. She wore tight blue leggings beneath a loose blue blouse flecked with scintillating points of light that flashed gold and silver. A belt gathered the blouse at her waist, which was just as well because it had no fasteners and lay open from throat to tails. Thus, though she was fully clothed, anyone with enough intelligence to outwit a Kowakian monkey-lizard could imagine what Erisi looked like naked, and the idea of having to share a cabin with her doubtless seemed wonderful to plenty of men.

Pity came when people saw how she treated him. Erisi berated him mercilessly—on those occasions she chose to acknowledge his presence consciously. Most of the time he trailed respectfully after her, paying for things she bought, carrying things she wanted carried, picking up after her, and apologizing graciously in her wake. While her conduct was far from graceless, she appeared to draw strength from the cruelties she inflicted upon him. Theirs appeared to be a symbiotic relationship where Corran endured abuse in return for sexual favors.

In the final analysis, despite Erisi's beauty, no one thought it was an even bargain.

Erisi tapped her foot impatiently as a stocky female Customs official wandered along from the previous docking foyer to where they waited. Erisi folded her arms and gave the woman a withering stare. At first the official hesitated, then she smiled slowly. The expression on her face all but broadcast her thoughts to Corran. *She's remembered* she *has the power here, at this moment, and will make Erisi pay for her disrespect.*

The official glanced at her datapad. "Ris Darsk?"

Erisi nodded coldly.

"I have a travel file with the appropriate visas for you, but not for him."

"He is Darsk Ristel." Erisi waved her left hand dismissively. "He is there."

"I only show one passenger."

Erisi reached out with one finger and punched a button on the woman's datapad. "There. Baggage."

A scowl settled over the official's face. "State the purpose of your visit to Imperial Center."

"It is a private matter."

An oily smile spilled over the scowl. "That is insufficient for our records."

Erisi glanced at Corran, then she produced a razor-edged smile that slashed into the official's confidence. "Mine is a pleasure journey here, though I anticipate very little of it."

The official turned toward him. "The purpose of your visit, sir?"

Erisi answered for him. "His is a business trip."

"Business and pleasure? Should it not be one or the other?"

Erisi shook her head slowly. "Not when my pleasure is his business. He is *telbun*."

The official's head drew back, trapping an extra chin against her throat. *"Telbun?"*

"Exactly. My *telbun* bore me here on Imperial Center so, in keeping with my family's tradition, I have come here with this *telbun* to conceive."

"To conceive? A child?"

"You understand."

"Telbun. I see." The official looked at Corran and he averted his eyes. *"Telbun."*

Telbun were drawn from the middle classes on Kuat. They were raised and trained by their families to excel in academics, social manners, and athletics. When they reached the appropriate age, they underwent a battery of tests that produced a ranking by combining scores for intelligence, grace, health, and genetic makeup. The upper classes of the great Kuat merchant houses then purchased *telbun* from their families for the purpose of parenting a child with a member of the merchant family, then raising that child. The child would be an heir of the merchant house, thereby getting all the benefits of its birth, while the *telbun*'s family would be greatly enriched by the fees paid for the *telbun*'s service.

The process, which divorced reproduction from emotional commitments, struck many, including Corran, as inhuman, but the Kuati aristocracy found it practical in a number of ways. It left their people free to enter into alliances and mergers without placing a child in jeopardy of being drawn into an enemy camp when whatever enterprise that brought two people together collapsed. It also prevented inbreeding between noble families and provided the children with a guardian/tutor with a very serious and tight bond to his charges. The children knew their *telbuns* provided one half of their biological makeup, but they only acknowledged their aristocratic parent as having a blood relationship with them.

The process was not easy on a *telbun*, but what did their feelings matter? They were property, nothing more.

The official hit a few buttons on her datapad. "You and the *telbun* are cleared. Beyond the airlock is your shuttle. Enjoy your stay . . . or whatever."

The woman moved off down along the ship's spine toward the next docking foyer. Erisi and Corran retreated to circle in the center of the docking foyer. The circle slowly rose toward the outer hull and the circular platform on which they rose locked into the floor of the airlock with a click. Corran felt bits and pieces of things shift below his feet, then the cylindrical airlock slowly rotated ninety degrees until the side opened onto a shuttle's hatch. Beyond the opening stood a female pilot who waved them aboard the modified *Lambda*-class ship.

The hatch closed behind them. "If you will be seated," said the pilot, "and strap yourselves in, I can take you to the Hotel Imperial."

Erisi nodded. "We are cleared for an entry vector?"

"Yes, Mistress Darsk."

Corran walked into the passenger compartment and took a seat in the last of four rows. Erisi cast a glance down a small corridor toward the cockpit, then came back and joined him. She said nothing as she strapped herself in, but she did rest her arm on his. The lights glistening on her blouse shifted color sequentially, as if a golden beach was being eroded by a silver wave.

The ship shuddered and popped as it disengaged itself from *Jewel*'s airlock, then it lifted off and its wings snapped down into place. As they did so, holographic displays lining the walls of the passenger compartment provided images that made it appear as if the whole ship had been made of transparisteel. The shuttle pulled up and away from *Jewel*, heading outbound from Coruscant for a moment. The screens filled with pinpoint images of distant stars.

Erisi kept her voice low. "Please forgive me for how rudely I have treated you."

"Whatever you desire, mistress."

She looked at him with a horrified expression at the dullness of his response, then that deepened as she realized that being alone in the ship's cabin did not mean they could not be overheard. Erisi leaned toward him, filling his nostrils with the sweet scent of *nlorna* flower perfume. She kissed him on the lips, lingering close enough to whisper, "You are *telbun*. You understand."

Corran nodded. "I am *telbun*. I understand." Her comment and his reply, fairly innocent and common given the relationship of their two cover identities, had been imbued with a different meaning for the two of them. It was a touchstone, a link back into their real identities. Whenever they needed to assure themselves that the other person was just playacting they were able to use the phrases and responses to do so. In this way Corran knew her cruelties were forced upon him by their situation, and she knew his indifferent responses did not reflect his true feelings for her.

Of course, I don't know what those feelings are, really. He liked Erisi enough as a friend and yet still found her very attractive. The degree of proximity forced by their roles had stopped short of physical intimacy, but had included living together throughout *Jewel*'s journey and the training before that. Erisi had made no secret, in the past, of her attraction to him. No one would have faulted them for sleeping together, given their circumstances, but Corran had held himself back from succumbing to her charms and the security of shared intimacy.

At first he told himself it was because he didn't want to let his guard down. If they were to make love their guard would be down. One slip, one fatal admission, an inappropriate name whispered in an unguarded moment of passion, could have spelled their undoing. Only by being apart could they guarantee mission security.

Those concerns eroded as they spent more time together. For a very short time he allowed himself to imagine that he would be betraying Mirax in some way if he slept with Erisi. He *did* have feelings for Mirax, but there were no commitments or obligations between them. For all he knew she had a lover stashed away in every starport across the galaxy—he doubted it, and was surprised at the spark of jealousy ignited at the thought—and if she did, it was no business of his. They were both adults and if they *did* eventually enter into a relationship, what had gone before would have to be dealt with as something that happened *before*.

His ultimate resistance stemmed from two things that fed back and forth into each other. The first surprised him when he discovered it, but he couldn't deny it—he thought of Erisi as being well and truly outside his social class—inescapably so. She came from a world where she was nobility. Money, opportunity, material advantages, and the best of everything were what she had been born to. While her joining the Rebellion spoke to true nobility in her heart, the fact was that she really enjoyed luxury and treated it as her due. He had seen that throughout the trip—she took to it like a Sarlacc to sand.

Despite being a *telbun*, the same luxury was available to Corran. He was surprised by his inability to get used to it. Whereas Erisi might think nothing of peeling a fruit and leaving the rind on the arm of a nerf-hide divan, Corran found himself worrying about spilling something or sweating on the divan, thereby ruining it. Erisi didn't care if it was ruined, whereas he did because he did not have access to the sort of money that would allow him to laugh off a demand to replace the couch.

Erisi's blithe disregard for money had all but given Corran fits. Erisi had ordered him to tip servants extravagantly, but he had a hard time rewarding indifferent or poor service as well as he did good service. And the servants on the ultra-deck were obsequious and sycophantic in the extreme. There were times he wanted to just lash out and bash them, but he knew they'd accept a beating, then thank him for administering it in such a skillful manner—doing whatever they thought would inflate the gratuities.

He knew he could never fit into her world, and he suspected she knew it, too. While the abuse she heaped upon him was exaggerated enough that he knew she didn't mean it, there were times the tone of her voice or the venom in her eyes seemed a bit too convincing. A small part of her realized his unsuitability as a mate, and that bit went to war with the part of her that liked him, producing enough anxiety that she dealt with him more sharply than she might otherwise have done.

Her resentment about his lack of ability to cope with the common elements of her existence made him want to show her he could adapt. Deep in his heart he knew he would fail ultimately because just as he and Erisi needed a touchstone phrase to remind them who they truly were, Corran himself needed a connection back to what he saw as real life. His family circumstances had never been affluent, but neither had they been impoverished. Like his father and grandfather, he had worked for the Corellian Security Force and he was proud of his background. If he and Erisi couldn't be together, then it was her loss, not his.

Erisi's hand tightened on Corran's arm. "Oh, my, look."

The shuttle had come about and gave them an unobstructed view of the planet. They sailed in beyond the sphere of Golan Space Defense platforms and the orbital solar reflection stations. The latter reflected sunlight down to the planet to warm zones near the glacial caps at either pole. While quite habitable, Coruscant's orbit took it far enough from the sun that capturing and redirecting solar energy was needed to keep the world temperate year round.

The shuttle was heading down and in toward the daylight side of the planet, but a crescent of night gobbled up a big portion of it. The lighted side had a spiky, angular quality to it, with towers rising up and grand canyons sinking down through a khaki and grey landscape. Skyhooks, massive stone islands flecked with green and purple gardens, floated lazily over the ferrocrete terrain. Corran could see nothing natural on that side of the world, just the rough scars of humanity's manufacture and constant reconstruction of the planet.

The nightside, by way of contrast, sparkled and shimmered with a full spectrum of colors that flowed through invisible channels. Millions of lights marked towers he could not see, and each light on them corresponded to one or two or four or a dozen people living in its proximity. Deep down at the base of the towers, winking in and out of life as buildings eclipsed his view, muted lights played out like those in ocean depths, hinting at life unseen and likely unknowable.

Approaching the line that marked the end of day and the beginning of the night, Corran saw a building that could only be the Imperial Palace. An arrogant edifice, it rivaled and mocked the Manarai Mountains to the south. Towers rose from it like coral spires from a reef and their sharp, angular construction made them seem as dangerous to Corran as the coral they reminded him of. Those towers, that artificial mountain, housed the bureaucracy and officials that could destroy planets with a rounding error in the budget. *It is a hive of evil.* He shivered. *No one will ever be safe until it has been purged.*

"Impressive, isn't it?"

Corran looked up and found the shuttle's pilot standing in the hatchway. "Shouldn't you be flying this thing?"

"We're on instrument approach to the Hotel Imperial. My droid copilot can handle it." She gestured at the vision of the planet. "You're lucky. It's a clear night. If there were storms, I'd be at the helm dodging lightning and skyhooks and you'd not see much."

Erisi lifted her chin. "My *telbun* and I . . ."

"You want the Emperor's suite. Someone else has a previous reservation."

Corran spoke slowly and carefully. "We thought it was arranged."

"It can be."

Erisi's eyes narrowed. "Will a thousand credits suffice?"

"As a down payment, yes."

Corran smiled. "You're our contact?"

The pilot nodded and Corran took a good look at her for the first time. He found her pretty, and her dark eyes were full of fire, but there was another quality about her that he couldn't place at first. He thought it had to do with her mood, and how quickly she had shifted from being just an anonymous pilot to their contact, but he recognized that mutability of personality as a mark of an excellent undercover operative. *Iella could change like that—affect a mood and suddenly she was someone else.*

As the woman drew closer he nailed it. Though her hair was white and gathered at the back of her head, he realized she reminded him very strongly of Princess Leia Organa. He'd not made the connection when she was the pilot—he knew he'd not really paid that much attention to her. It was obvious to him that she was *not* Leia Organa, but because of the resemblance he would have been willing to bet she came from Alderaan.

The pilot sat down in the chair in front of Corran and swiveled it around to face them both. "We've not much time here, but the cabin is clean, so we can talk briefly. I already know who you are. Here I'm known by the code name Targeter though as the pilot I go by Rima Borealis. That will do as a call name for now. We'll get you into the hotel and book you into a suite, but you'll live out of other rooms we have secured for you. New identities and identification cards will be supplied there."

Erisi nodded slowly. "We're not it, are we?" She pointed toward the Palace as their ship descended. "Just the two of us gathering the information needed to bring that down—that's a lot of pressure."

Rima shrugged. "I don't know, and I couldn't tell you if I did. Sorry." She patted Erisi on the knee. "I wouldn't worry, though. From what I understand, you Rogues are a thorn in the Empire's flesh. Now's the chance we have to shove it deeper and twist it a bit."

"Nice analogy." Corran smiled. "I like it."

"I thought you would." Rima returned his smile. "Nothing on this mission two Rogues can't handle, even if," she added with a shrug, "getting in to Coruscant is likely the easiest part of the whole thing."

16

Gavin Darklighter said nothing as the *Pulsar Skate* reverted to normal space. His silence did not result from previously warbled warnings by Liat Tsayv, nor was it born of the need for operational security that General Cracken's people had drilled into him. And it was not the result of his having his eyes closed so he couldn't see anything.

He could see.

What he saw was Coruscant, and that vision took his breath away.

Mirax turned in her seat. "Impressive, eh, kid?"

Gavin knew he'd not seen as much of the galaxy as some folks—*all of Rogue Squadron included, and the crew of the* Skate *as well*—but he didn't think of himself as a total nullwit or nerf-herder. He wasn't one of the Sand People, for example, and he knew plenty about sophisticated things, like flying an X-wing or slicing code in a computer. He might have grown up on a farm outside Anchorhead, but he'd been to town at least once a month, and his family was always invited over to the big house by his uncle for family celebrations.

He'd even been to Mos Eisley. *Once.*

But he'd never seen anything like Coruscant.

"It's just a city, the whole thing, one big, huge, really big city." Gavin spread his arms wide for emphasis, but hit hull before he thought he'd gotten the gesture right. "It's all city."

"Pole to pole, horizon to horizon, more or less." Mirax smiled. "There are spots on the glacier where things haven't been built over, but the only reason that's true is because the poles are frozen reservoirs. If you drink water down there, it was pole-frozen or shipped in from outside."

A light came to life on the console. The Sullustan pilot chittered at Mirax, causing her to turn around and hit three buttons. "*Merisee Hope* here."

"Coruscant Space Traffic Coordination on link here. Our files show you're transporting exotics? Our scan shows you have eight individuals on board."

"Affirmative. Three humans, five exotics."

"I copy. You are cleared on vector 34293AFX."

Liat gave Mirax a nod, so she spoke into the comm unit again. "We copy. Thank you, Coordinator."

Gavin saw her shut the comm unit off, then raised an eyebrow. "That seemed too easy."

"Suspicion is a good thing, just so long as you don't go overboard with it."

"Sounds like something Corran might say."

Mirax glanced back at Gavin, but he couldn't read the expression on her face. "He might say such a thing, indeed. And he'd be thinking our entry was too easy, too. The trick of it is that certain members of Coruscant's Space Traffic Coordination office have been bought and paid for. When the entry-monitor satellites beamed an inquiry to the *Skate* they got a transponder message that told them we were the *Merisee Hope*. That ship is a known slave-runner for one of the brothels on the edge of Invisec."

"Invisec?"

Mirax frowned. "I thought they briefed you before this run."

"Well, yes, they did, but I don't remember Invisec being mentioned before." Gavin shrugged helplessly. "What is it?"

"A chunk of the Imperial City that is popularly known as the Invisible Sector, primarily because most people don't want to admit it exists. It's large enough to swallow up three or four of the largest metropolitan areas from elsewhere in the galaxy, but here it's just one precinct out of many. Invisec is a contraction of the name and is used by folks who frequent it to refer to the area."

"You mean the Alien Protection Zone."

"Right, sure, if you want the Impspeak designation, but only the military uses that. Citizens don't talk about it, or call it *'there,'* or refer to it as invisible or unseen, or the witty ones confess slumming down there by saying they *disappeared* for a while. Invisec *is* largely made up of the APZ, but it extends around it and has little satellite sectors elsewhere in the city. Think of it like Mos Eisley, but uglier, nastier, and less hospitable."

Worse than Mos Eisley? Gavin blinked. "Is that possible?"

"That's the thing about evil, Gavin, it doesn't diminish when you spread it over a larger area. It's rumored Vader built a palace near Invisec because, for him, it was as attractive as a seashore sunset is to most folks. The black market thrives down there. Aliens who have work permits can leave Invisec and work in other locations. Those who don't are forced into working at the factories that have been built on the edges of Invisec."

Looking past Mirax and out through the cockpit viewscreen Gavin saw the dark city below rise up toward the ship. It seemed as if towers lunged to impale the *Skate* but the Sullustan pilot deftly steered the ship around them. Down and down the ship glided, flitting between towers and around through canyons, pushing lower and lower through layers of light and shadow until they reached a point where Liat had to turn on the ship's running lights or be left without a means for orienting the ship.

The Sullustan slowed the ship and brought it down below the overhanging edge of a building. Dark fungi and white lime stained the walls. Gavin couldn't identify the stone used to construct the building, but it seemed to be ancient and covered with odd, twisty runes like nothing he'd ever seen before. "What does the writing say?"

Mirax laughed. "That's not writing, Gavin, those are the trails of granite slugs. Hawk-bats tend not to get down this deep."

"Granite slugs and hawk-bats?"

"Hawk-bats look good riding the thermals—just as long as you don't suck one into an engine. They prey on granite slugs and get the occasional borrat. Borrats get as big as two meters long."

"Sounds like womp rats from back home."

"Sure, except these things have tusks, spines, armored flesh, and claws that can dig through ferrocrete. The only good thing about them is that they tend to be solitary." Mirax flipped some switches overhead. "And there are all sorts of extraterrestrial beasties that someone brought to Coruscant and let loose. Most are benign, but . . ."

Gavin shivered. *And why was it I agreed to this duty?*

The *Skate* slowly began an ascent, which Gavin thought would bump them against the bottom floor of the building above, but he discovered they were rising through an open hatchway in the overhang. "This is convenient."

"A lot of transport of goods goes on at the lower levels in the city—it keeps traffic lighter up above. This building used to be outside Invisec, but as the construction droids slice a piece off one side of Invisec, the unhomed push out and take over new areas of the city. It's a slow migration and Invisec generally gains two kilometers for every one it loses."

The *Pulsar Skate* drifted forward and put down its landing gear. It came to rest in the large, dark basement of the building, squeezed in between trash middens, hydro-reclamation processors, and the heart of the building's heating and cooling facilities. Liat killed the repulsorlift drives but left the external lights on, providing the only strong illumination in the facility.

Mirax unstrapped herself from the command chair and punched a button. Gavin heard a whooshing hiss followed by the sound of servomotors lowering the access hatch. It touched down with a metallic thump. "C'mon, kid, let's see what they have set up for you."

Gavin unfastened his restraining belts and followed her down the ramp and out into the building. The musty air filled his nose and dried it out. It reminded Gavin of how the air smelled just before a Tatooine dust storm hit with its full fury. He found the scent familiar enough to be reassuring.

Mirax preceded him down the ramp and crossed over to one of the trash middens. Dropping to one knee, she waved him over. "Grab this end of the crate and pull."

Gavin grabbed one of the handles on the duraplast box and slid it from beneath the trash. Mirax got the handle on the other end of the two-meter-long case and between them they lugged the heavy rectangular box over to a spot beneath one of the *Skate*'s lights. The rest of the Rogues descended the ramp and joined them.

Nawara Ven's black cape pooled around him as he knelt at the lockpad on the box. He studied it for a moment, then looked up at Mirax. "This looks to be what we were told to find here. It should have gear and identification cards in it. Should you be here when we open it?"

She shrugged. "You're probably right, I shouldn't be, but I've got two standard hours before the clearances for my exit identity become live."

Gavin frowned at Nawara. "We can trust her, you know."

The Twi'lek held a hand up. "I do not doubt her honesty, Gavin—but the less she knows, the better for her. In the same way, our not knowing the particulars of her escape vector and identity means we cannot reveal it if we run into complications."

Mirax patted Gavin on the shoulder. "Not to worry,

Gavin. I've got navigational calculations to do. May the Force be with you all." She retreated up the ramp, then it ascended after her.

Nawara punched a combination into the lockpad. The lock clicked and the Twi'lek slid the cover off. The gear inside had been packed into numbered boxes that Nawara pulled from the case and handed to the appropriate individuals. Gavin accepted box one and wandered away from the others to open it.

Inside he found a folded change of clothes, a small satchel in which they could be carried, a hundred credits in various forms, a small hold-out blaster, and a packet filled with identification cards. He tore the packet open and poured its contents into his hand. He had a drawcard in his alias so he could pull money from a transaction account as needed, a basic medical record card containing a medical history that would allow doctors to treat him without knowing who he really was, and his new identification card.

His cover identity was that of Vin Leiger, a young man from a Rimworld who had gotten into trouble. He'd hooked up with a Shistavanen—conveniently played by Riv Shiel—and had left home. The two of them had scraped by on a number of worlds by using Vin's apparent innocence to trick locals into trying to take him for all he was worth. Shiel—who would go by the name Shaalir Resh—would rob the con men targeting Vin, then they would move on.

A chill ran down Gavin's spine as he ran through all the details of his new identity. Vin Leiger, he realized, had a more complete history than he did himself. It struck Gavin that it was utterly absurd for him to be trying to pass as an outlaw from another world. It was even more absurd for him to be a member of an elite Rebel squadron on a spy mission to the Imperial homeworld. *How can I be here?*

He remembered standing on the edge of the pit where his family lived, looking out at the wastes of Tatooine, wondering if Luke Skywalker had ever stood where he stood and had seen what he'd seen. It was quite a contrast to the scene below where his mother and siblings cleared away the debris from his sixteenth birthday celebration. Security, warmth, love, all existed down in the hole, while everything outside it was hostile, inhospitable, and unforgiving.

His father had come up and had stood there with him. "You've got the Darklighter look on your face, and at your age, too." His father sighed. "I knew this day would come, just not this soon."

Gavin had looked down at his father. "What do you mean?"

"Us Darklighters have a point in our lives when we look outside ourselves. We look outside our lives. Some of us, like my father, never do it until the end, and then they regret all the things they didn't do. Your uncle Huff looked outside once upon a time and chose to ignore what he saw. That's why he's become a food magnate here. By building up his little empire here he's too busy to see what's out there."

Gavin could once again feel his father's rough hand on the back of his neck. "Your cousin, Biggs, had the look at your age. He was determined to go to the Academy and become a hero with his name written big in the stars. He succeeded, better than he ever imagined, I suspect, though I'd have settled for a bit less success and a bit more life for him. And now you, Gavin, my eldest, you have the look."

"There's something out there for me, Father." Gavin had shrugged. "Maybe I'm dreaming, but it feels like my destiny is out there."

"There's only one way for you to find out."

His father's reply had surprised him. "Do you mean you would let me go off and join the Rebellion?"

The elder Darklighter sighed heavily. "I couldn't stop you any more than Huff could stop Biggs, but Huff tried. When he saw he couldn't win, he secured Biggs an appointment to the Academy—that way he was in control of his son's fate. Biggs went, of course, because that's what he had to do, but he resented his father's meddling. There was a rift there, and that eats at Huff every day of his life.

"Well, I'm not going to stand in your way. You're welcome back here whenever you want to come, and no matter what you do, or don't do, or run from, you'll always be welcome here. You're a Darklighter. Going out there is what you must do, so go with my fondest wishes that the Force will keep you safe and whole."

Gavin had smiled and continued to stare out into the distance. "I feel as if the whole universe is opening up to me, and that all I have to do is step forward and I can make a difference. The feeling is powerful and exhilarating. Is that how you felt when you *looked*, Father?"

"I never looked until now, Gavin. I was always too afraid, and what I see now is a lot of pain and hurt." He smiled up at his son. "And regret I won't be out there with you. Whatever you do, remember who you are, what you are. A Darklighter's destiny is waiting for you out there. This Rebellion, it's been without a Darklighter for too long. It's time that problem was solved."

So now I'm with the Rebellion, on a dangerous mission to find the weaknesses of a fortress planet. Whose vision was more accurate, Father, mine of destiny, or yours of pain and regret? He shook his head. *At least back there with you I have a safe haven. This mission is part of seeing to it that everyone has a safe haven and the freedom to discover their own destiny. I think you'd probably tell me that with a Darklighter involved, we'll succeed. I hope you're right.*

Shiel's hand landed heavily on Gavin's shoulder. "Time to move, Gavin."

"I don't know any Gavin, Shaalir." Gavin stuffed his clothes into his satchel, tucked the blaster into his belt, and pocketed the identification cards and money. "The name's Vin Leiger and I'm here to find out what makes this world spin, and then find a way to make it stop."

17

Wedge Antilles realized that the mission he and Pash Cracken had been given was the most difficult of all to complete. He suspected the other members of Rogue Squadron had been assigned tasks like mapping out power grids or locating shield generation stations. Pinpointing those locations would be vital if any invasion was to succeed, but that data would be useless unless he and Pash succeeded and came away with a positive report.

They had been charged with the duty of assessing the loyalty of the populace on the planet. Iella Wessiri had been able to provide them with her impressions of the general mood of the world's population, but she freely acknowledged she was more pessimistic than another might be. "Paranoia has a way of coloring your thoughts about the world."

Wedge smiled as they moved out of the Galactic Museum's Sith artifact room. "Paranoia may be an effect of the things in that room. Ghastly stuff . . ."

"But seductively powerful." Iella glanced down wistfully. "Not as crude as a cubic meter of credits, but those things appeal to something even more base than greed."

"My thoughts exactly." Because of his mission parameters Wedge had decided touring the various Imperial facilities open to the public should form the basis of their survey, and in the week since his arrival they had covered a lot of ground. He had expected the Empire to put its best face forward and display things that would denigrate and demean the Rebellion, and he'd not been disappointed. By learning what it was the Empire wanted its citizens to believe about the Rebellion, he could then assess whether or not the Imperial propaganda efforts were successful.

The museum had proved very instructive in this regard. The bottom two floors provided extensive displays of the flora, fauna, and mineral treasures from throughout the Empire. Several displays did provide notations that this plant or that animal had been made extinct on their native worlds by "outlaws and malcontents," and included among such beasts were Ewoks—and Imperial taxidermists had taken great pains to make them seem helpless and even more cute than they were in real life. However, despite such propagandistic comments, the displays were impressive and reminded Wedge there was much more to the Empire than he'd consciously acknowledged before.

The first two floors were clearly designed to impress and overwhelm visitors with their magnificence, so the next four floors had been put together to capitalize on the favorable impressions made below. Those floors covered the cultural and social developments of the Empire. One whole floor had been given over to the Emperor and his life. Holograms of people who had known him served as tour guides at each display while droids admonished the people to keep moving on. All the displays, from items shown to the descriptions that accompanied them, were slanted toward making the viewers believe everything the Emperor had done had been for their specific good.

The final tableau presented on that floor made this point abundantly clear. It showed the Emperor lying in state upon a bier in a dark room. He looked far younger and more handsome than Luke had described him, as if the moral rot and evil in him had never been able to ooze out and reveal itself. The Emperor appeared just to be sleeping, ready to rise up if the Empire needed him again.

A holographic image of Darth Vader sizzled to life when Wedge had approached. "Behold my Master and weep. He has been stolen from us by those who embrace hatred. The Emperor learned that the Rebels had stolen plans for an Imperial Planetary Ore Extractor and intended to use the one they were fabricating at Endor on inhabited planets. He assembled his fleet, and heedless of personal danger, he had me take him to Endor. He infiltrated the half-completed extractor, offering these Rebels his forgiveness and a hand in friendship. They rejected him and attacked his fleet. My Master had no alternative but to destroy this Death Star himself, perishing in the process so his citizens could live on. I was slain with him, but my death did not distress me, for it came in service to my Master."

As Vader spoke, a fanciful holographic simulation of the battle at Endor played itself out against the backdrop of the chamber. An outnumbered and outgunned Imperial fleet drove a dagger into the heart of the Rebel formation. The pinpoint accuracy of Imperial gunners laid waste to the Rebels. As that war raged outside, the Emperor appeared looking beatific as he pleaded with an unseen Rebel host. His expression melted into sorrow and pain, then his eyes blazed and his fists knotted. Suddenly his image exploded, taking the Death Star with it. The explosion tore into the Rebel fleet, leaving only small, weak ships to flee.

The whole presentation had sent a shiver through Wedge. He had been at Endor—he had fired the shot that helped destroy the Death Star—yet this telling of the story felt as compelling to him as the true history of what had happened. It suggested a benign purpose for the Death Stars and made the Rebels out to be monsters for thinking to use one on an inhabited planet. By doing so, and by suggesting the Emperor had gone there to prevent that sort of perversion, the fear that lingered in everyone's heart concerning the destruction of Alderaan was shifted into fear directed at the Rebellion. The Emperor had sacrificed himself to save everyone else, so only the most boorish of louts would not show gratitude of some sort toward him.

As he moved on to the Hall of Justice with Iella he found himself amazed at how easily the Empire had been able to warp the truth into a story that sustained the realm. "The people who create these exhibits are very good at what they do."

"That was never more evident as it is with this area concerning the Jedi." Iella linked her arm through Wedge's as they strolled on. "Were it not for the Emperor, we would be slaves to a tyrannical Jedi state."

The history of the Jedi Knights was presented in a linear fashion, moving from right to left around the room. The thousand-generation saga had been condensed such that it gave emphasis to the legendary Jedi Masters of old, then suggested a gradual deviation from that noble tradition as the Knighthood grew. The corruption had begun—Wedge gathered by implication—when human Jedi Masters had taken on nonhuman disciples. The Jedi Knights went from being the guardians of the Old Republic to the secret masters of its future. They used their powers to manipulate and direct the Republic's leaders.

After the resolution of the Clone Wars, the Jedi began to move toward an open grab for power. Senator Palpatine circumvented them and deposed their puppet. In overthrowing the corrupt Old Republic, the Emperor stripped from the Jedi their political power and laid their evil bare for all to see. The Jedi denied the truth he revealed, all except one of their number. His fellows tried to murder him, but he survived their treachery and rose to assist the Emperor in rooting out the evil that had ruined the Knighthood. He was Darth Vader and, said the display, never had there been a greater champion for the high ideals of the Empire than he.

Wedge smiled. "At least that last bit is true—Vader was Imperial through and through."

"Notice how they have the true line of Jedi Knights dying with Vader at Endor? No mention of Luke Skywalker, but the implication is that he is heir to the corrupt tradition." She shook her head. "I wonder if that is too subtle?"

"Appeals that play to fear can be subtle and still very effective." Wedge turned and looked back toward the far corner of the room. "It looks to me as if this chamber once opened onto another one, but the entrance has been sealed up."

"I've seen an old version of a holographic museum tour—we have people who archive those sorts of things just to see what's been changed. Once upon a time, back in the days of the Old Republic, there were three more chambers that extended back there with mementos of famous Jedi Knights and their exploits." Iella shrugged. "It's been sealed up for over thirty standard years. Rumor has it that most of the things in there now are memento mori, and the descriptions of some are enough to make the Sith artifacts look absolutely benign."

Pash Cracken met them outside the Jedi exhibit carrying a small sack. "Are you two interested in getting out of here?"

Wedge didn't answer immediately because his attention was drawn to something beyond Pash. The museum had been constructed in such a way that the circular foyer rose all the way up to the roof, giving each floor a crescent-shaped opening onto it. The northern wall, through which the public entered the building, had been constructed of transparisteel, providing a commanding view of the Imperial Palace and the walkway that linked the Museum with the Imperial Justice Court.

A vicious dark, roiling cloud was coalescing in the kilometer or so between the museum and the Palace. Golden lightning shot through it, then arced up into the air. A brilliant energy thread linked the cloud with the lowest of the planetary shields, then seconds later an explosive rumble of thunder sent a tremor through the building. More lightning flashed at the heart of the cloud's dark depths and the cloud began to drift toward them.

Wedge looked over at Iella. "That's a nasty-looking storm. Are we safe here?"

"Sure," she said, taking her hands off the steel railing. "A compressor probably blew in one of the buildings down there. Water vapor escapes into the air, condenses, and starts spitting energy. There's lightning rods all over the place on these towers and skyhooks, so we should be safe. You'll know it's a really bad storm when the skyhooks detach their tethers and move off."

Down below Wedge saw all sorts of people streaming into the foyer as the storm approached. Beneath the dark cloud he saw a shimmering sheet of rain scourging the buildings. "Such quickly developing storms must make weather prediction here very tough."

"I've heard it said that any meteorologist who is right thirty percent of the time here on Coruscant is barred from shipping on the submarine gambling vessel *Coral Vanda* or from any other casino because she's just too lucky. In reality, though, no one has any reason to actually go outside, so the weather matters little."

A bolt of lightning struck very near the museum and the lights dimmed for a moment. Pash smiled. "*That* could be an inconvenience."

"True."

Wedge pointed at the sack Pash had in his left hand. "I take it you found something interesting in the museum's souvenir mart?"

"I have here the most popular items, as indicated by a very friendly salesclerk." Pash peered down into the bag. "I have a statue of the Emperor made from cold-cast Corusca Stone resin—if you project a laser through the base it will give you a series of pictures of the Emperor displayed on your wall. I promised my father I'd bring him something, and that's it."

Wedge nodded solemnly. "He'll love that."

"I hope so. I also got two holopad display disks that will project the two most popular segments of the Emperor's life story: the Clone Wars and the one titled 'Sacrifice at Endor.' I was assured they were the hottest sellers and especially popular with tourists who would be heading back into the outlier worlds."

"Interesting." In their early discussions of how best to accomplish their mission, Pash had suggested to Wedge that one way to determine the beliefs held by others was to watch what they spent money on. The popularity of the statue suggested that a good number of people did revere the Emperor, though the image of Pash's father displaying it like a trophy in his office suggested that even the Emperor's detractors would find a use for such a thing. The holopad disks, on the other hand, suggested an interest in the events that happened before and around the founding of the Empire and the events that marked its decline. The 'Sacrifice at Endor' piece was significant in that it confirmed the Emperor's death and could be brought to distant worlds to lay any doubts to rest. The fact that it showed the Rebel fleet as having been broken, and suggested evil motives on the part of the Rebels themselves, was not that great a concern to Wedge. While Imperialists could use the program to show how the Emperor cared for his people, the chances of it convincing anyone that the Rebellion had died at Endor with it were slim indeed.

Well, this is a start. It would seem that people are beginning to come to grips with the fact that the Emperor is dead. How ever he died—by his own hand or through Luke's intervention—the fact is that the Rebellion was sufficiently strong to put him in mortal danger. To a greater or lesser extent everyone on this planet must wonder how much of the Rebellion has survived and how it will come to affect their lives.

Wedge smiled. "I think those will do just fine. Everyone will be happy with them."

"I hope so." Pash jerked his head back toward the

building's central core and the lift tubes. "The storm will be past shortly. Shall we head down and out?"

Wedge nodded and started toward the lifts when a woman grabbed his elbow. He turned with a polite smile on his face and she launched herself into his arms. "Darling," she shouted, then kissed him full on the lips. "I'm so glad I caught up with you!"

Wedge got his hands on her shoulders and pried himself loose of her embrace. He started to sputter, then he saw who she was and a chunk of Hoth settled itself in his guts. *Mirax!* "Yes, love, we were just getting ready to look for you. Where have you been?"

"I missed some connections and couldn't get out when I wanted to." Mirax forced a light laugh and smiled at Pash and Iella. "You know me, I always push my luck with my travel plans. Things just fell apart this time, and I don't have a clue as to what I shall do now. Perhaps, my dear, you do."

18

Though the week he'd already spent wandering through the upper precincts of Coruscant had allowed him to become accustomed to constant observation, Corran could not shake the background sense of being watched. Of course there were reasons for people to watch him. He sat at a tapcaf table on the edge of a promenade in the Imperial Palace's Grand Corridor accompanied by two strikingly beautiful women. Erisi with her short black hair and Rima with her longer white hair proved enough of a contrast to each other that eyes were naturally drawn to them. That he, a lone man, should be blessed with their company made him the object of a certain amount of envy, as did the apparent leisure with which all three of them sat at the table and chatted away idly.

Corran and Erisi had been given two areas to study in their survey of Coruscant. They were to cover basic security and peacekeeping as well as medical services and facilities. Having been a security officer, Corran knew what to look for by way of force allocation, morale, discipline, response times, and tactics. Much of the week had already been spent in passive observation of the Coruscant constabulary and the stormtrooper contingents that worked with them.

Coming to the Palace's Grand Corridor had been the final and crowning expedition in their survey of the upper, most public levels of Coruscant. At first Corran had absolutely balked at taking such a risk because he felt security there, in the heart of the building from which the government was run, had to be maintained at the highest level. The chance of detection there was greatest, yet the need for study there was equally great. He knew that any attempt to take Coruscant might well end up with a running lightfight through the halls and corridors of the Palace, so any information about its security would clearly save lives.

And in this place Rogue Squadron could have dog-fights with a whole wing of TIEs.

The Grand Corridor had immediately impressed him with its scope and size. The corridor itself ran on for kilometers and the open areas at the floor level could easily have accommodated a Star Destroyer. Banners of all colors and designs hung from balustrades and arches. Each one represented a world in the Empire and there were more of them than Corran figured he could count in a lifetime.

Purple and green *ch'hala* trees lined the main floor and each of the upper levels. Their bark reacted to vibrations and sounds, sparking displays of color that splashed an ever-changing, opalescent mosaic on the grey granite walls and pillars. Corran had overheard from the numerous tour guide droids that *ch'hala* trees had been a favorite of the Emperor's and placed here at his specific request. Though he hated everything the Emperor had stood for, Corran had to admit that the *ch'hala* trees were what truly made this place grand.

The necessities of modern life did not intrude and spoil the majesty of the hall. Reader strips, like those scrolling out the latest news stories everywhere else on Coruscant, had been shielded so that anyone wanting to read their messages had to stand at a specific point on the floor to actually see the scarlet letters rolling by. Information kiosks were warded by *ch'hala* trees. Small alcoves scooped from the walls at regular intervals provided people a modicum of privacy for using the holo-link stations built therein.

Security appeared to be lax, but Corran picked up on things that Erisi clearly missed. Stormtrooper squads did patrol the main floor and passed certain checkpoints at fairly precise intervals. They appeared to be most concerned with breaking up or moving along knots of nonhumans. Those with legitimate reasons to be in the building were urged to be on their way, while those gawking at the magnificence of the Palace were directed to join escorted tours or to leave.

The upper galleries of the Grand Corridor appeared to be alien free, yet the mechanism for maintaining them that way was remarkably unobtrusive. Side passages leading to stairs or lifts narrowed considerably, forcing individuals to move through them no more than two or three abreast. Guards wearing a more stylized and esthetically pleasing form of stormtrooper armor maintained posts at these passages and gently redirected anyone who appeared to be lost. They did respond to questions, but only with the directions to the nearest visitor and information kiosks where the questions could be asked again.

The stairs themselves doubled back twice. This meant anyone who got past the guards on the lower level could be isolated on the middle staircase and dealt with. The landings on either side of the staircase appeared normal, but Corran knew of a dozen ways anyone traversing them could be trapped or, with a laser cannon emerging from behind a hidden panel, cut down with little or no risk to Imperial personnel. While quite fantastic in its design and execution, the Grand Corridor had not been created without an eye toward security.

Corran made some quick assumptions about other precautions that had to have been set up. He suspected that in the narrow corridors below there were weapons detectors. The technology for locating an inorganic object next to the flesh of or within the body of a living creature was old and unobtrusive. By detecting the disturbance a weapon made in the creature's bioelectric field or the planet's own magnetic field a computer could comlink to the guards the identity of the person carrying the weapon, its location on his body, and even the type of weapon he was carrying.

Other passive monitoring devices could be used to locate things like gas canisters or bombs by picking up on molecular traces coming off them. For all Corran knew the *ch'hala* trees could have been genetically altered to make them into botanical sniffers. The patterns of light flashing across their bark could have some sort of significance, alerting Imperial officials to danger without anyone in the Grand Corridor being the wiser.

You're definitely thinking too hard about this, Corran. He smiled and looked over at Rima. He caught her staring at him for a moment, but her eyes had enough of a soft focus that he knew she'd not been seeing or thinking about him. "Imperial Center to Rima. Hello?"

She blinked, then grinned sheepishly. "Sorry. I was thinking."

"That was apparent. What about?"

Rima hesitated and that caught Corran's full attention. Throughout the time he had spent with her he'd come to realize two things: She was incredibly observant and she seemed to forget little or nothing of what went on around her. Actually Corran couldn't remember having caught her out at having missed a detail about something, and he'd frequently been corrected by her. The only times she had previously hitched before answering a question were times when the answer had the potential of violating the security envelope surrounding the mission.

Rima's expression softened somewhat and Corran sensed she was about to open up a bit about herself. "I was thinking that we might actually have a friend in common. He was from back home, though I did not know him there. I was wondering how he was."

Corran smiled and picked up his cold cup of espcaf.

He'd assumed all along she was from Alderaan. She'd never confirmed this, nor had she denied it. He couldn't remember having said anything to her that told her his assumption, but from the look in her eyes, he had no doubt that he *had* said something, allowing her to phrase her question in such an oblique manner.

He lowered his cup and kept his voice neutral. "Do you mean Sel?" He abbreviated Tycho's last name, assuming that even if the conversation were being overheard, the intelligence value of one syllable was tiny.

"Yes, I was thinking of him."

Erisi smiled. "He is doing well. He recently got me out of a very tight spot. Quite a treasure."

"Really? That's good."

Corran caught a flicker of surprise and hurt in Rima's eyes. She covered it quickly, but he thought he recognized jealousy in her reaction to Erisi's flirtatious response to the question. *She and Tycho must have some history.* "I guess you know him better than either one of us. We're really just casual acquaintances of his."

Rima's eyes sharpened slightly. "Only casual acquaintances? I would have thought you two would have been fast friends."

"We could have been, but the man has secrets." Corran shifted his shoulders uneasily. Despite his original resolve to trust Tycho, reality had slowly impinged on him. The preparation for the mission to Coruscant had stressed trust and sharpened his sense of paranoia. At the core of the Tycho problem was the fact that no one save Ysanne Isard knew if Tycho was her puppet or not. Corran had emotionally begun to insulate himself from Tycho, but until now had not realized how far along that unconscious process had gotten. "Secrets establish a distance and undercut trust."

Hurt returned to Rima's eyes. "He's had a hard life."

"So haven't we all."

Rima's head came up. "You don't understand. His family died . . ."

"I *do* understand." Corran kept the volume of his

voice down, but let the emotions bubbling up in him pour straight through into his words. "I have no family either and do you know what? I saw my father get shot up. Murdered. And I couldn't do anything about it. I was a hundred meters away, watching him by remote, backing him up, when a bounty hunter walked into the cantina and lit up the booth where he was sitting with two other people. Killed them all and I couldn't do anything about it. I got there and held my father in my arms, but it was too late. You want a hard life, there's a hard life for you."

Corran's hands contracted into fists and Erisi leaned over to hug him. He stared openly at Rima, daring her to deny his pain. He wanted her to break, to lose that look of superiority she wore. He wanted her to admit that nothing Tycho had been through, even the destruction of his homeworld or his Imperial captivity, could have measured up to what Corran had endured.

Even as Erisi whispered, "I'm so sorry," in his ear, Corran knew he had overreacted and overreacted badly. *What's gotten into me?* He searched his mind for an answer, tracing back fleeting thoughts, and slowly came to a realization that surprised with its simplicity and amazed him with its power.

Tycho, in saving his life and in shepherding him through his introduction to Rogue Squadron, had moved into an august company in Corran's mind. Corran's father, his CorSec supervisor, Gil Bastra, and Wedge Antilles were the only other people that Corran saw in the guardian and mentor roles in his life. With his father and Gil both dead, Corran realized he had begun to rely on Wedge and Tycho to serve as touchstones and moral compasses for him.

The fact that Tycho could not be fully trusted had gone to war with the esteem in which Corran had held him. As he had mentally distanced himself from Tycho, he began to feel that Tycho had somehow betrayed him. The anger he felt toward Tycho, the anger that had triggered his outburst, had come from this sense of betrayal and

Corran's guilt at having elevated someone so untrustworthy to a rank equal to that of his father.

This is crazy. I have to sort all of this out. Tycho has not betrayed me or anyone else. I need to apologize to him and to Rima.

Before he could say anything, Rima began speaking in low, even tones. "I do not doubt the sincerity of the anguish you feel, and I am most sorry for you. As tragic as is your story, though, I think Sel's story can be considered of equal weight."

Corran wanted to tell her she need say nothing more, she need not explain, but the solemnity of her tone froze his words in his throat.

"He had graduated from the Academy and was assigned to a Star Destroyer—the *Accuser*. On the occasion of his birthday—something most TIE pilots celebrate because of their rarity—he was engaged in a realtime HoloNet connection to our home. His family was there: father, mother, brother, sisters, grandparents, and his fiancée. He was speaking to them when the transmission was cut off. That sort of thing was not unusual and he planned to chide his father about it since his father ran Novacom, the largest HoloNet provider on the world. The fact was that Sel never got a chance to do that because, as he discovered shortly thereafter, his family had died in a monumental catastrophe."

Corran's stomach collapsed in on itself like a neutron star. *Tycho was speaking to his family when Alderaan was destroyed. I saw my father die, but he saw everyone die. I was able to hold my father and give him a funeral. I was able to comfort his friends and be comforted by them. My father may have died alone, but I didn't have to endure his death alone. My life's as soft as a Hutt's underbelly by comparison.*

He heard Erisi stifle a sob and felt a tear moisten the side of his neck. He turned to face her, then saw a vision from the past that sent a chill straight through him. His hands came up to cup Erisi's face, tipping her chin upward, then he pulled her to him and kissed her fiercely.

He felt her start to pull away, but he restrained her gently and she flowed into his arms to return the kiss with a passion that all but melted what he felt inside.

Part of him wanted the kiss to end and wanted him to escape her arms. Corran resisted the idea of escape because he couldn't be certain of how he would spend his freedom. What he really wanted to do was insane on an Imperial scale. It would compromise the mission. It had the potential to delay or prevent the New Republic from taking Coruscant and finishing the Empire. It ran the risk of destroying everything the Rebellion had worked for.

But it would feel very, very good.

Over Erisi's shoulder Corran had seen Kirtan Loor. The tall slender body, the crisp gait, and the head held imperiously high were unmistakable. He'd memorized all those things about Kirtan Loor months before his father's death. Subsequent to it he had reveled in the fury and contempt they had spawned when he saw the man.

What Corran wanted to do at that moment, more than anything else in the galaxy, was to walk over, grab Loor, and pitch him from the promenade. He would have preferred being on a higher level to do so—a *much* higher level—but that problem could not be helped. He hoped the fall would kill the man, though from a mere ten meters up the chances were it would only break a few limbs and possibly rupture some internal organs.

Corran felt someone tap him on the shoulder and for the barest of moments thought Loor had spotted him. About the time he realized that hadn't happened—the fact that no stormtroopers were closing in and no alarms were going off cinching it for him—Rima said, "The danger is past. He's gone up another level."

Corran pulled back and gave Erisi a quick kiss on the nose, then looked over at Rima. "How'd you know?"

"Kirtan Loor's presence on Coruscant has not gone unreported. Correlating things I know about him and you were not difficult."

Erisi blinked her big blue eyes a couple of times, then

looked from Corran to Rima and back. "What was all that about?"

"You saved my life." He smiled at her. "Forgive the liberty I took, but . . ."

She caught her breath, then returned the smile. "I understand. If you ever need your life saved again, I'll be honored to be of service to you."

He patted her on the knee. "Thanks. I'll remember that." He turned back toward Rima. "I'm not afraid of him."

"I didn't think you were."

"I want to kill him." Corran reached out and tapped her lightly on the temple. "Do you know why?"

"I know many things, but not all things."

"I caught the Trandoshan who killed my father, but Loor let him go." Corran took in a deep breath and let it out. "He'll pay for that one day. Sooner than later, I hope, but don't worry, I have my priorities straight. His date with justice can wait, wait until we bring down the government that gives people like him the power to perpetrate evil on more worlds than we can count."

19

It occurred to Gavin that if his father had any idea he'd end up sitting in the Azure Dianoga cantina, he'd never have let him leave the farm. If Mos Eisley was considered the armpit of the galaxy, this part of Coruscant could be considered anatomically lower and decidedly less hygienic. In the dim distance, in an alcove between the bar and the doors, Gavin could see a Kubaz quartet playing trunkflutes and percussion, but the din caused by hundreds of aliens speaking all at once walled away the sound of their music.

Acrid green smoke drifted through the cantina's atmosphere, stinging Gavin's eyes and painting another layer of grime across his face. Down in the lower reaches of Invisec he'd taken to wearing all of his clothes in layers, rotating the inners to outers, and had been at it for the week since they'd landed. He felt he smelled like a dewback with bloat, but the worse his scent became, fewer were the complaints from the various aliens with whom they dealt.

The mission given to their team had been quite broad. The top two items on the agenda were to determine the level of control the Empire exerted over the lower reaches of the city—and the general mood of the alien population on the world—and to find out if the lower levels of the infrastructure would provide avenues of attack against the government. That seemed logical to Gavin because if Coruscant were built on a foundation the government didn't control, bringing it down would be just a little bit easier.

Since their cover story had Gavin and Shiel working as partners, they had traveled independently from the others and had spent a great deal of time exploring the tunnels and ruins at the bottom of the world. The Shistavanen wolf man had suggested they begin their exploration near the Invisec border because if there was no way to leave Invisec and penetrate the newer sections of the city, any invasion force that made planetfall in Invisec would be bottled up.

The border proved fascinating because of the mélange of building materials and architectural styles all jammed into a very small area. Where the huge construction droids had carved a swath that nibbled away at Invisec, the walls were formed of sheer ferrocrete with no preconstructed access ports to the other side. No matter how new these walls looked, all of them had been covered with colorful writing—most of it being anti-Imperial invective—or had been gouged by sharp claws or nibbled by sharper teeth.

Borrats appeared to be the pioneers that opened holes in these solid walls. The holes appeared to be about twice the size of a pilot's helmet, with claw marks that striated a cone shape going in and coming out on the other side. Clearly sapient beings had expanded on some of these holes, enlarging them to permit easy passage for most creatures. Some of the holes had been resealed, but the ferrocrete patches could be removed if they were chipped away at the edges, and in at least one case, a plug had been hinged so it looked normal from the far side and could provide easy access to areas outside Invisec.

The perimeter of Invisec where the residents were moving out and taking over buildings previously outside their sector was known in local parlance as the Outer Rim. There the holes through the ferrocrete walls were numerous and large enough to permit all sorts of commerce. Where the Imperials made an effort to stop the migration of aliens, all windows and doors had been sealed with ferrocrete plugs. Messages splashed on walls indicated points where people suspected the Imps had set up booby traps. Arcane sigils and graffiti in more languages than Gavin knew existed marked the sites of fights where Imps had killed people to prevent the sullying of new territory.

The Outer Rim clearly provided more opportunities for an invading force to push into the city proper primarily because the walls there were not as strong as the barriers on the other side of Invisec. That fact, however, would be the only bright spot in an otherwise very gloomy report. After days of wandering through the dark and twisted alleys and byways of Invisec, the vast scale of the invasion needed to wrest the planet from the Empire began to press in on Gavin. The planet had billions upon billions of people. The force needed to pacify the populace and maintain order while fighting against Imperial stormtroopers would have to be incredibly huge.

It would take more troops than the Rebellion has under arms. The shields make this place a tough nut to crack, but chewing up the meat isn't going to be any easier. Gavin hunched forward on the table in the corner booth and gripped his mug of lomin-ale with both hands. "Prospects don't look so good, do they?"

Shiel lowered a mug from his muzzle and wiped excess ale off on his sleeve. "If there's no prey, there's no reason to hunt."

Nawara Ven and Rhysati Ynr cut through the smoke and slid into the booth, forcing Gavin to slide around toward the center of the semicircle. The Twi'lek's clothes were worn in only one layer, were more conservatively cut and decidedly cleaner than the ragged things Gavin and Shiel wore. Rhysati wore a skintight, dark blue body stocking supplemented with knee-high boots, belts, chains, and other straplike accessories that accented her already considerable charms. Gavin forced himself to meet her stare, then blushed when she winked at him.

Nawara raised a hand and waved a serving droid over. "Churban brandy for me, or the closest synthesis you can manage. She will have a Durindfire, light on the phosphorescent agent." He settled a brain tail over Rhysati's shoulders as the droid scuttled off, then nodded to Ooryl and Aril Nunb as they joined the group. "All alive and well, I see."

Ooryl tapped himself on the chest. "Gand has traveled extensively and has found much exotica. Items are available from throughout the galaxy, at prices that reflect the distance they have been shipped, not any restriction on supply."

Nawara rhythmically tapped his fingernails against the scarred and stained tabletop. "Estimates on how long those goods would last?"

Aril cocked her head. "A month, perhaps more, provided Imperial interests did not stage raids. The Imps appear to monitor trading. Everyone seems to pay protection to the Imps, to Black Sun, and to local Invisec factions. If things were to get tight, some of the things here would be pulled outside."

Gavin exchanged a glance with Shiel. The wolf man had said that he would have opted to starve the Imps out by blockading the planet. He estimated it could survive for two or three months. Aril's estimation of the supplies in Invisec meant that the alien population of Coruscant would be hurt worse by a blockade than the Imps would. Given the anti-alien bias the Empire had, that sort of result wasn't surprising. *If Ysanne Isard was smart she'd ransom the Invisec population for supplies, or she'd just have them killed and take their supplies for the humans.*

The general din of the cantina faded and died as Imperial stormtroopers came through the doors. They wore the standard white armor seen across the galaxy, though they did have small pinpoint spotlights clipped to their right shoulders. Two soldiers remained at the doorway—

they were armed with heavy blaster rifles—while the rest of the squad broke down into a pair of three-man groups that began to work their way around the dark oval room. Back through the doorway Gavin thought he saw more troopers and a large vehicle, but the swirling smoke and general gloom made a positive identification impossible.

Aril kept her voice low. "Another sweep?"

Nawara nodded but remained silent.

The various alien denizens of the bar shifted around anxiously. The Gotal seated back to back with Nawara in the next booth over ducked his head, giving Gavin a clear view of the stormtroopers centered between the Gotal's horns. Gavin killed a smile as he recalled stories about Gotals being able to read minds. *It would be very interesting to be able to know what's going on inside those helmets, if anything at all is. I wonder what they're after?*

The knot of stormtroopers nearest the Rogues stopped at a table where two squid-headed Quarren sat conversing with a tall Duros. The leader of the stormtroopers demanded identification cards. He ran them one at a time through a slot on the datapad attached to the armor on his right thigh, then returned one card to the Duros.

"You two will have to come with us." The stormtroopers behind him brought their blaster carbines up to cover the Quarren.

"What have we done?"

"Routine inquiries. You have nothing to fear if you have done nothing wrong."

The Quarren, pulling their robes tightly around them, rose from their stools and scurried out. No one stared at them, but everyone seemed to be watching them go. Gavin could feel resentment rising in the room as it rose in him.

The second trio of stormtroopers found no one interesting to harass, so they backed to the door while the first set of troopers approached the Rogues' table. The leader demanded Gavin's identification with an outstretched hand. "Far from home, aren't you? ID, now."

Gavin fumbled for it, then turned it over.

The stormtrooper ran it through his datapad's slot, but didn't return it immediately. "I asked you a question, son. What are you doing here?"

"Ah, I, ah, I'm just here." Gavin fought to stop panic from choking him.

The stormtrooper snapped the ID card on the table. "I have reports that say you left home under strange circumstances. Maybe you want to come with us and return to your own kind. We won't let *them* hurt you."

"No, I'm fine here, really."

The trooper shifted his attention to Rhysati. "Identification."

She snuggled tighter beneath Nawara's brain tail and flicked her pink tongue salaciously over the grey flesh of the Twi'lek's throat. Nawara reached inside his tunic and held up an ID card between the second and third fingers of his right hand. As he lifted it toward the stormtrooper, Gavin saw the outline of a black triangular coin worth a hundred credits. "You don't really need to see her identification."

The stormtrooper took the ID card and neatly palmed the coin. He held the card up to compare the hologram with Rhysati, then tossed it down in anger when she turned her face toward him and winked. "Your kind makes me sick."

"As does your kind, which is why I'm with him."

That rocked the stormtrooper back on his heels for a moment and he seemed about ready to go for his blaster when a buzzing came from his helmet. He touched the side of it with his left hand, then turned to his two companions and jerked his head toward the door. Looking back at Nawara he said, "You're lucky this time, spoiler, but I'd be thinking about finding a new friend. It wouldn't do to have this one crying over your ashes, would it?"

"Perhaps not."

"Definitely not. Remember that."

The stormtroopers withdrew and darkness again descended on the Azure Dianoga. The conversational tone remained low, which allowed some of the band's music to make it over to the table. Over near the doorway Gavin saw some figures get up and begin to sway or writhe in time to the music, though the twitching of one person led him to believe that some of the notes were being played well outside the range of his hearing.

Aril appropriated Gavin's ale and downed a healthy swallow of it. "That was close."

"Gand has previously avoided such contact. Gand has seen Imperials rounding up others, both Quarren and Gamorreans."

Shiel nodded. "The kid and I saw a family of Gamorreans herded off."

"The stories we've heard indicate occasional sweeps taking in Gamorreans and Quarren on a weekly basis. They take a dozen or two." Nawara Ven scraped talons along his jawline. "Perhaps there has been an anti-Imperial uprising on Gamorr."

"That would explain the taking of Gamorreans." Aril's garnet eyes sparkled in the backlight of the glowing drink the service droid placed in front of Rhysati. "Why the Quarren?"

Nawara dropped a ten-credit piece in the slot on top of the droid's head and drew his brandy from the tray. "Quarren share the same world with the Mon Calamari, but the two populations are not wholly united. Perhaps they want to exploit the enmity between them."

A petite, black-furred female Bothan came walking over to their table and smiled invitingly in Gavin's direction. A diamond of silken white fur covered her from throat to navel—it being visible beneath her sleeveless jacket's loose lacing closures. White also sheathed her hands and carried on up to mid forearm. A blaze of white fur blossomed in the middle of her brow and splashed across her left eye and cheek to where it narrowed again at the corner of her jaw. Her light violet eyes shone brightly in contrast to the fur surrounding them, giving her a penetrating stare that sent a quick jolt through Gavin.

Nawara looked up at her. "Is there something I can do for you?"

"I think not, sir." She picked up Gavin's identification card, read it, and gently set it down again. "I noticed how you dared defy that stormtrooper, Vin Leiger, and I thought perhaps I would like to learn more of a man who can be so casual in a place where so few of his kind are found. I thought we might discuss this . . . privately."

It took Gavin a half second to remember *he* was Vin Leiger, but that was because he'd not recognized himself in her description of the encounter with the stormtrooper. *She must have somehow confused me with Nawara, but she's looking right at me.* "Um, I, ah, I'm here with my friends."

She nodded politely. "Of course, you would not want to abandon them. I understand." The Bothan glanced back over her shoulder toward where people were dancing. "Surely they would not begrudge my stealing you away for one dance?"

"Ah, we're discussing something right now. Perhaps another time, Miss . . ."

"I am Asyr Sei'lar." Her smile slackened slightly. "Another time, then?"

"Yes, certainly."

A Gotal seated in the next booth over turned around. "He's lying, Asyr. Your approach made him nervous and your retreat filled him with relief." As the horned humanoid came around to face Gavin he produced a blaster and pointed it at the Rogues. Out of the corner of his eye Gavon saw Asyr move and a small blaster appeared in her right hand. While he saw no more guns, he heard a crescendo of safety switches being snapped off, so he instantly rejected the idea of digging for his puny hold-out blaster.

Nawara's voice took on an edge, the sort of edge Gavin imagined it had when the Twi'lek had fought for his clients in court. "Would someone care to explain what my friend has done wrong here? Is it a crime to refuse to dance in the Azure Dianoga?"

"Not at all, but his relief shows him to be as much a bigot as the stormtroopers who just left here." Asyr tapped Gavin's ID card with the muzzle of her blaster. "If he'd not lied, if he'd accepted my invitation, we'd have known he's like your woman—someone to whom species makes no difference. Since he's a bigot, we have other uses for him."

"And those would be?"

The Bothan smiled coolly. "The Imps have been kidnapping people from Invisec and they've not returned them. Something has to be done, so we have formed the Alien Combine. We need someone to take a message to the Imps to let them know we'll tolerate their predation no longer. Your friend has elected himself to fill that post and this will be one time when a dead man *will* tell a tale."

20

Kirtan Loor's ears popped as the lift ascended to the rarefied precincts where Ysanne Isard lived. *She does not live, she* lairs. As much as he hated her intrusive holovisitations to his tiny office, being summoned to see her personally was even less of a cause for celebration. And even though all of the news he had relayed to her had been very positive, he did not see her as someone who would invite a subordinate to her office to congratulate him on his successes.

To eat him alive, perhaps, but not to congratulate him.

The lift slowed, then stopped, and the doors slid open. He stepped out and paused, raising his arms away from his body. Though the scarlet-armored Imperial Guards on either side of the lift and at either end of the short corridor did not move or even seem to pay attention to him, he knew rash or casual movements could prove lethal in their territory. He waited, then lowered his arms and walked down the corridor to his right. After a couple more turns, passing several more guard stations, he arrived at the door to Isard's office and it slid open soundlessly.

Though he stood half a head taller than she did, Loor always felt dwarfed by her. That impression had nothing to do with her physical presence, though she was a strikingly handsome woman, and her mismatched eyes did lend her an exotic air. Instead it was the way she stood, how she moved, and how well she wore the scarlet uniform that confirmed her right to rule. Though she made no claim to the title of Empress, she was very much Imperial in her manner. In a time when the Empire was crumbling, that was enough to leave her in charge.

Isard waved Loor into her office. As he had on each previous visit to it, he marveled at the sheer emptiness of the cavernous room. Whereas other Imperial officers and bureaucrats managed to cram their cramped offices with treasures from countless worlds, Isard reveled in the greatest luxury of all on crowded Imperial Center—uncluttered space. The external transparisteel wall gave her a view of the world she ruled as the sun set on it and the red strip edging the room's blue carpet appeared to be just an extension of the red sunset.

"You wished to see me, Madam Director?"

Isard hit a button on a remote and shields slowly descended to eclipse the sun. She let the office fall completely dark before slowly bringing the lights up. "I did indeed wish to see you. General Derricote now wants Sullustans for his experiments?"

"He does. They were his second choice. He would have preferred Wookiees, but I explained to him the foolishness of killing off a valuable labor source."

"Did you think to explain to him the foolishness of choosing Sullustans?"

Loor nodded. "I did, but he countered that since SoroSuub had chosen to back the Rebellion, punishing them is hardly out of the question. I suggested he should use Ewoks as a substitute, but he actually has some sound scientific reasons for wanting to work with Sullustans. The Quarren are an outlink to some of the more aquatic species, Gamorreans to another set of creatures, and the

Sullustans, he says, will be a bridge race to Shistavanen, Bothan, and similar species."

Isard frowned. "I would prefer avoiding the slaughter of Sullustans—like Wookiees they are useful. However, if their sacrifice will give me dead Bothans, the advantage outweighs the immediate disadvantage. Perhaps we should quarantine a breeding stock of Sullustans so they can repopulate their world."

Her reasoning seemed logical to him, which surprised Kirtan Loor. On one hand she was plotting a way to slaughter millions of creatures in a most horrible way, yet on the other she was concerned with having enough of one species left alive to repopulate devastated worlds. While he had no love for Sullustans, and did see them as being inferior to humanity, he did think of them as something more than grain that could be poisoned and fed to rats, with some pristine kernels held back as seed stock.

Was there a time I would have seen this as insanity? That question lurked in his brain and he was surprised that he did not have a clear answer to it. *Does it truly matter? These are extraordinary times, and they call for extraordinary action.*

"Your precaution, Madam Director, is wise, but I wonder if it will be needed."

"You are approaching a subject obliquely, Agent Loor. Please be more direct." She clasped her hands at the small of her back. "You see a problem with Derricote's Krytos virus?"

"I do. It can be cured by bacta."

"I know."

"You do?"

"Yes, of course." Isard smiled slightly. "That a cure can be affected by the use of bacta was one of my original design parameters for the virus."

Loor's jaw dropped. "But I thought your goal was to kill the aliens here on Imperial Center so that when the Rebels came here they would be horrified."

"Oh, I expect that, but in a way you never imagined. The problem with your scenario is that it will not cripple the Rebellion." Her eyes sharpened. "Warlord Zsinj, Darth Vader, and even the Emperor failed to see that a single strike at the Rebellion will not destroy it. The Rebellion is a fire. You have to extinguish each and every hot spot, or you have to deny it fuel, so it cannot burn any longer. They settled on the former method, whereas I will use the latter."

"I am not certain I follow you."

"This is not a surprise." She held a hand up. "What do the Rebels do when one of their comrades is killed?"

"Bury him, burn him, whatever."

"And if one of their comrades is *wounded*?"

"Get him help." The simplicity of the question and the speed with which the answer came to him undercut its importance. He thought for a moment, then added, "Rescuing the man, getting him medical help, rehabilitating him, and getting him back into combat all require more resources than a memorial service."

"There *is* hope for you, Agent Loor." Isard's smile grew, as did the lump of ice in Loor's stomach. "The Rebellion has done a great deal with severely restricted resources, both in terms of matériel and personnel. If a trained warrior cannot be saved by medical intervention, the Rebellion has lost him *and* all the hours spent training him. While there are always more bodies willing to be sacrificed to tear down the Empire, training them is a strain.

"Another question for you: What will the Rebels do when they find people beginning to be sick with the Krytos virus."

Loor frowned. "They will heal them, if they can."

"Which means they will require unbelievably vast amounts of bacta. Just stabilizing a Krytos victim in the disease's incubation period—before the virus has begun to reproduce out of control—will result in the loss of a full liter of bacta. That doesn't seem like much, of course, since a bacta tank holds considerably more than that, but the losses will become significant as the disease spreads. Total production on Thyferra last year was seventeen billion liters. The amount needed to treat all the victims here on Imperial Center will require three quarters of last year's production. At the current prices for bacta, saving everyone they can will bankrupt the Rebellion."

"With no fuel they cannot burn." Loor stared down at the floor, then shook himself. "When Derricote gets the virus perfected, you'll turn the planet over to the Rebels."

"Exactly. And because the virus will not infect humans, I force the human Rebels to act to save as many aliens as they can. If they do not, because they are unaffected it will appear to their alien allies that they are just as unconcerned about aliens as they accuse us Imperials of being. Moreover, because elements of Rogue Squadron are here on Imperial Center now, we can begin to weave together lies that will implicate them in spreading the virus."

"No one would believe that of them."

"No one would believe they would free vicious criminals from Kessel and send them to Imperial Center, but they did." Isard slowly rubbed her hands together. "While that morsel will be a lie, it is a lie that the Bothans will use as a pry bar to work more power into their hands. Those aliens we do not kill or drive away into a self-imposed quarantine will see the wisdom of repudiating their alliance with treacherous humans. The Rebellion will tear itself apart from within."

Loor gave himself a few moments and let all she had said sort itself out in his brain. "Am I to assume, then, that you do not want the members of Rogue Squadron we have identified swept up?"

"No, I want them to scout out the world and decide on one or another plan of attack to take this world away from us. As long as they are seeing what we want them to see, and our agent keeps us apprised of their timetable, they are useful to us. We cannot allow them to act before we have sufficiently infected the alien population of the world. If they strike prematurely, they will never take the world and our efforts to gather them here and present to them the Krytos crisis will fail."

Isard closed her eyes for a moment, then nodded. "You will send out the appropriate code phrases to alert our agent that you desire a meeting, face-to-face."

"Isn't that risky?"

"I think it is vital. Arrange for it this evening—you will go yourself."

"But . . ."

Ysanne Isard's light laughter came laden with sharp barbs. "You are afraid of Corran Horn finding you, yes?"

Loor knew denying the truth in her question was foolish. "He would kill me if he had the opportunity to do so."

"But the chances of your running into him here, on Imperial Center, are what, one in trillions?"

"Corran Horn has an annoying facility for beating those kinds of odds and showing up where he is least wanted." Loor's frown deepened into a scowl, but not because he resented the fear he had of Corran Horn. That fear was well founded and useful, just as the fear of a rancor might keep someone away from its lair. If Corran had the opportunity to kill him, he would take it and likely succeed.

What bothered Loor more than that eventuality was Ysanne Isard's willingness to put him in jeopardy by sending him out to meet the traitor in Rogue Squadron. So far information generated by the spy had only been used actively once. That use had resulted in the death of Bror Jace, but things had been arranged so that everything appeared coincidental. That *could* have been enough to leave Corran without suspicion, but if it was not, then Loor's sojourn could lead to a confrontation and his death.

To her I am expendable—an opinion I do not share. While she can take chances with me, I cannot afford to take chances myself. Fortunately I am not entirely without resources of my own here on Imperial Center. I will have to take precautions myself. I must prevent Corran from having a confrontation he devoutly desires and one I heartily wish to avoid.

Isard studied him with no mercy in her eyes. "Horn is not what should concern you—assuring our spy of our support is. Without timely and reliable reports, things could collapse and that would not please me."

"Yes, Madam Director."

"Oh, and order the collection of some Sullustans. Keep General Derricote happy." She hesitated for a moment, then smiled. "Or, at least, keep him productive. The Empire is a house afire and he is the means to smothering the blaze. When his work is done, the Rebellion will have ceased to be a problem. Then and only then will we be able to begin to restore the galaxy to the way it should be."

21

Though Mirax's appearance surprised Wedge and had
him a bit off balance, Iella took it immediately in stride.
She looped an arm through Mirax's and smiled sweetly.
"We have some catching up to do, so you boys just follow along and don't you dare try to overhear us."
Though her smile remained in place, and she kept a light
tone in her voice, Wedge read tension and wariness in her
eyes.

"As you wish, ladies." He sketched a short bow, then
followed them to the lifts. They descended in one cage,
then headed out onto the rain-slicked promenade. Iella
and Mirax chatted and laughed as their path meandered
around, entering buildings, stopping at vistas, and going
from point to point of interest while always descending.
Wedge could tell, from the way they traveled, that Iella
made some choices at random, but others with a purpose.
With the frequent stops and passes through clothing bou-
tiques that made *him* feel uncomfortable, Iella made it
very difficult for anyone following them to go unnoticed.

Wedge realized that being forced to wait amid racks
of women's clothing samples made him uneasy because of
more than his gender making him feel utterly out of place

there. For the past seven plus years he had been at war. While there had been relaxing times and he'd been given leaves, he'd never slipped out of his identity of being a pilot. Without family to visit—his parents were dead, and because of his connection to the Rebellion, visiting any other relatives would put them in jeopardy—he'd taken time *off* but not time *away*. Wandering through the byways of Coruscant was as close as he had come to what others might see as normal life since his parents were killed.

He smiled. Even the time he had put in as a touring hero for the Rebellion had been far from normal. He found himself whisked around from planet to planet, banquet to banquet, wearing a dress uniform he didn't even know the Rebellion *had*. At receptions and parties and dinners he found himself congratulated for his part in the Rebellion by creatures he never knew existed before. Gifts had been bestowed upon him, honors given him, and opportunities provided him to do things he'd never had the courage to even dream about as a child.

He watched as Iella and Mirax played with a garment-fabricator holo-unit, lengthening and shortening, trimming and coloring dresses they'd never order. They laughed and were having fun. *Just the way normal folks do when enjoying a normal life.*

The word "normal" stuck in his brain for a moment and he realized that "normal" was a goal for most folks that had no definition. When Rogue Squadron's chief tech, Zraii, ran diagnostics on Wedge's X-wing, normal was defined by a series of benchmark readings established in Alliance specifications and Incom performance manuals. There was a way to determine if the fighter was performing normally or not. And if it was deficient in some way or other, that defect could be corrected.

Normal in terms of *life*, on the other hand, was not so easy to determine. For Mirax, hauling contraband between worlds was normal, yet to someone like Iella or Corran, that was grossly abnormal behavior. For his parents normal life had been owning a fueling depot and raising a family. *That* version of normal, or some minor variation of it, seemed to fit most folks' view of what life *should* be.

But does that mean that anything else is not normal? For him, living the life of a pilot fighting against the Empire seemed normal. Moreover, it seemed to be a life that was based on reality. The Empire, weakened though it was, cast a pall over the entire galaxy and until it was eliminated, the home, job, and family sort of normal would always be in jeopardy. A hint of wrongdoing could shatter the cocoon of normalcy most people tried to spin around themselves and disrupt their lives forever.

Wedge and Pash trailed silently in the women's wake as they moved on. Iella seemed to move a little more deliberately, and as they emerged from a stairwell onto a promenade that hung out over an urban canyon with a river of shadow filling it, a repulsorlift cab came to a stop. The doors opened and Iella motioned them all into it. Wedge didn't recognize the driver, but that somehow made him feel better about the situation than not.

Without instructions from Iella, the driver took the vehicle away from the building and down. The route he flew seemed as twisted and circuitous as the one Iella had employed, but the journey ended quickly. The driver dropped them on another walkway, but this one was several kilometers down and away from where they'd been picked up, leaving them submerged in the thick shadows of the undercity.

Iella led them along to an alley, then down it and into a building. Three floors up she opened a door and led them into a sparingly furnished room. Its most impressive features were the two large picture windows that dominated the far walls. They provided a rather panoramic view of the intersection that the apartment overlooked, or underlooked, depending upon one's perspective.

Iella closed the door, then nodded toward the two couches that faced each other in the center of the room. "Please be seated."

Mirax sat with her back to one of the windows and

let a slight smile play across her lips. "Which do you want first? The story of why I'm here on Coruscant, or how I managed to find you?"

Iella shrugged easily. "Which one will convince me you're not an Imp?"

Wedge frowned. "Mirax is clean. I've known her all my life. She's no Imp."

"Convince me."

Wedge started to say something, but Mirax cleared her voice. "I can handle this, Wedge, honest." She smiled. "I appreciate the caution, especially here. I'll start with the museum and work back only as far as needed, that way you won't know more than you need to."

Iella nodded. "Coruscant is a world that has billions of people on it. The chances of your being in the right place to spot someone you know are astronomical. Even luck or believing in the Force doesn't begin to cover those odds."

"Quite true, but I had a house edge on the wager." Mirax jerked a thumb toward Wedge and Pash. "They're snubfighter-jockeys. Sooner or later they'd have to go to the Galactic Museum and check the display that talked about Endor. It's ego and these pilots can breathe vacuum easier than they let slip a chance to see what lies the enemy is telling about them. Corellian pilots are notorious egotists, so staking out the museum seemed natural."

Wedge arched an eyebrow at Mirax. "You think I'm egotistical?"

"Wedge, I love you like a brother, so it hurts me to say this, but you're *so* egotistical you think you can keep your ego under control. Most of the time you do, which is your only saving grace. And the times you don't, well, I've not been on the receiving end of a display, but I imagine there are some Imps who would regret that experience, *if* they were alive to think about it."

Despite the slight sting of her words, Wedge knew there was more truth in them than he really wanted to acknowledge. In the second run at Borleias he'd let himself be outraged at the tactics the Imps thought would stop him from completing his mission. *That* was *quite the display of ego and they paid a dear price for letting me indulge myself.*

He turned toward Iella. "Well, at least you can tell she knows me."

"From that explanation I can tell she knows Corellian pilots. I had a partner who was a hot hand with an X-wing. If he ever joins the Rebellion, he'll give you a run for your credits." Iella looped a lock of brown hair back behind her right ear. "Since you didn't run Commander Antilles in to Coruscant, you didn't know he was here. That means you brought more pilots in and were figuring they'd visit the museum. Probably more from Rogue Squadron."

Mirax inclined her head to the left. "You certainly could conclude that scenario is accurate."

"Oh, I'm sure it is." Iella sat down on the arm of the couch opposite Mirax. "Your presence means your exit identity was blown, which means the rest of the pilots could have been compromised somehow."

Mirax looked up at Wedge. "Are you and I the only folks from Corellia who don't sound like we were trained in deductive reasoning by CorSec?"

Iella patted Mirax on the knee. "I *was* trained in deductive reasoning by CorSec."

"So you were part of CorSec?"

"Yes, why?"

Mirax sighed and held her hand out. "I'm Mirax Terrik."

Iella's hand stopped short of sliding into Mirax's grip. "You're Booster Terrik's daughter?"

Mirax's hand dropped back to her lap. "I bet you liked it better when you thought I was an Imp agent."

"You'd lose the bet." Iella kept her hand held out. "I'd just joined the force when Hal Horn put your father away. Booster was smart enough that I can believe his daughter was sharp enough to stake out the museum. And he was lucky enough that I can believe you succeeded in your long shot. I'm Iella Wessiri."

Wedge waited for recognition to flash in Mirax's eyes, but she shook Iella's hand without any sign she recognized the name or knew of the woman. *Perhaps Corran never spoke to her about his partner or never named her to Mirax.*

Iella freed her hand from Mirax's and sat back on the couch. "This all complicates things incredibly, but we're on top of them right now, so it's not a crippling emergency. This place is a safehouse. I've called in someone who I expected to use to help debrief you and interrogate you, if necessary. We'll still need the debriefing, of course, but we need it to determine where to start assessing the damage to our operation here. Your problems could have a perfectly innocent explanation, but because they involve the Empire, I doubt that entirely."

"I don't know what happened really." Mirax shrugged. "I made the arrangements as per usual with a broker. That gives me an identity code and a window for an exit vector. I enter three flight plans or so, get clearance on them, then head out. This time, when I tried to use the ID to enter the flight plans from a public datapad, things locked up. I cleared out and Imp Security landed on the place. It was down in Invisec so it created quite the stir. I turned around and burned some favors my father had earned with Black Sun to get my ship and crew taken care of. Since then I've been looking for a friendly face."

Iella's brown eyes focused on the window behind Mirax for a second. "Sounds like the Imps got the controller who was entering the ID codes. Your broker insulated you from direct discovery, but when you used the code they found you. We can get some slicers backtracking things and see how bad the situation has become. That means bringing in folks who have skills I don't, and for that, we have to wait."

Pash sat down beside Mirax. "While we wait I think we've a more serious problem to figure out how to handle."

Mirax frowned. "What can be more serious than the

Imps knowing members of Rogue Squadron are on Coruscant?"

Wedge smiled. "If the Imps find out *why* we're here, they can take steps to make the conquest of Coruscant impossible. That, my dear Mirax, is about as serious as it gets."

22

As unsettled as things were, Corran felt glad when they headed back to the Hotel Imperial. Erisi, Rima, and he made fairly good time through the city. A freak storm over near the museum slowed them down by cutting power to a moving sidewalk. Like most of the other pedestrians they stood around waiting for it to be repaired, contenting themselves with watching the storm or reading the news as it scrolled past on the readers. Corran noted that while public transport could be disrupted by storms, the news and propaganda machine flowed onward without a hitch.

No one spoke very much as they traveled back to the hotel, but Corran caught Erisi watching him and giving him brave smiles to shore up his feelings. He appreciated the effort, but it only served to remind him what sort of fool he'd made of himself. He almost asked her to stop, but somewhere deep down inside he knew the humiliation was good for him, trimming back ego and forcing him to be more thoughtful.

As they walked along, he reached out and rested a hand on Rima's shoulder. "I do want to apologize for what went on back there."

A curtain of white hair slid in back of her shoulder, brushing across the top of his hand, as she looked in his direction. "Perhaps I owe you an apology also."

"Not at all."

"I do." Pink, blue, and silver highlights flashed through her hair as a moving sidewalk conveyed them through a tunnel lit with a random pattern of neon lights. "Everyone from my world carries around some survivor guilt. We do not want to be pitied, but at the same time the sacrifice our people paid seems to demand respect. Among us there are those who have lost a great deal more than others . . ."

"But you have all lost everything."

"True, but someone who was with his family in service on another planet has lost less than those who had kin die. Sel, in seeing everyone go, his story is tragic." Rima glanced down at her open hands. "All of us recall where we were when we heard the news and the tragedy's impact hit us full at that moment. Sel had thought nothing was amiss, then he learned the significance of what he had experienced. The hours in which he considered it nothing mock him and haunt him."

In the same way does my failure to avenge my father haunt me. "You were right, his life was hard."

Erisi rubbed her left hand along his spine. "I think what she means to say is that her people are pitied for something over which they had no control. The gulf between pity and respect is vast. When their tragedy is denigrated, and that seemed to be what you were doing, you strip away respect and reduce them to a pathetic state. And while they do not want to be pitied, their actions cannot be judged without bearing in mind the tragedy that underscores their lives."

Corran slowly nodded. *Working in the Rebellion provides two things for Alderaanians: vengeance and a means to earn the respect they desire from others. They seek the vindication I felt when I brought Bossk in for my father's murder, and they're fighting to avoid what I felt when Loor let him go.*

He smiled. "We were both wrong."

Rima shook her head. "We were both underinformed and that condition has been corrected."

"Agreed."

They got off the moving sidewalk at one of the Hotel Imperial's middle entrances. Erisi pointed toward the doorway as Rima slowed her pace. "You will join us for dinner, yes?"

"Can't." She gestured vaguely back along their line of travel. "There's something I have to check on. I'll be in contact tomorrow morning."

Corran and Erisi bid Rima farewell and took a lift down to their room. They said nothing to each other, but Erisi stood a bit closer to Corran than she normally did. He didn't mind that terribly much because her obvious concern told him he wasn't alone and had, in her, a friend upon whom he could rely. He also read other confusing things in her eyes and posture, but his emotional state was chaotic enough that making sense of much of anything was impossible.

He opened the door to the room and preceded her in. Hitting a light switch he saw no one and confirmed that things had been left the way he positioned them in the morning before they headed out. The triangular nub of a black sock was still caught in the edge of a drawer and the closet's slide door had been left open to a point that was even with a pair of Erisi's ecru slacks.

The door clicked shut behind him, then the lights went out. He turned and felt Erisi's hands slide along either side of his chest, then close gently around his back. Corran felt her body press against his and the feather-light brush of her lips on his forehead, nose, and lips. She pulled him close and again dropped her mouth to his, kissing him with the fierce passion they'd shared in the Grand Hall.

Making no conscious decisions to do so, he let his arms enfold her. His left hand slipped beneath the hem of her jacket and gently stroked her back. His right hand came up and held the back of her head. He breathed in deeply, filling his nose with the spicy scent of her perfume. As she broke off their kiss, arching her head back, he traced his tongue from the hollow of her throat to her earlobe.

Erisi lazily pulled him along with her as she slowly drifted toward the room's bed. Corran understood her intention and realized he should have resisted the temptation she offered. Rational arguments tried to trip a circuit breaker in his brain, but they all failed. Operational security wasn't important because if the Imperials decided to take them there was no way for them to elude capture. Sleeping together or separately would not save them if the Empire knew enough about them to know where to find them.

Both of them being members of Rogue Squadron was no bar to involvement. Nawara Ven and Rhysati Ynr had fallen in love and that had not proved an impediment to their skills and performance. Corran and Erisi were of legal age, sound mind, and both consented to what they were about to do. Even the fact that the two of them were from different worlds and different cultures had no bearing on what they were going to do. *That we are here, now, is all that matters.*

The word "now" began to ricochet around in his skull, releasing all sorts of memories. When he'd been in CorSec he'd heard his father or Gil Bastra or himself tell rookies that most criminals were stupid because they lived for *now*. Living for *now* meant they didn't look ahead to the consequences of their actions. They didn't take precautions, didn't plan, and as a result, what they did fell apart on them.

Things went deeper than just that as well. He remembered his father weeping on the anniversary of the death of Corran's mother. "One of the reasons she was a good woman, wife, and mother was because she didn't think about herself first. Not a selfish bone in your mother's body. Everyone else came first and what she wanted was saved for later because we needed her *now*. And now she has no more later, and there seems little reason in having a later without her."

Erisi stopped moving backward and Corran felt the foot of the bed against his shins. She slowly sank back on the bed and drew him down with her. He resisted slightly, lowering her softly onto the quilted coverlet. He saw her in soft shades of grey from the dim light splashing in through the window. She was a seductive vision, a dream made real and warm and he fought to use that image to quiet the thoughts raging through his mind.

Powerful though that image was, a feeling of disaster dissolved it. Corran remembered his own relief at not sleeping with Iella back when he was with CorSec because, aside from destroying her marriage, the affair would have changed forever their relationship. The friendship and trust they had developed working together could have never been reclaimed. It was true that they might have stuck together and been stronger for getting together, but their attraction had been as much circumstantial as it had been real, which made for a poor foundation for any permanent relationship.

And this is circumstantial, too. Corran heard Mirax on Noquivzor telling him that Erisi would not be good for him and he'd seen how truly different they were as they came into Coruscant. He'd developed doubts about any relationship with her then, and this situation *now* did not invalidate those doubts. *She's attractive and I'm attracted, but something is not right here.*

Something inside him felt very *wrong.* His father had told him countless times to trust his feelings and to play his hunches. Corran had taken his father's advice and had learned to live by what he felt, or to later regret going against those feelings. He had gone against his gut feelings before, and with much less in the way of inducement to do so, but those situations had never turned out right in the end.

Corran let himself fall forward, but he kept his elbows locked and held his chest and head above Erisi. "I can't."

Erisi flashed him a shadowed smile. "I think you're doing fine."

"Seriously, I can't." He bent his right arm and flopped down on his flank beside her. "It isn't going to work."

Rolling up on her side, she reached over and stroked his check. "What's wrong? What did I do wrong?"

"It's not you." He took her hand and kissed her palm. "It's not that I'd like nothing better than to be here with you, but . . ."

"This is just now, Corran. I need this, you need this. It won't change who we are. No obligations. No recriminations. No regrets."

Her words poured soothingly into his ears. He had no doubt she meant them and that they would be true for her. "I hear you, Erisi, and I believe you, but I don't know that I'd be able to leave it in the past. It might not change who we are or what we mean to each other, but I'd bet against it given my past history. As I said, it's not you, it's me."

He rolled onto his back, then sat up. "You have to figure I'm an idiot. We've gotten very close a number of times and I keep pulling back."

He felt her hand on his back as she sat up beside him. "Actually, while it is frustrating, I do find this hesitation one of your more endearing qualities."

"Decisiveness in men is so off-putting, after all."

Erisi laughed easily. "Your sense of humor is attractive as well, except when you use it as a shield."

"Sorry."

She kissed his shoulder. "You see, Corran, few are the men who allow their emotions to have a part in their decision-making process. Most are expediently logical—emotions motivate them, but do not guide them. With most men there would be no hesitation—if emotions were going to come into play, it would be afterward. Your ability to factor emotions into your choices ahead of time makes you rather unique and worth pursuing."

"Or a big waste of time."

"Not so far."

"I'm just warming up. You'll see. Give me time."

Erisi sighed beside him. "Perhaps that is the best idea, right now, no matter what we think we want. What we *need* is time alone."

He smiled in the direction of her silhouette. "How can you be so logical? Aren't you supposed to be feeling scorned right now?"

"Perhaps I should, but then I don't always allow myself to be ruled by emotions." She shrugged. "We've just come to a decision to postpone making a decision about us and the nature of our relationship. Depending upon the decision made, I might be scorned, but I don't think that emotion is worthy of either one of us."

Corran nodded. "Yeah, you're right there, on both counts."

"Well, I'll leave you here, then . . ."

"No." Corran reached over and squeezed her leg just above the knee. "I'm fairly used to taking walks to sort things out. I've got a key, so I can let myself back in. I don't know when I'll get back."

"I'll head out and get some food. I should be here when you get back unless some Hapan princeling comes along and sweeps me away to make me the queen of some distant planet. Then won't *you* be sorry?"

"Actually I think I would be." Corran stood, then leaned down and kissed her on the forehead. "Thanks for understanding."

"Thank you for letting me understand."

Guided more by emotion than any sort of rational thought, Corran left Erisi behind in the room, entered a lift, and hit the lowest numbered button he could find. It took him well below the level where they had last seen Rima. The walkway onto which it dumped him didn't look that bad, though it was deeper than any place he'd been since his arrival on Coruscant.

Shoulders hunched and hands jammed deep into the

pockets of a brown bantha-suede jacket, he started wandering. It didn't matter to him where he was going, but just that he was going. Walking demanded little in the way of mental activity, so it gave him time to think and he'd done scant little of that which was unconnected to the mission for well over a month.

He tried to trace the source of his discomfort, but no easy answer presented itself. Certainly the pressure of being on Coruscant had a lot to do with it. Though precautions had been taken against discovery, something as simple as his nearly being sighted by Kirtan Loor showed that no matter how much care one took, there were times when luck just ran out.

Corran smiled. Back in CorSec they'd adulterated an old Jedi aphorism about luck to answer criminals who claimed they'd been caught because of bad luck. The Jedi Knights maintained there was no such thing as luck, just the Force. In CorSec they'd told criminals there was no such thing as bad luck, just the Corellian Security Force.

Now there's not even that. In news he had seen scrolling across readouts throughout Coruscant he learned that the Diktat had dissolved CorSec and had allocated most of its resources and some of its personnel to the new Public Safety Service. It didn't take much to see the change was a purge of people with questionable loyalties to the Diktat, but whatever its purpose, it erased yet one more link he had to his past.

His hand rose to his breastbone, but the gold medallion he normally wore was not there. General Cracken's people had said that by keeping it he could seriously compromise security, so he'd put it away in Whistler's small storage compartment. He knew the droid would keep it safe and, for him, knowing where it was had almost the same effect as actually wearing the good luck charm. *And the Jedi whose face appears on that coin would say there's no such thing as luck, so clearly it can't be a good luck charm.*

It occurred to him that he was losing his focus on life. Back when he had been with CorSec things had been simple. He knew who he was and so did everyone else around him. Though things were not all black and white, the number of grey tones were limited. There wasn't too much for him to handle, which made it that much easier to focus on what he was supposed to be doing.

In cataloging the chaos that had dominated his life over the past five years or so, it was easy to tote things up in the negative column. His father had died. He'd left CorSec and his friends had vanished. He'd slipped in and out of various identities while on the run. After months of training and fighting for the Rebellion—escaping death by the narrowest of margins over and over again—he got stuffed onto Coruscant and nearly got spotted by one of the few people on the planet who could recognize him. He wasn't flying. He didn't have his good luck charm and he found himself missing Whistler, Mirax, Ooryl, and the others.

He shivered. *If I only look at things on the negative side of the balance sheet, I'll keep imposing reasons on myself to remain unfocused.* The key to getting his focus back was to isolate those things he could control and work with them. Anything else didn't matter because he couldn't influence it. Only by doing as much as he could to manipulate the variables under his control could he keep himself in position to make decisions instead of finding himself without options.

What that means now is concentrating on my mission. I'm here to learn about security and that's what I should be doing. He nodded, then slowly began to realize that his wanderings had taken him farther and lower than he would have consciously chosen to go. Coronet City on Corellia had some seedy spots, but they appeared positively immaculate and safe compared to where Corran found himself. While his location did provide him with a datapoint for his mission—namely that there was no active Imperial security to be seen this deep down—it was a small speck of silver lining in a large cloud.

He decided to get his bearings and moved in off the street. This required him to thread his way through various makes and models of speeder bikes hovering in a wall in front of a cantina. If there was any lettering painted on the wall or door to indicate what the place was, it had long since faded too much for Corran to read it. A series of holograms flickered in sequence showing a stormtrooper's helmet breaking into four uneven and rather messy sections. What it meant mystified him until he walked inside and down the steps and saw a sizzling orange sign that proclaimed the place to be "The Headquarters," or, at least, did so when all the letters chose to buzz to life.

Corran had chased fleeing Selonians through sewers with better atmosphere and more consistent lighting than the Headquarters. The narrow stairway broadened out into a foyer that ended where one side of the triangular bar blocked it off. To get farther into the cantina one had to pass through the choke points at either end of the bar. While a fair amount of dense smoke filled the air, Corran could see tables clogging the floor and booths back against the walls. Two curtained doorways were built into the back corners, leading to waste relief stations and, given the sort of clientele drawn to this type of establishment, providing access to dozens of bolt-holes.

Speaking of bolt-holes . . . Blaster bolts had dotted the walls near the entrance with a dense pattern of holes. Corran noticed they tended to be grouped about a meter up from the floor and tapered off past head height for the average stormtrooper. He found this marginally reassuring, though his gut did not agree with that sentiment at all. *The faster I can get out of here, the better I'll like it.*

He kept his gait casual and a bit loose. His hands emerged from his pockets slowly as he approached the bar, slipping into a spot near the end over to the left. A fairly powerfully built Quarren female in a sleeveless tunic planted her hands on the bar right in front of him. "I think you're lost."

In an instant Corran was back in CorSec making sweeps of various Coronet City cantinas. "If I wanted thinking, I'd not be in here. *Lomin-ale.*" He put enough of an edge in his voice to make her question the judgment she'd made of him. As she moved away to comply, with her facial tentacles twitching out a silent curse at him, he realized his clothes were too new for him to fit in easily. Most of the patrons wore cloaks, less out of a concession to fashion than because it concealed their identities, and not many people coming into a place like the Headquarters really wanted to be spotted.

She returned with a small glass of ale, half of which was foam. He tossed a couple of credit coins on the bar and they disappeared instantly in her grey fist. He sipped the ale and found it wasn't as bad as he expected, though it could have benefited from being colder. His was the only small glass being used in the place, which he took as a not-so-subtle measure of his popularity with the staff. He knew he'd not get served again, and he wasn't inclined to linger over his drink.

By the same token, if he just turned around and walked out, half the regulars would be all over him like chitin on a Verpine. Running away would have the same effect as flagrantly flashing credits around, or opening his jacket and letting everyone see he didn't have a blaster with him. He considered, for a moment, trying to buy a blaster from someone, but that would put him in direct contact with gun-carrying criminals who might decide killing and robbing him was easier than selling him a weapon.

Corran leaned on the bar and drank more of the ale. Realizing he was not in a good position, he started to look around and assess the threats suggested by the cantina's patrons. Dozens and dozens of criminal profiles flitted through his brain. He classified people based on their species, the amount of interest they showed in him, and the kind of hunches he got when he looked at them. The people inside seven meters provided him with two definite class-one threats, a half-dozen class-two threats, and one Gamorrean who appeared scared enough that Corran tried to attach the face to any warrants that had been outstanding when he'd been in CorSec. He came up blank, then started on the booths along the wall to the left.

What? Corran blinked his eyes and shook his head, then took another look. Through the swirling smoke, seated facing a tall, slender figure in a cloak and hood, Corran saw Tycho Celchu. *Impossible.*

He looked away, then back for a third time. The individual to whom Tycho was speaking stood, eclipsing Corran's view of the unit's Executive Officer. In doing so the figure also managed to destroy Corran's interest in Tycho because despite the dim light and the thick smoke, he knew the hooded and cloaked figure could only be one person.

Kirtan Loor.

Corran set his ale down and began to move around the bar. *Loor and Tycho! He is an Imperial agent! I have to get to . . .*

He slammed into a large Trandoshan and rebounded from the reptilian's chest. Someone clapped a hand on Corran's right shoulder and he felt the muzzle of a blaster jam into his ribs. The Trandoshan closed in on the left, pinning him against the man with the blaster. "You're going nowhere, pal."

Corran looked to his right and couldn't recognize the man holding the gun on him. What he did notice about the gunman was that he had a comlink clipped to the lapel of his jacket and a small lead to an earphone in his left ear. As Corran looked back to the left to see if the Trandoshan was similarly equipped he saw the cloaked figure disappear out one of the back entrances. Tycho was gone as well.

Depression blossomed full in the pit of Corran's stomach, yet he knew things could easily continue to get worse.

They did. Very easily.

Through the doorway that swallowed the cloaked man swaggered a person swathed in garish and gaudy clothes. The smoke would have been enough to conceal his identity until he drew closer, but the cantina's dim light allowed the diamond pupils in his eyes to shine brightly.

Corran shook his head. "What you see when you don't have a blaster."

Zekka Thyne didn't bother to smile. "Your thoughts parallel mine." He reached back and drew Inyri Forge from his shadow. As she came around him she handed him a blaster pistol. "Of course, now I *have* a blaster and am just full of ideas about what I can do with it."

23

Though he marched at the head of the parade, Gavin
Darklighter felt anything but happy. He'd been searched
and deprived of his hold-out blaster. The Gotal walked
behind him, occasionally poking him with a blaster, and
Asyr Sei'lar walked on his right. She seldom looked over
at him, but when she did he saw only venom in her violet
eyes.

The other Rogues had been dragged along in his
wake, with a thick knot of denizens from the cantina
traveling behind them. The Rogues had been allowed to
keep their weapons, but their power packs had been
taken away, reducing the blasters to oddly shaped clubs.
Shiel seemed the most angry, but Aril and Ooryl insulated
him from the individuals on either side so no violence
broke out.

Asyr led the way through a set of corridors and stair-
ways that provided easy and instant access to the city's
lower reaches. Unlike the pathways Gavin and Shiel had
located, this one appeared to have been built in place, not
hacked out of what construction droids had created. It
didn't seem that new—and certainly not as new as Asyr
had made the Alien Combine sound—so Gavin guessed it

had been built after a Hutt or some other criminal bribed the city planners to program it into a construction droid.

The journey ended in a large rectangular warehouse area that they entered through double doors in one of the narrow walls. Scattered throughout the space were all sorts of makeshift hovels. They had been cobbled together from ferrocrete blocks, duraplast packaging, broken sheets of transparisteel, and ragged bits of cloth. Dwellings for larger creatures formed the foundation of the makeshift apartment blocks. Smaller creatures like Sullustans, Ugnaughts, and Jawas occupied the upper levels. Gavin felt pretty certain things actually roosted up in the shadows ten meters overhead, but the light was too dim for him to see more than silhouettes moving about.

The Bothan led them to a central clearing. Wide roll-up doors had been slid down in place where they bisected the longer walls. The one off to Gavin's left had a hole cut in it large enough to permit transit by most humanoid creatures. A couple of Twi'leks and a Rodian bearing guns stood watch nearby. Since both of the roll-up doors were large enough to admit repulsorlift trucks, Gavin assumed they led out onto whatever passed for streets at this level of the city.

Asyr stopped Gavin at the center of the clearing. The rest of the aliens fanned out in a semicircle behind them to ring half the clearing. This left the rest of the Rogues halfway between Gavin and the circle. The Gotal came around from behind him and stalked forward to where a steel post had been set into the duracrete floor. He picked up the hammer that hung from a string and pounded it against the post's flattened top.

A heavy mournful tone rang from the post and filled the room. Gavin could feel vibrations play through the floor. All around curious faces peered out through holes, windows, and doorways in the hovels. The Gotal hit the post again, summoning more people to come out of their homes. He hit it a third and final time, then let the hammer drop.

Gavin heard the whir of an engine and looked up as

a box drifted forward and slowly down. Cables lowered it from the mobile winch moving along tracks out away from the far wall. Lights came on inside the box, revealing windows and a doorway. As the floating building came to rest against the floor, the doorway opened and a male Devaronian stepped forth. The black cloak he wore nearly shrouded all of him—what little of his rotund belly and chest it didn't cover made a bright scarlet stripe down his middle that matched the tone of his flesh.

Asyr bowed her head in his direction. "Dmaynel, we have brought you one of the bigoted men who has traveled into Invisec to mock us. He is the one we should use as the message we wish to send to the Empire."

Light reflected white from the Devaronian's sable horns. He stepped forward and took Gavin's chin in his hand. His fingernails pressed hard into Gavin's flesh, but Gavin did not flinch nor try to pull away. He stared down into Dmaynel's dark eyes and did his best to hide his fear.

The Devaronian smiled, then released him and stepped back. "You have chosen wisely, Asyr. He is youthful and even handsome by their standards. His body will say all we want to say, and more."

"Indeed," said Nawara Ven, "it will let them know they are superior to all of us in every way they think now and new ones as well."

"Who are you?"

The Bothan scowled. "These five were with this Man."

Dmaynel looked past Gavin. "And you five are his friends?"

"We are, and proud to be so." Nawara Ven appeared at Gavin's left hand. "I have known him for well over six standard months and consider him one of the best friends I have ever had."

The Devaronian folded his arms across his chest. "It is rare among us to find one who so openly professes his friendship with a bigot."

Nawara smiled. "And what proof do you have that he is a bigot?"

Asyr snarled. "He refused to dance with me."

The Twi'lek opened his arms. "Of course, how could I have forgotten? Refusing to dance is a sign of being a bigot. What if I had refused your request? Would I have been a bigot?"

"You were with *her*."

"The human female, yes." Nawara nodded slowly. "So you would say I would have had a reason to refuse you."

Asyr nervously smoothed the fur on her face. "Yes, you would have."

"Is it not possible, then, that this Man had a reason to refuse you?"

"He did. He is a bigot."

"You draw a conclusion that is not supported by evidence, my dear." Nawara opened his hands and lifted them up to take in all the aliens watching. "Is there no reason other than bigotry that might explain his action? Perhaps he is not a good dancer. Perhaps he has someone he loves far away from here. Perhaps he is allergic to Bothan fur."

Asyr thrust a finger toward the Gotal. "But Mnor Nha said he felt relief when I went away. He was relieved he would not have to touch me and associate with me."

"She is telling the truth, Dmaynel. That is what I sensed."

Nawara drew himself up to his full height and turned to face the Gotal. "Tell me, Mnor Nha, did you sense relief from this Man when the stormtrooper departed from our table?"

The Gotal hesitated, then nodded. "Yes."

"So when one threat removed itself, this Man felt relief." Nawara turned back and smiled at Asyr. "Could it be, fair Asyr Sei'lar, that this man felt you as threatening in some ways as a stormtrooper?"

The Bothan's head came up. "I am no stormtrooper."

"Perhaps not in form, but in impact, I think you are." The Twi'lek patted Gavin on the shoulder. "My friend here is young and you are very beautiful. You approached him. You flattered him. You expressed interest in him and you were persistent. You stalked him, all of which must have quickened his pulse. You clearly saw something in him that he was not certain truly existed, which certainly would make him anxious. Your departure meant he never had to discover how disappointed you would be when you discovered he did not live up to the image you carried in your mind. Relief at your departure would only be natural."

Gavin nodded in agreement with Nawara's assessment and saw heads among the spectators also bob away. *Nawara's hitting close to one part of the truth so he can leave the rest of it alone.* Rather obviously Gavin's relief could be explained in terms of his being on a covert mission from the Rebellion, but revealing that fact would blow the operation. As much as the Alien Combine had been organized to protest Imperial misconduct, he knew there had to be at least one Imperial informant among the creatures assembled in the warehouse.

"He was threatened by *me*?" Asyr's violet eyes narrowed. "That's nonsense. How could anyone think of me as threatening?"

"How indeed?" Nawara exaggerated a frown. "Could it be that he has heard it was the Bothan people who bravely sacrificed themselves to carry news of the second Death Star to the Rebellion? How could he find a member of the species that caused the Emperor's death threatening? No, of course, you're right, that is not possible.

"The larger question to ask, of course, is why would he find you or me or any of us threatening right now? Could it be that his random selection, his being sentenced to death for an offense that is poorly defined; could that possibly remind him of the Empire you hate so much? Could it be the idea of being used to convey a message to people he does not know sounds very Imperial to him? Could it be that your action in this regard makes it difficult for him to differentiate between you and the Empire?"

"Absurd!"

"It is, Asyr?" Nawara looked up and out at the aliens staring down at the center of the room. "If you act like the Empire, you will be seen as the Empire."

The Devaronian waved that idea away. "He is one of *them*. Kill him and leave the body for them."

"No! He is one of *us*." The Twi'lek shook his head vehemently. "You are protesting death and mistreatment by the Empire, but Humans have suffered as much at the hands of the Empire as any of us. Yes, Mon Calamari, Gamorreans, and Wookiees have all been enslaved, but none of them had their homeworlds destroyed as Alderaan was destroyed. And who is it who has struck the most mortal blows against the Empire? The Rebellion, yes, but the Men among them. How many of us were part of the Rebellion and shed our blood at Yavin? How many of us froze on Hoth or died at Derra IV?"

Someone in an upper gallery shouted down, "We were there at Endor. A Mon Cal led the fleet at Endor. We have contributed to the war against the Empire."

"He's right," Asyr crowed. "We were there at Endor—without Bothans, Endor would not have happened. A Sullustan piloted the *Millennium Falcon* and it killed the second Death Star. Your points are for naught."

Nawara smiled slowly. "Yes, we were there at Endor, but Men fired the shots that destroyed that Death Star. Men killed the Emperor. Even so, the point you bring up to protest mine makes my case for me. We would *not* have been at Endor except that the Men who began the Rebellion, the Men who bled and died for its first victories, the Men who allowed us in, brought us in, welcomed us with open arms. You accuse this Man of bigotry because he felt relief when you left him alone, yet you are willing to treat him as a loyal son of the Empire when you already know that to do so is to discard any possibility that he hates the Empire just as much as you do."

Dmaynel shrugged casually. "If he hated the Empire that much, he would be out fighting it, not here hiding at its heart."

Nawara hesitated for a second and Gavin shook his head. *Don't blow mission security. It's better they kill me and our mission remain secret than to let the Empire know we're here. Too many people would hear the explanation for us to be safe.*

The Twi'lek stroked his chin. "And what if his loyalty to the Rebellion can be demonstrated?"

Dmaynel shrugged. "The Rebellion is far away. It will be years before I have to deal with them, and by then, this one will be forgotten. Right now he can serve notice on the Empire that we will no longer tolerate their predation upon us. Kill him."

The Gotal took careful aim with his blaster, but before he could pull the trigger, earsplitting explosions and bright flashes buckled the metal door to Gavin's left. The metal ribbon flopped down over the Twi'leks and Rodian standing guard. A cylindrical Ubrikkian HAVr A9 Floating Fortress cruised forward. The repulsorlift field pressed the door flat against the floor causing dark fluids to gush out from beneath it. The blaster cannon turret atop the vehicle spun to the right and the two spotlights on either side pinpointed the Devaronian. In the vehicle's wake two dozen armored stormtroopers poured into the warehouse.

Light from the machine's cockpit control panel revealed an image of the Fortress's Commander holding a comlink up to his mouth. "This is an unlawful assembly. You will lay down your weapons and disperse peacefully when given leave to do so. If you do not, my orders are clear. So are my fields of fire."

24

Wedge smiled as the white-haired woman walked through the door Iella had opened. "The Provisional Council must be serious about taking Coruscant. They have you here." He offered her his hand. "It's been a while, Winter—and you'd know exactly how long it's been, right?"

"I would, Commander Antilles, which is why, like you, I'm here." Winter shook his hand, then greeted Iella. Turning to face Pash, she nodded. "You would be General Cracken's son."

"The legendary Winter. I'm honored." Pash bowed in her direction.

Mirax stood and shook Winter's hand. "I'm Mirax Terrik."

Winter nodded. "And the reason I was summoned here." She looked over at Iella. "Nothing in our files indicates Imperial involvement with her."

Pash frowned. "Being my father's son, I have a question that you may not want to answer, but I have to ask. Commander Antilles and I were with Iella and Mirax the whole time we were coming here and we didn't see Iella make contact. How did you know to come here?"

Winter's expression became more serious, heightening

her resemblance to Princess Leia. "The account number Iella used to gain access to the datapad in the dress shop was special. Various things about the dress design selected, such as the colors, were sliced into municipal computers. At certain points around the city—in this case on a moving sidewalk—a pattern of lights communicated to me enough information that I knew to come here. There are backup systems to handle things if there is no response, but everything worked well, so it was no problem."

Wedge nodded appreciatively. "It's nice that you can slice into Coruscant's central computer."

Winter shook her head. "We can't. The safeguards there are too heavy for us to get in cleanly and out again. The central computer is attached to roughly a dozen auxiliary computer centers that are intended as backup, but are used primarily for low-level administrative and commercial applications. We can get into them and do so on a regular basis, but none of the patches we've tried to insert into the central computer have made it."

Iella sat back down. "If we could bring the central computer down we'd be set because it controls all the important things, like the shields and ground-based fighter defenses."

"The shields are the key." Wedge perched himself on the arm of the couch next to Mirax. "If they go down I tend to think most of the citizenry would support a change in government."

Winter sat beside Iella. "Overall security here is not as tight as I might have expected it to be under Ysanne Isard's control. That goes for the Imperial Palace, too. I was seated on the promenade nearly four hours drinking espcaf and saw nothing special. We almost had a problem when an Imp Intel officer just happened by. I was afraid one of my companions was going to attack Loor, but he kept his temper under control, just barely, but under control."

Iella's eyes narrowed. "Kirtan Loor is here, on Coruscant?"

Winter nodded.

Mirax raised an eyebrow. "Sounds like the kind of reaction Corran would have had to Loor."

Iella's jaw dropped. "You know Corran?" Mirax looked up and stared blankly at Iella for a moment, then blinked with astonishment. Both women then turned to Wedge."

"Corran's here?" Mirax asked.

"And he's in Rogue Squadron?" Iella added. "Is Whistler still with him?"

Wedge held his hands up. "I don't know exactly where he is, but he *is* on Coruscant. Iella, I know you were his partner in CorSec. I didn't mention his being in Rogue Squadron because you didn't seem to have that information yourself, which means New Republic Intelligence didn't let you have it. Operational security and all that."

Winter nodded. "Corran Horn is here, but he has no droid with him."

Mirax frowned. "How did you know Whistler was a droid?"

"Two years ago Corran Horn ran from CorSec taking an X-wing and an R2 unit with him. He was spotted as a prospect then, but we lost track of him. A year and a half later he joins Rogue Squadron, implying he has great skill as a pilot. This implies practice flying while he was on the run. This means he kept his R2 unit, so I decided Iella's question was about a droid, since X-wings have notoriously little capacity for dragging pets or other people around in them."

Mirax sat back. "You're good."

"Thank you."

Wedge winced. "Corran's here with Erisi."

Mirax growled. "The bacta queen."

Iella glanced at her. "The way you said that . . . but you're Booster Terrik's daughter. You and Corran couldn't be . . ."

"We're just good friends."

Iella laughed. "Not the first time I've heard that said in exactly that way. The stories I could tell you."

"Without Corran here to defend himself, I don't think that's a good idea." Wedge looked over at Winter. "Mirax's exit identity was blown by the Imps, leaving her stuck here after she dropped off what was probably the rest of my squadron."

"All of them, even Ooryl. They're in Invisec, or at least that's where I left them."

"Thanks. What we're trying to determine is if the Imps picked Mirax up at random, or if the security on this operation has been blown. Any problems with Corran and Erisi?"

"None." Winter thought for a second. "I had a team watching them for the first couple of nights to see if any Imps showed an interest in them, but that turned out negative. Those teams were shifted to monitor Imp sweeps in Invisec. They seem to be picking up Gamorreans and Quarren, but no one is certain why."

As Winter spoke staccato flickers of color outside prompted Wedge to look toward one of the windows. Bright flashes of red and green blaster bolts lit the thoroughfare outside. He studied the tableau for a moment, trying to make sense of it, then his jaw dropped as his brain sorted out what he was actually seeing. "Everyone down!"

Having no time to explain his warning shout, he grabbed on to the arm of the couch and wrenched it over backward. Mirax's hands shot out to both sides as she fought to balance herself, with her left hand locking in a death grip on Pash's shirtfront. She pulled her legs up and in to protect them, inadvertently making it just that much easier for Wedge to tip the couch over.

Over he went with it. He slipped to the side, ducking in toward Mirax, barely managing to pull his left leg in to safety. His hands came up to cover his head and he expected a nasty bash when he hit the floor, but that was the least of his worries. *I hope the couch will be armor enough!*

Outside, the speeder bike he had seen flying toward the window finally hit. It broadsided the wall of transparisteel with a solid thump, bursting through to spin into the room. The rider went one way and the speeder bike the other, between them sowing a glittering rain of lethal crystalline shrapnel throughout what was supposed to be, ironically enough, a safehouse.

25

Corran let himself sag toward the man on his right. The man jabbed him again with the gun to shove him away. Corran moved to the left but when he could no longer feel the gun in his ribs he took a step backward. The man on his right pulled the blaster's trigger, sending a scarlet bolt of energy into the Trandoshan's belly. It opened a smoking hole there, hurling the reptile back onto a table that collapsed under his weight.

Corran's left hand dropped over the top of the blaster and pulled. At the same time his right elbow came up and out, catching the shooter between mouth and nose. Twisting slightly, Corran pulled the man around between him and Zekka Thyne. He tore the blaster from the man's grip, then gave him a sidekick that propelled him toward Thyne.

Without waiting to see what happened, Corran spun and ran a zigzag course toward the doorway. The whine of blaster fire filled the room. Bolts burned past his legs and over his head, lighting little guttering fires on either side of the doorway. Remembering what he'd observed on his way in, Corran dove forward into a somersault, then came up to his feet at the base of the shadowed stairs.

Shifting the gun to his right hand, he brought his arm up and fired back over his shoulder to discourage pursuit.

Bursting out through the doorway, he kicked a Rodian off a speeder bike, settled himself in the saddle, and dropped it into first gear. Cranking the throttle, he shot off and headed for the nearest canyonlike intersection that would allow him to lose himself in the city. He instantly regretted not having shot up the other speeder bikes in front of the Headquarters, but a glance back at his pursuit suggested returning to do that now would be suicide.

If I'm going to die, I'd prefer it on my terms, in my time. Doing what he'd done back in the cantina had been stupid, but that was the only option he had when being faced with death. There had been no doubt in his mind—or the minds of anyone else in that cantina—that Thyne was going to kill him. That knowledge was the reason Corran knew the man on his right would hesitate before shooting—robbing Thyne of his kill would be as fatal as being Corran Horn in that situation.

Corran clutched and shifted with his feet, then gave the bike more throttle with his right hand. Using his thumb he hit the suicide-cruise button, keeping the throttle constant, then shoved the blaster down onto a pair of snap-clips that held it perfectly at the muzzle and trigger guard. With his left hand he rotated the vector-shift back, canting the forward directional vanes up, and hung on as the speeder bike climbed toward a hovering skyhook.

I don't remember the Incom Zoom II being this responsive, but it looks like the Rodian had this one all tricked out. Good thing for me, I guess. He hunkered down and rotated the speeder bike to put its bulk between him and the blaster bolts being shot by his pursuit. The Incom speeder bike didn't have any weaponry built onto it. The small data display between the throttle and vector handles constantly had stuff scrolling across it, but it was all in Rodian, which meant Corran had no idea what was going on. *As long as I go fast, does it really matter?*

Rolling the bike and playing with the vector-shift, he straightened it out and sent it screaming along through one of the upper canyons. He aimed the speeder bike well away from the mountainous Imperial Palace and cut around a skyhook tether. Shifting his weight and giving the vector-shift nudges now and again, he kept the speeder bike juking and bouncing as the wind tugged at his hair and blaster bolts streaked scarlet past him. Some of them were heavier than those a handheld blaster could produce, letting him know that some of the machines were military surplus and in good working order.

He glanced back, but in the darkness all he could see was blaster bolts coming at him. The riders coming up behind were getting better with their shots and Corran realized that flying up high and in the open was playing to their strength. *I need a tight course with few shots available. That means down!*

Hanging on tightly he inverted and cranked the vector-shift back. The speeder bike dove through the night, flashing past level after level of apartments, malls, offices, and grand promenades. Chopping the throttle back, Corran threw his weight to the left and hooked the bike around and back up through a narrow space between two towers. Leaning back to the right, he came around the cylindrical tower and shot off down an alley.

A scattering of blaster bolts scored the walls around him. Corran broke left, then cut the throttle back and shifted into neutral. A tug on the vector-shift brought his bike around in a flat spin that he killed by goosing the thrust to kill his momentum. Hanging there in the air, he filled his hand with the blaster and braced his hand on the speeder bike's chassis.

Two speeder bikes cut into the alley, racing full bore after him. Corran's first two shots hit the rightmost bike on the nose. The bike's control panel exploded in a silver shower of sparks. The blast lifted the driver and pitched him head over heels off the speeder bike's rear end. The bike itself immediately began a smoking dive toward the planet below and the driver slowly tumbled down in its wake.

He shifted his aim to the second bike, but the driver had already begun to pull up. Corran's two shots hit his target, one on the driver's leg and the other on the connector post fixing the sidepod to the speeder bike. The vehicle did not split apart and the driver veered away as if he'd had enough, so Corran rehomed the blaster and set off again.

Something on the data monitor squawked at him. He knew it was Rodian but he could no more understand the spoken tongue than he could read the written language. *The guys on the bike and sidepod are comlinking with the others. They'll coordinate and they know this city better than I do.* His hand snaked up to where he usually wore his good luck charm but he felt nothing. *On my own.*

He refused to despair and instead set the speeder bike at a moderate pace and took it down farther and farther into the lower reaches of Coruscant. He had no idea where he was, but that did not matter to him as much as being aware of where his pursuit was. Fortunately for him they tended to announce themselves with blaster shots that sizzled past close, but never seemed to tag him.

With three on his tail, he dove into a black hole at the bottom of a canyon, then came around and shot back against his previous line of travel. Trimming his speed he ducked and dodged his way through a tangle of support girders, then dove back out of them and came up and around through a hole in the roof of a passage. Cutting back on his throttle, he locked the speeder bike in a gentle circling pattern that flew around the hole. He drew the blaster and waited. *One has to be coming soon.*

One of the three *did* jet up through the hole, but he came out riding a rocket. Corran snapped a quick shot off at him but missed. *The way he came out means he was warned.*

A speeder bike swooped at him from above. Something bright flashed at the front of the sidecar, then he felt a thump on the aft end of his bike. The whole speeder bike jolted, then started flying backward. Because of the way he'd locked his controls, the bike began spinning through an awkward spiral that almost pitched him to the ground.

Dropping back into the saddle—literally willing himself back into it—Corran shifted to neutral and adjusted the vector control to kill the roll. *They've got a line on me.* He twisted himself around and tried to see the line so he could shoot it, but it was too slender for him to spot in the darkness. Given no choice, he shifted his aim toward the main body of the Ikas-Ando Starhawk and triggered three shots at the lump a meter or so below a fist that had been thrust victoriously into the air.

The Starhawk's pilot slumped forward over the front of the speeder bike and Corran immediately felt his bike begin to slow. Dropping back down into the saddle, he shifted the Zoom II into gear and punched the throttle forward. Coming around to his right, he sailed on past and below the hovering Starhawk. Twenty meters out from it he felt a tug and his bike slowed.

Damn, the sidecar guy didn't release me. All speeder bikes came with a deadman switch that returned the throttle to zero thrust if it was released. That prevented the speeder bike from racing along if the person at the controls died, fell off, or somehow could no longer pilot the bike. It was a safety precaution built into the machines, but as with the one Corran had stolen, it was possible to put in a suicide-cruise switch that would keep the throttle set despite having no hands on it.

Corran cranked his throttle up full, but the drag from the Starhawk was making him far too slow. The trio of bikes that had chased him down were pacing him, but their drivers had clearly decided to call in other help to box him in. *I have to get rid of this thing. I have to cut that line.*

Corran sent the Zoom II into a dive, hauling the Starhawk after it. He sped on through level after level, then came out into a huge intersection of canyonlike airroads. *Damn, back out in the open.* His pursuit began to close, shooting again. Corran tried to make the bike dance as before, but with an air-anchor attached to it, he was having no luck at all.

Snarling with frustration, he pointed the speeder bike straight at the building on one corner of the intersection. He aimed at a lit rectangle on one of the lower levels, intending to whip the trailing Starhawk into the illuminated sign there. *It would be poetic justice if it were an ad for Starhawks.* He expected the impact would batter the bike to bits. If it didn't, *well, there are plenty more walls.*

It wasn't until he got close enough to see people sitting in the room move that he realized it wasn't an advertising billboard but a window. He wanted to veer off, but blaster bolts on both sides bracketed him. He thought for a second about going straight through and out through the other side, but he knew the transparisteel would rip him apart. *Get out of the way!*

At the last moment Corran hauled the speeder bike around in a sharp left turn. The Starhawk trailing around after him hit the window. He felt a hard jolt, then his speeder bike shot off across the intersection and parallel to another building's front. He glanced back and thought for a moment that he was free of the Starhawk, then a slight tremble in the bike's frame matched sparks on the building wall.

Of all the luck! Instead of the transparisteel severing the cord that bound him to the Starhawk, the sharpness of the turn had snapped the weakened connectors between the sidepod and the Starhawk itself. The pod's occupant had vanished, but Corran couldn't see where he'd gone. The pod itself trailed after him like a balloon after a child in a stiff wind, but the advent of a half-dozen more speeder bikes into the intersection gave him no chance to try to shuck it off.

The trailing pod gave him all sorts of trouble because of the potential it had for anchoring him to pillar or post. He tried to keep his turns crisp, but he had to avoid narrow alleys and keep his speed under control. If he went too fast the pod would whip around, bashing into walls and throwing the aft end of his speeder bike around. If he slowed, the pod still shot forward. The elasticity of the line connecting it with his bike meant it shot it toward him unless he broke from his line of flight.

The trailing speeder bikes and swoops kept him hemmed in. He knew he was being herded toward a specific point, and he desperately wanted to avoid going there, but he didn't have many choices. He did dive and sideslip to smash the pod against walls and break it loose, but it stayed with him. *If I survive this perhaps I'll send the Ikas-Ando people a testimonial on the durability of their sidepods . . .*

Cruising around a corner, Corran saw bikes closing from above and behind, trapping him in a wide alley that ended in a solid wall a hundred and fifty meters on. It had no other outlets save up and what appeared to be a closed loading gate at the base of the wall toward which he sped. *This is it, my run ends now.* The only choices open to him seemed to be slamming into the wall and dying, or fighting and dying.

He thought about slowing to fight, but the whistling pod behind him reminded him of the folly of that idea. *It'll go through me faster than . . . hey, that's an idea!* Corran pointed the speeder bike directly at the loading gate and kicked the throttle up to full. Twenty meters out, he cranked the vector-shift back, nosing the speeder bike toward the sky, and reversed thrust. The combination pitched him forward, then brought the front of the bike up to bash him back into his seat. As the bike inverted and the pod sailed through beneath it, Corran grabbed the blaster pistol and dropped a dozen feet to the ground.

The pod hit the loading gate's roll-up door with enough force to cave in the metal barrier toward the middle and rip it from the tracks on which it hung. The speeder bike, with the suicide-cruise switch engaged, slammed into the falling ribbon of metal, then flew on over the crest of it and on into the building's interior. It tugged on the pod, but the pod had become trapped by the door, so the cord parted, freeing the speeder bike to careen farther on.

With blaster bolts raining down around him, Corran dove for cover inside the building. Speeder bikes swooped past him as he twisted around and got just inside the doorway. Bringing his blaster pistol up, he tried to pick out targets, but found far too many to choose from. This confused him for a moment because while he distinctly remembered being chased by Zekka Thyne's Black Sun villains, he could see no way stormtroopers could have anticipated his journey and set up the ambush into which he had ridden.

26

The peal of metal striking metal and the scream of the door being torn from its rails snapped Gavin's head around to his right. Beyond Asyr he saw the door opposite the Imperial Fortress come crashing down, then a riderless speeder bike flew into the warehouse. Blaster bolts stippled the door and scarlet energy darts shot from incoming speeder bikes toward the stormtroopers.

As shock faded and the stormtroopers began to return fire, Gavin dove to the right and tackled Asyr Sei'lar. She snarled and clawed at his back as they went down, but he held on and rolled her toward the edge of the circle and behind debris. A dying Duros—his chest featuring a blackened hole at the center with flames burning around it—collapsed on top of them. Gavin shrugged him off and filled his hands with the blaster pistol the Duros had dropped.

Gavin came up on one knee and triggered two shots at a stormtrooper. One glanced off the man's thigh armor, scoring it with a black stripe, and the other passed between the man's knees. The stormtrooper came around, leveling his blaster carbine at Gavin. *Oh, no, just like on Talasea.*

A hand grabbed him by the shoulder and pulled him down. The stormtrooper's fire scythed up through where Gavin had been and one bolt passed through the hem of Gavin's coat, but didn't draw blood.

Having released her grip on his shoulder, Asyr leaned out around the ferrocrete blocks shielding them and snapped off two shots at the stormtrooper. Both hit him in the torso, turning him around and dropping him to the floor. There he twitched and slapped his hands at the holes in his armor, but he did not rise up again.

Red and green energy bolts crisscrossed in the air, filling the warehouse with the stink of ozone, melted armor, and burned flesh. The Fortress's heavy blaster cannons pumped out bolts that methodically blasted into the lower levels of the makeshift dwellings. Shadowed interiors flared scarlet for a moment, then exploded in smoke and dust. The upper floors would collapse on the lower, burying people alive.

Gavin came up to fire again, but Asyr yanked him back down as a speeder bike just missed clipping him.

"Keep your head down unless you want to lose it."

"A minute ago you were planning to have me killed."

She flashed him a smile. "A bigot wouldn't have saved me."

Gavin shoved her aside with his left hand and triggered a line of shots at a stormtrooper peeking out from behind cover. "We can't stay here."

"C'mon, run to the open door." Nimbly she rolled up onto her feet and started off. She scattered shots in the direction of the Fortress. He couldn't see what she was shooting at because of the dust and the smoke, but he ran right along behind her and shot in the same direction she did. Blaster bolts sizzled back through the pall at him, but nothing came within a meter of hitting him.

As nearly as Gavin could tell, the volume of blaster fire heading in at the stormtroopers grossly exceeded the amount coming back from them. What the Imperial fire lacked in volume it made up for with accuracy and power. Through the smoke Gavin could see bolts from pistols and carbines glancing off the Fortress's armor whereas its return fire stained the smoke with the color of blood and exploded whatever it touched. People ran screaming, others staggered and fell. He looked for anyone he could recognize, but saw none of the other Rogues among the refugees.

He reached the street outside and found himself abruptly dragged out of the river of fleeing people and to the left. He pulled his right arm free from the other man's grasp, then smiled. "Corran?"

"Good to see you, too, Gavin."

Asyr, who was standing next to Nawara and Rhysati, frowned. "Gavin?"

"Long story." Gavin looked at the others gathered beside the door. Between them, Shiel and Ooryl supported the Devaronian, Dmaynel Kiph. His black blood oozed like oil from a wound in his right thigh. Everyone else looked fine. "Where's Aril?"

Nawara shook his head. "Don't know."

Corran glanced at the people running from the warehouse. "She's small. We could have missed her."

Rhysati nodded. "There have been a lot of Sullustans running away."

Gavin brandished his gun. "We can't leave her."

Another explosion rumbled from within the warehouse. Corran shied away from the opening. "The Fortress is moving up. We can't go back in."

Bits of masonry debris pitter-patted over Gavin's coat and stung his face. He wanted to go diving back into the fight, but his belly began to throb where he had previously been gut-shot by a stormtrooper and that made him hesitate. Guilt immediately assailed him because he had been the cause for the Rogues to be in the warehouse. Part of him knew the Imperial operation had to have been one that was planned long before he was dragged down for a trial, but logic couldn't defeat the fear he felt for Aril and the others inside.

Two speeder bikes shot back out of the warehouse, followed by a third and then a fourth. After them came two Imperial stormtroopers on speeder bikes of their own. The lead Imp bike fired a shot from its laser cannon and melted half the control surfaces on a Starhawk. The speeder bike went down hard, spilling the rider to the ground. The second bike swooped low toward the downed driver.

More smoothly than Gavin would have thought possible, Corran's blaster pistol came up and around. He snapped off three quick shots. One missed the second Imp speeder, but the other two hit and boosted the driver up out of the saddle. The armored figure fell ten meters to the ferrocrete street, rolling up in a lifeless heap next to his prey. The speeder bike glided to a hover in midair above him, out of reach and benign.

Nawara pointed up as a half-dozen stormtroopers on speeder bikes dove down through the alley. "Reinforcements, let's move."

Asyr pointed to a doorway set flush with a wall off to the right. "This way."

Corran waved them on, then darted out and ran toward the downed bike driver. Gavin followed him, directing a scattered pattern of covering fire back into the warehouse. He reached the rider a moment after Corran did and realized the rider was a woman. She tugged her helmet off, spilling brown hair over her shoulders. A blue forelock had been pasted to her forehead by sweat.

"Leave me alone!" she snarled at Corran.

"No way, Inyri." Corran grabbed her by the shoulder of her jacket to pull her along, but just ended up keeping her off the ground when her step faltered.

"My knee," she gasped, "I can't."

Gavin handed Corran his blaster, then swept her up in his arms. "Let's go."

Inyri struggled against Gavin for a moment, then hung on as stormtroopers started shooting at them from all directions. The Rogues who had gone over to the doorway Asyr had pointed out returned fire on the stormtroopers emerging from the warehouse, momentarily driving them back. Corran, with a blaster in each hand, triggered a flurry of shots at the first speeder bike as it came around to make a pass at them. He didn't hit the pilot, but he made the man shy off and slam his speeder into the alley wall.

The speeder exploded, spilling fire down the wall and into the alley. It sparked a momentary lull in the shooting that Gavin used to complete his run to the doorway. He got inside quickly and stumbled forward, but kept his feet. The backlight of blaster fire from the other Rogues provided him with enough light to find his way a bit deeper into what appeared to be a cluttered stockroom of some sort. Despite the smoke in the air, Gavin detected a heavy chemical scent.

Up ahead Asyr cracked a door open, letting a sliver of dim yellow light slice through the gloom. Janitorial supplies filled the shelves in the room, though dust covered all of them. As he moved out into the corridor with Inyri, he saw enough grime to confirm that the supplies were seldom used in the building.

Asyr cut across the corridor to a stairwell and led them down. Ooryl and Shiel followed with Dmaynel, leaving Nawara, Rhysati, and Corran to form the rear guard. Though no one seemed to be pursuing the group, Corran and the other two gave the wounded folks a good head start before they followed.

Gavin didn't recognize any of the tunnels or passages they took, nor the buildings they cut through, though they all looked pretty much like those he and Shiel had seen in their survey of Invisec. Finally they moved up a few levels and were admitted to an apartment where an Ithorian led them through a fairly conventional room to a thickly overgrown, junglelike area of heavy humid air, dripping water, rainbow-colored plants, and artificial lighting.

Asyr pointed Ooryl and Shiel toward a bluish-green mossy patch and they deposited Dmaynel there. "Houlilan, take care of Dmaynel. This other one is hurt, too, but not badly."

Inyri shifted a bit in Gavin's arms. "You can let me down. I can stand. I just banged my knee up when I fell."

Gavin eased her onto her feet and supported her as she balanced on her left foot. "Are you going to be okay?"

She nodded, wincing only slightly as she tried to put weight on her right leg. "I guess you think I should be grateful."

Asyr looked surprised. "They saved you from death or worse at Imp hands. Thanks are warranted."

Inyri shrugged. "Thank them? Never. They're the reason I'm here. If they'd not interfered with my life, I wouldn't have been in trouble."

Corran frowned from the doorway. "You had a choice. You didn't have to leave Kessel."

Asyr pocketed her small blaster and folded her arms. "There's definitely something going on here that I don't know about. Do I want to?"

Gavin shook his head. "Probably not."

"For your own sake," Nawara added.

Inyri smiled cruelly. "These are the people who brought Black Sun back to Coruscant."

The Bothan covered her surprise well, then stared right at Gavin. "True?"

He shrugged. "I'm afraid so."

Asyr frowned. "Freeing folks from Kessel explains why you've got no love for the Imps, but I don't think the Rebels will think much of your doing that either. Makes the galaxy kind of small for you. That's a big problem."

"Not really, not at all." Corran handed Gavin back his blaster. "As things go, that's really a minor problem."

"A *minor* problem?" Asyr's frown deepened. "Do I even want to know you people?"

"Probably not." Gavin smiled at her. "We're Rebels—pilots in Rogue Squadron."

"And you're here on Coruscant?" Asyr's amethyst eyes widened. "I begin to see your perspective on things."

Corran nodded. "Let me help you get the full hologram. We're here to figure out how to liberate Coruscant. In comparison with *our* mission, *any* other problem is a minor problem."

Aril Nunb had decided to feign unconsciousness when they dragged her from the rubble, but the cracked ribs on the right side of her chest were painful enough to make her squeal when a stormtrooper pulled on her right arm. He hauled her to her feet, then shoved her toward the group of cut and bleeding refugees standing behind the Floating Fortress.

Aril didn't think she'd blacked out when things started happening, but she couldn't be certain. She remembered the stormtroopers arriving, then the far door going down. She'd broken for the exit along with the other Rogues, but a blast from the Fortress had exploded part of a hovel to her right. She thought only the shock wave had knocked her down, but the ache in her ribs suggested she'd been hit solidly by flying debris. Then she'd seen a Sullustan toddler begin to scream and thrash in a midden. She'd bent to help him out when the rest of the building came down.

She glanced back at the pile from where they had pulled her, but she saw no child. Aril turned to look forward again, but she saw no child among the hollow-eyed survivors. Those that could cry did, others licked their wounds; many stared off into space.

A Too-Onebee glanced in her direction, then pointed off to the left. Aril mutely followed the directions and found a group of Sullustans huddled together, segregated from the other refugees. A number of children clung to adults, hiding behind legs or burying their faces in a parent's neck. Aril couldn't see the child she had gone after. She had a hard time actually recalling the child's face, which told her she'd probably been concussed.

Instead of letting herself think she'd failed, she arbitrarily picked out one child and decided he had been the one she had tried to help. She nodded in his direction, but he just hid further behind his father's leg.

Someone grabbed her left arm. Aril looked up into the jowly face of a man who stood a good forty centimeters taller than she did. He was quite heavyset, yet his brown eyes shone with a cunning that removed him from the class of man she would have called bovine. He wore his thinning black hair in a short military style cut, which was in keeping with his General's uniform.

"You seem healthy. A good specimen."

Aril lightly tapped the right side of her chest and winced.

The man dropped his thick-fingered hand to her flank and probed her ribs. She squeaked out a protest. His touch, while clinical, was also forceful and hurt. "Cracked ribs maybe, probably just bruised." He looked down into her eyes and turned her head to the left and right. "You look fine. Don't worry, I'll take care of you."

He straightened up. "Diric!"

An older, dull-eyed man in a bloodstained orderly's uniform spun on his heel. "Yes, General Derricote?"

Derricote patted Aril on the shoulder. "This is one we're taking with us. Put her with the others."

"She makes a dozen and a half, sir."

"Good." Derricote pointed to the orderly. "Go with him. You will have the best of care. In fact, I daresay, you will have the best medical care available for the rest of your life."

27

Admiral Ackbar closed his eyes for a second, then nodded to his aide. "I suppose the tide is high, so I cannot escape it. Please show Councilor Fey'lya in."

The human aide departed, giving Ackbar a moment of silence in which he could prepare for the coming confrontation. *No, Ackbar, if you assume bitter water, you'll not taste the sweet.* The Admiral refused to consider the Bothan a rival for power, primarily because Ackbar himself had no desire for power in any political sense of the word. He had risen to his position at the head of the Alliance military because of his intimate knowledge of Imperial doctrines—learned while he was Grand Moff Tarkin's slave—and because the Mon Calamari had contributed their considerable fleet to bolster the Rebel Navy for the battle at Endor. Once the Empire was defeated and his services were no longer needed, he would happily retire to Mon Calamari and spend the rest of his days living through tide cycles.

He realized his refusal to see Borsk Fey'lya as a rival probably was shortsighted, but he could not afford the distraction. With the death of General Laryn Kre'fey at Borleias, the Bothans had lost their most celebrated military leader. The Bothans had no other candidate to offer as viable for running grand operations like the taking of Coruscant.

Which meant any Bothan agenda had to go through Ackbar.

Which is why Fey'lya has come to me now.

The hatch to Ackbar's cabin on *Home One* opened and Borsk Fey'lya entered the dimly lit office. Ackbar started to adjust the lighting upward, but the Bothan shook his head. "Be comfortable, Admiral, I can see well enough in this light."

The subdued tones of Fey'lya's voice, and the conciliatory nature of his words, immediately put Ackbar on his guard. "You honor me with your visit, Councilor."

Fey'lya held a gold-furred hand up. "Please, the formality of titles is unnecessary between us. We have not always been on the same side, nor do you probably consider me a friend, but you do acknowledge the bond we share within the Rebellion."

"Of course." Ackbar nodded slowly. "You came to speak to me about Noquivzor."

"Indeed. The reports I have gotten were sketchy."

Ackbar sat back in his eggshell repulsorlift chair. "You have the basics: one standard day ago Warlord Zsinj showed up in the system with the *Iron Fist*, launched a wing of TIEs, and proceeded with a planetary bombardment. Our base there was hit hard, though since most of it was underground, the damage was not as extensive as Zsinj undoubtedly would like to think."

Fey'lya's purple eyes glowed luminescently in the half-light. "We met on Noquivzor approximately seven standard weeks ago. Do you think this was a misguided assassination attempt?"

Ackbar thought for a moment, then shook his head. "Unlikely. If he killed the Rebellion leadership he would make himself a target. I suspect he thought he was attacking Rogue Squadron, to pay them back for hitting his ships. His facility for carrying a grudge is all but legendary. We made no secret of where Rogue Squadron was staying primarily to keep the Empire looking at Noquivzor instead of closer to home."

"How badly was Noquivzor hit?"

Ackbar's eyes half closed. "We had major damage to the barracks complex. Multiple floors collapsed one atop another. We will be a long time digging bodies out. Rogue Squadron lost a significant portion of their support staff. The hangar complex, on the other horizon, escaped damage. When we get them back from Coruscant they will have ships to fly."

"Even the worst plague will spare some of the virtuous." The Bothan slowly shook his head. "Warlord Zsinj is becoming more of a problem. If we do not strike back at him and hit him hard, he will be emboldened and hit us again."

"Agreed, but where do we hit him? He's as elusive as the *Katana* fleet. The galaxy is a big place and even with back-plotting and reports coming in, pinpointing his location is all but impossible. To find him would demand a full fleet operation, and that would mean we delay the Coruscant operation indefinitely."

"But if we were to do that and try to hunt Zsinj down, we would suddenly open ourselves to more reprisals by him and might give Ysanne Isard the opening she needs to strike at us." Fey'lya smoothed the fur around the mouth with his left hand. "Fighting on two fronts is folly."

"Truly spoken." Ackbar cocked his head slightly. "You would not be here if you did not have an idea to offer, for this discussion merely verbalizes facts plainly in evidence to anyone who has read the reports."

A hurt expression stole upon Fey'lya's face, but the intelligence in his eyes robbed it of its intended effect. "To escape a rancor, one is wise to ignore the bite of a flea."

"Meaning?"

"We cannot shift our focus from the Empire. What I propose is a bold strike at Coruscant."

"We're not ready."

"We must be." Fey'lya opened his hands. "We are already staging for it and nothing in reports from Coruscant give any indication that Isard is increasing her defenses. She must know we are not ready so she thinks she has time to prepare. If we go now, soon, she will be taken unawares."

"You grossly underestimate Iceheart if you think she is ever unprepared."

Fey'lya's head came up and his jaw opened in a predatory grin. "You are not protesting the plan as utter madness. Your thoughts parallel mine, don't they?"

Ackbar sat forward again, his barbels quivering. "We are at a critical junction. Iceheart's preparations for the invasion she has to know is coming have been insufficient. Reports from Coruscant are favorable. Because of recent developments it appears it is possible to unite disparate parts of the Coruscant population to give us a partisan force on the planet. They are poorly equipped, but can be disruptive and distracting."

"Can they disrupt and distract enough to bring the shields down?"

"I do not know." Ackbar shook his head. "I have sent a message to Commander Antilles directing him to formulate and prepare to implement a plan to do just that, with the resources he has on hand. Once I receive a reply that indicates he has such a plan prepared, I will give him a target time for when it has to go into effect. When the shields go down, we will arrive at Coruscant."

The Bothan's eyes narrowed. "You allow for no slippage in his plan. What if he cannot bring it off in time?"

Ackbar's jaw opened in a smile. "I have had a report which makes this plan viable in the event that Commander Antilles and his people fail to bring the shields down. You may recall that in recent months the Interdictor cruiser *Black Asp* ran afoul of Rogue Squadron? Their Captain, a woman named Uwlla Iillor, filed a protest over the transfer of her flight operations officer from her command. The protest was ignored and, apparently, was enough to prompt her and her staff to decide to defect.

This gives us an Interdictor cruiser, something we have not had before.

"Depending upon the course we choose, the journey from Borleias to Coruscant will take approximately twenty standard hours. My intention is to send the *Black Asp* in early and have it jump to the outer edges of the Coruscant system. If the shields are not down, the Interdictor will power up the gravity well projectors and drag our invasion fleet from hyperspace prematurely. If the shields are down, Iillor will do nothing and allow us to revert from hyperspace right on top of Coruscant."

Fey'lya slowly nodded. "Elegantly simple but decidedly effective. You clearly trust this Captain Iillor. You do not think her coming over is one of Ysanne Isard's deceptions?"

"No. Captain Iillor cites interference by Imperial Intelligence with her command as the primary reason for her defection. General Cracken has cleared her and has his people working on her staff. Within a week the *Black Asp* will be operational with an Alliance crew."

The Bothan nodded. "The ship will be renamed?"

"The crew has chosen a hopeful name: *Corusca Rainbow*."

"An omen, to be sure."

"That is my hope." Ackbar gave Fey'lya a wall-eyed look. "You will propose this plan to Mon Mothma?"

"In both our names, yes." Fey'lya smiled. "With her support and the two of us backing it, the Provisional Council cannot fail to make it operational."

"Good." The Mon Calamari nodded. "Then I just have to see that the operation does not fail."

28

Kirtan Loor dropped to one knee before the holographic image of Ysanne Isard but did not bow his head. "Thank you for replying to my request so quickly, Madam Director."

She arched an eyebrow at him. "Displays of ego and spirit always attract my attention, Agent Loor."

"Good, then I can take it that you will be reprimanding General Derricote?"

"Why?"

Loor blinked, then narrowed his eyes. "Why? Madam Director, he took it upon himself to go into Invisec and select subjects for his experimentation who were transported directly to his lab. He violated every known security procedure we have in doing that. The Sullustans he took were not properly screened so we do not know who they were. The other captives spoke of an Alien Combine and the Sullustans might have been able to supply more useful information on that organization."

Isard dismissed his protest with a sneer. "I have told him you are to be allowed to interview his subjects."

"Oh, yes, but he immediately injected them with the newest strain of his Krytos virus. The interviews would have to take place with my people in isolation suits, which means the subjects would know they were never getting out. Their motivation to cooperate would be gone. And if he's right, if this strain has an incubation period of two weeks, the subjects would be well into dementia and death before analysis would let us conduct other interrogations."

"That is not your concern at this moment, Agent Loor. General Derricote's Krytos project is of paramount importance. This new strain could be the breakthrough we need to prepare Imperial Center for the Rebels." Fire flared in her molten left eye. "That idiot Zsinj attacked the Rebels to salve his own wounded pride. He doesn't realize that if they were to mobilize their entire fleet and devote it to hunting him down they'd have him inside a year. The fool thinks he is powerful, but he doesn't realize all he has done is to force the Rebels to move more swiftly to take Imperial Center—too swiftly."

Loor sat back on his heel. "There is no indication of impending operations according to our spy in Rogue Squadron."

"I know that, but I also know their leadership. They mean to wipe us from the galaxy and they cannot do that if they end up chasing after every Moff who decides he should be the next Emperor. Imperial Center is the key to power in the galaxy. They know that and they know the sooner they sit Mon Mothma on the Imperial throne, the easier their crusade will be."

The audacity of launching a strike at Imperial Center surprised Loor, but he knew the leaders of the Rebellion often saw the impossible as necessary and their successes against the Death Stars had made them think they could succeed at anything. Isard had purposely left Imperial Center vulnerable, but only so the Krytos virus could cause the Rebel Alliance to collapse. If it were not ready, her plan would fail and the Alliance would be stronger than ever.

"I will monitor the situation, Madam Director."

"Oh, yes, you will." She stabbed a holographic finger

at him. "The Rogues can plan all they want, but nothing can actually be *done* for two weeks. I am going to deploy this version of the Krytos virus so it can be introduced to the planetary water supply starting now. We will see if Derricote's predictions on its speed and lethality are correct, and assuming they are, we will save ourselves two weeks of waiting. If the Rogues strike too soon, all will be lost. Two weeks minimum—a month would be better. Develop the resources you need, do whatever you must, but see to it that the Rogues do nothing substantive before I want them to."

"It will be done, Madam Director." Loor bowed his head, but when he looked up again her image had vanished. He stood, slowly, and a smile spread across his features. "Develop resources and do what I must. By your order."

He walked from his dark, cramped office down a short corridor to another room. The door whisked up into the ceiling, revealing a dark room with a figure bound to a chair and flanked by two stormtroopers. Loor walked in and took the man sitting there by the chin, eliciting a snarl from him.

Loor laughed, releasing the chin, then backhanded the man across the face. "Displays of spirit can be painful."

"Nothing you can do will hurt me, Loor."

"Ah, you do remember me. I should be flattered, Patches." Loor looked down at Zekka Thyne and hit him again. The man's head rocked back, but the red eyes stared up at him, full of defiance. Striking Thyne had a cathartic effect on him, but Loor refused to indulge himself. "Fortunately for you, I remember you as well."

"You'll get nothing from me, Loor."

"But you have nothing I want, Patches." Loor tapped fingers against his own breastbone. "I have something to offer you, however. Rogue Squadron brought you and other Black Sun scum to Imperial Center, then they followed you. There is only one implication for this, which is to suppose you and they are preparing for an assault on Imperial Center."

"I know nothing about that."

Loor grabbed an ear and twisted it cruelly. "You're listening now, not speaking."

Thyne stared vibroblades at him but remained silent.

"Good." Loor released him. "You will be my eyes and ears within the Alliance community here. I want to know their plans. I want timetables, suppliers, personnel rosters, anything and everything. If you give me what I want, I let you live."

"If I walk out of here, you will never be able to get me again so your threat means nothing."

"Oh, I won't be the one to kill you. Not firsthand, anyway. What I *will* do is allow Black Sun slicers to obtain files that even go back to my CorSec days noting how you were working for me. They will implicate you in the downfall of Black Sun here on Imperial Center. Your fate will be decided by your brethren, not me."

That threat damped some of the defiance in Thyne's eyes. "Do not be disheartened, though, Patches, I would not surrender you unless forced to. These stormtroopers will conduct you to a place to which you will say you escaped after your speeder bike was brought down. We've been combing the area constantly for the last three days. You will tell your compatriots that you were in hiding and finally managed to escape. They will believe you."

"No one will believe I hid."

Loor looked over at one of the stormtroopers. "He's right. Before you leave him inflict a nonfatal abdominal wound—one he could survive and one that won't hamper him too much."

"You don't need to do that."

Loor smiled. "Oh, but I think we do. Verisimilitude. If you can't believe you would have been hiding, no one else will. People are suspicious, especially people like Corran Horn."

"Then this will be another thing I owe him for. If it weren't for him, I'd not be in your custody."

"Indeed," Loor nodded confidently. "And just to show you that I'm not a monster, I'll give you a gift. If you find a convenient time to kill Corran Horn, do so. I consider him a threat to you and your operation. His elimination, therefore, will please me no end."

29

Corran hated waiting. It seemed that since he'd left the rest of the Rogues with the Ithorian he'd done little but wait. After departing from the Ithorian's jungle—which was just one apartment within a whole complex filled with such apartments so the Ithorians could live together, as was their wont—he had used a public comm station and had called a number Rima had given him. The recording at the other end asked him to punch in a personal code, which he did, then he was given instructions on where to go.

Being careful to see he was not followed, he went to the location indicated. He found himself at a biopod hotel run by a Selonian. The tall, slender creature showed Corran to a small pod midway up on a wall of pods. As Corran climbed in he estimated the cockpit of his X-wing was larger. He dialed the external opaquing for his door up to full, then lay down in a pod that measured two meters in length, a meter in height, and a meter in width.

He immediately adjusted the temperature up—it was set low enough that he figured a Sullustan had been the last occupant—and opened a channel on the comlink to let music fill the pod. The datapad display unit above his face flashed through a series of instructions concerning fire exits, the location of refresher facilities, and the locations of nearby culinary establishments. He watched that until one advertisement showed a Gamorrean digging a paw into a bowl of something pink that pulsed, at which point the need for locating food became moot.

He remained at that location for two days before Rima came for him and took him to another place that was better suited to his needs, though it was in need of a great deal of repair. Plasteel sheets covered one of the apartment's walls. The furnishings, while hardly worn at all, were tattered and torn. The carpet had some blood in it and transparisteel occasionally crunched underfoot. The interior wall opposite the plasteel wall had been heavily dented by an oblong, vaguely cylindrical object.

Corran looked at her. "Is this the place where a speeder bike came crashing through the wall?"

Rima stared at him, somewhat stunned. "How do you know about that?"

"I was driving the bike that sent it into the window." Corran ran his hand over the impression in the wall. "The others wouldn't have told you about that. The Rogues didn't know and the Black Sun people aren't much for talking about their defeats. I'd imagine they have turned the story into something about rescuing the aliens from the Imps, right?"

"I do not know." Rima shrugged easily. "My primary concern has been seeing to it that you and Erisi are taken care of. I apologize for quarantining you two, but I don't know how much has been relayed to Imperial Intelligence."

"I don't know either, but I made some basic arrangements before I headed out and called the emergency number you gave me. Inyri Forge was going back to the Headquarters. That is one place Fliry Vorru can be found. It was my bad luck that Zekka Thyne was there the night I visited. That's what initiated the chase that ended with my running into the Imperial raid on the Alien Combine.

"The other Rogues have the Headquarters as a touchstone. I gave them no way to reach me and I have no way to reach them save through using Inyri as a cutout. I imagine the Alien Combine also has a way to reach the other Rogues. Has there been any word on Aril?"

Rima shook her head.

Corran frowned. "Does that mean there's no information or there is, but I don't need to know it?"

"There is no news." Rima's shoulders sagged just a bit. "There was a lot of confusion in the aftermath of the raid. Some reports have suggested a group of Sullustans were led off early on, but we've no confirmation of that, nor any indication they are in any of the prisons here. They vanished and so has Aril."

"People tend to do that." Corran's hands knotted into fists. "One thing that's important, I need to talk to Commander Antilles."

"Who?"

Corran smiled wearily at Rima. "I'm here, the other Rogues are here." *Including Tycho.* "Commander Antilles has to be here and I need to speak with him. I saw something the other night that he needs to know about."

"If it is that important, perhaps I need to know about it?"

Not with you being as close to Tycho as you seem to be. Corran shook his head. "You don't need to know, Rima, sorry. Squadron business."

"Very well." The white-haired woman shrugged. "Stay here until I return for you."

"As ordered." Corran drew the blaster from the makeshift holster he'd fashioned in the lining of his jacket. "Can you get me some spare power packs for this thing?"

"I'll see."

"That doesn't sound very hopeful. What if stormtroopers raid this place?"

"Ask if you can borrow some from them." Rima gave him a grim smile. "All they can say is no."

He waited two more days, spending his time working up a line that would convince stormtroopers to surrender their weapons to him. He found it a singularly frustrating occupation because, since they tended to be much larger than he was, he knew he could not intimidate them. Appealing to their humanity seemed a dubious prospect, as did appealing to their sense of fair play.

He spent the vast majority of time in the apartment going over the earlier events and trying to draw conclusions from all of it. First and foremost he was certain he'd seen Tycho Celchu talking with Kirtan Loor. That meant the operation on Coruscant was busted wide open. With Tycho on Coruscant the Imps clearly had full descriptions and datafiles on everyone in the squadron. He had to assume they were under surveillance or would soon be watched.

The fact that he'd stumbled across Tycho and Loor meeting in public *did* bother him a bit. If Tycho was an Imperial agent—as had been everyone else who'd ever been at Lusankya—why wouldn't the meeting have been held in an Imperial facility? The obvious answer to that question was that Tycho hadn't appreciated his Lusankya experience and was being wary of trapping himself in an Imperial stronghold. He was smart enough to know the Imps couldn't be trusted, so he was probably gouging them for sufficient credits to buy some far-away world and live like a Moff for the rest of his life.

The fact that their mission had so clearly been blown really left the Rogues only one choice: leave immediately. He felt he had collected enough information about the general level of security on the planet to be useful, but he also expected all that to change in the near future, if it had not changed already. He had to assume that whatever any of the Rogues had learned was of dubious value, and therefore, their mission was a bust.

The only way to salvage any of this is to go home and start fighting against the Empire again.

Before he could come up with another plan that would be effective, but also before he'd admitted defeat to himself, Rima came for him. She resisted answering his questions about their destination and seemed abnormally taciturn and withdrawn, but she did give him power packs for his blaster, so he chose not to press her for information. He did wonder what had gotten into her, but he chose not to ask questions on the street. When they slipped into the Headquarters he found other things to occupy his attention, especially his being ushered down the back corridor to a side room where Wedge sat waiting for him.

Corran snapped to attention and saluted as Rima left the room. "Horn reporting, sir."

Wedge returned the salute, then smiled and gave Corran a back-slapping hug. "It's good to see you're alive and well, even though the last time I saw you, you were doing your best to kill me and a number of other people."

What? "Excuse me, sir?"

"I was in the apartment where you sent a speeder bike through the window." Wedge held a hand up and Corran saw some half-healed cuts on it. "Nothing major, but there's not much bacta down here, so I have to heal the traditional way. Did find some ryll tincture that killed infection, though."

"If I had known, I'd . . ."

"No one save the driver was badly hurt, so don't worry." Wedge inclined his head toward the door. "Winter tells me you wanted to talk with me? Something you could only tell me?"

"Winter?" Corran frowned for a second. "Ah, you mean Rima . . ."

"Right. We'd met before. She and Tycho are friends."

"So I've gathered, which is why I wanted to talk to you." Corran clasped his hands at the small of his back. "Five days ago, right here in the Headquarters, I saw Tycho Celchu talking with Kirtan Loor, an Imperial Intelligence agent."

Wedge looked surprised, then frowned and slowly shook his head. "Five days ago?"

"Yes, sir."

"That's impossible."

"I know what I saw, sir." Corran jerked a thumb back toward the bar. "I saw him as sure as the Emperor is dead." He tried to make his statement sound certain, but he was getting feelings of confusion and sorrow from Wedge's expression. "Really, I did see him."

"That's impossible, Corran. Five days ago Warlord Zsinj attacked our base at Noquivzor. The barracks complex got hit hard. They're digging through the rubble now but they don't expect to find survivors." Wedge hesitated for a moment, then swallowed. "Our support staff was devastated. Zraii survived, but that was the only confirmation they'd give me."

"What about Whistler?" Corran blurted out the question before he realized how callous it made him sound. "He's only a droid, but . . ."

Wedge patted him on the shoulder. "I understand. I don't have word of him directly, but Zraii was working on our fighters in the hangar, so I have to suppose most of our astromechs were there with him. The hangar escaped serious damage. If any news comes through, I will let you know."

"Thanks." Corran took a deep breath and tried to sort everything out in his mind. "So what you're telling me is that if I saw Tycho, I saw a ghost?"

"That's about the size of it."

"And you told Rima, er, Winter? That's why she was so quiet."

"I just got word myself and broke it to her as gently as I could. We're still hoping—bacta can do miracles if there's even the remotest spark of life—but things do not look good." Wedge sighed. "Of course, that's the least of our worries right now."

"Oh?"

Wedge nodded. "Zsinj's attack is driving the invasion schedule forward. We have a new mission and you're here to help plan it out."

"I'll do my best, sir."

"Let's hope we can *all* do our best, and then some." Wedge slowly exhaled. "We've got to come up with a plan that will let us, with a minimal amount of lead time, take over or destroy whatever we need to bring down Coruscant's shields and leave the world open to invasion.

30

Corran followed Wedge from the small room into the hallway and farther along to an even larger room. The first people he saw there were the Bothan Asyr and the Devaronian he'd helped to escape from the warehouse. They were already seated at the large round table in the middle of the room. As he came around Wedge he saw Fliry Vorru looking very Imperial and Zekka Thyne looked pale and in a bit of discomfort.

Looks like not everyone escaped unharmed.

"Corran!"

"Iella!" Arching his back, he picked her up in a hug and hung on tight. "I can't believe you're here."

"Gil did this to me. The identities he set up were on Coruscant." Iella pulled back away from him, but kept his hands in hers. "I can't believe it's you."

If seeing Thyne hurt had made Corran feel good, seeing Iella made him feel . . . *almost whole. I've spent too long with nothing and no one from my past aside from Whistler. It was as if that world didn't exist.* He smiled. "Where's Diric?"

Iella's smile froze for a second, then she glanced down. "I don't know."

"I'm sorry. What happened?"

"A year ago or so he was picked up in an Imp sweep and never came home. I bolted, made some Alliance contacts, and joined the Rebellion. There's been no word and after this amount of time . . ."

Corran nodded and hugged her again. Diric Wessiri had been an interesting man. Old family wealth allowed him to lead a life of leisure. He viewed life as a collection of phenomena to be studied and experienced, but he was not one to let those experiences change him. He was easily twenty years Iella's senior, but they fit together like oxygen and hydrogen. Diric didn't always agree with things CorSec did, but he made an attempt to understand what had been done, and that quest for enlightenment had impressed Corran.

This is not the time to tell Iella that Gil is dead and that Loor killed him. There will be opportunities later, I'm sure. "Diric was special, but so are you. It's great to see you again despite everything else."

"I agree." Iella squeezed his hands gently. "And Mirax asked to be remembered to you."

A smile blossomed on Corran's face. "She's here? How?"

"The *Skate* brought the rest of the squadron here and couldn't get away." Iella frowned. "I would have thought the others had told you how they got here."

"We were a bit busy when we ran into each other."

"No kidding. Mirax has threatened to give you speeder bike lessons. First rule, she says, is stay away from buildings."

Corran laughed aloud. "Yeah. We'll have to discuss that more."

Thyne snarled. "How long is this chummy crap going to go on?"

"Patches, someday when you have a friend you'll learn this is what you do when you haven't seen each other for a while." Corran released Iella and she moved off to take a seat next to Winter.

"Well said, Lieutenant Horn." Vorru folded his hands

together on the table. "However, time is of the essence, I gather. Shall we get things under way? Commander?"

Corran took a seat beside Wedge, placing Winter on his right hand. Iella sat next to her, then the two aliens and finally Vorru and Thyne. Corran noticed that Thyne held his right hand and forearm protectively over his stomach. *Gut-shot. Painful. Good.*

Wedge stood. "I want to keep this as simple as possible. Since the warehouse incident we have all come to agree that working together to oppose the Empire is preferential to each going our own ways. Each of our groups has strengths and weaknesses, most of which overlap to minimize our exposure to the enemy. We can all agree that we will fare better on Coruscant once the Empire is overthrown and accomplishing that end is a goal of the Rebellion.

"Originally Rogue Squadron was sent here to recon Coruscant and gauge the vulnerable points for later exploitation. The problem is that Warlord Zsinj is testing both the Empire and the Rebellion. The Imperials know that to attack him is to weaken themselves to the point where they cannot prevail. The Alliance knows that to pursue Zsinj would dilute our strength so that a strike at Coruscant won't be possible for years, perhaps even decades. This means the Alliance will have to strike in the very near future and they want us to open the gates to Coruscant."

Fliry Vorru tapped a fingertip against the tabletop. "Bringing down a planet's shields is not an easy proposition."

"Agreed." Wedge leaned forward on his hands. "The central computer complex here is the key. Is it fair to assume Black Sun's slicers have not been able to insert code into the master programs that control the planet?"

The white-haired man sat back in his chair. "I believe the discussion of that point is premature."

"Oh?"

"Quite so, Commander." Vorru nodded toward the representatives of the Alien Combine. "Their stake in this is quite clear. The Imperial regime is decidedly cruel and inhumane in dealing with them. The liberation of this planet would benefit them enormously. And you Rebels, well, you would be achieving a goal you've been focused upon for at least seven years. I mean, Winter dear, it is every Alderaanian's dream to replace your lost world with Coruscant, is it not?"

Winter's eyes glittered coldly. "The Alliance's goal is to see the death of the evil that destroyed our world. Alderaan cannot be replaced and certainly not with this transparisteel and duracrete mausoleum for an Empire."

Wedge folded his arms. "Your point, Vorru?"

"My point, Commander, is that the Alliance is not likely to be any more favorable to Black Sun than the Empire was. Less, in fact, I suspect. I want to know what is in this plan to reward me and my people for their cooperation."

Corran snarled. "Why don't you start with your liberation from Kessel?"

Vorru smiled delicately. "You would gladly see me back there, would you not, Lieutenant? If your plan succeeds you might find yourself appointed Minister of Security. If the cursing about you and your family done by Thyne here is any measure of Horn efficacy, I think I prefer having Ysanne Isard opposing me. What I would like, Commander Antilles, is some guarantee of clemency for those of my people who work to help you overthrow Isard."

"And if that is not possible?"

"Relocation to a world of my choosing, a world that will be made part of your Alliance with me at its head."

"A world you will turn into a haven for crime?" Iella looked disgusted.

Corran shook his head. "He's smarter than that. He'll solicit bribes from worlds so he doesn't end up there. He'll be rich enough to buy a star system or two."

Vorru opened his hands. "I seek a world where I can live out my days in peace and you think poorly of me. I find it hard to believe you hold the rehabilitative qualities of Kessel in such contempt."

"Enough." Wedge held a hand out to forestall Corran's reply to Vorru's unctuous comment. "I'll give you my personal guarantee you and your people will not be held responsible for crimes committed while you are acting in concert with us. That doesn't mean a sociopath like Thyne here is free to slaughter innocents. We're only going to hit legitimate military targets. The streets start running with blood and I'll burn your people down myself. I think this is the best offer you're going to get."

"It's acceptable. For now." Vorru nodded. "And, no, our slicers have not been able to get into the main computer."

Thyne shifted uncomfortably in his chair. "We should just blow it up. Everything will stop and the shields will come down."

"No they won't." Winter frowned. "Damage to the main computer system will transfer control to satellite facilities. While they are not as well guarded as the main facility, they will not be easy to take over. There is also a possibility that crucial systems, such as shield control, could get shunted to another satellite center if there is trouble with one. In other words, to get the shields down that way we'd have to guarantee a strike at *all* of the satellites as well as the main center, and we don't know for certain where *all* of those subsidiary centers are."

Vorru smiled. "I can furnish you with those locations, but your reservations about so explosive a plan are justified. It strikes me that something more subtle would be preferential."

Asyr laid a hand gently over one of Vorru's. "I don't understand why it is so difficult to slice code into the main computer. There are billions of transactions and messages that go through the system on an hourly basis. Something ought to be able to get through, shouldn't it?"

Wedge shrugged. "Seems like it, but I guess not. Winter?"

She tucked a strand of white hair back behind her

ear. "The Imperial computers operate through a very restrictive language that has a hierarchical command and access structure. Programs that go in to be effective across the system have to be authorized at the highest security levels. These levels are ultra-secure. Programs are scanned for content and that content is compared to their access levels. If a system program comes in without an access code that is cleared for entering system programs, it's dumped."

Corran frowned. "If you were able to wrap a program up in the right disguise, it would get through, right?"

"Presumably, but we don't have the right codes. Those codes are changed by the hour and old memory cores are swapped out daily and destroyed within a week—though after a day's worth of use they're pretty well ready to be junked anyway. Each night clean new memory cores are placed in the computers and trillions of exabytes of transactions are transferred to the new cores. This happens throughout the system."

Asyr nodded. "The production facility for the Palar memory cores is on the Invisec border. Nasty work making the things. All sorts of noxious chemicals go on the data retention surfaces, then a lot of energy gets used in formatting the cores. We lose people every day in that plant."

Wedge folded his arms. "If they're getting new cores daily, how does the transfer of data occur? I mean, if an old core is replaced with a new core, how does the data from the old core get onto the new core?"

"They have two banks of cores and the data is transferred from one to the other. The process doesn't take that long." Winter smiled. "The Imperial Senate's computer system used the same security system, but on a much smaller scale. Half a standard hour is all it should take to complete the operation."

Corran sat back. "What happens to the transactions that occur while the transfers are taking place?"

"They get caught on a subsidiary memory bank and

queued up to be sent into the main banks when the appropriate cores are free. Then those cores send the data over into the new banks."

"Okay, Winter, now what sort of program governs the transfer of data between the banks?"

She looked at Corran oddly. "Pretty basic stuff, universal to every system really. It goes into cores when they're formatted. What are you getting at?"

"Data goes from the first bank to the second, right?"

"Yes."

"And it goes fast because, presumably, it was checked as it came in and anything bad was discarded, right?"

"Yes."

"So if something on one of the subsidiary cores was shot over into the security core during the transfer, it wouldn't be checked by the second bank, right?"

Winter began to smile. "And altering the transfer code on one of the subsidiary disks so it would send a Rebel program over when the secure transfer was taking place, instead of blocking that transfer the way it's supposed to, wouldn't be that hard . . ."

"Because," said Asyr, "we have access to the plant where the cores are manufactured and we can alter the code used to format the memory cores."

"Right." Corran beamed. "We send over a program that causes us to be given clearance codes and addresses for the shield maintenance programs and we can bring the shields down at will."

Vorru bowed his head in Corran's direction. "CorSec's gain was Black Sun's loss. You have a devious mind—it is a pity you decided to use it to hunt us."

Corran winked at him. "That's the trick of it—I can't stand the thought of a criminal who's dumber than I am profiting by his crimes. Neither could my father, which explains why we shortened Patches's career."

"If your father was *that* smart, he'd still be alive."

Corran refused to be goaded. "This operation is a little bit more important than punching holes in your fantasy life, but the time will come."

Thyne started to get up, but Wedge pushed him back into his chair. "Stay down."

"Make me."

Vorru's right hand struck fast and slapped Thyne on the belly. The younger man howled, then, as he doubled over, Vorru grabbed him by his neck and slammed his forehead into the table. Thyne, glassy-eyed, rebounded and Vorru flung him from his chair. "For some people discipline is a *lesson*. For others it is a lifetime."

A shiver ran down Corran's spine. *He goes from gracious to vicious in less time than it takes for darkness to come in when a light goes out. And Thyne is out like a light.* He exchanged a knowing glance with Iella and saw her shake her head.

Wedge looked at the man on the floor, then shrugged. "We have enough, I think, to begin some planning. Winter, if you can have your slicers begin the programs we'll need, that will be a big help. Asyr, we'll need the basic security setup at the Palar plant, plus the routines and any computer security information you can get us." He looked at Vorru. "And you . . ."

"I will find out if any of the computer core technicians have any interesting vices we can exploit or an interest in exploiting the vices we have to offer."

"I think that will be fine." Wedge smiled. "In two days we will meet again and see how close we are to making the plan work."

31

Kirtan Loor's hands convulsed into fists. *Who is more stupid, a fool or someone who relies upon a fool?* Zekka Thyne's initial report about a planning meeting for what the Rogues would be doing to bring Imperial Center down had seemed promising. Thyne had told him who had attended and it had pleased Loor to learn Iella Wessiri and Corran Horn had been reunited. The fact that he'd not known Iella was living right under his nose did not thrill him, but her location had been outside his area of immediate interest until she became part of Rogue Squadron's operation.

The datafiles that the Imperial Intelligence organized crime division had sent over to him had provided interesting information on Fliry Vorru as well as the Devaronian, Dmaynel Kiph, but of Asyr Sei'lar they had no record. Though he had been chastened before by Ysanne Isard about drawing unwarranted conclusions, Loor decided Sei'lar was probably a member of some Bothan spy network. The possible existence of an independent Bothan Intelligence operation on Imperial Center suggested the Alliance was not a wholly unified front, which meant

Iceheart's strategy for dividing and destroying them piece-meal had even greater merit.

What angered Loor was Thyne's deception—a deception that became quite apparent from subsequent reports. Thyne had said the first meeting had merely been organizational and had not produced any sort of a working plan. In the five days since that meeting, though, Thyne had been given certain tasks to perform that ran outside the usual duties he had within Black Sun. Initially he had overseen the collection of all sorts of data from the Black Sun's gambling and spice operations on Imperial Center, but he only collected the datacards. He had no idea what information they contained.

After two days of that he had been shifted over to equipment procurement. While his activities provided Loor with an interesting window on the black market availability of almost anything, it did not give him the sort of information that would be useful for countering the Rogues' operation. Thyne was overbuying weapons and having them delivered to any number of sites. In this Loor recognized an effort to provide far too many sites for Imperial Intelligence to adequately cover.

It seemed clear to Loor that Thyne had been isolated by the command group and given jobs that, while valuable, were not crippling if bungled. Thyne was not the only person buying weapons on the black market so Loor had to conclude that perhaps *none* of the arms Thyne had collected would be used. Loor would have decided Thyne's cover had been blown, but Vorru's file left little doubt about how the man would have been dealt with if Black Sun knew Patches was working with the Empire.

Several things seemed obvious to Loor. The first was that Thyne had managed to show himself to be unreliable. He assumed this was because Thyne clearly would have loved to supplant Vorru as the head of Black Sun and Vorru, just as clearly, would want to prevent that from happening. Thyne's animosity for Corran and Iella could have also made him a liability in any planning councils. Loor had decided that Thyne had been ejected from the initial meeting before plans had been discussed and only later learned that Thyne had been concussed and amnesia blanked the substantive part of the meeting.

The spy within Rogue Squadron had not been present at the meeting. The spy's subsequent reports had been singularly useless. The planning council had compartmentalized the jobs needed to complete the operation, so the spy's activities proved less enlightening than Thyne's. Having Rogue Squadron personnel maintain a low profile did make sense, since they were not as familiar with Imperial Center as other members of the conspiracy, but it made their activities useless as indicators of what was going to happen.

The only saving grace in all of it was that things appeared to be building slowly. Isard had told Loor that nothing could happen before two weeks—the incubation period of the new strain of the Krytos virus. The Sullustans taken in the warehouse had been injected with the virus ten days earlier so he was very close to his deadline already. Isard said she'd already introduced the virus into the water supply, so countless creatures were already ingesting it. Loor himself had taken to boiling water and only drinking wines imported from other worlds—even though the virus was not supposed to infect humans, he wanted to take no chances.

Loor sat back in the shadowed depths of his office and rubbed a hand against his forehead. The key to taking any planet was to lower its shields and drop troops. While a planetary bombardment might cause a lot of damage, only troops on the ground could take and hold real estate. Without the shields going down, that couldn't happen, so the shields had to be the logical target for the Rogues.

The obvious target for taking the shields down was to attack the shield generators themselves. Loading a landspeeder full of Nergon 14 and having a suicide bomber run it into a generation station seemed the most expedient way of dealing with the shields. Two facts argued against that as a strategy—the sheer number of stations would require a metric ton or two for the Rebels to obliterate them all and the Rebels had not, to his knowledge, purchased any Nergon 14 so far. More importantly, destroying the shield generators would work against their future efforts to hold the planet.

A strike against the power generation stations had similar problems. There were even more of them than there were shield generation stations. The planet's electrical grid was coordinated such that an area that lost its local power plant would immediately have energy supplied by others in nearby sectors. Flickering lights would be the only sign of disruption. In his months on Imperial Center Loor had only seen lights flicker when one of the powerful local thunderstorms broke over a building where he was.

The obvious target was the computer that controlled everything on Imperial Center, but Loor had seen prisons that had less security than the central computer. The center had its own platoon of stormtroopers and the barracks within a fifty-kilometer radius had orders to respond to alarms there with all speed and firepower at their command. The facility itself had been built with more demanding specifications than those of any other building on the planet, including the Imperial Palace. Rumor had it that if the Death Star had been used against Imperial Center, the computer center would have been a recognizable and salvageable piece of debris.

An armed strike on the computer center would seem doomed to failure, but the presence of Rogue Squadron did make it a bit more viable. If they had fighters—and fighters of various types were available on the black market—they might be able to intercept and down some of the incoming troops. That would give the attackers more time, though the outcome would still be dismal for the Rebels. The ground-based TIE fighter squadrons in the area would be able to counter the fighter threat, so placing them on alert was a precaution he would suggest to Isard.

Perhaps the most difficult part of guarding against

the Rebel action was balancing on the razored edge of Isard's plan. She wanted to give Imperial Center to the Rebels, saddling them with responsibility for a population that would drain them of bacta and fluid capital, effectively hobbling them and pinning them in one place. If his precautions against Rebel action were too obvious, the Rebels might do something unusual, giving them the planet before she wanted them to have it or, worse yet, convincing them to scrub their invasion. The idea of facing her anger if things went wrong filled Loor with dread.

Still, there are only four more days until her minimum deadline, two and a half weeks until the maximum. I'm close to success. Loor nodded slowly in the darkness. "If Derricote delivers what he promises with this Sullustan group, the Rebels will take a dying world and their movement will die right along with it."

32

Corran wetted a small cloth swab with ethyl alcohol and rubbed it over the focal end of the BlasTech DL-44 Heavy blaster pistol. He peered at it closely, then gave it one more light pass with the cloth. As the alcohol evaporated, he saw Gavin reflected in miniature. "Ah, Gavin, this is the third time you've asked me if you could ask me a question."

The kid blushed as he snapped the trigger assembly for his SoroSuub S1BR into the receiver housing. "I know, sorry." Gavin kept his voice low enough that no one in the warehouse space aside from Corran could hear him. "I wanted to ask you about, um, you know."

Corran winced. He *didn't* know, but that sort of thing was only said as preface to a question about killing or sex. Since Gavin had long ago become an ace and had acquitted himself well in the firefight in the warehouse across Invisec, Corran assumed the question had to be about sex. *His parents should have told him about this before they let him go off to war, shouldn't they?* Corran looked around to see if Wedge was nearby, figuring he would do a much better job helping Gavin.

He couldn't see Wedge anywhere. Corran shrugged

his shoulders and eased the concentration element into the barrel of the blaster pistol. "What's your question?"

Gavin set his face in what he clearly thought was a serious expression, but the general youthfulness of his features undermined the effort. "On Tatooine, well, in Anchorhead, well, in the area around the farm, it was small and so . . . We didn't have a school the way you did on Corellia, see, we all took classes via a local HoloNet and sent lessons in on datacards, you know . . ."

Corran fit the barrel assembly together and snapped it into the gun's frame. "Gavin, are you trying to tell me you don't know how to kiss a girl?"

The young man pulled his head up and blinked, then frowned. "Anchorhead may have been small but not *that* small."

"Kin don't count."

Gavin blushed. "I wasn't related to everyone around there, you know."

Corran raised his hands and smiled. "I know, I know, I was just giving you a hard time. What is it that you want to know?"

"Well, you've been around a lot. And you come from Corellia." Gavin's voice dropped precipitously. "You've seen, you know, two people get together, but they're different, right?"

"Do you mean like Erisi and me? We come from different worlds, but we're both human—though we haven't gotten together."

"No, I mean like Nawara and Rhysati."

"Oh." Corran nodded slowly. Throughout the galaxy the permutations of relationships between two or more individuals were legion, as were the rules, formal and otherwise, that governed their conduct. Prohibitions on relationships between races and classes and castes varied from planet to planet, but the rules governing interspecies relationships tended to be largely similar. The majority of them were set by official Imperial policy—a policy CorSec officials had called "look but don't touch."

"Exotic and different can be very attractive, Gavin.

There are some folks who absolutely draw the line on dating outside their species while there are others who seem to be interested in experiencing anything and everything they can." Corran shrugged. "I guess I don't think it's *wrong*, but it just may not be right."

"I don't think I follow you."

"I wasn't very clear. Look, would you like to have children someday, have a family?"

"Yes, I think so."

"Okay, what if the person you fall for isn't capable of having children with a human?"

"I would, well, um, I don't know."

"There are other problems, too, and we're not talking the possible difficulties and dangers of making love, either."

"Dangers?"

"Sure. Suppose the person you're with is used to giving and getting gentle little love nips—with ten-centimeter-long teeth?" Corran hooked two fingers over like fangs. "Your hide isn't as thick as a Gamorrean's, so you'd be leaking."

"I hadn't thought about that." Gavin frowned and his shoulders slumped. "I mean, I don't think that will be a problem."

"Some species don't live as long as we do—though amid present company, life expectancy isn't that big an issue." Corran picked up a new heavy blaster and began to disassemble it for cleaning. "There are a lot of things you can take into consideration, Gavin, but it pretty much boils down to the same thing relationships between humans do: if you and the other person get along, problems can be worked out."

Gavin nodded. "So have you ever, you know . . . ?" The young man's voice trailed off as color rose in his cheeks.

Corran felt two hands on his shoulders and looked back to see Iella's smiling face above his. "Has Corran ever *what*?"

Corran shrugged his shoulders. "Nothing."

Mirax appeared on his left and leaned on the table between Corran and Gavin. Her dark hair had been pulled back into a thick braid. "The look on Gavin's face doesn't suggest it was nothing, CorSec."

Iella's hands tightened playfully on the back of his neck. "Come on, Corran, there's not much you haven't done."

A smile blossomed on Gavin's face and Corran suddenly felt outnumbered. And reluctant to answer Gavin's question. He knew it wasn't because of Iella's presence—she already knew the answer and could even tell the story better than he could. And he figured Gavin would find it amusing and make him less nervous. Clearly Gavin wanted to hear that Corran had dated an alien because the boy obviously had an interest in someone, and from the glances Corran had seen and the stories he'd heard, Gavin was thinking a lot about the Bothan, Asyr Sei'lar. While Corran thought she was a bit worldlier than Gavin could handle, he was willing to bet the farm boy from Tatooine could learn fast.

He found his reluctance to say anything came from Mirax's presence and his feelings toward her. Erisi and Rhysati had been paired together for their part of planning the operation, giving Corran time apart from her. It allowed him to put Erisi into perspective. Even though they were of the same species and even were attracted to each other, something deep down inside told Corran that their getting together would be *wrong*. *Not wrong, a disaster!*

Everything that made Erisi wrong seemed to make Mirax right. She understood him because of their common background. Granted their fathers had been enemies—Corran characterized them as *chronic* enemies instead of *mortal* enemies—but that gave them a bond he would never have with Erisi. Ultimately with Erisi he knew he'd have felt like a pet, whereas with Mirax he felt like a friend and equal.

During the planning operations Corran, Mirax, Gavin, and Iella had gone out and secured a lot of supplies for the operation. Things were scarce and, if available at all, were high priced. More than once Corran wished Emtrey had been on Coruscant to help with procurement, but Mirax proved every bit his equal in obtaining things. Whereas the droid might have used an instant analysis of a trader's wares to figure out his markup and squeeze him until his prices became reasonable, Mirax charmed, cajoled, wheedled, and even threatened. She'd learned every trick in the book from her father and Corran thought old Booster would be proud when he learned about her exploits.

But there is so much about her I don't know, like her reaction to learning I dated outside my species. Fear that she might see such an action as making him unclean or unworthy killed any quip he might have tossed at Iella. He looked up at Mirax but saw no suspicion or disappointment in her face.

Gavin fit two pieces of the blaster rifle together and tightened down a restraining bolt. "I wanted to know if he'd ever dated someone who wasn't human."

Iella laughed. "Well, there were plenty of women he dated who weren't human, in spirit, that is."

Mirax sniffed lightly. "But why bring the bacta queen into this."

"I never dated Erisi."

"No, you just pretended to be her Kuati impregnator, then kissed her in full view of the Grand Hall of the Galaxy in the Imperial Palace." Mirax shook her head. "Clearly no relationship there at all."

Corran laughed. "The way you tell it, I might have actually had fun."

Iella lightly cuffed the back of his head. "You always did complain about the easiest duty, Horn."

"Believe me, I'd take Chertyl Ruluwoor over Erisi gladly."

"Oh." Iella raised an eyebrow. "That's interesting."

Gavin frowned. "What's Chertyl Ruluwoor?"

Mirax straightened up and tapped a finger against her chin. "Sounds Selonian."

"It is." Iella smiled broadly. "Tell them, Corran."

"No, you tell them. You tell it better."

"You don't mind?"

"If I have to be mortified, I'd prefer not to do it to myself."

Mirax swung around and seated herself on the edge of the table. "This sounds wonderful." She winked at Corran, then looked up at Iella. "Go ahead, he'll survive it."

"True, it's not like it's the first time he's heard this." Iella smiled and Corran knew she'd put a good face on the incident. "Chertyl Ruluwoor was a female Selonian who had been sent to our unit to get some training. It was a cultural exchange program. She was tall—at least two meters—and slender. Selonians are all very lithe and she was covered with relatively short black fur that glistened a silver-blue when the light hit it right. Definitely gorgeous, definitely humanoid, but definitely not human.

"The Annual CorSec Awards Ball was coming up and she didn't know anyone. Selonians tend to be a very private sort of people and the only ones you see in public are sterile females. They run things in their society and maintain a family unit with fertile males and females, but she was all alone. The unattached male officers in our branch put together a pool to see who would take Chertyl to the celebration. Each man was required to buy a ticket for five credits and the winner—whom everyone considered a loser—would get the pot to compensate for the evening."

Mirax frowned. "It strikes me that the whole process was the wrong way around."

Corran smiled. "The Awards Ball pool is a tradition dating from a time when the Director had a daughter who, as decorum dictated, could not go to the Ball unescorted. The Director refused to order someone to ask her to go, though he did order participation in the pool. Most years the prize is someone in the squad who has volunteered to be 'won,' with the money going to the Survivors and Orphans fund."

"This year, though, the prize was Chertyl and she

knew nothing about it. Most everyone who knew what was going on thought it was barbaric, but they hid behind tradition."

Gavin smiled. "And Corran won, right?"

"You could say that." Iella gave him a gentle punch on the shoulder. "What he did was talk to the women who really wanted to go to the Ball with the other officers and gave them the impression that the whole thing had been rigged—whatever ticket their guy had would be selected as the winning ticket. The only way their man could get out of winning would be to get out of the pool. When pressed Corran allowed that he could be bribed into taking on just one more ticket—but it would have to be a secret. The women pressured their men to get Corran to take their tickets. By the time the pool winner was chosen, Corran had *all* the tickets."

Mirax beamed at him. "Quite enterprising, sir."

"Well, I knew I'd be miserable because of how my life was going at the time, so I saw no reason for anyone else to be away from the person they wanted to be with."

"But you did something noble. That's good."

"It gets better, Mirax. Corran gave the pool and the bribes to the fund, then went all out and showed Chertyl the time of her life. He hired a repulsorlimo, found out what kind of flowers were considered appropriate by Selonians, and flew out in his X-wing to the only import florist on Corellia who had them in bloom to get them. He even got a new formal dress uniform tailored up for the occasion. And he proved he cleans up very well.

"For her part, Chertyl was nothing short of stunning. She had that long, sleek physique that enabled her to wear a slinky gown over which light slithered. She wore a necklace of silver and aquamarine and a bracelet to match that looked like light playing across her fur. Every woman who saw her was instantly jealous and Corran was the envy of all the men. And, to make it worse, they actually enjoyed each other's company. That was about six months after his father's death and things had been rough for Corran, so the whole situation seemed perfect."

Being unable to stop a smile from tugging at the corner of his mouth, Corran nodded, and discovered he was disinclined to kill the smile. *That evening was a lot of fun. I put enough energy into it that I got to leave my life behind for a while.* "It *was* great."

Gavin leaned forward. "So what happened?"

Corran looked up at Iella. "Spare the salacious details, please."

Mirax smiled. "You can elaborate another time, Iella."

Iella shrugged. "Though Chertyl was infertile it didn't mean she was incapable. Apparently she had enjoyed the evening as much as Corran had and they continued to celebrate after they left the Ball. Is that circumspect enough for you?"

"It will do."

"Was it . . . ?" Gavin began to blush.

Corran gave him a wink. "Better."

Mirax raised an eyebrow. "Than what?"

"Imagine finding a pile of rocks, deciding to throw them out, dropping one, and having it split open to reveal a Corusca gem embedded in the middle."

"Oh, my."

"And with each stone after that, the Corusca gem is more lustrous and beautiful than the one before it."

"I see, very special indeed."

"And each of those stones, when fitted together, creates a brilliant, exquisitely carved sculpture."

"I've got the hologram digitized and analyzed here, Corran. Thanks."

Gavin blinked. "Wow."

Mirax's brown eyes narrowed. "So if it was as great as all that, how come you're here and not in some den on Selonia?"

Corran winced. "Well, there was one little, microscopic problem."

Iella nodded. "The chemistry wasn't right."

"Sounds like it was perfect to me." Gavin grinned broadly.

"Personal chemistry, yes, Gavin, was perfect. Personal *bio*chemistry was not, however." Iella rested a hand on Corran's shoulder. "The reason the lucky charm Corran wears is on a gold chain is because his sweat is acidic enough to tarnish something like silver. It's within normal range for a human, mind you, but just on the acidic end. And that was sufficient to get through the waxy surface on Chertyl's fur and irritate her skin. And as it turned out, Corran was mildly allergic to her fur."

"It was much like being sunburned all over for the both of us."

Mirax giggled for a second, then made herself appear sober and saddened. "That's horrible."

Corran shrugged. "Unfortunately, it's life." He looked over at Gavin. "There you have it, kid. My advice, see what happens. It can't hurt, except in rare cases."

Gavin set the blaster rifle down and stood. "Thanks. I'll take your advice, if you'll excuse me."

"Good luck, Gavin." Corran waved him on his way, then smiled up at Iella. "Nicely told."

Mirax's brows furrowed. "How much of that was true?"

"All of it, every bit."

She frowned. "That's so sad, though."

Corran shook his head. "Not really. We both knew we were living out a fantasy, but it wouldn't have worked in the long run. I had no desire to move to Selonia and become part of a broodhome. Chertyl knew she couldn't bear the children I'd want. We remained friends and both have wonderful memories. In fact, that was the best ending I had for any of my relationships."

"True, Corran, but that's because you never listened to my advice about the women you were interested in." Iella shook her head. "Disasters, every one of them."

Mirax smiled. "And what is your impression of the bacta queen?"

"Her? All wrong for Corran. Attractive, sure, but just not his kind of woman."

"My thoughts exactly. I've told him so, but he doesn't listen."

"Never has."

Corran held his hands up in surrender. "Stop, please. You may not think Erisi is right for me, and I don't really think so either—a conclusion I came up with on my own, too, I might add. Regardless, though, she doesn't deserve this. Ysanne Isard wouldn't deserve this."

Iella glanced down at him. "Actually, Ysanne Isard *does* deserve this."

Corran thought for a moment. "Yeah, you're right, she does, carry on. By the time you're done, I'll have finished cleaning all these blaster pistols. Then we'll be ready to do the job that really needs to be done."

33

Though General Derricote's office was no larger than his own, its stark white color made Kirtan Loor feel more vulnerable. He would have preferred waiting to deliver his message to the Director from his own office, but the delay the trip back would necessitate would not be acceptable. Ysanne Isard would be furious with what he had to say, so he saw no reason to compound her anger.

On one knee, he refused to look up when her image burned to life in the General's office. "What is so urgent, Agent Loor?"

"General Derricote's estimates of the incubation period for the Krytos virus in Sullustans was generous."

"What?" Loor could not see Isard's expression, but her voice sounded as it might if he had told her that the Rebels had just showed up with a Death Star. "Generous in what way?"

"Generous in his favor. He promised you ten days until the Sullustans began to sicken, but a dozen appears more correct. And . . ."

"There is more?"

"Yes, Madam Director. The virus has resisted airborne transmission. Contact with virus-laden fluids and tissues will still infect another individual, but fluid contact is still required."

"This is impossible, Loor, and I hold *you* responsible for all this. Look at me!"

Loor lifted his face and saw molten fury roiling in her left eye. "General Derricote gave me false information."

"He did that at Borleias, but you found him out."

"But I didn't have to be tracking Rogue Squadron's activities on Imperial Center at the time. I was worried about your deadline, which came and went today." Loor hesitated and found himself cringing in anticipation of her reply.

"The deadline was based on a ten-day incubation period followed by a week-long terminal cycle. This throws everything off." Isard's image towered over him. "What are the transmissibility figures? Is the virus jumping from species to species?"

"Flesh contact with ten ccs of viral fluid results in a twenty percent infection rate and the virus is viable for thirty-six hours outside a host, longer if the conditions are warm and moist. The virus can be frozen and thawed without lost of viability or lethality. If the virus is actually injected or injested, as little as one cubic centimeter is enough to infect a subject."

"And species migration?"

"General Derricote projects . . ."

"Projects! I want results, not projections." Isard's hologram slammed a fist into an open palm but the sound relayed by holo-link sounded muted and weak. "Order Derricote to begin replication of the current virus strains and release all of them into the water supply."

Loor again bowed his head. "I anticipated your request. Derricote says that in four days he should have sufficient supplies to take care of the planet."

"Tell him he doesn't have four days. Full replication and production begins immediately and batches go into the water supply when they are complete. I want it done now. I will tolerate no more mistakes, his or yours, do you understand?"

"Yes, Madam Director."

"And one more thing, Agent Loor."

"Yes, Madam Director?"

"Your last report on the Rogues indicated this evening appears to be when they are taking their first step at liberating Imperial Center. It is too soon. I won't have it. Scatter them, kill them, deal with them. This time tomorrow I do not want to have to worry about them."

"As you wish, Madam Director!"

Isard's image vanished revealing Derricote standing in the doorway to his office. He applauded politely. "That was a wonderful performance."

Loor snarled inarticulately and came up quickly. He buried his left fist deep in Derricote's stomach, then clouted him on the side of the head with a roundhouse right. The heavyset man stumbled sideways and slammed into the wall. He tipped shelves, overturning countless boxes of datacard journals, then abruptly sat down on the floor and wallowed in them.

Part of Loor basked in the disbelief on Derricote's florid face, but even that feeling of elation did not dull the rage in his mind. He grabbed a handful of Derricote's tunic and hauled the corpulent man to his feet. "You have placed me in mortal jeopardy because of your incompetence."

"Incompetence!? We are traveling paths that were previously shunned here. I have done the best I could. The fact that my efforts do not live up to specifications designated by those who have no idea about the true nature of . . ."

Loor slapped the man hard with his open hand, then tugged him out of the office. "First, your technicians are to start manufacturing the Krytos viruses in their myriad forms and start injecting them into the water supply. Now! You have lied about how long it will take to kill aliens and I'm not sure I trust your transmission figures so I want as much virus as available being used now as possible. Including the experimental versions."

"But . . ."

"No buts, General, just *now*." Loor's nostrils flared. "What else have you lied to me about? Is it as deadly as you say?"

"You have seen the results, Agent Loor."

"Yes, I *have* seen the results, but not all of them." Loor dragged Derricote stumbling after him through the laboratory to the hallway where the victims were kept. Loor tossed him on ahead and Derricote spilled to the ground in the sanitized corridor. "I will not pay for another of your mistakes, General."

Glancing to the right, Loor could see Quarren beginning to melt, so he turned away and studied a huddled group of Sullustans. They clustered around two small children who were vomiting violently. Half the adults tore at their own hair, pulling it out in great clumps. Some reeled away, others just fell and trembled as if being shaken by a Cyborrean battle dog.

Loor looked back down at Derricote. "Madam Director wants bacta to cure the Krytos virus."

"It will."

"Have you tested the Sullustan version for a cure?"

"No, there is no need to waste bacta . . ."

Loor kicked the man in the thigh. "Wrong answer, General. Get up here."

The General stood and Loor shoved him toward the transparisteel wall. "We will test the efficacy of bacta on the virus, General." Loor looked at the Sullustans and saw one adult desperately mopping vomitus from a child's face. "Those two, the child and the adult. Test it on them. I want them to survive, General, do you understand me?"

"Mother and child? How touching."

"Don't mock me, General. The child is younger and the disease has clearly ravaged it far more than the adult. And that adult, she is caring for the child. She can tell others how to care for victims of this virus, accelerating the desired effect on the Rebellion." Loor shoved a comlink into Derricote's fat hand. "Get your people in there now and save them. Do it."

"Or?"

"Or I give you a taste, here and now, of what the Rogues will face tonight." Loor smiled coldly. "I guarantee, General, you'll like it no better than they will."

34

Everything was going perfectly, then the Trandoshan dropped the memory core. Wedge's heart caught in his throat—it clearly intended to escape him altogether, but the forced smile and gritted teeth prevented it from getting away. The box landed on a corner that immediately crumpled, and there was no mistaking the moan of metal bending out of shape.

The Imperial technician's face drained of blood. "Oh, now there is trouble."

Wedge raised a hand. "Perhaps not, friend."

"I have no time and this incident will have to be reported and checked out."

"I think, perhaps, I have a solution to your problem."

"I hope so, for your sake." The small technician sniffed and looked around nervously. "If there is trouble, I will not be found at blame—you and your *alien* help will be held responsible."

The loading process had gone almost without a hitch. Each core had been packaged in individual boxes and a diagnostic datacard had been placed in a clear plastic container fastened to the box. The technician had selected forty Palar memory cores from the fifty-five available at the plant. Each datacard was checked and then a quarter of the boxes were opened and probes were run on these randomly selected cores. If the data on them matched the data on the card, the lot was assumed to be good.

The auxiliary cores were slightly different and only ten of them had been produced. Three of them had been formatted with the special codes and had serial numbers where the last two digits added to ten. The Trandoshan doing the loading had been told to drop a core if none of the specially prepared ones had been selected, but one had.

The one he dropped.

The Trandoshan trundled back to the remaining five boxes and picked one of the other two that had the Rebel coding on it. He started to lift it up, but the technician put his hand firmly on the box and pressed it back down to the ground. "No, you clumsy vermin, you will not select the core. My choice."

Wedge slapped the Trandoshan hard across the arm, stinging his hand on the creature's leathery hide. "Back away, Portha. Your clumsiness will be reported."

The big, lizardly Trandoshan hissed and shuffled back away from the boxes to stand over by Pash. The technician nodded slowly. "Thank you. They so seldom understand our problems."

"Indeed." Wedge scratched at the beard he had grown to help disguise himself. "You are quite right to make the choice yourself, but there is insufficient time to run the diagnostics yourself. Their cards have already shown you that they are clean, but you want it clear that you were scrupulous in making your random choice. If not, well, I doubt your superiors would be impressed."

"That would be very bad indeed."

"And we can't have that, so choose you shall. Several times, so there can be no doubt of the randomness of the choice. You'll see." Wedge smiled and spread his hands out. "There are five here. Pick three."

The man frowned for a second, then pointed to the first one and the last two.

Wedge motioned Gavin over. "Take the other two away."

Gavin slid the two designated units away into the depths of the factory's warehouse floor. Wedge hastily rearranged the remaining trio into a single line. *One of these is the unit I want him to take, two are not.* "Pick two more."

The man designated the two on the end. "I choose them."

"Good." He pointed to Pash. "Take that one away. Now pick one." Wedge wanted him to pick the first box, but the technician tapped the second one.

Wedge nodded, smiled, then turned and scowled at Gavin. "What are you waiting for? Get it into the truck with the others." As he gave Gavin the command, Wedge rested his foot on top of the chosen memory core. "Hurry up, the man's on a schedule, a tight schedule."

"Don't drop it," the technician snapped.

Wedge sighed. "The exotics here work hard, but you can't trust them—then I get a man like him who isn't much better."

The technician nodded as he watched Gavin carry the box to the repulsorlift truck and slide it into the back. "It's the fault of the Rebellion, you know."

"Do you think?"

"Of course. When the Emperor was still ruling there was no doubt about how things were to be done. Now . . ." The man shrugged his shoulders eloquently and Wedge nodded emphatically. "The people nowadays have stopped thinking because sloppiness no longer earns the sorts of rewards it did before."

"I think you are quite correct." Wedge smiled and rubbed his hands together. *Had you been thinking at all, my friend, you'd have seen that I forced your choice of box. You made the choice, but I decided what the choice meant. Had you chosen the two sliced cores at first, I would have discarded the other three. The illusion of choice has you satisfied.* He made a mental note to thank Booster Terrik for having so long ago taught him the value of letting people deceive themselves by showing him how to force a choice.

The technician made an entry on his datapad. "Even the stormtroopers are slipping. They tried to prevent me from coming into this sector this evening, but I would not be dissuaded by them, no, sir. I bulled on through and they let me go!"

"Stormtroopers?" Wedge shook his head, then pointed at Gavin. "Do you hear that, son? Even stormtroopers are becoming so undisciplined that you could join them. Perhaps those outside could tell you where their recruiting office is."

The technician looked surprised. "Son? Is he your boy?"

"Takes after his mother." Wedge guided the man toward his repulsorlift truck. "Don't want to keep you."

Suddenly sparks shot from the loading dock side door and rained down from the warehouse ceiling. A halo of brilliant white fire surrounded the door, then imploded leaving a smoking hole through which stormtroopers began to run. Duracrete and steel rained down from above as teams blasted their way in through the roof and descended on slender lines. Out past the nose of the computer center truck Wedge saw a Mekuun Hoverscout's blunt prow batter the far gate. It bounced back, fired one burst with its laser cannon, then came on again over the molten remains of the gate.

Wedge gave the technician a shove forward, then spun on his heel and started running back into the warehouse's shadows. He hurdled a line of memory cores, then cut left and back right as blaster bolts exploded all around him. Leaping over another line of crates, Wedge crouched down behind cover. From his right Iella slid him a blaster carbine, then activated her comlink. "Shiel, Ooryl, Wedge is clear. Open up."

From deeper in the warehouse both the Gand and the Shistavanen started firing with a pair of Merr-Sonn E-Web Heavy blaster cannons. The weapons were mounted on tripods and had very specific fields of fire.

Ooryl raked a stream of fire over the loading dock and out at the Hoverscout. The scarlet blaster bolts burned their way up over the vehicle's nose and punched through the cockpit windscreen. The cockpit exploded in fire and smoke.

Shiel concentrated his fire on the stormtroopers descending on the lines from the roof. The high rate of fire allowed him to track his shots and pick stormtroopers off the lines. Wedge and Iella added their fire, but concentrated it near the holes to shoot people just beginning their descent.

The exit over at the far corner of the factory exploded. Wedge hit his comlink. "Corran, report." He got nothing in reply and could see nothing but fire and twisted metal where a stairway had once been. The original evacuation plan had designated that stairway and the area beyond it, which Corran, Mirax, and some of the Black Sunners were holding, as their primary exit. *Not anymore.*

He looked at Iella. "Plan two. Fall back."

She passed the signal along via her comlink. Portha, Pash, and Gavin pulled back from their positions first while Iella and Wedge provided covering fire. Once they were set, Iella and Wedge pulled back, but they didn't get far. Even with covering fire from the heavy blasters and the others, the stormtroopers managed to concentrate enough fire to make it impossible for him to move.

Lying prone on the ferrocrete, with his left cheek pressed against the cool floor and sparks from burning crates stinging his right cheek, everything seemed to collapse in on him at once. Wedge knew that being in the warehouse in Invisec on Coruscant was utterly and completely insane—more so even than sending snubfighters out to destroy a Death Star. He should have been in an X-wing if he was going to be fighting Imperials. Having a firefight with stormtroopers was still one of the best ways he knew of committing suicide, and he was afraid he was going to prove it in the next three or four minutes.

In setting up their operation they had taken into account what would happen if a stormtrooper patrol happened to make a sweep of the Palar factory—and the two heavy blasters should have been more than enough to take care of the threat. The presence of so many stormtroopers meant they'd been sold out at least twice—once so the Imperial operation could be planned and again so the scouts they'd had outside the plant wouldn't warn them of the impending raid. *Corran said having Thyne organize the lookouts was a big mistake.*

More blaster bolts scorched the air above him. *If I don't do something fast, we're done.* Wedge pushed up on the bottom of his comlink and gave it a twist, setting the device on a new frequency. "This is Rogue Leader. Things are breaking up here. Track and recover on this signal. Come ready to shuck stormies."

"I copy."

Iella crawled over to him and glanced at the comlink. "Do I want to know?"

"I don't like working without backup." He smiled, then ducked his head as a blaster bolt scorched the air. "If we hang on we may get out of this fine."

"You're the Rebellion's hero, so I'll trust you." She gave him a confident smile. "Thyne sold us out, I'd bet."

"No takers." Another trio of bolts burned through the air above them. "Can't wait here. Let's move."

"How?"

Wedge grinned. "Call Shiel. Get him to use that cannon to burn us a path through this maze."

"Consider it done." Iella gave Shiel the command and the line of thick red bolts cut over and down. Memory cores exploded casting fiery debris everywhere. The memory platters whirled through the air, hit, and rolled throughout the warehouse. Smoke already coated the ceiling with a grey cotton cloud, but more rose to take it from benign to a darkly menacing thunderhead.

As nearly as Wedge could determine later, Shiel's firing on crates to clear a path for Iella and him was interpreted by the computer technician as an attempt to destroy the memory cores in the back of the repulsorlift truck. Whoever was driving it started the engine and ran power into the repulsorlift coils. The truck rose from the warehouse floor and started forward gingerly. The aft end began to drift left, but that was clearly preparatory to swinging around the burning Hoverscout.

Suddenly the truck lurched forward. Its right front fender slammed into the edge of the loading dock access port. The truck spun around to the left and backed into the burning Hoverscout. It rode halfway up onto the military vehicle before the repulsorlift coils shorted, dropping the truck down to crush the Hoverscout.

A titanic explosion shredded both vehicles and sprayed shrapnel throughout the loading dock area. The blast's shock wave sent crates flying and tossed Wedge around like a Chadra-Fan wrestling with a rancor. He landed hard on a crate, shattering it and the memory core it had contained. At the same time he felt something pop on his left side and got a sharp pain with each breath. *Ribs, but at least I can still move.*

He grabbed Gavin's proffered hand and got to his feet. The two of them sprayed blaster fire into the black cloud choking the far end of the warehouse, but very little in return fire headed in their direction. The stormtroopers clearly had gotten the worst of the blast, being closest to it when the Hoverscout's magazine of concussion missiles had blown.

Iella, Pash, and Portha had taken up stations around the doorway heading deeper into the factory complex. Beyond it Nawara Ven and Shiel were wrestling with their heavy blaster cannon. Rhysati and Erisi were out in front with Ooryl close behind. He sported a blaster carbine.

Wedge winced as he waved everyone on. "Go, go! This place is crawling with Imps. We were sold out so now we have to get clear."

Gavin's eyes grew wide. "But you're hurt, sir."

"I can still move, Gavin, and that's what we have to do." Wedge shoved him on ahead. "If we don't we're all going to be hurt a lot more."

35

Waiting in the plant supervisor's office Corran had a bad feeling about how things were unfolding out in the warehouse. The supervisor's holopad had been wired into the warehouse surveillance holocams. Wedge, the technician, Pash, Gavin, and Portha all marched around on the desktop like pieces in a hologame. Though everything seemed to be going well for his team, he couldn't shake the feeling that they were somehow losing.

Mirax sat behind the heavy steel desk and watched Wedge force the technician's choice of a new core with a big smile on her face. "Oh, the smuggler you could have been, Wedge Antilles! He's got this guy thinking he's made a totally random choice when Wedge had a core picked out from the beginning for him to take."

"I'll take your word for it." Corran paced back and forth behind her. The supervisor's office had two doors. The one at the front of the office led to a waiting room with a window that overlooked the warehouse. The other door, built into the office's back wall, led to a private stairwell and the private parking area below the warehouse floor. To avoid being spotted through the window, Mirax and Corran had taken up a position in the office.

Down below, in the parking area, Inyri and several other Black Suns waited with airspeeders to whisk the Rogues away.

"Take it easy. We're almost home free."

"I'll believe it when we're away from here and Winter's people can test the code." He again dropped a hand to the heavy blaster he wore on his hip, just to check how it was seated in the holster, then looked at the blaster carbine he held and made sure the safety switch was off. "Wait, what's that?"

"I don't know." Mirax leaned forward and poked at a sparking light at the edge of the hologram. "Someone's burning through the door!"

Corran smelled smoke and knew he was too far from the loading dock to be getting it from there. *Something else is burning. Too close.* He reached out with his right hand and roughly shoved Mirax from her chair. "Get down."

The wall between the waiting room and the office exploded inward. He saw it fragment and fire poured through the cracks. The pieces of wall disintegrated, breaking into smaller and smaller bits until they were nothing but pebbles and dust. The fire blacked the aluminum studs, ripping them free from the floor and ceiling, then propelled them into the office, gnarling and twisting them as they flew.

The force of the explosion lifted Corran off his feet and blasted him into the office's rear wall. Wallstone sagged and buckled, studs bent, but the wall did not collapse. The door leading into the stairwell crumpled and tore free of the hinges, allowing a great deal of the explosive force to blow out through it. The desk slammed back against the wall and Corran's legs fell across the top of it. His head and shoulders tipped down, his feet came up, and he crashed to the debris-strewn floor with blood streaming from his nose and an incessant ringing in his ears.

Through the dust and smoke he saw what appeared to be a quartet of stormtroopers dropping through a hole in the floor and standing on the ceiling. Dazed as he was it took him a moment to realize his perspective came from his still being upside down. Slightly more surprising than that discovery was the far more welcome realization that he still held the blaster carbine in his left hand.

He let his body sag to the right, then he rolled forward onto his stomach. The world swam into focus a moment later. He slid his right hand forward and got it wrapped around the weapon's pistol grip. His left hand moved up to grasp the barrel and he tightened down on the trigger.

His first shots hit a stormtrooper in the knees and dropped him back into his fellows. Only one of them turned toward him, the other two looked out at the warehouse floor that was lit by back and forth fire from dozens of blasters. The stormtrooper who had made the correct guess brought his carbine up and over, but only managed to trace a line of fire across the wall above Corran's head.

Corran walked his fire up the stormtrooper's midline, burning three holes navel, heart, and throat before a fourth knocked the man's helmet flying and dumped his body to the floor. The helmet bounced off the back of one of the other stormtroopers and clipped the helmet of the last one. Both men spun, their weapons coming around with deliberate and lethal intent.

Corran managed to rip off a burst that hit one of them in the thigh, then his blaster carbine stopped firing. The man he'd hit spun around and went down to one knee, but still appeared to be full of fight. Corran hit the power pack release button and reached down into his pants pocket for a replacement, but all he felt was tattered fabric and his own flesh.

Next to him the desk rose two centimeters off the floor, then tipped forward. It rolled awkwardly, half eclipsing him, and caught the full force of the last standing stormtrooper's fire. Corran rolled to his right, trying to take advantage of the cover. As he did so, Mirax rose up on one knee and scythed blaster fire back and forth across the last two stormtroopers. Her shots took the standing man in the middle, doubling him over, and blew apart the helmet of the one Corran had only wounded.

Corran saw her look down at him and saw her lips move, but he couldn't hear her past the ringing in his ears. He took a guess at what she was saying and forced a smile through the blood he could taste on his lips. "I'll live. They used concussion munitions but the wall stopped us from being knocked out." He scrambled up on his hands and knees. "Let's get out of here."

Mirax crawled over to the open doorway and slid down the door to the first landing. Corran followed, then the two of them ran down the remaining flights. Corran kicked the door to the basement garage open. Mirax went through low and he followed. What they found made her curse and the only good thing about it was the fact that he heard her oath.

Off to the right, heading out through the shadows, he saw four airspeeders going away. From the left, racing down a ramp and into the garage's dark interior, came six Imperial stormtroopers on Aratech 74-Y military speeder bikes. Five peeled off their formation to go after the airspeeders and one swung around toward them.

"Mirax, go!" Corran cast aside the useless carbine and drew his blaster pistol. She darted off toward the left and got behind one of the garage's massive pillars. She waved him toward her and made to come around and cover him, but a laser bolt from the speeder bike gouged a chunk of duracrete from near her head.

He shook his head and ran toward the approaching speeder bike. He cut to the right, snapped off two shots, then ducked his left shoulder and rolled to the side as the speeder bike's laser bolts sizzled over his head. He came up into a crouch with only twenty meters separating him from the speeder bike. As his blaster came up he saw the stormtrooper's right hand curl back, cranking the throttle. The bike roared forward and Corran knew the man intended to impale him on the spikes that jutted forward of the speeder bike's vector-control surfaces.

Corran twisted to the right, willing his body to flow out around the sharp spearhead mounted on the front of the craft. The vector-control surface shredded the left side of his jacket, passing just beneath Corran's left arm. He tried to bring his blaster around to get a shot off at the stormtrooper, but all he managed to do before the stormtrooper's knee caught him in the hip and spun him to the ground was slam the weapon down hard on the driver's left hand.

The blow to the man's hand jerked the vector-control back making the speeder bike's nose veer sharply upward. It struck sparks from the ceiling and a moment later the bike's tail joined in producing fireworks as it scraped along on the ground. The forward control surfaces buckled and curled in as the bike jammed them hard against the ceiling. The bike began to invert, spilling the rider, then bounced against the floor and ceiling before it stopped and hovered.

The stormtrooper skidded along on his armored back, spinning around like a top. His legs finally smacked up against a pillar stopping his spin. He shook his head and tried to climb to his feet, but Mirax stepped out from behind the pillar and dropped him with a kick to the head.

"Now what, Corran?"

A muffled explosion from above shook the garage. Dust and peeling paint fell from the ceiling. Smoke and dust billowed out of the doorway from above. "I know we're not going back up there."

She frowned. "Okay, one choice down. Care to pick another?"

He shrugged, then saw blaster bolts darting through the garage. One of the airspeeders had turned off at the last moment and was racing back toward them, with a speeder bike in pursuit. The airspeeder's driver neatly wound the vehicle around and through a complex course, never giving the stormtrooper a clean shot. Even so, because of the speeder bike's shorter turning radius, it ate up the distance between them, making it only a matter of time before he drew close enough to cripple and kill the airspeeder.

Corran pointed toward the pursuit. "Fire at the speeder bike. Let the airspeeder know there's cover over here."

"What are you going to do?"

"Get luckier than I've been already, I hope." Corran ran over to the hovering speeder bike, grabbed the control handles, and started pushing it toward one of the open rows between columns. He swung into the seat and checked the weapon's control monitor. *It's good to go. Now I just need a target.* He hit the thumb switch on the vector-controller and sent a ruby laser bolt screaming out into the distance.

Mirax laid down a solid pattern of fire that hemmed the speeder bike in and the airspeeder driver took full advantage of it. She whipped the wheel to the right and shot straight down a row toward the end where Mirax and Corran stood.

The airspeeder passed in front of the hovering speeder bike and the second it was clear, Corran hit the firing switch. The speeder bike's laser cannon spat out a steady stream of scarlet energy darts. He expected the pursuing stormtrooper to fly his speeder bike right through the hail of bolts, but the pilot cut sharply to the left and swung wide of Corran's trap.

Fortunately that left him in the open for Mirax. Her burst of fire caught the man in the left flank and knocked him from the saddle. He hit hard, with his helmet splitting like the rind of an overripe meiloorun. His body rolled along, almost coming upright again, when it collided with a pillar and fell back to the ground slowly.

The airspeeder came to a stop between Corran and Mirax. "C'mon, get in."

Corran looked somewhat agog at the pilot. "Inyri, you came back for us?"

"Stay if you like, Horn, or come with me."

Mirax grabbed Corran by the shoulder and dumped

him into the rear seat, then hopped in beside Inyri. "I think he got hit in the head. Go."

Lying in the back of the airspeeder, Corran swiped a hand across his mouth and it came away bloody. He tore a chunk of the lining out of his jacket and started mopping up the blood. "What happened back there?"

"I don't know." Inyri brought the airspeeder out of the garage and immediately started it climbing. "We were below waiting the way we were supposed to, then we heard a couple of small explosions and one big one from the office at the head of the stairs. There wasn't any percentage in staying around, so we took off."

Her voice took on an edge. "I wasn't really coming back for you. The speeder bikes had an angle on exit and I figured that being last in line I'd be the first to die. I broke off and thought to run back to the way they came in, then I noticed you were shooting at the bike on my tail. When you got him, the least I could do was pick you up."

Mirax patted Inyri on the shoulder. "Intentions don't count, what you *do* does."

Corran sat up in the back seat. The only way Imperials could have gotten to the memory core factory and raided it when they did was if they had inside information about what was happening there and when it was going to take place. Without thinking too hard on the matter he could identify twenty people who knew about the operation and that number could have expanded exponentially if someone stupid started bragging.

From those who might have sold the operation out he immediately discarded any of the Rogues, Mirax, Winter, and Iella. All of them, save Winter, had actually been in the factory. Wedge said Winter was incorruptible. While it was not in Corran's nature to believe that about anyone, the fact that Pash Cracken and Iella also vouched for her let him clear her.

Mirax looked out through the windscreen. "Where are we going?"

"Zekka picked out a location for us to meet if things

didn't go as planned. We'll link up there and then see who else has survived this debacle."

As Inyri whisked them along a twisty, mind-boggling course through the city, ascending and descending through levels and around buildings, Corran continued considering suspects. In the back of his mind he knew the exercise was futile because there was no way he could prove his suspicions. He also knew that the first person on his suspect list, Zekka Thyne, would also be the last person on it. Corran knew Thyne had betrayed them, he knew it in his heart, and he didn't really need proof for that conviction.

His being placed in the position of lookout was perfect from the Imp point of view. He protested that he wanted something more important but Vorru forced him to keep that job. Even though I thought letting him organize lookouts was a bad idea, I was relieved since I wouldn't have him with a gun in a place where my back might be turned. Heck, I was even glad he was disappointed with his assignment. Unfortunately, without proof I'll have a hard time convincing others he's the Sithspawn who gave us up to the Imps.

Inyri swooped the airspeeder down and brought it in through a small round portal on the shadowed midlevel of a building. A round plug of a door rolled in place after they entered. Lights came on in a hangar, revealing it to be empty except for a racked speeder bike off to the right. Inyri brought the airspeeder to a stop, letting it settle on the hangar floor.

"I guess we got here before the others." With her hands on the top of the windscreen, Inyri pulled herself up out of the airspeeder. "I hope they make it."

"I can vote for that." Corran clambered out of the back of the airspeeder and walked over to the speeder bike. He pressed a hand against the cold metal of its engine housing, then turned as the doorway into the interior of the building opened.

"You'll want to get away from the speeder bike." Zekka Thyne emerged from the building with a blaster carbine leveled in Corran's direction. "Get your hands up. Hmmm. I can see why you security types like saying that, such a feeling of power. You, too, Terrik. Inyri, take their blasters."

Mirax frowned. "What's going on here?"

Corran raised his hands to shoulder height as Inyri collected his gun. "Patches sold us out."

Inyri shook her head. "Impossible. He hates the Imps as much as you do—as much as any of us do."

Corran jerked a thumb toward the speeder bike. "The engine's cold. We got no warning because he wasn't there. Didn't want to take a chance the Imps would shoot him up."

"I knew you'd figure it out, just the same way I knew they wouldn't get you." Thyne sneered at him. "You and your father always were lucky. That's the only way you got me, your old man was luckier than I was."

"It wasn't luck. My father was *smarter* than you were. He still is."

"He's dead."

"My point stands." Corran shrugged. "What did you figure you'd tell Vorru after everyone else got wiped out in the raid? Or did you figure it wouldn't matter?"

Mirax slowly nodded. "He's got a plan to get away, Corran. He's going to sell you to his Imperial contact for safe passage and a new identity on a new world."

Thyne's smile broadened to hideous proportions. "Close, very close, except in one detail." The carbine rose to shoulder height. "Kirtan Loor just wants a corpse."

The whine of a single blaster shot filled the hangar and the bolt tinted everything with the color of blood. Thyne staggered, then slumped back against the wall. His legs collapsed and his carbine clattered to the ground. With both hands he tried to stem the steaming blood dribbling from his belly.

Corran looked over at Inyri, his gaze drawn to her because of the blaster pistol falling from her hands, then ran over to Thyne. Squatting down he could tell from the way blood soaked the man's clothes that there wasn't anything he could do for him. "Unless you have a bacta tank in there, you're dead."

"Then I'm dead. Just like your father." A wet cough wracked Thyne. "You want to know if I had him killed, yes?"

Corran shook his head. "No. I wouldn't believe whatever you told me and it wouldn't bring him back." *And since you really want to torture me with it, I won't give you the satisfaction of thinking I do want to know.*

Thyne grimaced against the pain that contracted his muscles. "Let me tell you this. Loor knows about you. He knew about you before he forced me to betray you. I sold you out this time, but someone else sold you out before me."

Corran's jaw dropped open. *Tycho! But Wedge said he'd died on Noquivzor so I couldn't have seen him here. Someone else? Who?*

Thyne forced a laugh. "There, I will haunt you."

"No, you'll just be dead and you'll die knowing you've warned me about an enemy I didn't know I had." Corran patted the man on the shoulder, pulling his hand back before Thyne could bite weakly at it. "You've just saved my life, Zekka Thyne, and that's something we'll both remember until death takes us."

Thyne's head lolled to the left and his body slackened. Corran stood and saw Mirax comforting Inyri. He started to open his mouth to say something, but Mirax caught his eye and shook her head to forestall his comment. He closed his mouth again realizing that the question he would have asked, though simple, probably would not have a simple answer. *Nor an answer I really have a chance of understanding.*

He didn't even know if he should thank Inyri for saving his life by shooting her lover. Corran admitted to himself that he'd not have thought she'd do that for all the stars in the galaxy. Her reaction toward him had been hostile from the moment they'd met on Kessel. Corran clearly remembered Inyri dispassionately handing Thyne a blaster so Thyne could kill him at the Headquarters.

Later she had seemed to resent his helping her escape from the Imperials after her speeder bike had been shot down.

Every clue she'd given him suggested that if Thyne had been slow in shooting him, she'd have gladly done the job rather speedily.

Inyri eased herself free of Mirax's embrace and sat back against the airspeeder's hull. The front end of the vehicle hid Thyne's body from her view though a thin rivulet of blood was meandering toward a drain in the center of the hangar floor. She hid her face in her hands, sobbed silently a bit, then wiped away her tears.

When she looked over at him, despite the red rimming her eyes, she looked eerily like her sister, Lujayne. "You want to know why."

Corran nodded. He'd heard enough preambles to confessions to know that she needed to talk more than he wanted to have her actions explained. "If you want to tell me."

"Coming from Kessel, it marks you. No one respects you because they assume you're a criminal. When you tell them you aren't they just assume you're a liar. Even the prisoners don't respect you—they all come from worlds that have more going for them than spice mines and a prison. If you're born there you can never escape Kessel."

Corran felt a tight knot forming in his stomach. When he'd first met Lujayne Forge he'd prejudged her because of where she had come from. Everything Inyri said was true, but her sister hadn't let that stop her. Lujayne had confronted Corran with his bias and made him see what he was doing. That experience with Lujayne had changed him. It had made him ready to look beyond where Inyri came from, but she'd prejudged and rejected him.

"Thyne helped me escape Kessel. He respected me. He made others respect me. He made *me* respect me. Yet in all the time I was with him I knew that he was not the sort of person I had been raised to respect. He was the antithesis of everything my parents had taught me was good and right in the galaxy."

Mirax nodded. "But he respected you and valued you in a way you never thought you'd find."

"Exactly." Inyri looked up at Corran. "Every time you would show up I'd be reminded of what I'd been raised to believe. I tried to keep you away, but in the middle of a lightfight you and Gavin run out and pull me out of the street. Thyne didn't do that. He didn't turn around and come back for me, but I missed the signs even then.

"Today he didn't warn me about what would happen at the factory. If you two hadn't been there in the garage, I would have died. And when we got here, his central concern was killing you, not the fact that I'd survived. I realized that Thyne did respect me, but only for my usefulness to him. He thought he could trust me implicitly, which is rare among the members of the Black Sun."

She shrugged. "So, he saved me from Kessel, but you saved me from the Imps and, through that, saved me from thinking I was worthless. That was worth more than Thyne's respect . . . or his life. I guess that favor you said you owed my sister has been redeemed."

"That favor I owe your sister, that's one that will take a lifetime to pay off. What you did here, as far as I'm concerned, nulls the datacard between us. We're even." Corran smiled, then shook his head. "Of course, we're still on Coruscant, we're being hunted by Imperial stormtroopers, and Thyne told me we have yet another traitor in our midst. Seems to me this is the perfect time to be settling up accounts and making sure all our affairs are truly in order."

Mirax nodded. "Never put off to tomorrow what you can do today."

Inyri raised an eyebrow. "Except, perhaps, dying."

"Good point." Corran headed toward the door into the building. "Let's get cleaned up and then we can go see if anyone else procrastinated their way past death."

36

If the Force is with us, Gavin thought as he ducked around a corner, *it's definitely the dark side*. Blaster bolts gnawed away at the wall, leaving the corner serrated and flaming. Looking to his right, he saw Ooryl and Nawara positioned inside a doorway, so he dove between them and rolled on past as they opened fire on the stormtroopers chasing them down the corridor.

Pursuit began almost immediately after they left the factory. They entered and moved through a number of buildings and thought they were in the clear when Portha shot a stormtrooper who challenged them. The storm-trooper went down but apparently lived long enough to report their location to his headquarters. Stormtroopers began to converge on the area, giving the Rogues few choices of where to run and even less time to consider them.

Wedge had insisted on going up, but the building they'd picked to give them access to the bridges on higher levels was probably the worst choice they could have made. A transparisteel and ferrocrete monolith, at the lower levels it stood absolutely alone, with no attach-ments, walkways, or links to other buildings. Up on the fiftieth level it branched out and gave them the access to other avenues of escape they desired, but getting to the fiftieth level proved to be the problem.

Coming up into a crouch, Gavin looked around and his heart sank. As with several previous floors, this one was an open square space centered on a lift and stairwell core. The floor-to-ceiling windows provided a lovely view of the shadowed levels of Coruscant—a view he found decidedly claustrophobic.

Especially with an Imperial Troop Transport gravtruck floating up to their level. An armored side panel snapped down on the truck's boxy cargo pod. A stormtrooper framed himself in the opening and tossed something at the window. It stuck for a second, appearing to be a black amoebic blob, then it exploded, spraying transparisteel fragments into the room.

Gavin had already dived to the floor, but he still felt the sting of the shards on his left flank and face. *We've had it.*

"Stay down," Wedge shouted above the din, "everyone stay down!"

Though he had no intention of making himself a target when trapped between two stormtrooper squads, he wondered if the Commander had snapped. Staying down was tantamount to surrendering, which would make sense except that the stormtroopers had never given any sign of being interested in taking prisoners. Looking to his left at the stormtroopers picking their way along the panel and entering through the broken window, Gavin didn't get the impression they were more inclined to shows of compassion than the other stormtroopers they'd fought so far.

Then something odd happened. The gravtruck tipped up at the front, spilling two stormtroopers from the walkway and tossing those in the back from their feet. A half second later the thing that had made the driver shy hit the front end of the gravtruck and exploded. The concussion of the blast shattered more windows and obliterated the gravtruck's cab. Beyond the floppy-limbed tumbling of broken stormtroopers, Gavin saw the gravtruck begin to break apart and slip from sight.

A sleek snubfighter shot up past their level, then came back around and flew directly toward the building. Though not as elegant as the next generation of starfighters, the black with gold trim Z-95 Headhunter came as a welcome sight to Gavin. Its blasters started blazing from each wingtip and sliced fire through the building's central core. Sparks shot from ruptured electrical conduits and water gushed from shattered mains. Walls evaporated beneath the assault, and of the stormtroopers who had been following them, Gavin could see no trace.

The Headhunter pulled back as a long black repulsorlift vehicle rose into place. Wedge got up and ran toward the window even before the gull-wing door to the vehicle's passenger compartment had fully opened. He waved the others forward and Gavin followed, but kept an eye on the downed stormtroopers and the central core to protect against further trouble.

"Gavin, go."

"After you, sir."

Wedge laughed, then winced. "Go, it's an order."

Gavin tossed his blaster carbine to Pash, then leapt into the vehicle and jammed himself between Erisi and the Trandoshan. Wedge followed and the vehicle dropped away from the building. Wind whistled in through the closing doors, and it wasn't until silence again reigned that Gavin heard the driver's voice. Once he did, Gavin recognized it and found the shocked look on the other Rogues' faces mirrored his own surprise.

Wedge nodded toward the driver's compartment. "Yes, Emtrey, I am hurt, but it's not serious."

Gavin shook his head and poked a finger in his right ear to try to clear it. "How can Emtrey be here?"

Rhysati nodded. "And who's flying the Headhunter, Commander?"

"Tycho."

Gavin's face froze as his emotions went from elation

to suspicion and the despair of betrayal. "How? He was killed at Noquivzor."

Wedge shook his head slowly. "No, he wasn't. The raid was real, but neither he nor Emtrey was there. Whistler was logging reports for both of them to make it appear like they were there. Both of them were actually here."

Iella raised an eyebrow. "You brought them here, why?"

"There are two things I've learned in the Rebellion. The first is that what any of us thinks is secret is really information that can be used to purchase other, more valuable information. If it were deemed expedient and useful for our presence on Coruscant to become common knowledge, say, to show a potential ally that we are taking steps to take the world, that ally would learn we were here. It would only be a matter of time before that information got into Imperial hands and we got into trouble."

Nawara nodded. "The fact that we were sold out today lends credence to this idea."

"And that brings me to my second point—the opposition can only plan to handle those things they know about. Tycho has been here as long as the rest of us have and has been working for me. I wanted one sabacc card that wouldn't change value on me and he was it. He'd been to Coruscant inside two years ago, knew how to get around, and, as we saw just now, has turned out to be very useful."

Emtrey's clamshell head swiveled around to the back. "Captain Celchu indicates we have no pursuit and are clear to our hideaway. He also has a message for you."

"Link him through."

"Wedge, I'd save this, but it's time-critical."

"Go ahead, we're all friends here."

"An urgent message came through for you while I was waiting." Tycho's voice grew somber. "We've got forty-eight hours to bring Coruscant's shields down."

37

Kirtan Loor bowed before Ysanne Isard. "Rogue Squadron is a threat no more."

Isard nodded as if she had only half heard him. "They are not dead, however."

"Not for lack of trying." Loor smothered the frown that struggled to make itself manifest. Her order to him had been to prevent Rogue Squadron from doing whatever it was they had planned to do. Killing them was an option, and he certainly could have had a squadron of TIE bombers fly in and level the Palar factory. Had he done so he had no doubt he would have been criticized for the overkill. "Their escape is regrettable, but our forces have seized their weapon and equipment caches. They are helpless."

Isard raised an eyebrow over her blue eye. "I hardly think the evidence justifies that statement."

Her stare sent a shiver down his spine, but Loor raised his head defiantly. "I agree, Madam Director, that the appearance of a Headhunter and a transport vehicle are disturbing, but extrapolating too much from that makes no sense. I think we will find the people who helped them escape were mercenaries or bounty hunters.

If Rogue Squadron had on hand the resources necessary to effect that rescue they would not have engineered a plan as weak as the one we disrupted."

"Weak?" Isard began to pace through the open expanse of her office. "I saw it as quite subtle."

"True. Analysis of some memory cores does indicate they contained programs that might have been able to insert security codes into the central computer that would have given the Rebels system-wide programming access. That *might* have enabled them to bring our shields down, but for how long? Overrides and failsafes in the system could have had the shields back up within an hour."

"Provided, Agent Loor, that they only went for the shields. You seem to think their effort would be either one employing brute strength, or one that is subtle and elegant." Isard shook her head. "Perhaps their first stage was meant to be subtle, but the second would be singularly crippling and enable them to destroy the central computer itself."

"I do not discount that, Madam Director, but I do not think you believe what you are saying." He held up a hand to postpone the angry reply her molten stare promised. "Bringing the central computer down would end *all* service on Imperial Center. All emergency services, all power, all water, all transportation. While that would be advantageous for them, the untold hardship it would visit upon the citizenry would work against them. Your plan to drain the Rebellion of bacta and money is predicated on their altruistic nature, which means you cannot believe they would be so crude."

The heat in Isard's stare slackened, then she nodded, once, and began to smile. "You surprise me, Agent Loor, with your insight. I had missed it before because of your inability to think through other things."

Loor cringed inwardly. "I beg your pardon, Madam Director?"

"Did you think you could run Zekka Thyne as your own operative without my becoming aware of it?"

"That was not my intention, Madam Director. He

was but a minor player and I thought not to bother you with insignificant details."

"You lie. He was useful in supplying you information, but you primarily wanted him to kill Corran Horn." The tall woman tapped a finger against her sharp chin. "It is just as well Thyne failed for I think I would like to meet this Corran Horn. It would be interesting to see why you fear him so."

"I fear him because he can be relentless. He hates me because I freed the bounty hunter who murdered his father. Though not a crime, it is something for which he will not forgive me. Were he disposed toward murder, I would already be dead. Now that he has joined the Rebellion, killing me would not be murder." Loor narrowed his eyes. "Playing with Corran Horn is playing with fire."

"I am Iceheart, I do not burn."

"Yes, Madam Director."

Isard watched him for a moment, then nodded slowly. "I find myself in a curious position regarding you, Agent Loor. A project under your direction, the Krytos project, has not succeeded according to my specifications. You have also, it appears, grown something of a spine and I am inclined to crush you down for having done so."

Fear clawed his heart but—and this surprised him—it found no real purchase there. It struck him that fear had been the motivating force for his life and the tool he used most often in dealing with others. He had first entered Imperial service out of fear of disappointing his parents. Fear of failure kept him pressing forward. Fear of embarrassment made him try to destroy Corran Horn and fear for his own life had marked his actions since Horn left CorSec.

He realized he'd lived in fear so long that he had become accustomed to it. As if it were an addictive drug, he required more and greater amounts to affect him. For the past two years he had operated at a high level of fear, at first because of Horn and then later because of Isard. Every threat Isard had thrown at him involved his termination for failure, and impending failure had seemed a constant companion for him. The pressure had not crushed him, and having lived through it, he was stronger for it.

Isard nodded slowly. "Very soon this world will become a festering pit of sick and dying aliens. I expect an inordinate number of Rebels will be here soon as well—them or Warlord Zsinj's people. For these and other reasons I will remove myself to my Lusankya facility. I have there the seeds of the Rebellion's complete destruction and they require cultivation.

"Imperial Center, on the other hand, needs slashing and burning. While I am content to let someone else take this world, I do not want their time on it to be easy. I do not want them to become complacent. I have determined, then, to leave behind a veritable web of Special Intelligence Operative commando and terrorist cells. I had not yet decided upon who I would sit as a spider in the center of that web, but it occurs to me that you would serve very well in that capacity. This spirit, this spine, it speaks well about your ability to act independently in my behalf."

Part of him, the cold, calculating, and *fearful* part of him, screamed for the offer to be rejected. If Isard was correct and the Rebellion would soon possess the planet, there was no reason he should stay behind. It would be better to go with Isard to Lusankya and face death at her hands every day than it was to remain on Coruscant to live a life in the shadows.

Another part of him correctly assessed the position. He would almost constantly be in danger. There would be no sanctuary, no safe haven. Even so, he would be the master of his fate—his decisions would determine whether he lived or died. That very prospect terrified him and yet, at the same time, it exhilarated him. Horn had left the sheltered life CorSec offered and he had thrived. This was Loor's chance to see if he, too, could stand on his own.

He pulled himself up to his full height. "You will make me, in effect, the Grand Moff of Imperial Center?"

"You will be the leader of the Palpatine Counterinsurgency Front. You will annoy the Rebels on Imperial Center as they have annoyed us throughout the galaxy. If you are successful, we will let the word of your movement spread throughout the galaxy. We want them focused on you so they will not be able to look too far ahead. Hobbling them by giving them this planet, then blinding them by making them focus on you means they will not see the snares I lay for them."

She smiled coldly. "They stand united now, but that is because they have a common enemy. The Krytos virus, the scramble for power here, and your PCF will help fracture this Rebel Alliance into its constituent parts. Once that happens, once they allow themselves to be divided, sweeping them away will be nothing."

Loor rubbed a hand over his chin. "If I succeed, what will my reward be?"

"*If* you succeed, you will do so because you will have mastered skills few people today possess." Isard's smile broadened, and even though he found the prospect of her being happy frightening, her amusement gratified him somehow. "In that case, Kirtan Loor, you will be in a position to *tell* me what your reward shall be, and to wrest it from me if I am foolish enough to deny it to you."

Which means you will have to destroy me somewhere along the line, but that is not unexpected. Loor nodded. "I understand your offer and all it entails."

"And?"

"And I accept it."

"Excellent. I have already sent two Star Destroyers and several of the ground-based TIE wings off to prepare the way for what will be a mass exodus when the opposition arrives. I will disappear then." Isard pressed her hands together. "To you I give the responsibility for Imperial Center, the Heart of the Empire. Ward your charge well and the glory that was Palpatine's empire will once again shine forth to illuminate the galaxy."

38

The location Tycho had found to serve as a hideaway surprised Wedge because it seemed quite unusual for Coruscant. Though he did not believe the room actually was beneath the surface of Coruscant itself, it had the sort of feel that made Wedge think of it as subterranean. The ceiling climbed up into a vault that had been finished to look as if it was part of a cavern, complete with stalactites hanging down. However, rust stains and lime scale added details that reminded him where he really was.

So did the moist trash midden in the heart of the room. It consisted largely of things slowly disintegrating to mush, but a few brightly colored plastic things spotted the corroded orange pile like mold. Nothing looked very useful and it all smelled rather bad, a fact that had Shiel feeling rather out of sorts. The moisture in the midden contributed to the room's microclimate, evaporating and then condensing on the ceiling to drip back down again.

Gavin seemed to be the only person who didn't mind being dripped upon. "On Tatooine I never even saw rain, much less got rained on." For the others the dripping water seemed to make their moods more foul and none became quite as foul as Corran's did when he saw Tycho.

Wedge had spotted Corran's anger rising up through his surprise. He pulled the younger man aside and away from the others. "Do you want me to apologize for deceiving you, Corran?"

Corran's green eyes flared. "You're my commanding officer. You don't need to explain yourself to me, sir." The hurt in his voice was unmistakable, but so was the implacability in his eyes. "I'm glad to see Captain Celchu was not killed at Noquivzor."

"Corran, I chose to keep Tycho's presence here a secret to safeguard him and to give us a weapon the other side knew nothing about."

"Wedge, I saw him talking with Kirtan Loor at the Headquarters."

"Tycho said he was there meeting with a Duros gunrunner named Lai Nootka. He didn't see you, but he wasn't meeting any Imp agent, that's for certain. Had he seen you and the trouble you were in, he would have helped."

"I bet."

Wedge grabbed Corran by the shoulders. "Look, he had instructions to contact you if something happened to me. You were going to be told, but only when it was necessary. It wasn't necessary until now."

Corran's head came up. "When Zekka Thyne was dying he said Kirtan Loor knew we were on Coruscant *before* he pressed Thyne into his service. There's a lying snake among us."

"And you believe what he said?"

"Shouldn't I?"

"Should you?" Wedge's brown eyes narrowed. "Why do you think Thyne said that to you?"

Corran hesitated. "He wanted to hurt me, sure, but that doesn't mean he was lying."

"No, but it also doesn't mean he was telling the truth, either. He reported what Loor told him." Wedge frowned. "We've not seen Aril Nunb since the warehouse. It is entirely possible she was interrogated before Loor confronted Thyne. Loor bluffed and Thyne believed him."

Corran slowly shook his head. "I worked with Loor for years and the one thing I never saw him do was bluff. The man's got a memory retention rate that rivals Winter's. Instead of letting a suspect guess at what he did or didn't know, Loor just started reeling facts off. He'd overwhelm a suspect with detail, proving how smart he was, so it would seem obvious to the suspect that sooner rather than later the truth would be found out. No, if Loor told Thyne he knew we were here, he did. And, remember, at the point she was taken, Aril didn't know anyone outside her group was here."

He has a point there, but he's still inferring a great deal from a dying man's last statement. "You think Tycho is the Imperial agent?"

"You know his history. What do you think?"

"I *do* know his history, but the whole of it." Wedge pointed over to where Tycho and Winter sat in close conversation. "I've watched him go through countless missions against the enemy. He has a facility for being in the right place at the right time."

"A bonus for a spy."

"Or for a hero. He's saved my life and he saved yours, as I recall, on numerous occasions for the both of us. I trust him absolutely. *If* there is a spy—and I don't find a spiteful tale told by Zekka Thyne very reliable—I'd sooner believe it was any one of us than I would believe it is Tycho. More importantly, though, I need Tycho and everyone else if we're going to bring the shields down tomorrow night."

Corran folded his arms across his chest. "So you're telling me to leave it alone even though his presence might jeopardize whatever we do?"

Wedge opened his hands. "Look, Corran, I respect your instincts, I really do, but I've been down here for fifteen hours more than you have. Our other caches have been hit by Imps. This is the only safe place for us. If Tycho had betrayed us, this place would have been hit, too. And, yes, the Imps could be holding off for some other reason, but I can't think of one aside from their not knowing where we are. That may not seem like much to you, but it's enough for me to hope we have a shot at accomplishing our mission here."

The younger man frowned heavily. "It *isn't* much, but right now it's more solid than anything I have. I'll try to keep an open mind here, but if the least little thing gets screwed up, I'm going to find out who did what and there will be hell to pay."

"I'll back you all the way."

"I guess that's as good as it gets, given the circumstances."

Wedge brushed a droplet of water off his shoulder. "That's not saying much here." He led Corran over to an area with a table and chairs set up under an overhang. "If I could have everyone over here, we need to figure out what we're going to be doing. Any and all suggestions are welcome."

The others gathered around the table. Aside from the members of Rogue Squadron the group included Iella, Winter, Mirax, Inyri, Portha, and Asyr. The Trandoshan and Shiel both remained on cots and did not join the meeting. Wedge could see both were sleeping, albeit fitfully in Shiel's case, so he decided not to waken them. *Better they rest now and are able to fight later.*

Wedge leaned forward on the table. "Our basic problem is the same as it's always been: The shields on this rock have to come down. We took one shot at getting a computer override established, but that didn't work. What do we do now?"

Winter raised a hand. "Things are not exactly the same as they have always been. The loss of the memory cores means the central computer has begun to delegate jobs to the subsidiary systems to conserve memory media. The disks they're using now are in sad shape—a lot more errors are creeping into things. They've got a construction droid building a new manufacturing plant as an adjunct to the computer center to bring the memory-core manufacture under Imperial control, but it won't be able to turn out product for another two days."

Wedge shivered. He'd seen construction droids work before and found their efficiency as impressive as he did their potential for destruction. Vast, huge machines, they combined the whole of the manufacturing cycle in one highly mobile package. The front end used lasers and other tools to dissect a structure. Little ancillary droids—some as big as a gravtruck—sorted through the debris and fed the appropriate bits of material into the constructor's gullet. There metal was resmelted, stone ground down to dust and reconstituted, then extruded in girders, blocks, sheets, and trim. The aft end of the construction droid then took the building blocks and, in accord with preprogrammed plans, created a new structure where the old one had been. Specialized subsidiary construction droids equipped with repulsorlift coils built the walkways that linked structures and worked on the delicate upper reaches of the highest towers on Coruscant.

"It's hard to believe that a factory can be built and running in three days, but that's progress."

Asyr growled. "I hope they evicted the tenants of the building they destroyed to make the factory. They keep forgetting to do that when they have one of those monsters take a slice out of Invisec."

Corran frowned. "If I remember correctly, the subsidiary computer facilities are not as well guarded as the central computer. This makes them vulnerable to an attack, right?"

"True, but using one of the computers to bring down the shields means we're only going to get a small portion of the shields down." Wedge shook his head. "This forces us to concentrate our assault teams in one place and allows the Empire to do the same with their defenses. This world is too well defended for the Alliance to take it by storm."

Gavin shot from his chair and clapped his hands together. "That's it! We take the world by storm."

Only the dripping sound of water violated the silence

that greeted Gavin's remark. Everyone stared at him and Gavin blushed.

Wedge nodded slowly. "What are you talking about, Gavin?"

"I'm talking about the storms we've seen here before. A cloud comes up and a lightning storm hits."

Corran shook his head. "Conjuring a storm up isn't that easy, Gavin."

"No, Corran, it is." Gavin raked his fingers back through wet hair. "My uncle on Tatooine is a food magnate who has a virtual monopoly on water rights and moisture farms. He wants all the water he can get. Hundreds of people have come to him with schemes to bring rain to Tatooine, and probably ten times that number have come up with schemes they intend to use to break Uncle Huff's control of the water market. Most he ignores, but occasionally he pays someone off. One of the guys he paid off was someone who had a plan to seed the atmosphere with chemical crystals around which water would condense. The water would form clouds and the clouds would produce rain."

Wedge straightened up. "Doesn't that presuppose there is sufficient water vapor already in the air? Aside from this place, Coruscant seems rather lacking in humidity."

"And when there is some, a storm forms almost instantly." Pash nodded at Iella. "We saw one of those fast-forming storms when we were at the museum."

Corran smiled. "Perhaps we could get everyone in the Black Sun and Alien Combine to put a pot on to boil at the same time."

Everyone laughed except for Winter. "Boiling is a good idea, but we need a lot of water set to boil all at one time. That requires lots of water and lots of heat."

Corran opened his hands. "So, where do we get that much water?"

Winter chewed on her lower lip for a second. "Water gets melted at the polar glaciers, then pumped through long aqueducts to pumping stations and deep reservoirs throughout the equatorial areas of the city. There's plenty of water in any one of the reservoirs."

"But how do we vaporize it?" Wedge scratched at the back of his head. "Thermal detonators are too inefficient, and repeated strafing runs to use lasers on it would take too long. We need a lot of heat, but we need it delivered all at once."

"I've got it." Asyr smiled proudly. "We use one of the orbital mirrors. They're designed to concentrate sunlight and deliver it to the planet to warm up the colder regions. We redirect one of them to focus on a reservoir and it'll vaporize the duracrete, transparisteel, and water in short order."

"The problem there, Asyr, is getting up to the mirror." Corran shook his head. "We'd have to get through the shields we want to bring down first, and that's not going to be easy, then we have to take the mirror. By the time we finished assaulting it, the Golan Space Defense stations would shoot it down or a TIE starfighter wing would come up and destroy it."

Iella looked over at Winter. "Are the mirrors crew-controlled or ground-controlled?"

"Ground-controlled. Mirror duty is considered punishment. The crews that maintain the facilities go out to repair damage from strikes by debris, but that's about it."

Wedge's eyes narrowed. "Presumably you're suggesting we take control of a ground station and redirect one of the orbital mirrors to vaporize a reservoir. That water vapor will condense into a monster storm that will strike with lightning all over the place, taking down the power grid. As the computers try to match power to demand, we should get a complete power grid collapse."

Iella smiled. "You got a better idea?"

"Unfortunately, no." Wedge frowned. "The weak link here, as I see it, is taking the control station."

"The orbital mirrors are controlled by the subsidiary computer centers." Winter glanced at her datapad. "The nearest should be SCC Number Four, just south of the Imperial Palace."

"Do we have enough people to assault it and get us in fast enough that we can do what needs to be done without interference?" Wedge looked around the table and saw frowns or blank expressions except on one face. "Lieutenant Horn, you have an idea?"

"Yeah, we evict folks from that center."

"What?"

Corran leaned forward, resting his elbows on the table. "There's a construction droid building a factory within a laser shot from that center, right? We get a crew in to take control of the factory and have it go rogue. It heads straight for the computer center. I don't think anyone is going to remain on station while a Death Star's little brother comes toward him gobbling up cityscape. It stops short of destroying the center, but our crew should be able to get in and get working on the orbital mirror. Moreover, we can have the construction droid spitting out a new central computer facility with some of our own code sliced into it. If we take the planet, we'll be up and running even if the Imps blow the old center."

"And if the Imps manage to stop the construction droid before it hits the abandoned computer center, they'll think they've muted our attack and thwarted us." Wedge nodded. "I see it. Emtrey, do you know how to run a construction droid?"

The droid's head came up. "I have had some experience with smaller manufacturing systems, sir, so I believe I can determine what we need to do."

Mirax raised a hand. "I've used one of the small ones to fabricate some storage areas for my father. Count me in on that crew."

"Right." Wedge felt a twinge of pain in his ribs. "With broken ribs I'm not flight ready, so I'll go on that one, too. Iella?"

"I'm with you."

"Good." Wedge rubbed his hands together. "Winter, you're the best slicer we've got here, so you've got to be going into the center. Tycho, Gavin, and Ooryl, you'll round out that crew."

Corran looked up at Wedge. "What about the rest of us?"

"You're flying cover."

"Commander, I don't think you're going to fit the rest of us in the cockpit of a Headhunter."

"True, which is why Tycho has procured six of them." Wedge smiled broadly. "Corran, you'll fly with Erisi on your wing, Rhysati and Pash will fly together and . . ." He looked over at Shiel. "Hmmm, Nawara, you might have to fly alone."

Asyr raised her hand. "Commander Antilles, I'm combat-qualified in a Headhunter."

"Excuse me?"

The Bothan looked down sheepishly. "You know me as Asyr Sei'lar, but what you don't know is that I'm a graduate of the Bothan Martial Academy. I graduated a year behind Peshk Vri'syk. He was good enough to join Rogue Squadron last year, and I was his equal when we were trained. It's been a while since I've flown, but I can handle the fighter."

Wedge raised an eyebrow. "What would a member of the Bothan military be doing here on Coruscant?"

"I'd rather not say, sir."

"I can understand that." Wedge nodded slowly. "Well, then, you've got number six with Nawara in five."

The Twi'lek shook his head and Wedge noticed his normally ash-colored flesh had taken on a creamy tone that, in some places, seemed translucent. "I think I'm coming down sick, sir. I'm not certain I'm flight capable. The ryll I've taken is helping a bit, but I'm still not feeling well enough to fly."

"I'm not formally qualified to fly, but I've done a lot of simming." Inyri bit her lower lip. "Lujayne used to train against me. She was better than I was and beat me regularly, but not all the time."

Corran smiled. "I've seen her pilot a speeder bike and an airspeeder. She does well in the tight confines of these urban canyons."

Wedge was tempted to take her up on her offer, but

he held back. "I believe what you've told me, Inyri, but I can't take responsibility for your first starfighter combat taking place on Coruscant. What I'd rather have you do is deliver Winter and the others to the computer center. That will take some fancy airspeeder flying because we'll be grinding a lot of stuff up in the area."

"Commander," Erisi began, "if we have Asyr or Inyri bring in some more people for the ground teams, we could free up Gavin, Captain Celchu, or Ooryl and give us six pilots."

"No, we're not bringing anyone else in." Wedge leaned forward again on the table. "Corran has brought to my attention the potential for betrayal. Zekka Thyne informed the Imperials of our plans for the factory. We're going to need all the time we have remaining to double- and triple-check our plans and equipment, then we're going. No one here is going to communicate with anyone outside just to make sure the Imps have no inkling of what we're going to do. This effort *must* succeed."

Gavin slowly shook his head. "Fourteen against a world. Those are long odds."

"Lieutenant Darklighter, I'm a Corellian. I have no use for odds." Wedge smiled broadly, putting as much confidence as he could into it. "No doubt the Imps have a sizable house edge here, but now the war has come to Coruscant, which means they're playing *our* game, and that makes everything even all over again."

39

Corran Horn tightened the straps on his life-support controller, adjusting the boxy device as he went to get it centered on his chest. He much preferred having the controller built into his command chair as it was on his CorSec X-wing, but the Z-95 was more primitive than that, so he had to wear it. He punched a button, putting the device through a self-check, then got a tone indicating everything was in good working order.

Mirax smiled broadly as she came walking over and succeeded in forestalling the dread her black Imperial uniform sparked in him. "We're getting ready to head out. Are you okay?"

Corran nodded. "Yeah. We've gone over all the Headhunters from nose to stern and they check out."

"So I gather. I recall seeing you and Erisi in close conversation."

Corran felt hot color rise in his cheeks. "That was a prelude to a group discussion. We ended up adjusting the sensor packages and zeroing the blasters at 150 meters. We figured that dogfights would be close and shots of over 150 meters in the canyons here are going to be rare."

"Take care of yourself out there."

"Hey, my job is making sure to keep TIEs and others off you." Corran reached out and tapped the tip of her nose with his finger. "Look, it will be crazy out there. In all likelihood Rogue Squadron will get a few more heroes inducted into its Hall of the Dead . . ."

Mirax gave him a smirk. "Corran, if this is one of those 'tomorrow we might die so we should be together tonight' speeches, your timing is lousy since tomorrow is now and last night ended when this morning started."

"I know." Corran laughed at the nervousness he felt. "I guess what I'm trying to say is this: Before Coruscant I found you interesting and attractive. Since we've been here I've gotten to know more about you, to see how you react under pressure and how effortlessly you seem to get along with others. I admire the qualities that I've seen in you and, well, if we both come out of this, I'd like the opportunity to get to know you even better."

"Corran Horn, are you asking me out?" Mirax's dark eyes sparkled. "Or was there some pool that you lost?"

"If there'd been a pool, I'd have bought up all the tickets." He sighed. "Mirax, we've got enough things going against us, like our respective backgrounds, that the chances of things working out are bad."

"But we're Corellians, so what use have we for odds?" She pressed a finger to his lips, then leaned forward and kissed him. "And just to let you know, you're not the only one who's been impressed here, so you're on. You're taking me to the biggest and best victory celebration the New Republic throws on this rock." Mirax tapped a finger against the box on his chest. "Life-support gear optional."

"I'll be there." He kissed her in return, then looked up and saw Wedge heading over to the black airspeeder Emtrey was to use to get them to the construction droid. "You better get going."

"The Force be with you."

"And with you." Corran smiled as she ran off. He felt particularly lucky and hoped that sensation would continue throughout the mission, then he turned and found himself face-to-face with Tycho Celchu. "Captain."

"I'm glad you'll be flying the black and gold Headhunter. I think it's the best of the lot, which is why I used it the other day. I just checked it out, everything looks fine, and I know I can trust you to bring it back in one piece."

"I'll do my best, sir." Corran refused to look him in the eye. "If you will excuse me, sir."

"No, wait a minute." Tycho shifted to the right to block his path. "I want you to know you're wrong about me. I didn't meet Kirtan Loor the night you saw me. I'm not working for the Imps."

Corran exhaled slowly. "Captain, Wedge has asked me to let it go, and so I will, for now, but there are too many odd things here to make me leave it alone forever."

"Such as?"

"Such as your being here when Alliance Intelligence thinks you're buried in rubble on Noquivzor. Such as my seeing you here with an agent of Imperial Intelligence. Such as your vacation at Lusankya." Muscles bunched at the corners of Corran's jaw. "Such as Bror Jace being ambushed and killed by Imperials after you obtained permission for him to travel and plotted his course for him."

Tycho's face slackened slightly. "But that's all circumstantial. Nothing is proven."

"Nothing's proven *yet*." Corran looked him square in the face. "The fact that there's no solid evidence against you just means you're real good."

The other man's blue eyes sharpened. "Or, Lieutenant Horn, it means I've left no evidence because I'm completely innocent."

"I guess we'll see about that, Captain Celchu." Corran rested his fists on his hips. "When I return, I'm going to make ferreting out the spy in our midst a hobby. I'm good at that sort of thing, very good."

Tycho opened his hands. "And you're honest, so I know I have nothing to fear."

His calm reply surprised Corran. There was an utter defenselessness about it he'd never encountered before.

He wasn't certain how to take that remark, so he shunted it aside. "Well, Captain, if you *do* have anything to fear, I'll find it."

"Fly well, Corran." Tycho gave Corran a nod, then walked off. Beyond him Corran saw Pash Cracken looking in his direction, but he turned away quickly and rubbed at an invisible spot on his red and green Headhunter's cockpit canopy.

Corran walked past him toward his own fighter. Erisi glanced up from where her blue Headhunter with red trim sat, then walked over on an intercept course. Corran forced a smile on his face. "Set to go, Erisi?"

"Yes. I still wish we were flying together."

"I'd be happy to have you on my wing." With Asyr's joining the flight, Wedge had adjusted assignments so Pash flew with the Bothan and Erisi joined Rhysati. That left Corran alone, but he'd been alone before in combat zones and both he and Wedge knew anyone other than Pash Cracken would have a hard time keeping up with him anyway. "With me flying solo we can lull the Imps into a false sense of security."

"The last thing they'll feel is regret." Erisi smiled easily at him. "Are you feeling well? You're not coming down sick like Nawara and Shiel, are you?"

Corran shook his head. "No. I'll be fine. I, ah, I just had a confrontation with Tycho. The Empire owns him, I can feel it. I told him that when I got back I'd dig up all the clues concerning the spy in our midst and prove *he* was involved in getting Bror Jace ambushed and jeopardizing our mission here."

"I can see how that might have you out of sorts." She reached out and stroked his arm. "If there's anything I can do to help you, let me know."

"Thanks, Erisi, I appreciate it." He winked at her, then stepped back and let a loud whistle echo through the cavern. "Let's go, Rogues. It's time to get moving. Our people will be in position inside fifteen minutes, which means our prey will show up shortly thereafter. Shoot straight and fly fast."

40

The datapad's stuttered trilling attracted Kirtan Loor's attention. He walked over from where he had been inventorying weapons to be distributed to his command and tapped a button on the datapad. The nature of the sound had told him the message was urgent and of a high priority as well. The message the datapad displayed lived up to its billing.

So an Interdictor cruiser has been spotted at the fringe of our system. Those ships are too big and too valuable to use as scouts. Either it is meant to decoy some of our forces out away from this planet or it is the vanguard of an invasion fleet. He knew, without a doubt, the latter case was the truth, but that prospect did not fill him with the dread it might have six months earlier. His reason for existing now required a Rebel invasion and conquest of Coruscant. *Our shields aren't down, so they must mean to make a fight of it or . . .*

Loor hit some more buttons and checked to see if any warnings had come in from the Rogue Squadron spy. He saw nothing, but curiosity and caution caused him to delve a bit deeper. Using a security override program he discovered all messages from the agent inside Rogue

Squadron had been reclassified to "Isard Eyes Only." She had engineered it so all those messages were routed to her first so she could decide their disposition. Loor knew if he challenged her on it, she would say it was done so he would not be distracted during his preparations.

At another stage in his life he would have wasted valuable time and energy trying to work a way around Isard's action, but no more. What the spy had to say was no longer important to the conduct of his mission. Isard wanted Coruscant to fall into the hands of the Rebellion, so it would. Since he already knew who the spy was, re-establishing contact at a later date would not be particularly difficult, should the need arise.

Best if I assume that the Rogues are up to something. Fine. I wish them all the Force-inspired success they desire. Once they win, once they drop their guard, then we will hit them and hit them hard. He laughed aloud and returned to his work. "Not much longer from now the Rebels will have what they most desire. And shortly thereafter they will learn they don't really want it at all."

The black airspeeder raced through the night-dim streets on a course that brought it parallel to the construction droid's path, then Emtrey cut the wheel left and pulled back. The airspeeder climbed rapidly, then the nose eased down and Emtrey steered in toward the flat landing surface built behind the droid's control center. "I will have us down in fifteen seconds, sir."

Wedge fitted the mask over the right side of his head. He spoke the command that inflated the air bladders that clamped the helmet in place. "How do I look?" he croaked.

"Very Imperial, Colonel Roat." Iella gave him a nod.

Mirax looked less comfortable with his disguise. "You look very cyborg."

"Good. That lessens my chance of being recognized." Wedge rode out the slight bump as Emtrey put the vehicle down on the construction droid. A faint hum filled the air, but it grew to a hideous din when the airspeeder's gull-wing doors opened. Wedge got out of the speeder first, then helped both Mirax and Iella disembark.

A man wearing a red helmet and an orange jumpsuit waved both hands at them as he came running over. "You can't be here. Get going or I call for stormtroopers."

Wedge leaned forward and frowned, tapping the metal over his right ear. "I cannot hear you."

"I SAID . . ."

"Too much noise."

The workman frowned, then bid all of them to follow him with a curt wave. He led them into a small foyer just outside the command center. The door closed behind them, cutting the noise almost to nothing. "You can't be here."

"I am Colonel Antar Roat and these are my aides. I have come for a safety inspection."

"I don't know anything about that."

Mirax gave the man a withering stare. "Of course not, idiot. If you did, this inspection wouldn't be a surprise, would it?"

Iella held a hand out. "Your identification and work permits please."

"Wait." The man went for the identification cards and held them out. "I should check with . . ."

Iella snatched the datacards from him. "Compounding the possible charges against you? Is there a conspiracy between you and your cohorts? How much do they pay you for your part in the smuggling operation?" Iella paced around him like a Thevaxan Marauder stalking prey.

"What smuggling?" The man's hands came up as he turned to face her. "I don't know no . . ."

Wedge's boxy right hand crashed onto the back of the man's head, dropping him to the ground. Iella immediately turned to the interior door while Mirax let Emtrey into the foyer. The droid held blaster carbines for each of the others and passed them out carefully. Iella checked hers, then passed the downed man's identification card through the coded slot.

The door buzzed. Iella jerked it open and Wedge and Mirax hurried through it, brandishing their weapons at the trio of men lounging at a hologame table. Beyond them, filling the walls of the rectangular command center, monitors, gauges, dials, and lights displayed an unending amount of information about every phase of the construction droid's operation. The multicolored lights tended mostly to be green, which underscored the sick pallor of the men's flesh tones.

"Lie down on the floor and no one gets hurt." Mirax pointed her carbine at the men and smiled. "I ask once—after that I have the droid pitch your bodies off the front and you'll end up as compost in some Ithorian's indoor garden, understand? That's it, hug that deck and you won't have to be enlightened."

Iella held the door open as Wedge went back through and dragged the unconscious man into the cockpit. The other three looked shocked to see him down, but his snores reassured them somewhat as to their own fate. Iella used some synthetic binders to fasten their hands behind their backs and link their legs together. "They can be tightened, gentlemen, so rest easy and there will be no need to make you more uncomfortable."

While Iella took over covering the men, Wedge removed his mask and joined Mirax at the command console. "Can you drive this thing?"

Mirax tipped her head to one side, then the other, hesitated, then nodded. "It's a bit more complex than the one I've used before, but I think Emtrey can help me through this. Emtrey, bring this monster around on a new heading for our target."

"Yes, Mistress Terrik. There, new course is set."

The main viewscreen showed a nighttime landscape of lights and shadows begin to scroll across as the construction droid executed a ninety-degree turn toward the south. In the distance, between two stocky office towers,

Wedge made out the squat form of Subsidiary Computer Center Number Four. "Right on target."

"Good." Mirax looked up and hit a glowing red button. The light started flashing red.

"What's that?"

"All government buildings are required to have evacuation alarms in the case of a catastrophe."

Wedge smiled. "Like a construction droid bearing down on it?"

"It's easy to see how you got that squadron command, Wedge." Mirax poked him playfully in the stomach with an elbow. "The alarms are going off in every building for ten kilometers along our line of advance. The same evacuation alarms are required in residential areas with a relatively high assessed value. Not so in places like Invisec."

Emtrey turned from his position. "Sir, I have inserted the auxiliary code into the blueprints here. Our computer center is begun."

The buildings in their path immediately came alive with lights moving at a variety of speeds. Wedge scanned the console and punched a button, shifting the image over from visible light to infrared. He saw traces from all manner of speeders heading out and away. A solid mass of gold tinged with red at the top and bottom surged across the bridges connecting the doomed towers with safer buildings.

The console's comm unit came alive. "This is the Ministry of Planning and Zoning. Construction droid Foursixnine, do you have a problem? We're showing a deviation of your course."

Wedge hit the reply button. "No problem here, we just have new plans. With Coruscant being under new management, we wanted to get things started early to ease the transition."

"What are you talking about? Who is this?"

"Rogue Squadron Contracting. X-wings are faster, but they don't build things as nicely as this does. Antilles out." He hit the comm, terminating the conversation. "There, think that will make us a target?"

Iella laughed. "If it doesn't, that's just one more example of why the Empire is too stupid to survive."

Captain Uwlla Iillor of the New Republic Interdictor cruiser *Corusca Rainbow* glanced at the chronographic display built into the arm of her command chair, then up at the holographic representation of Coruscant hovering in the middle of the bridge. The display indicated there were only twenty standard minutes left before the Rebel fleet would be within range for her to pull them from hyperspace. If she did not, they would continue on into the system and arrive around Coruscant to do battle for the Jewel of the Empire.

The hologram of Coruscant—which was based on Imperial Traffic Control data broadcast to the system—showed the world as a translucent sphere studded with a rainbow of lights. Superimposed over that were two spheres made up of hexagonal tiles. As long as those spheres were there, indicating the presence of shields around Coruscant, Captain Iillor was under orders to power up her ship's gravity well projectors and pull the fleet from hyperspace prematurely. The situation was desperate enough that Admiral Ackbar had even said a partial shield failure would be sufficient to let the fleet continue on in, provided Captain Iillor felt the shield outage was significant.

The decision she had to make was even more difficult than the choice to defect with her ship and crew to the Rebellion. While Ackbar had been clear in his instructions to her, she knew the conquest of Coruscant would significantly cripple the Empire and correspondingly enrich the New Republic. That she had been placed in such a position of trust and power showed her how different the Republic was from the Empire and because of that difference she didn't want to make the wrong decision.

Lieutenant Jhemiti, her Mon Calamari First Officer,

held a datapad out for her inspection. "Projector crews have run full system diagnostics on their equipment and we are ready to power up when you give the word."

She glanced at the times appended to each diagnostics run. "The crew is slow. We can't have that."

The Mon Calamari opened his mouth in a smile. "Few believe we'll be activating the gravity well projectors, Captain."

Iillor raised an eyebrow. "And why is that, Lieutenant?"

Jhemiti hesitated for a moment. "Rumor has it that the people we have on the ground are Rogue Squadron. They've killed Death Stars. They'll accomplish their mission."

"Ah, yes, Rogue Squadron." The Captain smiled slightly. "Let me tell you, Lieutenant, I've fought Rogue Squadron. They drove this ship off. They cost me almost all of my TIE fighters, too, in doing so. Were anyone else down there, I would take their failure for granted. With them, I am willing to allow the possibility they will succeed."

Jhemiti blinked and the gold flecks in his red scales sparkled. "But Rogue Squadron *is* known for accomplishing the impossible."

"If reputations alone won wars, Lieutenant, Darth Vader would still live and you'd still be a slave." Captain Iillor nodded grimly and looked at the chronometer again. "There are eighteen minutes on the clock—eighteen minutes for a squadron to strip a planet of its defenses. We'll let them have every second we can, but we will be ready to do our duty if they cannot do theirs."

41

Gavin jammed his hands against the dashboard of the airspeeder as Inyri flew through the cloud of dust being raised by the construction droid. Even in the enclosed cab of the speeder he could hear the warning klaxons blaring at Subsidiary Computer Center Number Four. As they broke free of the grey cloud he got a good look at all the vehicles jetting away from the computer center and all the people fleeing across bridges to other towers.

Inyri sideslipped the speeder to center it on the balcony situated fifth-floor front. From information supplied originally by Black Sun, Winter had determined the control center they needed was located on the fifth floor. While they expected the whole facility to be abandoned, they assumed a general security lockdown would make entering at the first floor and working their way up difficult.

"Brace for impact." Inyri cut power to the engine and began to slow the speeder, then let it sail straight over the balcony and into the office beyond it. The transparisteel wall disintegrated into one crystalline wave that washed up and over the speeder's windscreen. A desk exploded at the front bumper's casual caress and the room's far walls

•

buckled, letting the speeder skid to a stop in the waiting room attached to what had once been the CEO's office.

Gavin slapped the quick release for his restraining belts and kicked his door open. He slid from the speeder and brought a blaster carbine up. The klaxons obliterated any sounds the opposition might have made and the dust curtain between him and the rest of the building hid possible foes. Hunkered down in the shadow of his opened door he could see nothing, but with each passing second he came to believe everyone had evacuated the building.

Tycho cut to the right, Gavin went left and advanced. Things appeared clear from his new vantage point, so he waved the others forward. Ooryl came up with Winter following close behind him. Inyri brought up the rear, constantly checking back toward the outside to make sure no one followed them in.

Winter was the key to their success because the datapad she held contained the code that would move an orbital mirror to target the nearest water distribution plant and reservoir. Once beyond the area of devastation created by Inyri's entry, they were able to move along quickly. All the doors along the corridor to the control center were closed. Gavin tried to open all those on his side of the corridor but they were all locked tight. Tycho indicated the situation on the right was the same, but that is what they had been led to expect after the plant was abandoned.

They reached the door to the computer center without opposition. Gavin took a moment to glance through the transparisteel viewport in the heavy door. The room looked empty of life to him, though the computers themselves had lights flickering across their dark surfaces. Holographic streams of data scrolled up from desktop to oblivion above a dozen workstations. Aided by a thin mist hanging in the air, the light from them cast green and red shadows over the rest of the room, making the dimly lit room seem sinister.

Winter dropped to her knees and attached a cable from her datapad to a computer port on the doorjamb.

"The sequencer programs I have will open the door in no time. First, though, I need to run a diagnostic and see what sort of combination I want."

"Good luck." Gavin dropped to a crouch and watched the corridor that led farther into the complex. He positioned himself so his body shielded Winter. He felt a twinge in his belly from an old blaster wound and hoped it was not some sort of ill omen for the future.

The datapad beeped and Winter swore. "Sithspawn."

Tycho crouched at her shoulder. "What?"

"They've flooded the control room with gas. Looks like Fex-M3d." Winter raised a fist but refrained from punching the door. "It's in a diluted form so it won't kill you if you get a lungful, but it'll put you out."

Gavin jerked a thumb at the door. "To the left, on the wall, there's a clear case that has breather masks in it. If we could get in, we could get them."

"That's the big *if*. The case is coded, just like the door here. By the time a sequencer got it open, you'd have to breathe and you'd be down." Winter shook her head. "Looks as if this system was installed within the last two weeks, after we were given the data we used to make our attack. There's nothing we can do. We can't get in. It's over."

His hand on the stick, the Z-95 Headhunter cruising through the duracrete canyons of Coruscant, Corran Horn felt more alive and free than all the soaring hawkbats on the planet. He would have much preferred to be flying his X-wing, and he felt awkward flying into combat without Whistler backing him up, but flying again made him happy enough that he could forgive Whistler his absence. *No place for him in this Headhunter anyway.*

The Headhunter suffered in comparison with the X-wing. It lacked the maneuverability and speed of the X-wing, though the shields and hull had the same integrity. The Headhunter did not have hyperdrives and, consequently, did not need an R2 unit. The Headhunter's triple blasters and concussion missiles were not the equal of the X-wing's four laser cannons and proton torpedo launchers but they didn't exactly leave him defenseless, either.

Against the Imperial starfighters he'd be facing the Headhunter had the potential to be troublesome—both for him and them. In atmosphere the TIEs lost some of their maneuverability. Their lack of shields made them vulnerable to his attacks, but the fact that they'd be swarming meant being able to stay with one long enough to kill it would be difficult. Locking in on one target would make him a target.

He glanced down at his sensor display. "Hunt Leader here. I have twelve, that is one-two, starfighters coming in on the droid. Time to engagement is thirty seconds. Shoot straight and call for help."

Corran got a series of acknowledgments over the comm. Pulling back on his stick he started the Z-95 climbing. Pushing the throttle full forward he rocketed up like a ship intent on escaping the planet. A quartet of TIE starfighters came up after him but before they could close to range and start shooting, he rolled the Headhunter to starboard. The fighter came up and over, then dove back in the direction from which the TIEs had come.

Halfway through the dive, he pulled the fighter through a 180-degree snap-roll left, then swooped out in a long glide that brought him in over the construction droid and into the rest of the TIEs. He spitted the leader on his targeting crosshairs and gave it two bursts of blaster fire. The dozen energy darts stippled the eyeball with hits. It began a lazy roll that ended abruptly as it slammed into a tower and exploded.

The pilot of the next TIE followed his leader through the roll, clearly not realizing one of Corran's shots had pierced the cockpit and killed the pilot. He tried to pull up and away at the last second. His hexagonal port wing clipped the corner of the tower and sent the TIE into a corkscrew spin that spiraled down into a fiery explosion deep in a dark canyon.

Standing the Headhunter on its port S-foils, Corran added enough left rudder to snap the ship into a dive past the construction droid. He pointed the fighter's nose straight at the bottom of the urban trench and started down. He chopped his throttle back to zero and used the stick to roll his ship until the canyon stretched to infinity off each wing, but crowded him above and below.

Two TIEs dove after him and closed fast. Corran made minor adjustments on his position, forcing them to stick with him to target him. Their first shots missed, sending green energy lances down to flare brightly in the darkness, but they began to get better. Then they got close enough that they hit his aft shield, prompting him to take action.

He rolled the Headhunter ninety degrees to port, hemming himself in on either wing, then he pulled back on the stick. At the same time he punched all the power being generated by his engines into the repulsorlift drive. The Headhunter's nose popped up, leveling him out a hundred meters above the canyon's bottom. Momentum from the dive kept him going forward and away from the TIEs.

One eyeball pilot made a serious mistake by not rolling before he tried to follow the Headhunter. His maneuver was intended to bring the TIE around in a sharp, right-angle turn—a maneuver that would have worked in the vacuum of space and placed him right on Corran's tail with a killing shot. In atmosphere, however, the maneuver brought his starboard wing around in direct opposition to his previous line of flight. The hexagonal panel snapped, with the top half sheering through the ship's ball cockpit. Still going full out, the TIE fighter hammered the ground and exploded.

The second TIE pilot rolled first, then swooped in after Corran's Headhunter. The speed of the dive forced the pilot into a wider turn than he clearly wanted. The lower edges of his wings struck sparks from the duracrete street. Fighting inertial forces, the pilot did everything he could to make his fighter climb. Finally the ship began to win in its battle with gravity and began to come up.

Up into one of the numerous walkways connecting one building with another. The TIE plowed into a central portion of the span, splintering the permacrete section it hit. The fighter exploded, shattering windows and sowing shrapnel throughout the area.

Reversing thrust and applying some rudder, Corran brought the fighter around in an end for end swap that left him looking at the fires burning in his wake. *Not a bad start, four down, but it's only a start.* He eased the throttle forward and started a gentle climb to the unobstructed reaches of Coruscant's atmosphere. He glanced at the shipboard chronometer and fuel gauge.

"Fifteen minutes to get the shields down and a half hour of flying time. That's forever if we succeed and little more than a heartbeat if we do not."

Wedge's comlink buzzed at him. "Antilles here, go ahead."

"Tycho here. We have a problem—gas in the computer center. We need Emtrey. Now."

"I copy." He looked up at Mirax. "Will this thing keep going by itself?"

She nodded. "The droid will stop at the outer edge of the computer center if"—she pointed at external view monitors showing TIEs on strafing runs—"they don't stop it first."

"If we can leave this thing alone, they need us in the computer center."

Mirax held her hands up. "Let's go."

Iella led the way back into the entryway. She started to push the door open, then quickly ducked back. A spray of blaster bolts dotted the interior of the door with burn marks.

Wedge ran over to where she sat on the floor. "Are you hurt?"

"I'm fine."

"What was that?"

She shook her head. "I couldn't see clearly but given the size of those burn marks I'd say some stormtroopers have an E-web heavy blaster set up on one of the nearby towers. They've got the door covered and covered well." Iella shrugged. "Unless we get some help, we're going to be stuck here for the rest of our lives."

42

Gavin's stomach began to fold in on itself as he heard Wedge's voice come out of the comlink. "Sorry, Tycho, we're pinned down here. Unless we get some help, we're going nowhere."

"I copy, Wedge." Tycho looked over at Gavin. "You and I will go see if we can help them out."

Ooryl raised a three-fingered hand. "Ooryl . . ."

Tycho shook his head. "I want you here to help Inyri guard Winter. The kid and I will go."

The Gand nodded, then his mouth parts snapped open. "Ooryl does not question your orders, Captain. Ooryl merely wants to know how this Fex-M3d works."

Winter slowly straightened up. "You breathe it in, it gets into your bloodstream and binds to neuroreceptors, preventing nerves from passing information. If you get a strong enough dose your autonomic nervous system shuts down and you stop breathing. You suffocate."

The Gand's mouth parts closed again. "Ooryl understands. If you will all back down this hallway, Ooryl will open the door, open the interior case, and bring you back respirators."

Gavin's jaw shot open. "But you'll die."

The Gand shook his head. "Ooryl does not respire."

Inyri blinked. "What?"

Ooryl tapped his chest. "Gands do not respire."

"But you talk."

"Yes, Inyri Forge, but respiration is not required for speech. Ooryl's body has a muscular gas bladder that allows Ooryl to, among other things, draw in gases and expel them at a controlled rate through pieces of Gand exoskeleton that vibrate and approximate speech. Ooryl gets the metabolic ingredients Ooryl needs through ingestion, not respiration. Fex-M3d will not affect Ooryl."

Tycho thought for a moment, then nodded. "Here's what we'll do. Ooryl will wait here until we retreat. Inyri, you'll turn the airspeeder around and bring the engine up. Point the exhaust jets down this hallway and we can use them to push the freed Fex-M3d deeper into the building."

"It will also point the airspeeder in the right direction for our escape."

"Good point, Inyri." Tycho looked over at Gavin. "Depending upon how many masks there are in the room, you and Inyri may have to wait outside. If there are enough, we all go down and hold the center."

"Got it."

Tycho slapped the Gand on the arm. "Wait until we get clear, then go."

"Ooryl understands."

Gavin retreated with the others. They sealed themselves inside the airspeeder. Inyri brought it up and around, giving Gavin a good view of the firefights going on outside. TIE fighters swooped and dove. Green laser bolts flashed through the sky thick and furious. Countless burn marks scored the flanks and front of the construction droid, yet it loomed ever larger as it came on toward them.

Winter twisted around in the seat. "He's in."

Gavin turned to look. The room's door appeared open. A greenish-yellow mist rolled out and carpeted the hallway in haze. The airspeeder's exhaust pushed it farther down the hallway, but there always seemed to be more of it pouring from the computer center.

The sharp report of an explosion brought all eyes forward again. A pair of blurred Headhunters raced past, flying through a collapsing ball of fire and debris. More laser bolts poured in at the construction droid, but there was no sign they had any effect on the titanic machine. And as bad as things looked in the air outside it, the cold efficiency of the way the droid dismembered the building in front of it was even worse. Their vantage point let the Rogues peer into the construction droid's maw and Gavin imagined what he saw to be the vision seen by billions of Alderaanians before their world exploded.

A thump on the hood of the airspeeder made Gavin jump and bang his head on the roof. He hunched down and rubbed his head. "Emperor's bones!"

Outside the Gand looked surprised, then held up four masks. "Ooryl has been successful."

Tycho reached forward from the back seat and patted Gavin on the shoulder. "Ready to go?"

"Sure. Maybe I can get a light dose of the gas and it'll slow my heart." Gavin got out of the airspeeder and pulled his mask on. It immediately felt hot on his face, but he tugged on the straps, fitting it tightly to his face. He took his comlink from his jacket lapel and snapped it into the receptacle near his right ear.

"I'm set, Tycho."

The Alderaanian Captain gave him a nod. "Come on, then. Let's go see if we can make it rain."

As Corran's Headhunter came up through the towers he caught Wedge's message to Tycho. "Hunter Lead here, Commander. Got a problem?"

"Seems so, Corran. Tower east of us has an E-web trained on us."

"Collateral targets?"

"Don't know, but the building should be evacuated except for troops. Get them gone."

"As ordered. Stand by." Corran throttled the black and gold fighter up and aimed for the stars. Before he got there, but after he had left the towers of Coruscant behind, he came up on his starboard wing and started to circle. From up there it was relatively easy to spot the stream of fire coming from a nearby cylindrical tower and lancing out at the construction droid.

Corran extended his loop and let it take him over and around the computer center. He dove and leveled out, coming in on the tower while running parallel to the construction droid's course. He shot past the droid and came up slightly. Heavy blaster fire lanced out at the construction droid from the tower. Corran let loose with a quick burst of fire, raking it across the side of the building.

His flight took him past his target, so he started to turn around again when fire came at him from the building. The blaster bolts splashed harmlessly against his rear shield, but Corran immediately rolled the Headhunter and turned back away from the side of the building he'd attacked. He leveled out, then dove and came around on a new attack vector. He switched his weapons' control over to concussion missiles, linked two, then climbed up over the construction droid's blocky outline.

His crosshairs settled on the genesis of the red stream directed against Wedge's droid. He got no target lock—an E-web and stormtrooper crew didn't conform to any target profile in the Headhunter's combat computer. Regardless, when he hit the trigger, two blue missiles streaked out and hit dead on target.

An argent explosion blew through that floor of the cylinder. The silvery disk spread out through the entire level and beyond, incinerating most of what was in there and scattering the rest of it out over the city. Yet, even for all that violence, the concussion missiles failed to damage the structural supports, leaving the tower intact above and below the level where little fires burned brightly in the night.

Corran keyed his comm unit. "Will that do it for you, Commander?"

"Thanks, Corran. We're leaving to see some friends."

"I copy. Want an escort?"

"If you've got nothing better to do."

Corran smiled. "At your leisure, sir, I live to serve."

Gavin had positioned himself so he could watch the door and still see what Winter was doing from the corner of his eye. Once they'd gotten into the room she'd plugged her datapad into the computer console and very quickly had a representation of Coruscant floating above her workstation. Her fingers flew over the keys and suddenly small cubes appeared to float around the world arranged in three rings. One circled the equator while the other two split the distance between the equator and the poles.

Seeming as insectoid as a Verpine because of the mask she wore, Winter nodded to Tycho. "These are the Orbital Solar Energy Transfer Satellites." She pointed to a glowing red dot riding just above the equator. "This is our target. It's night here now, but several orbital mirrors are high enough to give us what we need."

More typing and a small label appeared attached to each of the floating cubes. Gavin couldn't read them at that distance but he assumed they were unit designators that would allow Winter to send orders from the computer to the station.

"We'll use OSETS 2711. First step is to have the mirror opaque itself. Then we focus it here and start it reflecting again."

Tycho nodded. "Can you also bring up on this display the Golan stations and ships in orbit?"

She shrugged. "I don't know, probably, but if I do it might attract some attention. First things first."

"Go to it." Tycho stood behind her and rested his hands on her shoulders. "This world needs a bath, so start boiling the water."

•   •   •

Life could have been worse, Lieutenant Virar Needa thought to himself. The Captain Needa who had once commanded the Imperial Star Destroyer *Avenger* had only been his cousin, and one generation removed at that. Darth Vader had executed Lorth Needa for incompetence after Hoth, while Virar was still at the Imperial Military Academy. His cousins had all vanished, along with his aunt and his grandparents on the Needa side of the family, but at least he'd remained alive and been allowed to continue in service to the Empire. *It could have been worse, I could be dead.*

Of course, service on an Orbital Solar Energy Transfer Satellite was about as close to death as someone could get in the Imperial Navy without having shots fired at him. Others, including the rest of the six-man crew, saw OSETS service as punishment, but Virar Needa saw it as noble duty. After all, he was entrusted with the care of a facility that made life on Imperial Center possible. Without OSETS 2711, Imperial Center would be just that much more uncomfortable, and if the people who ran the Empire were uncomfortable, well, then things would just begin to fall apart entirely.

A mild tremor shook the station. The others looked up from their sabacc game in the lounge. He saw fear in their eyes because they had no idea what was happening. He did because of his four years of experience with OSETS 2711. That's why he was a Lieutenant and in command.

He raised a hand. "Don't worry, that's just the mirror panels rotating to opaque the surface."

One of the cadets looked up. "Why would they be doing that, sir?"

Needa smiled at him. "Well, Pedetsen, I would guess it is because another station is off-line for repairs and we're going to take over its duty. We'll have our direction adjusted . . ." He held a hand up, then cocked his wrist and pointed his index finger just as the altitude adjustment jets started a burn. "There you go."

"Thank you, sir."

Needa nodded and went back to looking out the viewport. Below him he saw the dark face of a sleeping Imperial Center. It scintillated with a variety of lights that ran like phosphorescent blood through shadowy flesh. He smiled and tried to burn the vision of the planet into his brain. *It always looks so pretty from up here—a potential it fails to live up to when I am down on the ground.*

The jet burn went on a bit longer than usual and this disturbed him. Not because he realized anything was wrong, after all, the care of OSETS 2711 was what kept him alive, so nothing could go wrong. He couldn't and wouldn't conceive of that possibility. No, the longer than normal burn, he decided, meant they had built a new reception facility for the energy OSETS 2711 was sending down. That he'd not heard of the plans to do this meant they were top secret. The use of OSETS 2711 to power this top secret, vital, new site meant someone down there had finally decided to reward his unswerving and unfailing loyalty.

The tremor again coursed through the station and Needa smiled. "That's the mirror reflecting again, boys. We're giving them everything they want. Our contribution to this day will never be forgotten."

43

Corran Horn snapped the Headhunter up on its starboard S-foil and pulled back on the stick. He feathered the throttle back, slowing his fighter, and pulled it through a tight turn. Leveling off he triggered two blaster bursts that blazed through the air in front of a TIE starfighter. The eyeball broke off its run on Wedge's airspeeder. The black vehicle slid into the gaping cavern marking what had once been a fifth-floor office.

Corran rolled the ship left, dropped into a dive, then came back up and over the computer center. "Hunter Lead here, anyone need help?"

Asyr's voice came back through the comm. "I show six more interceptors vectored in on us. Estimated time of arrival, five minutes."

"I copy, Five." Corran glanced at his scanner and saw the group she was indicating. "See if you can pull the fight more in this direction."

"As ordered, Lead."

Leveling out, Corran began a slow loop to the east. All of a sudden a golden dagger of sunlight stabbed down through the night. The wedge of light focused on an ostentatious building fitted with columns and a cascade of ever broadening steps. The building grew in brilliance until it shone like a beacon. For the barest of moments it even rivaled the exalted edifice of the Imperial Palace.

Then the building began to melt.

Window casings began to smoke and glow, then the pressure from the superheated air inside the building blew them out. Pennants flying from the top of the building burst into flame. Huge iron doors went from black to orange, red, and finally white before they began to waver and collapse. Columns began to wither and the building's sharp edges softened.

The building began to sag in on itself, then it swelled at the center. The roof rose up volcanically, then an explosion shook the building. Half-molten granite blocks split apart and sloughed to the side like rotting vegetable matter as a gout of steam shot skyward. It billowed out and thickened as it hit the layer of cooler air above it. The expanding vapor darkened precipitously, then Corran saw golden highlights illuminate it from within.

The first silvery lightning bolt slashed down at the Imperial Palace. Corran laughed aloud. "Even the elements want the Empire dead!"

He keyed his comm unit. "I hope you can hear me, Wedge. You've got one fantastic storm brewing out here. Keep it going."

The image of Coruscant floating in front of Captain Uwlla Iillor on the bridge of the *Corusca Rainbow* began to change. Beneath the twin shields the datastream began to sketch in an angry red storm centering itself over the Palace district. Gold pinpoints marked lightning strikes and quickly became so numerous that flecks of red floated like islands in a golden sea.

Jhemiti inclined his head toward the image. "The storm appears to be fierce."

"The worst Coruscant has seen in generations, I would imagine." She leaned forward and studied the image through half-closed eyes. "Rogue Squadron must have caused this storm somehow. It becomes a weapon of fantastic power, but it is very difficult to direct."

The Mon Calamari nodded. "Perhaps the Jedi Knight . . ."

"Can control it? I doubt the Emperor could have controlled a storm of this magnitude. This I take as a good thing because it means the Empire cannot stop it."

The inner shield sphere flickered and went dark. Jhemiti pointed at the holographic projection. "There, the shields are coming down."

"Perhaps." Iillor looked at the chronometer. "We have five minutes until the fleet comes through. Begin initial power up of the gravity well projectors."

Jhemiti's eyes half shut. "But the shields."

"The shields still exist." Captain Iillor gave her First Officer a cold stare. "We'll give Rogue Squadron time to finish their mission, but if they cannot, we will finish ours."

Wedge came around the corner and into the computer center after getting an all-clear from Gavin. Because the construction droid had the same anti-intruder system installed on it, Mirax, Iella, and he had been able to appropriate breathing gear from it before they made the run to the center. He immediately crossed to the workstation where Winter sat while Iella and Mirax took up defensive positions near the door.

"How are things going?"

Tycho looked over at him while Winter typed furiously on her datapad. "Good and bad. The storm is fierce enough that skyhooks are detaching and moving off. Better yet, the inner shields have come down. Unfortunately, it appears their collapse has resulted in a shift of resource allocation programs within the computers. The storm is taking some power plants off-line, but others have been directed to shunt their output through previously unused conduits."

Wedge frowned. "You're telling me that the destruction of one layer of shields has diverted power through backup systems to reinforce the remaining shields?"

Winter nodded. "No one knew the backup system of conduits existed—no power ran through them so folks scouting for places to tap the grid never found them. In essence, this is a whole new power grid. It allocates power to essential services, of which this center is part, but it means that main shield isn't coming down."

This is not good. Wedge leaned with one hand on the workstation. "Can you pull a map of this grid up?"

"Not available."

Emtrey tottled over. "If I might suggest, sir . . . ?"

"Please do, Emtrey."

"Lightning will travel along the easiest course from the ground to the clouds and vice versa. The new grid, and especially its substation transfer points, will leak a certain amount of power. Lightning strikes will cluster at these points, so a plot of strikes should show you where the grid is."

Winter's fingers played quickly over the datapad's input surface. The globe flattened out and golden pinpoints started to dot the resulting grid map. The image became localized to the Palace district and enlarged, but the strikes still bled together into a golden network. Wedge saw dark spaces fill in on the map with each staccato thunderclap from outside.

Tycho pointed to a solid cluster that appeared to be the hub from which many gold spokes spread. "That's likely a substation. The whole purpose of this storm was to hit and knock out power stations. This one looks invulnerable to lightning. So much for our plan."

Wedge shook his head. "The grounding that will protect it from lightning won't help it against missiles. Winter, can you pinpoint that substation?"

"Done."

Tycho looked over at Wedge. "You're going to send someone in at that target with the storm raging above it?"

"The airspeeder I came in doesn't have missiles or I'd go."

"Yes, but you're a Corellian. You have no respect for how truly hopeless some tasks really are."

"Right."

"So you're sending Corran."

"Right again." Wedge slapped Tycho on the back. "There's no pilot I know of for certain who can outfly lightning, but I'd sooner bet *on* Corran than against him."

Corran brought his fighter around on the heading Winter gave him. "You want me to fly into *that*?" Six kilometers distant, the lightning strikes came in sheets, not individual bolts. "It's very ugly over there."

"I copy, Corran, but it's got to be done. Take heart, the target is twice the size of the conduit on Borleias."

"Oh, you should have said that from the start." Corran nudged the throttle forward. "On an inbound vector."

"You have four minutes."

"I'll keep that in mind." Corran took the fighter into a dive and tried to sink as low as he could in the duracrete chasms. The storms had already begun to kick up high winds, but the buildings tended to break them up. He did hit some nasty sheers when he flew through intersections, but the worse of them occurred at the largest intersections, giving him plenty of time to recover.

He started to come up and out of the urban maze two kilometers away from his target. Rain immediately lashed his fighter. It beat so heavily on the cockpit canopy and shook the ship enough that it wasn't until he saw his shield indicator go from green to yellow that he realized someone was shooting at him. A glance at his aft monitor showed two Interceptors coming up on his tail.

Corran rolled and started a dive that he aborted almost immediately. Rolling again violently, he righted his craft and kicked in power to the repulsorlift drives. The drives cut in on cue and bounced his fighter up over a crumbling skywalk between buildings. *With power going down, they don't have their little lights on.*

Behind him something exploded and his aft sensor indicated he only had one squint on his tail. A pair of near misses, with green bolts shooting past his starboard S-foil, told him that the Imp pilot behind him was good. Coming up on his left wing, he pulled a hard turn around the corner of a building, then rolled 180 degrees and cut back around another. The figure-eight maneuver got rid of his pursuit for the moment, so he came back around and set up to make his run on the target.

The Headhunter sliced through the air amid a cacophony of thunder and a forest of lightning bolts. Corran knew there was no way to dodge a bolt—one second it would not be there and the next it would. The lightning strikes silhouetted darkened towers, helping him steer around trouble. In that way they proved more helpful than harmful, but he knew one solid strike and his controls would fry. *They will fry, fighter won't fly, and I will die.*

Turbulence in the air began to bounce him around. The stick tried to pull itself out of his grasp, but he hung on firmly. Flying through rough air he had to strike a balance between becoming rigid, which would lock things up and crash him, and being too flexible, which meant he'd lose control of the stick and the fighter would crash. He trimmed his speed and did his best to keep the fighter on target.

More green laser blasts shot past. *At least the turbulence is making me tough to hit.* He shoved the stick hard to the left, then rolled right and pulled back. After two seconds he rolled left again and hauled back on the stick. Leveling out right, he hit rudder and brought his nose in line with the aft of the Interceptor. His quick turns amounted to taking a long time to cover the distance the squint covered swiftly in its swoop. He ended up behind it and fired.

The blaster bolts clipped the starboard wing on the Imperial fighter. It rolled right and got out of his line of fire. Corran could have followed it and killed it, but he'd closed on his target, so he switched over to concussion missiles. He set them on single fire, rolled, and dove in on the target. He dropped the targeting box on what appeared to be the base of a massive obelisk honoring the Emperor and let fly.

The concussion missile streaked out and hit the base of the statue. It exploded, casting rock in all directions. The obelisk cast a massive shadow up over the face of the Imperial Palace, then it tottered and fell. Hitting the ground, it shattered into a thousand pieces, but Corran saw no secondary explosions. *Ruined a monument, but nothing else. One more run better do the trick.*

Wedge stared at the map. He'd seen Corran's attack run and had a track of the missile going into the target, but the lights didn't go out and the image didn't die. "What happened? He hit it, didn't he?"

Winter nodded. "Right on target, but not enough power. He's cracked the outer case. Another shot or two should do it."

Tycho shook his head. "It better just be one more shot because that's all he's got."

Wedge pointed to a green Interceptor icon coming in and around toward Corran's red Headhunter icon. "Provided he gets one more shot. Can't you do something about that squint, Winter?"

She looked up at him. "That squint was the source of the data on the missile hit. You really want us to be blind out there?"

"No, of course not." Wedge looked down for a moment, then clapped his hands. "You're getting datafeeds from him? You have his identification number and internal identification, right?"

"Can't get this data any other way. We're inside the Imperial system, so getting that data is easy."

"Good. I've got an idea. Tap into Coruscant Traffic Control and get the Taxi, Hangar, and Maintenance programs set up with his numbers." Wedge keyed his comlink. "Corran, listen to me. Your first hit was good, but you need to pack more into the next one. Here's the plan . . ."

• • •

Corran closed his mouth. "I copy, Wedge." He punched a couple of buttons on his console. "Telemetry coming your way. You know, you're always stealing my data for runs. Can I start getting Pathfinder pay?"

"Sure, I'll add it to your back-pay file. Squint's coming up on your tail. Get ready."

"As ordered, sir." Corran let a smile spread across his face. *According to the boss I want you with me as tight as possible, but still loose enough that you aren't going to burn me down.* Corran unconsciously pressed his hand to his throat, but the medallion he normally wore wasn't there. *It's with Whistler. That'll have to count for luck for now.*

Coming around on another attack vector against the target, Corran let the squint drift onto his tail. Loosening his grip on the stick ever so slightly, he let the air bounce him around a bit. Green laser bolts played out all around him. With a flick of his thumb he shunted all forward shield energy to the rear shields, then he tightened his grip and rolled ninety degrees to the left. He remained diving in at the target, but was ready to pull out at the last minute.

He spitted the hole the earlier missile had made with his targeting reticle. "Control, three, two, one!" He hit the trigger, then pulled back on the stick for all he was worth. "Missile away."

Winter punched a button on her datapad. "Link established and flowing."

Captain Iillor looked at Jhemiti. "Thirty seconds and counting. Bring the gravity well projectors to full power on my mark."

Corran's concussion missile sailed in at the target. Throughout the short flight the targeting computer built into the missile took sensor readings, compared the coordinates they supplied with those of the target, determined if it should explode or not yet, and reported the whole process back to Corran's Headhunter. A million times a second it went through that same process, constantly updating its position relative to the target and relaying the data to the Headhunter.

Corran's Headhunter, in turn, sent that information on to Winter's datapad. There it remained for a nanosecond, then flowed into the Imperial computer network. It routed itself through several key systems and finally poured into Coruscant Traffic Control. The data then fed into the Taxi, Hangar, and Maintenance programming that, because of the override and emergency data flags Winter had provided, sent it back out to the Imperial Interceptor closing on the Headhunter.

The chief benefit of computers is that they can automate boring and routine jobs that need not concern a human. If an X-wing fighter needed to be moved from a landing pad to a hangar position, or on into maintenance, the R2 unit assigned to that X wing could perform that simple task without the need to trouble the pilot. Since TIE fighters do not use R2 units, other programs had been created to supply travel routes, coordinates, and speeds to a TIE fighter so it could be moved about without a pilot.

In this case, the course supplied to the Interceptor on Corran's tail was the course the missile was traveling. The destination was the missile's target coordinates and the speed was as close as the fighter could manage to approximating the missile's speed. The implementation of such programming required an override code, which had been supplied. Because of the potential problems caused if such codes were to fall into enemy hands, the pilots could override the automatic programming, provided they hit the correct console buttons in the appropriate order.

Doing that required approximately 2.5 seconds of the pilot's undivided attention.

The Interceptor pilot's attention was anything but undivided.

The concussion missile caromed off the edge of the breach its predecessor had opened and exploded. It blasted a hole in the shielding of the energy conduit. Shards from the conduit and its shielding sprayed the interior of the conduit, severing some cables, merely nicking others. Sparks flew and several circuits shorted out. Power died in several buildings for a second, but other lines accepted more power and the shields remained intact.

Then the Interceptor hit. While it was not traveling as fast as the concussion missile, it did mass significantly more than the projectile. It was able to build up a considerable amount of kinetic energy that it transferred to the target upon impact. In addition, the crash compacted the Interceptor's fuel cells, compressing the fuel that subsequently detonated. The Interceptor's crushed hull sheered through the power conduit, severing the thick bundle of cables running through it, and the explosion that followed tangled and fused lines that had never been meant to touch.

Outside Corran's cockpit, Coruscant went black.

"Ten, nine, eight," Captain Iillor counted down.
    "Look!"
    Her eye came up off the chronometer. The last shield sphere flickered.
    "Seven, six, five . . ."
    The shield sphere died.
    "Kill the projectors, Lieutenant Jhemiti." Captain Iillor looked out toward the planet sparkling like a star in the distance. "Now the battle for Coruscant begins."

44

Still basking in the glory of his redemption, Lieutenant Virar Needa stared out the viewport at Imperial Center. He saw lights on the world flicker and die, but even that unusual a thing happening did not penetrate the aura of well-being in which he cocooned himself. Clearly, it seemed to him, those responsible for the power problems on Imperial Center would be banished to oblivion and he would be free to ascend into the positions they vacated.

As he stared out into space he saw the stars ripple along a wide front. Ships began to revert from hyperspace and his heart rate picked up as this happened. He always enjoyed ships entering and leaving Imperial Center space. He took great delight in cataloging them by type and later correlating a sighting with news from the war against the Rebels.

A smile spread across his face as two large ships materialized. He recognized them instantly as Imperial Star Destroyers. As they reverted they executed a turn to starboard, putting them into a geostationary orbit. *That's standard procedure, as the Captains of the* Accuser *and* Adjucator *know quite well*.

His ability to recognize the two ships pleased him,

which is why he wondered about the underlying sense of unease slowly seeping into his heart. About the time one of the long, gently curved Mon Calamari battle cruisers reverted and swung into the line, he recalled the *Accuser* and *Adjucator* had both been captured at Endor by the Rebels. The fact that a number of Mon Cal ships were pulling into line with them meant . . . Needa paled. *At the moment of my greatest glory, the Rebels have come to ruin me!*

More and more Rebel ships poured from hyperspace. Big ships, small ships, snubfighters, freighters, frigates, and corvettes, each of them pulled into line with the heavier ships. The battle cruisers and destroyers formed a central layer, with ships diminishing in size and strength as they stretched out from equator to pole in the northern hemisphere.

Instantly the black void of space came alive with turbolaser and ion-cannon fire. Toward the bottom of the viewport Needa saw a Golan Space Defense station. The lozenge-shaped platform launched spread after spread of proton torpedoes while its turbolaser batteries sprayed green energy projectiles at the invaders. The return fire it took splashed harmlessly against its shields, or so it seemed at first, though Needa noticed the shield sphere slowly shrinking.

This cannot be! He turned from the viewport, raking fingers back through brown hair. "To your battle stations, men! The enemy is upon us!"

Pedetsen looked up from the sabacc game. "Begging your pardon, sir, but a mirror doesn't have battle stations."

Needa's jaw worked up and down a couple of times as he mulled over the cadet's comment. *True, but we must do something.* "Arm yourselves. We won't go down without a fight."

The darkness in the computer center only lasted for a couple of seconds, but it seemed like eons to Wedge. It was time enough for remnants of childhood fears of darkness to meld with adult fears of failure. The darkness left him blind and opened the doorway to any number of possible and horrible futures. For all he knew the power to the subsidiary computer center had been severed by Imperial stormtroopers who were even now preparing to enter the room and resume control of the facility.

The lights came back up again. The holographic map wavered and popped, then stabilized. Elation filled him for a moment, then he realized that having power available meant failure. *Or does it?* "Why do we have power?"

Winter hit two keys on the datapad. "Reserve generators came on-line here after the external power was cut."

"And power is down? And the shields?"

She hit more keys and the map expanded up from the tactical one showing the Palace district to the orbital one showing the planet as a whole. There was no indication of shields anywhere. "They're down."

Wedge keyed his comlink. "Corran, you did it."

"I just aimed, Wedge, you sliced the victory together."

"We can argue who gets stuck with credit later. Be careful, you still have TIEs flying around you."

"They're all vectoring up, Wedge."

"What?"

"We have company."

Wedge pointed to Winter. "Slice me into Traffic Control. I want to see what's orbiting out there."

"Will do." Winter's fingers flew over the keys and the sphere that was Coruscant suddenly became surrounded by a shell of orbiting stations, satellites, and ships. The Rebel fleet formed a concave cap over part of the northern hemisphere. Within its range floated a number of Golan stations as well as several Star Destroyers racing to oppose the Rebels.

"Can you get me better visuals? Is there a feed from that mirror you can pull?"

She shook her head. "No visual feed from it and all

of the military ships have gone independent of the ground, so I can't get their visuals either. We know where they are, but we don't know what they're doing."

A few holes opened in the Rebel formation. Wedge knew that the ships lost were small—most likely converted freighters with weapons grafted on—but their losses disturbed him. Just looking at the situation, the size of the Rebel fleet and the paucity of defenders, there was no way Imperial forces could defeat the Rebels. *Slow us down and hurt us, yes, but keep us off Coruscant? No. That's clear, which means everyone who dies up there today doesn't need to.*

Tycho pointed to one of the space platforms. "I'd bet that's a Golan III. Our heavy ships can't concentrate on it until they eliminate the destroyers. It's not quite as heavily armed as the *Victory*-class destroyers, but it's got to be the source of most of the damage to the fringes of the fleet."

"You can't slice into any ground-based missile batteries to use against that thing?"

Winter shook her head. "Aside from Corran and the other Headhunters, we have no weapons here. It would be nice if the Golan station would shoot streamers down into the atmosphere and into our thunderstorm, but I wouldn't count on that happening anytime soon."

Tycho shrugged. "Look on the bright side, Wedge . . ."

"Is there a bright side?"

"Sure, if it had targeted us, we'd be slag."

"That's not what I'd call particularly bright, Tycho." Wedge brought his head up. "But it could be. It could be very bright indeed."

"Go down without a fight, Lieutenant Needa?" Pedetsen frowned in Needa's direction. "One proton torpedo and we go down without even a whimper. I'll take two."

Needa blinked in confusion. "You want us hit with two?"

"No, I want two more cards." The cadet glanced at his cards, then up at Needa. "Of proton torpedoes I want zero."

"The Rebels have come!" Needa pointed at the viewport. "We must do something!"

Pedetsen shook his head and laid his sabacc cards on the table. "Sir, if we do anything, we'll die. Now either side might have a use for dead heroes, but I don't think the heroes will get much out of it. On the other hand, whoever takes Imperial Center—or maybe we should call it Coruscant—will have use for an undamaged mirror and a live crew."

Needa glanced back at the fleet. "But those are the Rebels."

"You think they can find us worst duty than this?" Pedetsen smiled. "They'll probably hail you as a hero."

"What?"

"Hey, it was your cousin who was martyred by Darth Vader after he let Han Solo escape Hoth. After all, your cousin had Rebel sympathies that he only confided in you, which is why he let Solo escape. Your having been punished with this duty proves the Empire suspected him, but could prove nothing."

That is one way to interpret the facts of the case, I suppose. Needa frowned. "Do you think the Rebels would believe that?"

"I don't know, but I think if we're dead, you won't be able to convince them that you and your loyal crew have been waiting for them for ages." Pedetsen raked a pile of chips toward himself and started to shuffle the sabacc deck. "Your choice, sir. Do what you think is right."

Needa thought for a second, frowned, then nodded. "I think I choose not to choose. If we do something, we risk death. We can't do anything anyway, so there is no reason to choose."

A tremor shook OSETS 2711. Needa braced himself against the bulkhead as the mirror started to shift. "We're moving."

"I know, Lieutenant." Pedetsen smiled. "Looks like someone just made your mind up for you."

On *Home One*'s bridge chaos reigned. Hundreds of voices competed with one another, each filled with urgency. Admiral Ackbar sat at the center of it, listening intently to comm feeds from his group commanders. The two Imperial Star Destroyers entering the battle were the *Triumph* and the *Monarch*. Already *Emancipator* and *Liberator* had begun pounding the ships. *Triumph*'s shields had collapsed on one side, prompting the Captain to execute a roll that brought undamaged shields up between the destroyer and the Rebels.

Though the *Triumph*'s difficulties heartened Ackbar, the Golan Space Defense platform off the port stern sickened him. It had engaged many of the smaller ships in the fleet and was hammering them mercilessly. The Commander on the platform had targeted ships with multiple proton torpedoes while saving his turbolasers for snubfighter defense. TIE fighters coming up from Coruscant seemed content to fight beneath the umbrella of his fire. The fact that the station could not move made it marginally less lethal than the Star Destroyers, but in the time it took for them to be taken out of action, a lot of smaller Rebel ships would die.

He looked up at the Quarren who had just appeared beside his command chair. "What is it, Commander Sirlul? Something about the station?"

"Perhaps . . ." A tremolo distorted her words as she pointed out the port side viewport. "The mirror is moving."

"Why would it . . . ?"

Before Sirlul could offer a possible answer to Ackbar's question, the mirror's panels swung and locked into reflective position. The whole structure contracted slightly, sharpening the solar beam. Though the reflected light remained all but invisible in space—only showing up where it shone upon and incinerated debris—

its brilliant focal point could easily be seen. It appeared as a bright dot on the edge of the Golan III station.

Silvery lines, like cracks forming in ice or rootlets spreading through the earth, began to appear at the edges of the circle. Delicate and almost brittle, they snaked away from the station and drifted into space. The bright spotlight shifted right ever so slightly, leaving in its wake a black crescent. The argent rootlets clung to the crescent's outer edge while opposite them some of the rootlets spun off into space.

The Quarren clasped her hands at the small of her back. "At its focal point the solar beam is approximately 12.5 meters in diameter. Roughly the length of an X-wing."

The hole on the end of the station grew as the beam shifted slightly. Already half the turbolaser batteries had stopped firing. Ackbar could easily visualize the destruction as the beam pierced bulkhead after bulkhead, burning from one end of the station to another. A sheet of metal would glow red, then white, then evaporate. The solar beam would stab deeper, igniting whatever it touched, then begin on another bulkhead.

Ackbar looked up. "When the platform stops shooting send the *Devonian* and *Ryloth* over there. I want our people on that station to assess it and help those who have survived."

"Sir, the *Ryloth* and *Devonian* have less than one hundred troopers on board. The station has over a thousand."

"Not anymore, Commander." Ackbar half closed his eyes as something near the center of the station exploded. "Those who are left aren't going to be hostile. They'll want to get off that thing and we will oblige them. Send them to the other Golan stations, let them tell the story of what happened to their station. It'll give their Commanders a lot to think about and maybe, just maybe, save a lot of lives on both sides."

45

Corran glanced at the fuel indicator on his command console. It showed he had another ten minutes of fuel. A return to Tycho's base would only take two or three minutes and refueling would take a half hour or so. He wasn't certain if with the fleet orbiting above the Palace district, Wedge and the others in the computer center would face danger from Imperial forces, but in many ways that question was moot given his fuel supply. He suspected the others were not in much better shape.

"Hunter Lead here, report with fuel status."

Everyone else in the flight reported being in the same situation he was. "What we will do is this: Everyone take a long-range scan of the area. If we have no immediate things to worry about, we head in, refuel, and come back out."

"I copy, Hunter Lead," came the replies.

"Corran, I caught that, too." Wedge's voice paused for a moment. "Winter shows no activity in your vicinity and we look pretty secure here, too. Head in and hurry back."

"Will do, Wedge. Horn out." Corran brought his Headhunter around in a vast circle, letting the others fly in on a more direct route toward their hangar. *First up, last in.* He smiled. He knew the others didn't need him to provide a good example. The fact was that the five of them had accounted for over a dozen Imperial starfighters and Interceptors, proving the Rogues had not lost their edge and that Asyr Sei'lar was a good pilot in her own right.

He punched his sensors over to long range and immediately picked up a number of signals on his scanner. Corran keyed the comm unit. "Pash, I'm picking up nine or ten hits."

"I copy, Corran. Looks like small civilian vessels. The exodus is beginning."

Corran ruddered his ship to port and dove down to do a flyby on one of his sensor contacts. It did in fact appear to be a luxury yacht, with gentle flowing lines and a gaudily painted hull. Like the other ships it was heading northeast to slip beneath the edge of the Rebel umbrella. The ships would sail around to the daytime side of the planet and head out into hyperspace from there, using Coruscant's mass as a shield to prevent the Rebels from attacking them.

Corran was certain the vast majority of the people heading out firmly believed the Rebels would steal their wealth, dispossess them of their treasures, defile their sons and daughters, torture, maim, and kill resisters, and commit any number of other crimes against them. He didn't think plunder and raping were foremost in the minds of most Rebels, but here at the core of the Empire the belief in lies used by the Emperor to justify his dictatorship ran deep among some folks. And even those who knew better than to believe such lies did truly feel they had something to fear since the idea of bringing Imperials to justice had always been one of the Rebellion's more appealing tenants.

He found himself of two minds about the fleeing people. Part of him wanted to bring them to justice. He could easily have sideslipped his Headhunter and blasted the hyperdrive engines from the hull of the yacht. That would trap its occupants on Coruscant and force them to face retribution for their crimes against their fellow citizens.

The other part of him sympathized with them. The Empire had forced him to flee from Corellia, carrying with him little more than a change of clothes. He even had to surrender his identity, as would these refugees, for to remain who he was would have left him vulnerable to the Empire's hunters. He had been forced to change who he had been and had been forced into an entirely different lifestyle just to preserve his life. Because of the constant fear of discovery, of being made to run again, that life seemed more punishing than any prison term or even execution. *Better no life at all than one lived in constant fear.*

He didn't know if he'd heard those words before or composed the line himself, but it struck him that those words embodied the nugget of Rebel opposition to the Empire. Mon Mothma and the other leaders had enough foresight to look ahead and plan out the course of the campaign against the Empire, but for people in his position, the fight was one to defeat the forces who made them fear. The fact that after each battle, each victory, there was just that much less to be afraid of became almost tangible and served as a very sweet reward indeed.

Corran nudged his stick back and climbed up away from the fleeing yacht. *Run, but always know you cannot run far enough.*

He started to bring the Headhunter around on a course to the hangar, but he saw an anomalous blip on his sensor screen. He initiated an identification program, but the contact faded and returned, depriving the computer of enough solid data to make a match. It seemed to settle on an unknown fighter and a Super Star Destroyer. "Pash, what have you got for a contact at 352.4 degrees?"

"Nothing. Do you have something?"

"Yeah, but it's weird. Probably a storm ghost. I'm going to check it out."

"Want a wing? I can abort my approach."

"Negative, I'm just doing a flyby. If I need help, I'll need you all ready to go." Corran glanced at his fuel gauge. "One pass, then I'm in."

With the Golan Space Defense platform gone, Admiral Ackbar sent a signal to the fleet that started an evolution of the battle. Originally the Rebels had expected two or three times more by way of Star Destroyers than had appeared to defend Coruscant. That only the *Triumph* and *Monarch* remained to oppose them surprised him because neither ship had a particularly illustrious reputation or crew. At last reports *Emperor's Will* and *Imperator* had also been part of the Coruscant defense force as well, and their participation in the battle would have made things much more difficult.

Liberator, *Emancipator*, and *Home One* formed a line moving past *Triumph* and *Monarch*. The two lines exchanged fire and missiles, savaging each other. Shields held at first, then, inevitably, crumbled. Beneath them the ships' heavy armor had to absorb the force of the missile blasts and laser bolts. Some shots, guided by the Force or the product of pure chance, hit turbolaser batteries or torpedo launch tubes, vaporizing them, crushing them, and destroying them. Others just nibbled away at a ship's hull or superstructure. Molecule by molecule they weakened the barrier between the ship's interior and the void.

As always with war the best strategy was to hit without being hit back. With ships the size of Star Destroyers and heavy cruisers, avoiding being hit was, at best, difficult. The closest that could be managed in that regard was to minimize the number of weapons bearing on the ship. With the two lines passing broadside to each other, the ships were exposed to the maximum possible damage inflicted by the other side.

At Ackbar's signal another Mon Calamari heavy cruiser, *Mon Remonda*, turned from its position in line behind *Home One*, and pointed its bow toward Coruscant. It surged forward, cutting across the Imperial Star

Destroyers' line of flight. In doing so it was able to bring all of its starboard firing-arc weapons to bear on *Triumph* while the Star Destroyer could hit it with its forward arc weapons.

Mon Remonda's gunners began to pour fire in on *Triumph*. The Imperial Star Destroyer had already lost its shields, so the turbolaser strikes played easily up over the spine of the ship. Even more devastating were the hits by the Mon Calamari cruiser's ion cannons. Their blue lightning chased all over the destroyer's hull. Explosions trailed in the lightning's wake.

The same time that *Mon Remonda* moved to strike at *Triumph*, the umbrella force began to separate. Assault frigates—a fanciful name for refitted freighters—began to close a net around the two Imperial warships and their smaller support ships. While they could not sustain the sort of damage the heavier ships were taking and survive, the Star Destroyers' ability to strike at them had been diminished by combat. The smaller ships closed in, firing away at the destroyers. There were so many of them that the gunners who could target them could not target *all* of them.

Other heavier ships—Corellian corvettes, gunships, and a variety of bulk cruisers and Mon Calamari cruisers—pushed up and out away from Coruscant. They used distance to let them see over Coruscant's horizon and spot other Imperial forces that could have been hidden on the world's far side. They remained out of range of the Golan Space Defense platforms, yet close enough to respond quickly to any situation that demanded overwhelming firepower.

Starfighters and troop carriers began their runs to the planet. The outcome of the battle in space was important, but without troops on the ground to take, hold, and secure facilities and impose order, Coruscant would remain unconquered. Ackbar suffered under no illusions about Coruscant and its defenselessness. That the shields were down he felt was nothing short of a miracle, but he couldn't count on how long they would stay down. He had, as nearly as he knew, a narrow window in which to insert his troops, so he pushed them forward as quickly as seemed prudent.

Commander Sirlul reached over and tapped a command into the keypad on the arm of Ackbar's command chair. A holographic schematic of *Triumph* appeared before him. Multiple systems were outlined in red, including the bridge. "*Triumph* has lost power and is beginning to slide back into the atmosphere."

Ackbar hit his comlink. "Ackbar to Onoma."

"Onoma here, Admiral."

"Cease firing on *Triumph*. Use your tractor beams to pull *Triumph* along and accelerate its orbit so it won't decay. We want to save the ship if we can." Ackbar looked at *Monarch* and could see it taking as much damage as *Triumph* had. *Between it and* Triumph, *we might be able to salvage most of a Star Destroyer.*

"Order acknowledged, sir. Onoma out."

Sirlul glanced over at Ackbar. "Captain Averen of *Monarch* has sent a truce-byte out to everyone."

"He will surrender unconditionally?"

"If there are conditions, they will be insignificant."

Ackbar nodded. "Conduct the negotiations."

"Yes, sir."

"And when you're done with that, Commander, I have another job for you."

"Yes, sir?"

Ackbar pointed at Coruscant. "Find me someone down there who can surrender that world to me."

Wedge had Winter bring back up the Palace district tactical map. "Corran, we're getting nothing on this contact you report."

"Contact is weak, Wedge. It oscillates back and forth, as if running between buildings. The computer can't make any sense of . . . wait a minute!"

"What's going on, Corran."

"I've lost throttle control. I'm speeding up!" The

green arrow representing Corran's Headhunter began a slow dip toward the planet. "Initiating emergency shutdown of fuel injectors one and two."

That will cut fuel back to half, slowing him. Wedge looked down at Winter. "Can you help him?"

"I can try."

"Negative, Winter, cut the override code you're using. I need to shut those two injectors down."

"I haven't used an override code, Corran."

"Yes, you have. I'm locked up. No control."

Wedge dropped down to stare at the data scrolling across the screen on Winter's datapad. "What's happening?"

Near panic flooded through the comlink from Corran. "Manual override is not working."

"Punch out, Corran! Eject!"

"Can't. Inverting! Nothing I can . . ."

Static filled the comlink channel as the green arrow dropped from sight. Wedge heard an explosion and listened to its echoes rumble as the holographic image of the building Corran's Headhunter had hit slowly collapsed. He saw the building implode, but he felt it in his stomach. A void formed deep in his guts, swallowing the elation he had felt moments before and having more than enough room to devour the pain and guilt trickling through him.

Wedge bounced a fist off the holopad workstation, then tore off his gas mask and hurled it across the room. He didn't know if the gas in the room had fully dissipated yet, and part of him hoped it had not. He'd been fighting for more than seven years to oppose the Empire. Friends had come and gone—mostly *gone*—in that time. He'd grown cynical enough to keep his distance from new recruits because he knew they died earliest and if he didn't befriend them it wouldn't hurt him as much when they died.

The truth was, though, that the distance didn't really insulate him, it just allowed him to think their deaths didn't hurt as much. But Corran, as much as the rest of the Rogues and a little bit more, had managed to close that gap. No, they didn't always get along, but disagreements didn't dull respect and admiration. Corran was a good pilot and a smart man who treated loyalty as the sacred foundation of friendship. Corran was like Tycho and Luke—all of them knew the horrors and pressures and anxiety of war, and all of them knew the sense of satisfaction at having completed a mission.

Even though they fought against Imperial stormtroopers and pilots, it sounded somehow evil to take pride in killing other living creatures. And it wasn't really the killing of which they were proud, but of surviving. They took pride in the fact that they had stopped someone from killing their friends and, in doing so, loosened the grip of an evil Empire on a fearful populace. Only those individuals who had gone through what they had could truly understand it all and only those who understood it could really, truly, understand why war and killing should never be anything but the last resort.

A hand landed on Wedge's shoulder and he spun, knocking Tycho's arm aside. "I lost another one."

"Maybe." The outline of his gas mask had left red lines on Tycho's face. "But maybe, just maybe, Corran managed to punch out before the ship went down. Maybe he's lying on top of that pile of rubble just waiting for someone to help him."

And maybe he's buried so deep we'll never find him. Wedge drew in a deep breath, then nodded. "You're right, that's probably what happened. He's probably waiting for us right now."

"He's a Rogue, after all."

"Right, come on." Wedge headed for the door. "He's a Rogue and we take care of our own. No matter the circumstances, no matter the situation, we take care of our own."

46

Wedge Antilles found the duracrete and transparisteel barrow improbably neat. The off and on rain for the last four days had washed the dust away and granted the fractured pieces of pseudogranite sharp edges that looked almost decorative. Nothing moved in the mound, nothing showed colors outside reflective silver, black, and grey. The hill of debris rose less than seven meters above the level upon which he stood because the falling stories had telescoped into the floors below.

And somewhere in there are the mortal remains of Corran Horn. Wedge shook his head. The building Corran had hit had been on the line of the construction droid's advance, so when Mirax used the warning beacon to get the computer center evacuated, this building had likewise emptied of people. Most of the newly unhomed already picked up on Rebellion phrases and said that the Force had truly been with them when they got out. And yet others had determined that Corran, knowing his Headhunter was going down, had deliberately driven it into a tower he knew had been evacuated. They said that made him a hero.

As if that's what it took for him to be a hero. As if

nothing else he had done would have made him one.
Wedge realized his hands had knotted into fists again. He
forced them open, as he had found himself doing numerous times since Coruscant had fallen. When it came down
to it, because of the efforts of his people, Coruscant had
not been drenched in blood. In fact, aside from the casu-
alties in the space battle and limited actions on the planet,
virtually no one had been injured. "Yet another miracle,
another sign the Force was with us."

Wedge hated the mocking tone that came with his
words. People all around had gone berserk with joy when
Coruscant fell. Even he had celebrated, albeit a bit subdued, because Aril Nunb had been found alive and nearly
well in Invisec. Her return did not cancel the pain of
Corran's loss, especially with Mirax Terrik wandering
around as if her heart had been torn out and Iella Wessiri
not being much better off. The big hologram, the liberation of Coruscant, became hard to focus upon with such
an immediate loss.

While he pointed to Corran's death as the wellspring
of his anxiety and frustration, he knew he did so because
he did not want to consider the question that all members
of the Rebel staff had been asking themselves: Why hadn't
it been harder? To even consider that question somehow
seemed to cheapen their victory that was, by all accounts,
hard fought and won through superior planning and execution. Even so, an average deck of sabacc cards had more
computing power than the whole of the Imperial Naval
staff left to conduct the defense of the planet.

The inescapable conclusion that could be drawn from
the utterly inept defense of Coruscant was that Ysanne
Isard *wanted* the New Republic to take the world. The
Provisional Council had seen Coruscant as a symbol.
Once they took it they would have won the right to rule
the galaxy. There was no doubt that many worlds that
had proclaimed themselves neutral would indeed throw
their allegiance to the Republic. In that way the conquest
of Coruscant did hasten the fall of the Empire.

Coruscant also became a black hole from which the

New Republic could not escape. Just as taking it had been a goal for them, so taking it would be a goal for any other pretender to Palpatine's throne. The Rebellion that had survived detection by the enemy through moving their headquarters dozens of times now had bottled itself up. It traded flexibility and mobility for legitimacy and Wedge wasn't certain that was a trade made in their favor.

He also knew the conquest of Coruscant would not be without a price. Ysanne Isard had clearly traded the world for her escape from it—no one had found any trace of her and the reason for her evacuation seemed quite sound. Already rumors of a plague spreading through Invisec were flying thick and fast. Nawara Ven and Riv Shiel had undergone bacta therapy and were recovering. What little General Cracken had told him about Aril Nunb's debriefing suggested the virus might have been created by the Empire specifically to leave Coruscant a charnel house, but the conquest had aborted that plan. Virus had been found in the water supply, though Rogue Squadron's boil-off of a lot of water may have killed a vast quantity of the virus.

Wedge heard footsteps behind him and, expecting to see Tycho and Winter, was surprised when instead he saw General Cracken and Pash. Wedge began to smile, but Pash appeared hesitant and Airen intent, which led him to believe something serious was going on. "Good afternoon, General, Lieutenant. Is there something I can do for you?"

The elder Cracken nodded. "There's been some headway in the investigation of what happened to Lieutenant Horn. My people went over all the sensor traces we could find concerning the crash, as well as comm transcripts and the statements made by everyone who heard his last transmissions."

Wedge smiled genuinely. "This is good news. If you don't mind waiting a minute or two, I know Tycho will want to hear this, and it will save you telling it again." Wedge glanced at his chronometer. "He should be here momentarily."

Airen Cracken shook his head. "I'm afraid he won't

be joining you. He's been arrested for treason and the murder of Corran Horn."

"What? That's impossible." Wedge stared at the head of Alliance Intelligence. "Tycho would never do that. Never."

General Cracken held a hand up. "There are some things you don't know, Commander, and I shouldn't have to remind you that an arrest is not a conviction. It is just that we have sufficient evidence to arrest him and it was deemed appropriate to do so."

Wedge folded his arms across his chest. "What evidence?"

"He was absent without leave from his post at Noquivzor. He traveled from there to Coruscant, bringing with him an M-3PO droid full of highly sensitive data."

"He did those things on my order, General. Those orders were issued and sealed by me at Noquivzor."

The older man nodded. "So I have been told and so it says in your statement. If we ever get down to where your office was, I believe I will find those orders. However, until I do, his vanishing act looks highly suspicious, especially when coupled with other things."

"Such as?"

"Captain Celchu knew the command codes for the Headhunter Horn was flying."

"He knew them for all those Headhunters."

"Yes, but no other pilot threatened him with exposure for treasonous activities." General Cracken looked at his son. "Pash overheard a heated conversation between Horn and Celchu right before the mission began. Celchu told Horn he'd checked his machine out special."

Wedge's head came up and Pash winced at the harshness of his stare. "Is this true?"

"I wasn't spying, Commander."

"My son was not placed in your unit to spy. He just happened to be there." Airen frowned. "He didn't want to tell me about the conversation and has proved a most reluctant witness."

"I see." Rogue Squadron's leader nodded toward

Pash. "Corran was probably hot about all this. What was Tycho's reaction?"

Pash's tense expression eased. "He said he welcomed any investigation Corran wanted to make. He said he had nothing to fear."

Wedge raised an eyebrow. "That hardly sounds like a man with any fear of discovery."

"He wouldn't fear it if he'd disabled the manual override and had given his masters the command code for the Headhunter. What you did with that Interceptor, they did with Horn's Headhunter."

"You still haven't established a link between Tycho and the Empire."

"But we will, Commander." Cracken shrugged his shoulders. "We have means, motive, and opportunity. That's all we need for an arrest and trial."

Wedge just shook his head. "This is wrong, and you know it. After all we've fought for, to get to this point and arrest someone who's risked his life time and again for the Rebellion on evidence that's circumstantial at best is a crime itself. A crime worthy of the Empire."

"No, Commander Antilles, you're wrong." Anger sparked in the elder Cracken's eyes and jetted into his voice. "The Empire would have snatched Celchu, broken him down until he confessed, then they would have killed him. He would have disappeared and no one would have dared ask about him. That's how the Empire would have handled it. The way *we* will handle it is to have a trial and assess innocence or guilt publicly, openly, aboveboard, so there is no question about justice being done or not."

Cracken raised his head up and met Wedge's stare openly. "That, sir, is exactly what we fought for. You know it, and you know there's no other way to handle this situation."

Wedge hesitated, then closed his eyes and nodded. "You're correct, of course, General. We did fight for justice." He turned to stare at Corran's grave and thought of Tycho. "The pity is, even in victory, justice still eludes those who deserve it the most."

Epilogue

If there was a part of him that didn't hurt, Corran Horn couldn't name it. His chief complaint came from his shoulders. He could feel the binders holding his arms at the small of his back constantly exerting pressure to pull his elbows closer together. They sheathed his arms in metal from fingertips to elbows and were the kind of restraints that had been outlawed for CorSec's use.

He found himself lying on his stomach in the dark on a thin cot of some sort. He was naked, save for the binders, and the room was slightly chilled. A weak, barely noticeable vibration ran through the cot, producing a low hum that depending on how he turned his head, he could occasionally hear. He strained his eyes to determine if there was anything to see, but the utter absence of light foiled him.

Corran found his thoughts wandering, which made him think that he'd been drugged. That sensation, along with the binders, his nakedness, and the darkness, led him to the inescapable conclusion that he'd been captured by the Empire. The darkness and drugs kept him disoriented. His nakedness made him defensive—or was supposed to. He recalled a CorSec training seminar about methods used by kidnappers to keep their victims off balance and was able to pinpoint himself as the subject of such treatment.

The chill in the air and the vibration suggested he was on a starship heading out through hyperspace to some destination or other. He knew the Imps would be fleeing Coruscant, but for a moment he had no idea why. Then he remembered the Alliance fleet having arrived at Coruscant. *If they are running, we won.* He frowned. *But if we won, why am I their captive?*

He tried to remember what he could of his last moments on Coruscant. He'd lost control of his Headhunter and the manual override didn't work. Then a light had flashed on the console indicating the acceleration compensation unit had gone out. The ship flipped itself into a high g-force turn and he remembered nothing more. *Without acceleration compensation, I felt the full effect of the turn. Blood drained from my brain and I went out.*

Corran rolled onto his left side, then drew his knees up to his chest. He rocked himself a little bit and managed to get up onto his knees. The world immediately spun, which was a sensation that was made worse because the utter darkness gave him nothing to look at, nothing to occupy his attention. He brought his head down and rested it on the cot, but refused to let himself flop down again. It didn't matter that he felt terrible, he'd gotten to his knees and refused to retreat to his belly again.

Lights flashed on brilliantly in an instant, stabbing forked pain into his brain. He heard a door whoosh open and the careful, deliberate clank-clack of shoes on metal lattice steps, but he made no attempt to look in the direction of the sound. He refused to look, part of him knowing the individual had desired to make an entrance, and he congratulated himself for his restraint.

He waited until the sound of the footsteps stopped before he slowly brought his head up. He kept his eyes all but shut, letting eyelashes and welled-up tears protect his eyes against the light. Out of the corner of his right eye he saw a blot of red, so he slowly turned his head toward it and looked up. Even before he got to the mismatched eyes, he knew who she was and he hoped against hope she was a figment of whatever drugs they'd pumped into him.

Her first words came cold and even, tinted with just a hint of curiosity. "I would have expected you to be more formidable somehow."

"Clothes make the man," he said. At least he thought he said it. He did hear sound coming out of his mouth, a kind of harsh croaking that seemed closer to Huttese than Basic. Had he any spit to let gurgle in his throat as he spoke he'd definitely have been taken for a Hutt.

"Ah, the infamous Horn wit."

Corran opened his eyes wider and shuffled on his knees around to face her. "I left most of it back on Free Coruscant."

She brought her hands up and clapped gently. "I'm amazed a man in your condition can make jokes." She squatted down and caught him across the face with an openhanded slap he never saw coming. "I'm amazed a man in your situation *would* make jokes."

Corran played his tongue over his split lip. "Lieutenant Corran Horn, Alliance fleet, Rogue Squadron."

Ysanne Isard stood again but he didn't bother following her with his eyes. "Very good, defiance. I like defiance."

"If that were true, you'd find all you want on Coruscant."

"Indeed, perhaps I would. That is no concern of yours, however." Her low chuckle filled the room and made it seem even colder. "I'll have you know that your Rebel forces are indeed now in control of Imperial Center. What they have discovered, though they know not the depth of the problem, is that Imperial Center is a poisoned world, a sick world. It is a black hole from which they cannot escape. They have truly bitten off more than they can possibly chew and they will be choked to death because of it."

"I'm not inclined to take your word for all this."

Corran put as much disdain in the sentence as he could muster, but what she said disturbed him. Shiel and Nawara Ven and Portha had all become ill enough that they could not participate in the squadron's final action. He didn't think anyone could have gone forward with re- leasing some sort of plague on a world deliberately, but then he'd not thought anyone would use a weapon that destroyed whole planets on an inhabited world. The Em- pire had done the latter, so using a biological agent to de- stroy people and leave the world infrastructure intact just seemed like an economical refinement of Imperial doc- trine.

"I neither desire nor care about your belief in what I say. Ultimately what you think is immaterial to me. I have you, you are mine, and I will do with you what I see fit."

Corran brought his head up despite the pain. "What you did to Tycho Celchu to get him to betray me? He gave you the codes for my ship. That's how you got me."

She looked down at him and her eyes narrowed. "Oh, well done, Horn, well done. I would deny this, of course, but the latest word from Imperial Center is that Tycho Celchu has been arrested by Alliance Intelligence on charges of treason and murder. Specifically, *your* mur- der."

"Hardly an injustice, given the circumstances."

"Perhaps not, but I will find a way to use it. I will re- turn you to them after they have convicted and executed him. His wrongful death will gnaw away at consciences and undercut the Rebellion's illusion of moral superior- ity."

"I'll tell them the truth."

"The only truth you'll know is the truth I give you." Isard's smile slithered cruelly onto her face. "We are bound to Lusankya, my private workshop for people like you. By the time I am finished with you, your mind will be mine and your heart's desire will be what I wish."

Corran shook his head violently, hoping the pain would be enough to make him black out. It was not. "I will never betray my friends."

She laughed again. "I have heard this chorus many times before and it always sounds so sweet. You will betray them, Corran Horn, just as Tycho Celchu betrayed you. You will be the instrument of Rogue Squadron's death and will strike a mighty blow against the Alliance's precarious unity. When I am through with you, little man, you will become the instrument of the Emperor's vengeance and nothing and no one will be able to stop you."

About the Author

Michael A. Stackpole is an award-winning game and computer game designer who was born in 1957 and grew up in Burlington, Vermont. In 1979 he graduated from the University of Vermont with a BA in history. In his career as a game designer he has done work for Flying Buffalo, Inc., Interplay Productions, TSR Inc., West End Games, Hero Games, Wizards of the Coast, FASA Corp., Game Designers Workshop, and Steve Jackson Games. In recognition of his work in and for the game industry, he was inducted into the Academy of Gaming Arts and Design Hall of Fame in 1994.

Wedge's Gamble is his seventeenth published novel and the second of four Star Wars X-wing novels. In addition to working on the novels he has worked on the X-wing comic series from Dark Horse Comics, building a continuity between the two sets of stories.

He lives in Arizona with Liz Danforth and two Welsh Cardigan Corgis, Ruthless and Ember. In his spare time he plays indoor soccer, enjoys gaming, serves as the Executive Director of the Phoenix Skeptics, and does his best to remain caught up with the on-line traffic on GEnie.

The World of
STAR WARS Novels

In May 1991, *Star Wars* caused a sensation in the publishing industry with the Bantam release of Timothy Zahn's novel *Heir to the Empire*. For the first time, Lucasfilm Ltd. had authorized new novels that *continued* the famous story told in George Lucas's three blockbuster motion pictures: *Star Wars*, *The Empire Strikes Back*, and *Return of the Jedi*. Reader reaction was immediate and tumultuous: *Heir* reached #1 on the *New York Times* bestseller list and demonstrated that *Star Wars* lovers were eager for exciting new stories set in this universe, written by leading science fiction authors who shared their passion. Since then, each Bantam *Star Wars* novel has been an instant national bestseller.

Lucasfilm and Bantam decided that future novels in the series would be interconnected: that is, events in one novel would have consequences in the others. You might say that each Bantam *Star Wars* novel, enjoyable on its own, is also part of a much larger tale.

Here is a special look at Bantam's *Star Wars* books, along with excerpts from the more recent novels. Each one is available now wherever Bantam Books are sold.

SHADOWS OF THE EMPIRE by Steve Perry
Setting: between *The Empire Strikes Back* and *Return of the Jedi*

Here is a very special STAR WARS story dealing with Black Sun, a galaxy-spanning criminal organization that is masterminded by one of the most interesting villains in the STAR WARS universe: Xizor, dark prince of the Falleen. Xizor's chief rival for the favor of Emperor Palpatine is none other than Darth Vader himself— alive and well, and a major character in this story, since it is set during the events of the STAR WARS film trilogy.

In the opening prologue, we revisit a familiar scene from The Empire Strikes Back, *and are introduced to our marvelous new bad guy:*

He looks like a walking corpse, Xizor thought. *Like a mummified body dead a thousand years. Amazing he is still alive, much less the most powerful man in the galaxy. He isn't even that old; it is more as if something is slowly eating him.*

Xizor stood four meters away from the Emperor, watching as the man who had long ago been Senator Palpatine moved to stand in the holocam field. He imagined he could smell the decay in the Emperor's worn body. Likely that was just some trick of the recycled air, run through dozens of filters to ensure that there was no chance of any poison gas being introduced into it. Filtered the life out of it, perhaps, giving it that dead smell.

The viewer on the other end of the holo-link would see a close-up of the Emperor's head and shoulders, of an age-ravaged face shrouded in the cowl of his dark zeyd-cloth robe. The man on the other end of the transmission, light-years away, would not see Xizor, though Xizor would be able to see him. It was a measure of the Emperor's trust that Xizor was allowed to be here while the conversation took place.

The man on the other end of the transmission—if he could still be called that—

The air swirled inside the Imperial chamber in front of the Emperor, coalesced, and blossomed into the image of a figure down on one knee. A caped humanoid biped dressed in jet black, face hidden under a full helmet and breathing mask:

Darth Vader.

Vader spoke: "What is thy bidding, my master?"

If Xizor could have hurled a power bolt through time and space to strike Vader dead, he would have done it without blinking. Wishful thinking: Vader was too powerful to attack directly.

"There is a great disturbance in the Force," the Emperor said.

"I have felt it," Vader said.

"We have a new enemy. Luke Skywalker."

Skywalker? That had been Vader's name, a long time ago. Who was this person with the same name, someone so powerful as to be worth a conversation between the Emperor and his most loathsome creation? More importantly, why had Xizor's agents not uncovered this before now? Xizor's ire was instant—but cold. No sign of his surprise or anger would show on his imperturbable features. The Falleen did not allow their emotions to burst forth as did many of the inferior species; no, the Falleen ancestry was not fur but scales, not mammalian but reptilian. Not wild but coolly calculating. Such was much better. Much safer.

"Yes, my master," Vader continued.

"He could destroy us," the Emperor said.

Xizor's attention was riveted upon the Emperor and the

holographic image of Vader kneeling on the deck of a ship far away. Here was interesting news indeed. Something the Emperor perceived as a danger to himself? Something the Emperor feared?

"He's just a boy," Vader said. "Obi-Wan can no longer help him."

Obi-Wan. That name Xizor knew. He was among the last of the Jedi Knights, a general. But he'd been dead for decades, hadn't he?

Apparently Xizor's information was wrong if Obi-Wan had been helping someone who was still a boy. His agents were going to be sorry.

Even as Xizor took in the distant image of Vader and the nearness of the Emperor, even as he was aware of the luxury of the Emperor's private and protected chamber at the core of the giant pyramidal palace, he was also able to make a mental note to himself: Somebody's head would roll for the failure to make him aware of all this. Knowledge was power; lack of knowledge was weakness. This was something he could not permit.

The Emperor continued. "The Force is strong with him. The son of Skywalker must not become a Jedi."

Son of Skywalker?

Vader's son! Amazing!

"If he could be turned he would become a powerful ally," Vader said.

There was something in Vader's voice when he said this, something Xizor could not quite put his finger on. Longing? Worry?

Hope?

"Yes . . . yes. He would be a great asset," the Emperor said. "Can it be done?"

There was the briefest of pauses. "He will join us or die, master."

Xizor felt the smile, though he did not allow it to show any more than he had allowed his anger play. Ah. Vader wanted Skywalker alive, *that* was what had been in his tone. Yes, he had said that the boy would join them or die, but this latter part was obviously meant only to placate the Emperor. Vader had no intention of killing Skywalker, his own son; that was obvious to one as skilled in reading voices as was Xizor. He had not gotten to be the Dark Prince, Underlord of Black Sun, the largest criminal organization in the galaxy, merely on his formidable good looks. Xizor didn't truly understand the Force that sustained the Emperor and made him and Vader so powerful, save to know that it certainly worked somehow. But he did know that it was something the extinct Jedi had supposedly mastered. And now, apparently, this new player had tapped into it. Vader wanted Skywalker alive, had practically promised the Emperor that he would deliver him alive—and converted.

This was most interesting.

Most interesting indeed.

The Emperor finished his communication and turned back to face him. "Now, where were we, Prince Xizor?"

The Dark Prince smiled. He would attend to the business at hand, but he would not forget the name of Luke Skywalker.

THE TRUCE AT BAKURA by Kathy Tyers
Setting: Immediately after *Return of the Jedi*

The day after his climactic battle with Emperor Palpatine and the sacrifice of his father, Darth Vader, who died saving his life, Luke Skywalker helps recover an Imperial drone ship bearing a startling message intended for the Emperor. It is a distress signal from the far-off Imperial outpost of Bakura, which is under attack by an alien invasion force, the Ssi-ruuk. Leia sees a rescue mission as an opportunity to achieve a diplomatic victory for the Rebel Alliance, even if it means fighting alongside former Imperials. But Luke receives a vision from Obi-Wan Kenobi revealing that the stakes are even higher: the invasion at Bakura threatens everything the Rebels have won at such great cost.

STAR WARS: X-WING by Michael A. Stackpole
ROGUE SQUADRON
WEDGE'S GAMBLE
Setting: two and a half years
after *Return of the Jedi*

Inspired by X-wing, the bestselling computer game from LucasArts Entertainment Co., this exciting series chronicles the further adventures of the most feared and fearless fighting force in the galaxy. A new generation of X-wing pilots, led by Commander Wedge Antilles, is combating the remnants of the Empire still left after the events of the STAR WARS movies. Here are novels full of explosive space action, nonstop adventure, and the special brand of wonder known as STAR WARS.

In this very early scene, young Corellian pilot Corran Horn faces a tough challenge fast enough to get his heart pounding—and this is only a simulation! [P.S.: "Whistler" is Corran's R2 astromech droid]:

The Corellian brought his proton torpedo targeting program up and locked on to the TIE. It tried to break the lock, but turbolaser fire from the *Korolev* boxed it in. Corran's heads-up display went red and he triggered the torpedo. "Scratch one eyeball."

The missile shot straight in at the fighter, but the pilot broke hard to port and away, causing the missile to overshoot the target. *Nice flying!* Corran brought his X-wing over and started down to loop in behind the TIE, but as he did so, the TIE vanished from his forward screen and reappeared in his aft arc. Yanking the stick hard to the right and pulling it back, Corran wrestled the X-wing up and to starboard, then inverted and rolled out to the left.

A laser shot jolted a tremor through the simulator's couch. *Lucky thing I had all shields aft!* Corran reinforced them with energy from his lasers, then evened them out fore and aft. Jinking the fighter right and left, he avoided laser shots coming in from behind, but they all came in far closer than he liked.

He knew Jace had been in the bomber, and Jace was the only pilot in the unit who could have stayed with him. *Except for our leader.* Corran smiled broadly. *Coming to see how good I really am, Commander Antilles? Let me give you a clinic.* "Make sure you're in there solid, Whistler, because we're going for a little ride."

Corran refused to let the R2's moan slow him down. A snap-roll brought the X-wing up on its port wing. Pulling back on the stick yanked the fighter's nose up away from the original line of flight. The TIE stayed with him, then tightened up on the arc to close distance. Corran then rolled another ninety degrees and continued the turn into a dive. Throttling back, Corran hung in the dive for three seconds, then hauled back hard on the stick and cruised up into the TIE fighter's aft.

The X-wing's laser fire missed wide to the right as the TIE cut to the left. Corran kicked his speed up to full and broke with the TIE. He let the X-wing rise above the plane of the break, then put the fighter through a twisting roll that ate up enough time to bring him again into the TIE's rear. The TIE snapped to the right and Corran looped out left.

He watched the tracking display as the distance between them grew to be a kilometer and a half, then slowed. *Fine, you want to go nose to nose? I've got shields and you don't.* If Commander Antilles wanted to commit virtual suicide, Corran was happy to oblige him. He tugged the stick back to his sternum and rolled out in an inversion loop. *Coming at you!*

The two starfighters closed swiftly. Corran centered his foe in the crosshairs and waited for a dead shot. Without shields the TIE fighter would die with one burst, and Corran wanted the kill to be clean. His HUD flicked green as the TIE juked in and out of the center, then locked green as they closed.

The TIE started firing at maximum range and scored hits. At that distance the lasers did no real damage against the shields, prompting Corran to wonder why Wedge was wasting the energy. Then, as the HUD's green color started to flicker, realization dawned. *The bright bursts on the shields are a distraction to my targeting! I better kill him now!*

Corran tightened down on the trigger button, sending red laser needles stabbing out at the closing TIE fighter. He couldn't tell if he had hit anything. Lights flashed in the cockpit and Whistler started screeching furiously. Corran's main monitor went black, his shields were down, and his weapons controls were dead.

The pilot looked left and right. "Where is he, Whistler?"

The monitor in front of him flickered to life and a diagnostic report began to scroll by. Bloodred bordered the damage reports. "Scanners, out; lasers, out; shields, out; engine, out! I'm a wallowing Hutt just hanging here in space."

THE COURTSHIP OF PRINCESS LEIA
by Dave Wolverton
Setting: Four years after *Return of the Jedi*

One of the most interesting developments in Bantam's Star Wars novels is that in their storyline, Han Solo and Princess Leia start a family. This tale reveals how the couple originally got together. Wishing to strengthen the fledgling New Republic by bringing in powerful allies, Leia opens talks with the Hapes consortium of more than sixty worlds. But the consortium is ruled by the Queen Mother, who, to Han's dismay, wants Leia to marry her son, Prince Isolder. Before this action-packed story is over, Luke will join forces with Isolder against a group of Force-trained "witches" and face a deadly foe.

Luke stood in a mountain fortress of stone, looking over a plain with a sea of dark forested hills beyond, and a storm rose—a magnificent wind that brought with it towering walls of black clouds and dust, trees hurtling toward him and twisting through the sky. The clouds thundered overhead, filled with purple flames, obliterating all sunlight, and Luke could feel a malevolence hidden in those clouds and knew that they had been raised through the power of the dark side of the Force.

Dust and stones whistled through the air like autumn leaves. Luke tried to hold on to the stone parapet overlooking the plain to keep from being swept from the fortress walls. Winds pounded in his ears like the roar of an ocean, howling.

It was as if a storm of pure dark Force raged over the countryside, and suddenly, amid the towering clouds of darkness that thundered toward him, Luke could hear laughing, the sweet sound of women laughing. He looked above into the dark clouds, and saw the women borne through the air along with the rocks and debris, like motes of dust, laughing. A voice seemed to whisper, "the witches of Dathomir."

HEIR TO THE EMPIRE
DARK FORCE RISING
THE LAST COMMAND
by Timothy Zahn
Setting: Five years after *Return of the Jedi*

This #1 bestselling trilogy introduces two legendary forces of evil into the Star Wars literary pantheon. Grand Admiral Thrawn has taken control of the Imperial fleet in the years since the destruction of the Death Star, and the mysterious Joruus C'baoth is a fearsome Jedi Master who has been seduced by the dark side. Han and Leia have now been married for about a year, and as the story begins, she is pregnant with twins. Thrawn's plan is to crush the Rebellion and resurrect the Empire's New Order with C'baoth's help—and in return, the Dark Master will get Han and Leia's Jedi children to mold as he wishes. For as readers of this magnificent trilogy will see, Luke Skywalker is not the last of the old Jedi. He is the first of the new.

The Jedi Academy Trilogy:
JEDI SEARCH
DARK APPRENTICE
CHAMPIONS OF THE FORCE
by Kevin J. Anderson
Setting: Seven years after *Return of the Jedi*

In order to assure the continuation of the Jedi Knights, Luke Skywalker has decided to start a training facility: a Jedi Acad-

*emy. He will gather Force-sensitive students who show potential
as prospective Jedi and serve as their mentor, as Jedi Masters
Obi-Wan Kenobi and Yoda did for him. Han and Leia's twins are
now toddlers, and there is a third Jedi child: the infant Anakin,
named after Luke and Leia's father. In this trilogy, we discover
the existence of a powerful Imperial doomsday weapon, the hor-
rifying Sun Crusher—which will soon become the centerpiece of
a titanic struggle between Luke Skywalker and his most brilliant
Jedi Academy student, who is delving dangerously into the dark
side.*

In this scene from the first novel, Jedi Search, *Luke vocalizes
his concept of a new Jedi order to a distinguished assembly of
New Republic leaders:*

As he descended the long ramp, Luke felt all eyes turn
toward him. A hush fell over the assembly. Luke Skywalker, the
lone remaining Jedi Master, almost never took part in governmental proceedings.

"I have an important matter to address," he said.

Mon Mothma gave him a soft, mysterious smile and gestured for him to take a central position. "The words of a Jedi
Knight are always welcome to the New Republic," she said.

Luke tried not to look pleased. She had provided the perfect
opening for him. "In the Old Republic," he said, "Jedi Knights
were the protectors and guardians of all. For a thousand generations the Jedi used the powers of the Force to guide, defend, and
provide support for the rightful government of worlds—before
the dark days of the Empire came, and the Jedi Knights were
killed."

He let his words hang, then took another breath. "Now we
have a New Republic. The Empire appears to be defeated. We
have founded a new government based upon the old, but let us
hope we learn from our mistakes. Before, an entire order of Jedi
watched over the Republic, offering strength. Now I am the only
Jedi Master who remains.

"Without that order of protectors to provide a backbone of
strength for the New Republic, can we survive? Will we be able
to weather the storms and the difficulties of forging a new union?
Until now we have suffered severe struggles—but in the future
they will be seen as nothing more than birth pangs."

Before the other senators could disagree with that, Luke
continued. "Our people had a common foe in the Empire, and we
must not let our defenses lapse just because we have internal
problems. More to the point, what will happen when we begin

squabbling among ourselves over petty matters? The old Jedi helped to mediate many types of disputes. What if there are no Jedi Knights to protect us in the difficult times ahead?

"My sister is undergoing Jedi training. She has a great deal of skill in the Force. Her three children are also likely candidates to be trained as young Jedi. In recent years I have come to know a woman named Mara Jade, who is now unifying the smugglers—the former smugglers," he amended, "into an organization that can support the needs of the New Republic. She also has a talent for the Force. I have encountered others in my travels."

Another pause. The audience was listening so far. "But are these the only ones? We already know that the ability to use the Force is passed from generation to generation. Most of the Jedi were killed in the Emperor's purge—but could he possibly have eradicated all of the descendants of those Knights? I myself was unaware of the potential power within me until Obi-Wan Kenobi taught me how to use it. My sister Leia was similarly unaware.

"How many people are abroad in this galaxy who have a comparable strength in the Force, who are potential members of a new order of Jedi Knights, but are unaware of who they are?"

Luke looked at them again. "In my brief search I have already discovered that there are indeed some descendants of former Jedi. I have come here to ask" he turned to gesture toward Mon Mothma, swept his hands across the people gathered there in the chamber—"for two things.

"First, that the New Republic officially sanction my search for those with a hidden talent for the Force, to seek them out and try to bring them to our service. For this I will need some help."

"And what will you yourself be doing?" Mon Mothma asked, shifting in her robes.

CHILDREN OF THE JEDI by Barbara Hambly
Setting: Eight years after *Return of the Jedi*

The Star Wars *characters face a menace from the glory days of the Empire when a thirty-year-old automated Imperial Dread-naught comes to life and begins its grim mission: to gather forces and annihilate a long-forgotten stronghold of Jedi children. When Luke is whisked onboard, he begins to communicate with the brave Jedi Knight who paralyzed the ship decades ago, and gave her life in the process. Now she is part of the vessel, existing in its artificial intelligence core, and guiding Luke through one of the most unusual adventures he has ever had.*

In this scene, Luke discovers that an evil presence is gathering, one that will force him to join the battle:

Like See-Threepio, Nichos Marr sat in the outer room of the suite to which Cray had been assigned, in the power-down mode that was the droid equivalent of rest. Like Threepio, at the sound of Luke's almost noiseless tread he turned his head, aware of his presence.

"Luke?" Cray had equipped him with the most sensitive vocal modulators, and the word was calibrated to a whisper no louder than the rustle of the blueleaves massed outside the windows. He rose, and crossed to where Luke stood, the dull silver of his arms and shoulders a phantom gleam in the stray flickers of light. "What is it?"

"I don't know." They retreated to the small dining area where Luke had earlier probed his mind, and Luke stretched up to pin back a corner of the lamp-sheath, letting a slim triangle of butter-colored light fall on the purple of the vulwood tabletop. "A dream. A premonition, maybe." It was on his lips to ask, *Do you dream?* but he remembered the ghastly, imageless darkness in Nichos's mind, and didn't. He wasn't sure if his pupil was aware of the difference from his human perception and knowledge, aware of just exactly what he'd lost when his consciousness, his self, had been transferred.

In the morning Luke excused himself from the expedition Tomla El had organized with Nichos and Cray to the Falls of Dessiar, one of the places on Ithor most renowned for its beauty and peace. When they left he sought out Umwaw Moolis, and the tall herd leader listened gravely to his less than logical request and promised to put matters in train to fulfill it. Then Luke descended to the House of the Healers, where Drub McKumb lay, sedated far beyond pain but with all the perceptions of agony and nightmare still howling in his mind.

"Kill you!" He heaved himself at the restraints, blue eyes glaring furiously as he groped and scrabbled at Luke with his clawed hands. "It's all poison! I see you! I see the dark light all around you! You're him! You're him!" His back bent like a bow; the sound of his shrieking was like something being ground out of him by an infernal mangle.

Luke had been through the darkest places of the universe and of his own mind, had done and experienced greater evil than perhaps any man had known on the road the Force had dragged him . . . Still, it was hard not to turn away.

"We even tried yarrock on him last night," explained the

Healer in charge, a slightly built Ithorian beautifully tabby-striped green and yellow under her simple tabard of purple linen. "But apparently the earlier doses that brought him enough lucidity to reach here from his point of origin oversensitized his system. We'll try again in four or five days."

Luke gazed down into the contorted, grimacing face.

"As you can see," the Healer said, "the internal perception of pain and fear is slowly lessening. It's down to ninety-three percent of what it was when he was first brought in. Not much, I know, but something."

"Him! *Him! HIM!*" Foam spattered the old man's stained gray beard.

Who?

"I wouldn't advise attempting any kind of mindlink until it's at least down to fifty percent, Master Skywalker."

"No," said Luke softly.

Kill you all. And, *They are gathering . . .*

"Do you have recordings of everything he's said?"

"Oh, yes." The big coppery eyes blinked assent. "The transcript is available through the monitor cubicle down the hall. We could make nothing of them. Perhaps they will mean something to you."

They didn't. Luke listened to them all, the incoherent groans and screams, the chewed fragments of words that could be only guessed at, and now and again the clear disjointed cries: "Solo! Solo! Can you hear me? Children . . . Evil . . . Gathering here . . . Kill you all!"

DARKSABER by Kevin J. Anderson
Setting: Immediately thereafter

Not long after Children of the Jedi, *Luke and Han learn that evil Hutts are building a reconstruction of the original Death Star—and that the Empire is still alive, in the form of Daala, who has joined forces with Pellaeon, former second in command to the feared Grand Admiral Thrawn. In this early scene, Luke has returned to the home of Obi-Wan Kenobi on Tatooine to try and consult a long-gone mentor:*

He stood anxious and alone, feeling like a prodigal son outside the ramshackle, collapsed hut that had once been the home of Obi-Wan Kenobi.

Luke swallowed and stepped forward, his footsteps crunching in the silence. He had not been here in many years. The door had fallen off its hinges; part of the clay front wall had fallen in. Boulders and crumbled adobe jammed the entrance. A pair of small, screeching desert rodents snapped at him and fled for cover; Luke ignored them.

Gingerly, he ducked low and stepped into the home of his first mentor.

Luke stood in the middle of the room breathing deeply, turning around, trying to sense the presence he desperately needed to see. This was the place where Obi-Wan Kenobi had told Luke of the Force. Here, the old man had first given Luke his lightsaber and hinted at the truth about his father, "from a certain point of view," dispelling the diversionary story that Uncle Owen had told, at the same time planting seeds of his own deceptions.

"Ben," he said and closed his eyes, calling out with his mind as well as his voice. He tried to penetrate the invisible walls of the Force and reach to the luminous being of Obi-Wan Kenobi who had visited him numerous times, before saying he could never speak with Luke again.

"Ben, I need you," Luke said. Circumstances had changed. He could think of no other way past the obstacles he faced. Obi-Wan had to answer. It wouldn't take long, but it could give him the key he needed with all his heart.

Luke paused and listened and sensed—

But felt nothing. If he could not summon Obi-Wan's spirit here in the empty dwelling where the old man had lived in exile for so many years, Luke didn't believe he could find his former teacher ever again.

He echoed the words Leia had used more than a decade earlier, beseeching him, "Help me, Obi-Wan Kenobi," Luke whispered, "you're my only hope."

THE CRYSTAL STAR by Vonda N. McIntyre
Setting: Ten years after *Return of the Jedi*

Leia's three children have been kidnapped. That horrible fact is made worse by Leia's realization that she can no longer sense her children through the Force! While she, Artoo-Detoo, and Chewbacca trail the kidnappers, Luke and Han discover a planet that is suffering strange quantum effects from a nearby star. Slowly freezing into a perfect crystal and disrupting the Force, the star is blunting Luke's power and crippling the Millennium Falcon. *These strands converge in an apocalyptic threat not only to the fate of the New Republic, but to the universe itself.*

The Black Fleet Crisis
BEFORE THE STORM
by Michael P. Kube-McDowell
Setting: Twelve years after *Return of the Jedi*

*Long after setting up the hard-won New Republic, yesterday's
Rebels have become today's administrators and diplomats. But
the peace is not to last for long. A restless Luke must journey to
his mother's homeworld in a desperate quest to find her people;
Lando seizes a mysterious spacecraft with unimaginable weapons of destruction; and waiting in the wings is an horrific battle
fleet under the control of a ruthless leader bent on a genocidal
war.*

Here is an opening scene from Before the Storm:

In the pristine silence of space, the Fifth Battle Group of the
New Republic Defense Fleet blossomed over the planet Bessimir
like a beautiful, deadly flower.

The formation of capital ships sprang into view with startling suddenness, trailing fire-white wakes of twisted space and
bristling with weapons. Angular Star Destroyers guarded fat-
hulled fleet carriers, while the assault cruisers, their mirror fin-
ishes gleaming, took the point.

A halo of smaller ships appeared at the same time. The
fighters among them quickly deployed in a spherical defensive
screen. As the Star Destroyers firmed up their formation, their
flight decks quickly spawned scores of additional fighters.

At the same time, the carriers and cruisers began to disgorge
the bombers, transports, and gunboats they had ferried to the
battle. There was no reason to risk the loss of one fully
loaded—a lesson the Republic had learned in pain. At Orinda,
the commander of the fleet carrier *Endurance* had kept his pilots
waiting in the launch bays, to protect the smaller craft from Imperial fire as long as possible. They were still there when *Endurance* took the brunt of a Super Star Destroyer attack and
vanished in a ball of metal fire.

Before long more than two hundred warships, large and
small, were bearing down on Bessimir and its twin moons. But
the terrible, restless power of the armada could be heard and felt
only by the ships' crews. The silence of the approach was broken
only on the fleet comm channels, which had crackled to life in
the first moments with encoded bursts of noise and cryptic ship-
to-ship chatter.

At the center of the formation of great vessels was the flagship of the Fifth Battle Group, the fleet carrier *Intrepid*. She was so new from the yards at Hakassi that her corridors still reeked of sealing compound and cleaning solvent. Her huge realspace thruster engines still sang with the high-pitched squeal that the engine crews called "the baby's cry."

It would take more than a year for the mingled scents of the crew to displace the chemical smells from the first impressions of visitors. But after a hundred more hours under way, her engines' vibrations would drop two octaves, to the reassuring thrum of a seasoned thruster bank.

On *Intredpid*'s bridge, a tall Dornean in general's uniform paced along an arc of command stations equipped with large monitors. His eye-folds were swollen and fanned by an unconscious Dornean defensive reflex, and his leathery face was flushed purple by concern. Before the deployment was even a minute old, Etahn A'baht's first command had been bloodied.

The fleet tender *Ahazi* had overshot its jump, coming out of hyperspace too close to Bessimir and too late for its crew to recover from the error. Etahn A'baht watched the bright flare of light in the upper atmosphere from *Intrepid*'s forward viewstation, knowing that it meant six young men were dead.

The Corellian Trilogy:
AMBUSH AT CORELLIA
ASSAULT AT SELONIA
SHOWDOWN AT CENTERPOINT
by Roger MacBride Allen
Setting: Fourteen years after *Return of the Jedi*

This trilogy takes us to Corellia, Han Solo's homeworld, which Han has not visited in quite some time. A trade summit brings Han, Leia, and the children—now developing their own clear personalities and instinctively learning more about their innate skills in the Force—into the middle of a situation that most closely resembles a burning fuse. The Corellian system is on the brink of civil war, there are New Republic intelligence agents on a mysterious mission which even Han does not understand, and worst of all, a fanatical rebel leader has his hands on a superweapon of unimaginable power—and just wait until you find out who that leader is!

Here is an early scene from Ambush *that gives you a wonderful look at the growing Solo children (the twins are Jacen and Jaina, and their little brother is Anakin):*

Anakin plugged the board into the innards of the droid and pressed a button. The droid's black, boxy body shuddered awake, it drew in its wheels to stand up a bit taller, its status lights lit, and it made a sort of triple beep. "That's good," he said, and pushed the button again. The droid's status lights went out, and its body slumped down again. Anakin picked up the next piece, a motivation actuator. He frowned at it as he turned it over in his hands. He shook his head. "That's *not* good," he announced.

"What's not good?" Jaina asked.

"This thing," Anakin said, handing her the actuator. "Can't you *tell*? The insides part is all melty."

Jaina and Jacen exchanged a look. "The outside looks okay," Jaina said, giving the part to her brother. "How can he tell what the *inside* of it looks like? It's sealed shut when they make it."

Anakin, still sitting on the floor, took the device from his brother and frowned at it again. He turned it over and over in his hands, and then held it over his head and looked at it as if he were holding it up to the light. "There," he said, pointing a chubby finger at one point on the unmarked surface. "In there is the bad part." He rearranged himself to sit cross-legged, put the actuator in his lap, and put his right index finger over the "bad" part. "Fix," he said. "Fix." The dark brown outer case of the actuator seemed to glow for a second with an odd blue-red light, but then the glow sputtered out and Anakin pulled his finger away quickly and stuck it in his mouth, as if he had burned it on something.

"Better now?" Jaina asked.

"*Some* better," Anakin said, pulling his finger out of his mouth. "Not *all* better." He took the actuator in his hand and stood up. He opened the access panel on the broken droid and plugged in the actuator. He closed the door and looked expectantly at his older brother and sister.

"Done?" Jaina asked.

"Done," Anakin agreed. "But *I'm* not going to push the button." He backed well away from the droid, sat down on the floor, and folded his arms.

Jacen looked at his sister.

"Not me," she said. "This was your idea."

Jacen stepped forward to the droid, reached out to push the power button from as far away as he could, and then stepped hurriedly back.

Once again, the droid shuddered awake, rattling a bit this time as it did so. It pulled its wheels in, lit its panel lights, and made the same triple beep. But then its holocam eye viewlens wobbled back and forth, and its panel lights dimmed and flared. It rolled backward just a bit, and then recovered itself.

"Good morning, young mistress and masters," it said. "How may I surge you?"

Well, one word wrong, but so what? Jacen grinned and clapped his hands and rubbed them together eagerly. "Good day, droid," he said. They had done it! But what to ask for first? "First tidy up this room," he said. A simple task, and one that ought to serve as a good test of what this droid could do.

Suddenly the droid's overhead access door blew off and there was a flash of light from its interior. A thin plume of smoke drifted out of the droid. Its panel lights flared again, and then the work arm sagged downward. The droid's body, softened by heat, sagged in on itself and drooped to the floor. The floor and walls and ceilings of the playroom were supposed to be fireproof, but nonetheless the floor under the droid darkened a bit, and the ceiling turned black. The ventilators kicked on high automatically, and drew the smoke out of the room. After a moment they shut themselves off, and the room was silent.

The three children stood, every bit as frozen to the spot as the droid was, absolutely stunned. It was Anakin who recovered first. He walked cautiously toward the droid and looked at it carefully, being sure not to get too close or touch it. "*Really* melty now," he announced, and then wandered off to the other side of the room to play with his blocks.

The twins looked at the droid, and then at each other.

"We're dead," Jacen announced, surveying the wreckage.